SOMETHING YOU DO IN THE DARK

Something You

by DANIEL CURZON

Do in the Dark

G. P. Putnam's Sons, New York

To Bill H.

SOMETHING YOU DO IN THE DARK

1

Miriam and Roger sprang apart as the headlights of the circle of cars lighted up their partly nude skins. They looked humanoid with the brightness blinding them, burning out their eyes, the faces as pallid as unformed creatures under a log of wood. The men in the cars got out quickly, lifting their rifles easily with one arm. Roger started to bend down to pull up his pants, but one of the men shot at the ground nearby. "Leave 'em be, you fucker!" Roger stood upright again, stumbling back a few steps, tiny steps because his trousers were ensnarled around his ankles; his undershorts made a white blur on top of the trousers. He dropped his hands in front of his testicles, which moved up and down slightly, in rhythm with his much more heaving stomach. "What's the matter, boy?" one of the men spat out. "You ashamed of your pecker?" The others snorted, amused. They all seemed to be fat men, heavy-jowled, their belts sagging beneath their listless, overfed bellies. "Can't say nothing, eh?" another man said, and the others laughed again, even though the remark was not witty. "The cat got your ass?" With difficulty, Roger smiled an answer, feeling the sweat spilling across his ears, down his neck. He glanced at Miriam, who was sobbing softly, one breast exposed through her blouse, her skirt lying in the bushes somewhere—he remembered throwing it in fun. "Well, what are we going to do with them?" the man who seemed to be the leader said. "Shoot them here—or later?" Miriam exchanged a terrified look with Roger, and her hand went out involuntarily; he waddled a few steps closer to her, putting his arm around her shoulder. "Well, will you look at that!" the leader snarled. "Look, he's got his arm around that *woman!* What's the matter with you, creep?" It was not a question; no reply was expected, for the man turned immediately to the man next to him. "I want to throw up, you know! It makes me puke, puke all over." He sounded like a man whom sincerity had overwhelmed.

"But we're not hurting anybody," Roger protested meekly.

"You goddamn queer!"

"We're not bothering anybody out here in—"

"You bother me, that's enough. Coming out here in the park in the middle of the night to do your nastiness. Taking your clothes off and rolling around in your own slime, sticking your thing in her hole, pumping up and down like a . . . like a goddamn fucker! That's all you are, a goddamn *fucker!* Where's your shame? You ought to be shot to death."

Roger put his hands over his eyes and began to whimper, a jerking, sniffling noise that made him sound like an animal being killed. Miriam looked at his exposed genitals, now tightened in fear, and began to shiver. *How could she have done it, allowed herself to come out here with a man, a man?* Her face began to sting with the humiliation. She saw the men staring at the two of them, shaking their heads wearily, as if they had seen a hideous accident. "You even smell bad, you two. Don't you people ever wash? You heterosexuals are all alike, filthy and diseased. You spread your crud all over—or you'd like to, if we didn't keep you from it. I *pity* you two more than anything." The leader's voice dropped lower, a tone of spiritual advice in it. "You really have to help yourselves, see a doctor, or one of them head-shrinkers. You ought to get some treatment for your sickness; you can't go on like this, copulating . . ." He spoke the word awkwardly, as if the syllables made the inside of his mouth sore. "You *can* be helped, you know! Lots of your kind have been—you can get injections now. It's a bit painful—in the navel and all—but it's worth it, many times over. You don't have this perverted craving for . . . for"—he turned directly to Roger—"for women. What would your family say if they knew you was out here?"

"You won't tell them, will you? Please!" Roger waddled closer to the leader. "Please, don't!"

"I'm sorry, boy, but it's part of my job. As long as there are even a few of your kind left, we have to go and root you out. Society can't tolerate this sort of activity. You might get to the children, and. . . ." The leader's lips hardened at the idea; the eyes became cruel again. "You bastard, I ought to kill you right now." He raised his rifle to his shoulder, and Roger let out a high-pitched scream, but somehow it was oddly brief. It just stopped before it began, and his eyes widened.

"No, Sam, there's still the law." One of the other men put his hand fondly on the leader's shoulder.

"Yeah, you're right, Joe." The gun fell back into the crook of his arm. The leader lifted Joe's fingers from his own shoulder and kissed them gently. "I lost my head, I'm sorry."

"We understand, fella. It's these degenerates; they get to you. A decent man can't help but want to wipe 'em out. Probably should dig a pit someplace and throw 'em all in it and pour gasoline on it. We've worked so *blasted* hard to get this new society going right, and, by God, they aren't going to ruin it. If we don't take care of them, lock 'em up, they'll be contaminating the youngsters after they leave the hatcheries. There's already some teachers who are heterosexuals; they drop slight little hints about—jokes they call them—about boys sleeping with girls, touching breasts and all that filth! Pretty soon the kids'll go experimenting with that stuff and have babies on their own—all those germs, and the mongoloids that result!" He shuddered against his will. "There's no telling where it will end; we'll all be back in primitive days, when everybody was heterosexual!"

"You're right, Joe." The leader leaned over and kissed him

on the mouth. The rest of the men smiled at the affection, grinning at each other. After several seconds, the two parted, and one of the other men pointed his gun accusingly at Roger. "Why can't you find yourself a few nice boys to make love to. What's wrong with you anyway? We give you every opportunity and what do you do—sneak off to some woods with a girl! And what's wrong with you?" he said to Miriam. "There are plenty of girls to go around."

"We've said enough to them," the leader said abruptly. "Come on you two; we're taking you to jail." He motioned with the rifle for them to move toward the armored truck used for the Queer Raids, as they were called. "The courts can put you where you won't be any harm except to your own depraved selves."

"But they'll castrate me," Roger pleaded. "And they'll sew Miriam up, won't they?"

"That's only natural, what do you expect? If you violate the law, you gotta pay."

"But my friends, my job, the shame after I get out. I won't be able to show my face."

"Well, show your rear end then. People can't tell much difference anyway." The group laughed heartily at Joe's witticism.

"I can't, I can't face that!" Roger yelled. "Shoot me instead." He started to run away, but he fell down after a few yards because of his twisted pants. Miriam turned too and hurried after him, her one breast bobbing sensually in the cars' beams. She knelt beside his body, now covered with dust. "Shoot us both," she said defiantly. "I won't go back either."

"But you're still just kids. You can be treated; you don't have to go on like this, wallowing in perversion. . . ."

But Miriam turned her head away from the leader's words, and then very deliberately she placed her head on Roger's crotch.

"But we can help you; we can make you normal!" The leader's words dangled in the quiet June air. "For your own sakes!"

When the two refused to answer, the man let his shoulders slump ever so slightly before he motioned for the rest to come up closer to where the two perverts were lying. The boy glanced up frightened for a second before he buried his head in his hands. The rifles thumped against the men's bodies as they were aimed. And then the leader gave the signal, and they mercifully put the crippled ones out of their misery.

Cole languidly opened his eyes, looking up at the late afternoon sky through his sunglasses. This story never failed to satisfy him, especially when he was able to keep it going for ten minutes or more. Sometimes versions of it did not last as long, only a minute or two, and he felt cheated then. But today's fantasy had been a good one. He flipped over on his back to catch the rays of the flimsy August sun. *I guess I won't get a tan this year either*, he said lethargically to himself. *Maybe I could go to Florida. Or Bermuda. I can wait, though. I have waited these three years. What is one more tan or not? A tan ages a person anyway.*

He slipped the sunglasses up onto his stiff black hair so that he could rest his face more comfortably on his wrists. But then he felt something crawling on his waist, although he did not move. *Probably an ant.* Then very slowly he reached down and pressed the insect into his skin, feeling the segments of it break, ball up. He lifted his finger to his face to see what he had killed. It was a tiny green bug, some sort of hopper, its insides now a minute puddle on his fingertip. He watched as the delicate legs made a feeble effort to move. *I wonder how much pain it feels*, he thought to himself emotionlessly. *When a spider sinks his fangs into one of you, do you screech in agony? We think you don't feel anything because you're so small, don't we?* The insect stopped moving altogether, and for another minute Cole watched the dead thing on his fingertip. Then he pressed it very hard against his thumb. *You'd only live through the summer anyway, if you were lucky, if some bird, some other bug, some brother did not suck your sap before that.* He tried to flip the mashed creature away, but it stuck to his skin. He flicked again, as if trying to get rid of snot. The pulp landed somewhere out of sight, less than a yard away, swallowed up by one of the patches of grass in the motel's cement yard.

Cole flipped over onto his back again and stared down at his thin, white body. *What am I going to do now?* He looked at his legs: long, almost too thin, the black hairs that popped out all over them. He touched the tight skin of his chest and ran his hand across the well-formed torso. A line of dark fur pointed like an arrow down into his swimming trunks, and a slight mound where his "private parts," as his mother had called them, were located made him smile. *I'm all right there,* he thought. *Nothing spectacular, but serviceable.* The idea made him stir inside his trunks, just enough to make his body uncomfortable. *Only I'm so white,* he said to himself, as if examining a piece of cloth. He put his hands on his face, feeling the contours, as he had seen blind people do in movies. *My eyes are sunk in ridges,* he realized with a sudden panic. *That's why I look so evil, especially in certain lights.* His eyebrows felt thick, too thick, all twisted no matter how often he straightened them with a finger. *How many people have to comb their eyebrows?* he wondered. Tracing the facial areas that were pitted, he lingered over one especially deep acne scar. *A crater. And my nose is like a spear,* he noticed, touching it. *And it's much too long.* He pressed his whole hand against the length of his face to push the nose down, to make it flatter; he could feel the gristle moving silently. *We have no control over the way we look!* He spoke to himself with what he wanted to be bitterness, but somehow he was not bitter. *I look absolutely fine, absolutely perfectly mediocrely usual. Hundreds of men in veterans' hospitals would love to look like me. All those scarred people from automobile accidents, people with birthmarks, reddish blue veins showing on their faces, harelips, all the millions of subaverage average citizens would be delighted to have my face and body. But why aren't I handsome, breathtaking! Why don't people stare at me in admiration, nudging each other as I pass, so startling that they hate me because they cannot resist my appeal?* He smiled at his own words, words that he could see like typed lines across his brain. COLE RUFFNER WINS BEAUTY CONTEST. The line of type turned into a headline in the Detroit *Free Press*: COLE RUFFNER MAKES MILLIONS SWOON. He could see his realigned handsome face staring out of the shadows of a Sunday supplement: RUFFNER, MAN ABOUT TOWN, TELLS IT LIKE IT IS. What a stupid dope I am, he told himself in disgust. He folded his arms across his chest, then began picking at the long black hairs, paining himself as he made the flesh move up and down. *What a way to spend a Sunday! At a crummy motel in downtown Detroit, where it costs me eight dollars a day to lie here by myself, to soak my weight in this tiny pool, too full of chlorine and dead flies.* Cole looked up, startled, as a middle-aged woman in an aquamarine bathing suit came out of her motel room. A man about fifty followed her, carrying their beach towels. He had a very red face and was wearing underwater goggles across his balding head. The woman was going to fat, with her hips spread out like the bottom of a pear, and her red-tinted hair was too bright. The man spread the towels on two of the deck chairs as though he were afraid of picking up germs, as the woman took two cans of beer out of her large patterned purse and tore off the flip tops. *I wonder why his face is so flushed; he probably has to give it to her every night, maybe twice a day. She makes him grunt.* "Come on, Horace, you old bull, you can do better than that; I didn't marry you for conversation!"

Cole raised up a bit to see if the couple could read his thoughts, but they did not appear to notice him. They sat drinking their beers, saying nothing. *Is this how people pass their lives out of jail? Are they on vacation? Have they come here to Detroit just to be in this dismal sunshine? Is it a treat for them? They come down from Lapeer and think that they are having a good time? Or maybe instead he's a con man and she's an ex-madam of a brothel, hiding out for a few days, and their room just got too close for them.* He raised his head again to see if they looked any different from that perspective. But they did not. They continued to sit without uttering a word to each other, until the man muttered something that Cole could not understand. It must have been for a cigarette, since the woman took a package out of her purse and slid it across the table. *Perhaps they are Roger and Miriam thirty years later. Maybe they did not die when the men shot them but lived and crawled away, until they eventually recovered, the holes in their bodies closed over, sealing the bullets inside. The body is a marvelous camouflage for what's inside. Now they both carry five pounds of lead around within them, and they are very careful to subtract that amount whenever they weigh on a penny scale; it keeps them thinking they are not getting fat and old.*

When he looked at them again, the couple was talking, quietly, as if they had said the same things two hundred times before but they had long since stopped caring that they were boring to each other. *Maybe they are talking about their children, who live in Detroit and have asked them to come for a visit. However, it has turned out that they do not really have room for them, so they had to come to this motel. Later they are supposed to go over to their daughter's house for dinner, which will be very formal, and the parents will feel like outsiders. Then in a few days they will go back to Lapeer and tell their few friends what a nice trip they had.* "Sort of like me," Cole said aloud, but he forced the ideas back inside his mind. *I have nobody either, not even one person. I had to come to a lousy motel because no one knows me, certainly nobody who used to be my friend wants me, even for a few days.*

He thought of the letter that he had almost sent from the Detroit House of Correction to Bud Smallwood, his closest friend, whom he had known for more than two years. *Bud would not have bothered to answer. Probably married by now, doing well in his government job, afraid to be associated with a convicted homosexual. Or he would have written back to say that he wanted nothing to do with me.*

Of course I could not have written to my father. It would

*merely be an embarrassment if the wayward son tried to go back
there now, even for a visit; the prodigal son might even be
chased away, certainly no rings or robes—they would be considered too effeminate. The wonder is that my father did not
move away from the city after the scandal. Anyway, he sent
me a thousand dollars from the sale of my car, with a hundred
extra out of his own pocket. It was no substitute for love, of
course. It was better. Besides, the money probably was a bribe
to stay away.*

His mother was dead; she had died while he was in prison,
right after Christmas during the second year, and his father had
sent him a picture of the grave and a holy picture from the funeral. That was all, except for the brief note on the back of the
photograph. He could see his little, fat, fussy mother resting under the ground somewhere, wagging her head back and forth, as
she used to do, talking, talking, talking in a gossipy gush, her
hands waving. *I suppose I killed her, in a way. She helped put
me in prison, helped kill me, and I killed her in return. But
I'm not the first son to wind up disreputable. Why did she take
it so seriously? She was always such a silly, sentimental woman,
crying over a cake she had spoiled, a burned batch of doughy
Italian cookies. She believed that her love was enough to keep
away all pains, from everybody who was part of her family.
Yet she ought to have known better, been smarter, for her love
could not save anybody. All it did was compound the suffering
when it came.*

*Would it have done any good to contact my brother? No,
Edwin was too cold, too much older. He must be forty by now.
A telephone repairman with a wife and three children, growing
old in Toledo. I can't remember once ever having a conversation
with Edwin. We had nothing to say to each other, nothing. But
he may have helped me, out of some Catholic sense of duty.
Thank God for the eleven hundred dollars I have. Money can
save a man from too much humiliation. I can see myself sleeping in my brother's attic, a half-finished-off room, choking*

on the mouthfuls of food at the supper table, seeing him count the cost of each one of my bites, thinking that I would seduce one of his sons.

Cole sat up immediately when he heard the laugh, hurting his neck somehow. The fat woman at the pool looked over at him, hiding behind her mirrored sunglasses. *She wasn't laughing at me after all. Her husband must have told her a joke, something about two Negroes. . . .* Suddenly Cole became aware of the perspiration on his back; he was almost trembling. *And I thought I was impervious to opinion! Some fat lady's laugh sends shivers down my spine.* For a moment he felt like getting up and dragging her into the swimming pool, watching her heavy arms flapping in the chemically blue water as she sank gulping out her life, lunging for air that wouldn't come. He stretched back on the beach towel near the rim of the pool, his stomach muscles rising and falling too fast.

But I'm free now, by God! I earned the right to lie here, to think what I want to think. You'll never put me behind bars again. I swear it. He made himself remain quiet, directing the images into his mind. He had tried not to think clearly about the event for six months, for he had worn his brain out with reliving the scene, until he was weary, exhausted. But now he wanted to see if he could think about it again, even find some comfort in the details. *Three years ago? No, it couldn't be. Though sometimes it seemed longer than that—all those tedious, bland days of sitting in a cell. In August three years ago. Three years and three days ago:*

He drove through a public park, Rouge Park, to a "comfort station," even joking to himself about the name, thinking that all he wanted was a little comfort. The place was usually deserted after seven, but the attendants did not close it down until eight thirty. It was a well-known meeting place, for "quickies." The body built up its pressures, which had to be relieved. A fact of chemistry. There were always several men waiting inside, who leaned forward on the toilet stools to see who entered, not at all subtle. The officials of the park had removed the doors of the stalls to eliminate such sex acts, but the doorless stalls actually made cruising easier and prevented any sort of privacy, whereby the men would relieve their needs and depart, instead of lingering, startled by each opening of the outside door. Cole was on his way to a party given by Angie, a good friend, one of the girls who worked in his office. The irony was that he wanted to get sex off his mind, and he checked for police cars. None in sight.

He stood at a urinal, keeping his eyes down for a good five minutes, not especially interested in the older men sitting on the toilets. When he turned his head, one of them made slurping noises—disgusting, but they aroused him nevertheless. He started to face the man, when the door opened and a young man, very attractive, came in, right up to the next urinal. While glancing at Cole, he fumbled slowly with his zipper, and then began manipulating his penis, making the blood rush, beckoning with his head. Ordinarily, Cole would have waited, been much more cautious, but the man was so encouraging, and so attractive. Cole looked back over his shoulder at the other two men in the stalls, who obviously wanted him to take the offer. And so he did. He put out his hand, and when the man swung toward him, he cupped both hands around the sex.

The rest was blurred, somehow not completely formed in his mind. Mainly what he recalled was two men falling or jumping out of the ceiling, through a wire mesh. One of them must have injured his leg because he hopped around as he made the arrest. *It was really quite funny*, Cole told himself. *One detective hopping around like somebody playing hopscotch, shouting "cocksucker" over and over at him.* The handsome young man who was the decoy was washing his hands, saying nothing, wiping carefully, rolling the paper into wads as he tossed it casually into a wooden barrel.

They let the other two men in the booths go, hitting them a few times as a warning. But Cole they took to the unmarked Ford that was parked a few blocks away behind some willow trees. One of the men kept kicking him in the rear, at least seven or eight times, and Cole shouted for him to stop it, but all the man did was kick him harder. "There's some dirt on your clothes; I'm helping you, you cocksucker; I'm helping you!"

Inside the automobile the policemen shoved Cole to the far side, but they did not start the car right away, because the two in front were whispering to each other, while the biggest one, in the back seat with Cole, jabbed him gently in the ribs. "I'll let you go if you go down on me, kid," he said. "What do you say? All three of us—and we'll let you go." Cole could not tell from the tone if the man was serious or merely trying to humiliate him further. "Come on, son, go to it; you like to do it anyway. God, my leg hurts!" He suddenly stuck it over to Cole's side of the car. "You're gonna pay for my injury, kid, don't you forget it." He grabbed Cole's head and pulled on the hair, forcing the head down into his lap. But Cole resisted, his throat blistered, sick. The cop rolled the head around, back and forth, across his crotch. A warmish, vague musty odor mixed with tobacco. "Get to it, boy. This here boy don't know how to do nothing."

The two men in the front seat looked back at the words. "What are you doing to that kid, Keel?"

"Just giving him a chance to earn his freedom, that's all."

"Aw, don't you ever get tired of this?"

Cole tried to see their faces clearly, to see what they meant. Were they serious? But he could detect nothing in the dimness. Then the man in the back grabbed Cole's cheek in a hard pinch. "Get going, son, and watch them teeth." He pulled down his zipper, arching his back to do it. As he did, the car started and backed up. "Come on, we'll let you go afterward."

Cole looked up at the silhouetted forms in the front. "Will you? Really?"

"What do you think? We're good to faggots, aren't we, Ralph?" The three of them snickered so that Cole did not know what he was expected to do; he sat still. "Give me a blow job, what do you say?" Tentatively, he leaned forward, then sat back. "Come on, kid." The policeman patted his own legs on either side of the fly. Cole leaned down again toward the man's stomach. "That's the way, son. Do your duty." Cole slowly put his face into the man's clothes, his own sweat plastering his hair over his brow, a few pubic hairs brushing against his nose. "That's the way, fairy, tickle my pickle." The cop put his hand on the back of Cole's neck and squeezed, then pressed down. "Lick it." Cole could hardly breathe; he hesitated. "I said lick it!" His tongue went out and touched the stub, which tasted like salt and moist talcum powder. "Lick harder; give it a go." Cole's heart swelled inside him, achingly, and he thought he would vomit. But he opened his mouth and surrendered. After a few seconds, the cop yanked him up by the collar. "You ain't nothing but a whore, are you?" He pushed Cole's face away and fastened the zipper. "Pig, slimey pig. Faggot. Queer faggot freak! Sister man, you make me puke. Let's get this thing moving faster." The man gestured at the two in front.

"Keel, you're brutal," the handsome man said quietly.

"You ought to know, Parris, with your cock hanging out all the time. I think you get a kick out of it."

The other did not respond, and Cole, his mouth gone totally dry, asked, "Where are we going?"

"We got a judge that wants to see you, sissy boy. You're going to pay for your crime against society, including this pain in my leg." He rubbed at his calf. "You've got three witnesses who saw you—three. Don't you know sucking's against the law."

"But I didn't—"

"Hey fellas, he doesn't know that cocksuckers go to jail. Just like drunk drivers, only longer. You know, we ought to put up a sign like they do along the streets."

"Come on, cut it out, lay off," the handsome, younger man said.

"You give in to these queers, Parris, and you see what happens!"

For a while after that no one spoke, until the florid-complexioned man in the back said, "You happened along at a bad time, boy." Cole said nothing, but the man continued, confidentially. "Not talking, eh? Well, there was a queer murder a few days ago; some young boys, two of them, found shot through the back. Since we haven't found the killer yet, all of you faggots are gonna pay." He spoke as if the natural order of reward and punishment was being announced. "Why don't you speak up, fairy. The last one we caught, a couple of days ago, bawled all over us."

"Let me go. I—"

"Shut up, freak!" the man pulled his leg back to his side, scraping Cole's ankle as he did, but Cole made no further attempts to speak.

The courtroom the next morning was filled with people, primarily grubby-looking, even the officials. Cole was brought in with the other men from the jail, mostly drunks, a few assault cases. His clothes were rumpled from his having tried to sleep in them all night. He had not been allowed to call a bondsman. That morning a lawyer was appointed to defend him, a man who did not even ask him what had happened or bother to give his own name. He asked only if Cole had a job and how much money he made a year. Cole accepted the lawyer, not knowing what else to do, never having needed one before, not at twenty-four.

"What do you plead?" the judge asked, a leathery-faced old man.

"Not guilty, Your Honor," the court lawyer pleaded for Cole.

Then one of the arresting policemen, the limping one, read his account of the arrest, adding details that were lies, saying that Cole had grabbed the decoy, who was minding his own business, that the defendant had even exposed himself in a public place. The man's voice seemed extremely loud, carrying throughout the whole courtroom, but Cole was too embarrassed to look around to see. "The defendant also offered to bribe us by an obscene suggestion, Your Honor. But I won't go into the details since I won't press it," the heavy man said in conclusion.

"All right, what's your story?" the judge asked indifferently, scribbling some notes to himself as Cole talked.

Cole looked at his lawyer helplessly, wondering what he was

supposed to say. Should he deny everything? "What can I say, Your Honor? I seem to be on the defensive, don't I?" He grinned, not knowing why. Did he think that charm would work a miracle? But the judge was not charmed; he wrinkled his nose when he looked up.

"What is your defense, if any?"

The lawyer answered for him. "The defendant, Your Honor, is employed."

For some reason that seemed to make a difference in his guilt. "Where?" the judge asked Cole.

"I work in the Federal Building."

"Do you work for the government?"

"Yes, I'm a cartographer, a map-maker."

"For the government?"

"Yes."

"I see. Why were you in a public lavatory?"

"Why does anybody go into one, sir?"

"Don't be smart," the lawyer whispered to him, before he looked up to the judge. "The defendant was driving around, Your Honor, and stopped to use the convenience."

"He knows that toilet is notorious. Since he has a government job, he ought to be more responsible. If they didn't hire you people in the first place," he said accusingly at Cole, "then they wouldn't have to worry about your carrying-on."

"I wasn't bothering anyone."

"On the contrary, sir, this man was acting in a very obvious lewd and lascivious manner," the heavy man broke in.

"And how were you acting in the car?" Cole shouted at him. "What do you call that? Tell him what you made me do, tell him!"

"Stop shouting," the judge commanded. "We are not interested in what the officer did, but in what you did in that public lavatory."

"What do you mean you're not interested? He's guiltier than I am. Isn't he?" Cole turned to the other two policemen. "They know; they saw him."

"Well?" the judge asked them, but they shook their heads no.

"But you heard him last night! You do too know!"

When the two policemen again shook their heads, the judge said, "Enough of this. The case seems clear to me. Guilty as charged."

Then Cole went into a foolish rage. "You don't give a damn about justice. You leave my sex life alone, you hear me!"

His lawyer looked at him with contempt at his outburst.

"Have you said your piece?" the judge said sarcastically.

"I'm not guilty of any crime."

"Your conduct this morning here convinces me that you are a rather unstable person, and, according to your record, you were also picked up by the police at age nineteen for loitering. There's a pattern here. You need a bit of cooling off, it appears to me. It's persons like you who go stalking around these public parks, getting yourselves murdered, when you aren't committing the murders yourself. It's about time we put a stop to all of this. Six months in the Detroit House of Correction. Indecent Exposure and Lewd and Lascivious Behavior."

When a policeman came up behind Cole to escort him away, he shrugged off the man's hands. It couldn't be happening, it just couldn't be. He was dazed. Overhead a lazy blade-fan revolved, cooling nothing, just moving the oppressive heat around. "I won't go!" Cole yelled. Then he ran toward the railing that surrounded the judge's platform, toward the exit. Two other police officers came toward him from somewhere. To get away, he leaped over the railing but fell to the floor. He was up at once, grabbing papers from the court secretary's desk, throwing handfuls of paper at the advancing officers, more of them now. He lifted the shorthand typewriter the man had been using over his head with both hands. "Stay away, you bastards! Stay away!" The people in the courtroom were quiet, sitting staring at him from the blackish-brown rows that looked like pews. One man in the rear shouted encouragement to him: "Way to go, man. Give 'em hell." But before the words were finished, Cole was surrounded by men with pistols pointed at him, and he simply dropped the machine behind him; it merely bounced twice and settled back into an upright position, undamaged. His little demonstration cost him two more years in jail, for threatening a police officer and contempt of court.

Beside the pool, Cole laughed at himself, a small smirk that did not quite emerge from the mouth, a noise that could have been someone smothering. *King Kong Fights Airplanes on Empire State Building! King Cole Conquers Police! Why is it so funny now,* he wondered. *It was terrible then. Agonies and disasters become smart-aleck comments. Why can't my trial retain its form, remain the misery that it actually was? I have SUFFERED!* His self-smile dissolved, and he let his mind dwell on the faces of the three men in jail who had been the cause of yet six more months in prison:

One held his legs, another sat on his shoulders, and the third pulled down his trousers. It happened in the laundry room, amid all those soiled towels and briefs, little pieces of smut and hair dutifully soaped and bleached and rinsed away. He was tossed on a pile of laundry bags, his rear end lathered with a handful of detergent that the man had grabbed from a shelf. And then a sharp, slow pain as the man tried to penetrate him. All the man said was, "Hold still, buddy, and it won't hurt so much." *Cole wondered if he had really consented to the sodomy; he could have struggled harder. Nobody can be violated unless he wants to be, can he? But he had fought them.* The man clutched at his waist, panting, trying to work into a rhythm, but he never quite succeeded; he came in less than a minute. It was while the second man was greasing himself with the semen that they were discovered by a supervisor. All of them were given another six months for "unnatural behavior," Cole included. No one believed him at the hearing when he protested, sometimes screaming, that he had been raped. They thought he was lying, for, after all, he was the pervert, as everyone knew. The men who had attacked him were just normal men—all had wives. As they said in the director's office, they were just horny.

Cole made himself smile, savagely: *No wonder it's called a* penal *colony.* He flipped over onto his side.

However, the worst suffering had not been physical, not even the monotony of life in jail. It was the sense of isolation from everyone he knew. From Teddy one side of a sheet, in a large hand, saying that he was very sorry to hear about the misfortune and if there was anything he could do . . . from Teddy, his friend, his *lover* in fact. *It must have provided him with the excuse he wanted to break off our connection. I sensed it for several months before the arrest. The thing that probably bothered the bastard most was having to pay the whole rent himself! Though perhaps he was afraid of getting arrested too, as somehow an accomplice, guilty by association. Teddy never was very smart, a coward too. Why did I love him? He must have considered himself Florence Nightingale for sending that one lousy sheet of paper, signed "sincerely yours." I'm glad I ripped it into shreds.*

Teddy's probably still here in Detroit, still a waiter at that restaurant near downtown. Cole sat up, and the lady behind the sunglasses glanced his way again. *Teddy's not very far from here, and he's probably working now. I could drop in the place for dinner, pretend I have forgotten who he is, leave a small tip. Better yet, pennies. "Thanks for the memory, Teddy," I could whisper to him as I leave. Or a note near the pennies.* Cole grabbed his forehead, massaging it with his thumb and forefingers. *What's wrong with me? I should forget Teddy. He was shallow, I knew that. All he could think of was clothes, clothes and parties. Didn't even finish high school. Nothing to him but his handsomeness, and probably even that is beginning to go—he's— yes—twenty-nine now, the hair thinning, lines, delicate but permanent, streaking from beneath the eyes. Not even Dear John letters from him. He was always ashamed of his bad spelling. And he lacked nerve enough to write to say that he was leaving for somebody else; instead he would let the silence speak for him, trusting in the passing days. He may not even remember my birthday by now. The son of a bitch! Maybe he wouldn't even recall my first name. I ought to hit him in his pretty face.*

At least my mother wrote to me, probably never knowing exactly why I was in jail, never forming the shameful concept in her Old World mind. Her boy was in jail for some terrible reason; tragedies happened that way. Some boys got hit by cars; others were blown up in wars; her son was among these. Mothers had the chore of enduring such hardships; that was life, questioned with picturesque moans, but secretly accepted, even though it destroyed them. But then she died and I got a postcard from my father, an old one from a Howard Johnson restaurant, saying: "Your mother passed away as of the 27th of December. She did not suffer much." Nothing else except the picture of the grave a few weeks later, a bump covered with snow.

My father undoubtedly knows what I did, but feels absolutely no sympathy; he cannot tolerate such behavior; it is as if someone had made love to a corpse, and now no doubt he has blocked the idea completely from his mind, tells people nothing if they ask about his younger son, says that he is working in Detroit, is too busy to come to visit. Lying there, thinking about his father, he imagined the blood dripping from his own heart, drop by drop, as from a dagger of icicle.

In jail he had cursed all the people he knew, because he had been too ashamed to write to anyone but his mother. For hours he would lie thinking about them; then he had begun to draw obscene pictures: Bud Smallwood, his best friend, with his face inside a toilet bowl, Angie Fionda blowing a cardinal, his cousin Marilyn with her eyes missing, Carter Pearson and his wife picking each other's noses. They were the first such drawings he had ever done, and the more disgusting they became the more anger he felt, but after a time he had simply stopped thinking about them consciously; instead he had brooded, not always aware that he brooded, conscious of the fact now and then when he had slammed his fist against the wall beside his bed, when his teeth had hurt from pressing down too hard.

He had received another letter in prison—he remembered—

from his boss at the Federal Building, informing him that his contract with the government was being terminated because of his prison sentence, very carefully indicating that government employees could not be security risks. There was nothing personal in it, nothing even insulting, only a brisk, official end to his career. He would without question be in some file now, with black bands all around his photograph, he guessed. Or a big X drawn through his face. Confidential List of Queers! Homosexuals in Alphabetical Order! Personnel—Perverted! All those vast files in the Pentagon perhaps, somewhere, rows and rows of records, records that nobody ever looks at, except to keep people out of government jobs. *Nobody said I didn't do my job well,* Cole thought, with enough grimness to make his chest hurt.

Gazing up into the pale sun, he considered what he should do with his life. *I wonder who it was that informed my boss. Is there some little, shriveled man who spends the whole day writing cryptic letters to the employers of convicted men: "Dear Sir, your employee —— is temporarily detained for having been discovered in a lewd and lascivious position in a public lavatory. Said employee has been sentenced to two and half years in the Detroit House of Correction and may be reached there by mail. Faithfully yours, T. Tadpole Spiggot." And I tried to fool the boss by writing to tell him that I wanted to quit my job because of a personal problem. My personal problem is a public one!*

Cole returned to thinking about what he should do. *My bachelor's degree—at least that can't be rescinded. Or can it? No, I can at least hang on to that. And I can draw well. I might try a private firm like Rand McNally. But what if they require a reference? Perhaps making posters for some store, like Hudson's. What can I do with a degree in geography? Teach? No, that's too tiresome—and dangerous in many high schools. I'd rather starve. A salesman? Not that I'm a snob—or am I?—but selling shirts or garter belts seems so ordinary, and the pay is low, isn't it? Maybe I could go back to graduate school, to get a degree in*

Fine Arts or art. But I'm twenty-seven already. Can I go back to studying? Maybe some job would be better, easier. But I won't go begging at someone's door, my hat in my hand, he told himself viciously, turning over on the beach towel the motel provided. *I'm better than that; I won't have some mealy-faced, gloating creep tell me, "We're sorry, but you don't quite fit into our present plans." Or worse yet, one day a tap on the shoulder and my new boss will say, "Ruffner, you're through. We don't want your kind working here." I could drive a taxi, I suppose. Does anyone care what taxi drivers do?*

Perhaps I could get a job at Teddy's fancy restaurant. Good tips. But that would mean seeing Teddy, trivial, frivolous Teddy. Cole smiled at his words. He hated nelly quarrels, shrieking queens, like the two he had seen one time in a gay bar, making utter fools of themselves. *I won't be like that. I'm a man, no matter what anybody calls me. I am a man.* "Teddy, Teddy, how could you!" he muttered. "But I'd like you back anyway." He raised his head in resentment at the woman and her husband, still sitting beside the swimming pool, drinking their beer. He couldn't say Teddy's name over and over, the way he wanted to. *I wish you'd go away, you old bags,* he said silently to the couple. *What do you care what has happened to me? You'd snicker if I told you I loved a man. That or turn away. I hate your flabby old skin, your despicable cancer-ridden old snatch, your big breasts full of cancer, your dried-up old jabber. I hate you both. Go back into your motel room and screw and screw and SCREW! Nobody will arrest you. Be normal, by all means. Be good citizens. Nobody will put you in jail. Go give each other a fungus on your "genital areas."*

Cole slammed his body down, doing it too fast and cracking his head against the cement. Yet he did not make a sound, did not move, although the pain pulsated through the back of his brain. *Let me die, let me die, let the flash of pain descend into my heart and stop it, tangle it in knots, let me stop breathing.* But the throb remained, only gradually subsiding, leaving a dullness, a *knocking that matched his heartbeat.* "Oh, living, living!" Cole whispered to himself. He felt sick, the same way he had that night he had been arrested in the park.

Suddenly the heavy, red face of the man in the back seat jumped at him out of the sun. *You are a terrible man,* Cole realized quite coolly. *A horrible, distorted creature. You're probably still going out to entrap men, still pushing their faces in your sweaty lap. Someone ought to kill you, leave your rotting carcass in a stream, where dogs could urinate on it, some lusty lover could fling his used condom into your grinning mouth as you lie there, bloated, in the dark.* And then Cole felt his heart rush, spin. *It's my duty,* he thought. *It would be a moral act.* Yet he was very cautious not to move, not to call attention to himself. Surely the old couple could read his thoughts, could see the trembling flesh. When he peeked at them, he saw that they knew nothing. Then he lay back carefully and began to calm his mind. It took several minutes. After all, he had never planned a murder before.

2

The thought of murder had crossed his mind many times previously, while he had been lying in his cell, but he knew that it had been just one of his fantasies, a means of passing the time more than anything else. Yet now that he was out, the idea tasted good, actually better than before, in the impotence of prison. *The cop has already destroyed my life. So I'm entitled to destroy his. To hell with "starting anew," working hard to show that I'm a repentant, healthy member of society, as they would like. I'll be damned if I will wind up as a chapter in some minister's self-help best seller. Reclaimed Sinners, the title would be. "It was Mr. R's misfortune to have fallen into the wicked clutches of Sodom and Gomorrah. However, his tale is one that should encourage us all, unlike, unfortunately, the pathetic stories of so many of these, our afflicted brethren."*

Cole sat back in the taxi and lit a cigarette. *But first this other thing out of the way.* He had stopped smoking while in jail, but decided quite deliberately to take it up again. *It's my life—I earned it,* he thought, spitting a speck of tobacco off his tongue. As the taxi pulled away from the curb, he looked out its rear window at the building in which he had just rented an apartment —in Highland Park, just on the borderline between respectability and sluminess. Most of the tenants were college students at the University of Detroit, larking it up, visiting at all hours with great bursts of noise. The apartment had dark varnish on everything, floors, woodwork, dresser, even the lampposts in the room he labeled the bedroom; the other rooms were a kitchen, living room, and bathroom. Although it was much worse than the place he had shared with Teddy before he had been arrested in the park, he did not care very much; it somehow seemed fitting to him. *I'll think of myself as an old Russian countess come down in the world. The Countess Eugenie Colevsky—* Immediately he quelled the joke, not liking to feminize himself. "Let the rest of the goddamn world think that," he said.

"What?" The taxi driver looked back briefly over his shoulder.

"Never mind; just keep going." He was amazed at his own coolness. *And I think I've gotten smarter in these past three years. Before I would not have remembered to call ahead to see if Teddy was still living in the same apartment; I would have gone there to accuse him and somebody else would have answered the door so that I would have had to apologize or make up a lie while some man with a newspaper in his fist glared at me. No, this time I know where he is and that he'll be there. Perhaps I'm ready to commit my murder more than I realized.* He smiled to himself. *At three o'clock Teddy will be almost ready for work. They said he comes in at four thirty. How easy it was to trace him, because the manager of the restaurant was only too pleased to help "an old high school chum" find Teddy. No, he was not still living in an apartment downtown; he had a place on the east side of Detroit now, in a residential apartment building on Montclair, near Jefferson. Yes, he had the address. Good, I won't have to spoil my appearance by having a desk clerk ring his place first. Now I can ring one of the other apartments and be let in. His face will drop to his shoes when he sees me. A half hour ought to be sufficient.*

His gaze swept past two high-rise buildings along Jefferson. *How can there be so many rich people, to live in these? Of course I myself lived in one almost as good, and I was never rich. Still there must be people with thousands and thousands of dollars; they could toss money from their expensive, sliding-glass, enclosed balconies and hardly miss it, litter the swimming pools far below them. Well, they ought to throw themselves out of the buildings more often than they do, plug up the drains with their pink guts.*

The taxi drove on, past motels like the one he had stayed in for the past two days, past used car lots: DAN'S CARS, LOT'S LOTS, HARRY TYLOR'S TERRIFIC DEALS. Big, bright show windows in the new car dealerships, with rigorously upholstered salesmen waiting inside, the U.S. Royal Rubber Company, the Belle Isle Bridge. It seemed somehow proper to Cole that the city's biggest park lay right next to the factory that belched out hundreds of tons of soot, the dark particles sifting across to the Yacht Club, the yellow public beach, which always was filled with beer cans, broken bottles, wrappers, Kleenex. *People cannot complain about the filth; they put most of it there themselves,* he thought angrily. *But I don't care about other people,* he reminded himself. *They most likely don't even know the beach is polluted; it takes a hundred thousand repetitions on television before it begins to sink in, before they care at all, before they are able to form the idea into a cliché.*

The taxi passed a slow police car. One of the policemen looked at Cole indifferently. *If I kill my cop, how will I do it?* He looked at the back of the cabbie's head to see if the man knew what he was considering. *I own my own mind,* he insisted to himself. *Nobody can tell, nobody can read my mind.* Cole drew an X in the dust on the window beside him. *The mark of death. Maybe I'll write: "Stop me before I kill again" on a mirror, in lipstick. They will think it is some psychopath. I just hope that my cop is not already dead—a ruptured spleen, a heart attack. But how should I do it? I can't shoot him, because wouldn't I have to register a hand gun? Perhaps with a rifle. I could shoot him through the window of his house—split him into two hunks. Or follow him to a park during one of his entrapments, sneak up behind him and pump him full of shells, though that way I would have to contend with the others who would be with him; they might shoot me too. Could I poison him? Would I have to sign something to get quick-acting poison? And how would I get it into his coffee? No, too theatrical. And too difficult. If it looks like revenge, the po-*

lice are certain to review all those he has arrested—probably a large group. It must not seem sexual in any way, certainly not homosexual. How? Cole made another X in the window dirt. *So it is not so easy to commit a murder after all. I don't think I could stab anyone to death. That terrible thump after the first thrust, striking a bone, the blood squirting out. And then another thump. Another. And I'm not strong enough to strangle a man his size; he would kill me, no doubt, break my arm behind my back. Yes, what if he gets me instead?* Cole became aware of his prickly clothes, the threatening sweat. *What if I hit him with a car, run him over? It would seem to be a hit-and-run accident. Would there be witnesses? I could use a stolen car. I could find out where he lives, wait for him, never hurrying, and then slam into him. How fast would I have to drive? How do killers know all these facts?*

"Is this the place?" The cabbie's voice jolted him. The man was pointing at a yellow brick building in a changing neighborhood. Two girls were playing hopscotch a few doors down. Cole checked the address he had written down. "Yes, this is it." He didn't tip the driver. *Let him curse me all he likes; I need the money.*

Inside the vestibule, the six mailboxes looked sloppy and slick from years of handprints. The name "Ted Emmord" was typed on a slip of paper in one of the slots. *Be home, Teddy,* he hoped. Because the inside door was unlocked, he did not have to ring another apartment, and he went up to the third floor, to number five. The smell of strong, noxious paint drifted out of one of the apartments, and there were cobwebs high up in the corners. Although he felt cold, he was in control when he rang the buzzer.

However, Teddy did not answer the door; it was another man, about thirty, with sand-colored hair with streaks of natural straw-blond here and there. He was without a shirt, muscular, like a male model, elegantly rugged, virility worn like a cosmetic. He was even smoking a pipe. On his chin there was a bump, which made him look more handsome than if the features had

been regular. "Can I help you?" Of course he was a baritone.
"I thought Teddy Emmord lived here."
"Is he expecting you?"
"Not really. Is he gone out?"
"He's in the bathroom, getting ready for work. He has to work tonight."
"I know. Can I come in?"
"Sorry, sure." He moved aside to let Cole pass. "Who should I tell him?"
"Tell him just an old friend." He was not going to be denied the shock. The man puffed significantly on the pipe, eyeing Cole. "I'm not his trick before work, if that's bothering you," he said, flopping into a chair, uninvited. "He knows me."
"He ought to be out in a minute or two."
"Nice place he has here." Cole meant it ironically, for the colors were extreme flashes of paisleys, the drapes and one chair a mixture of fuchsia and orange—Teddy's taste when left to himself. The rest of the furniture obviously came with the apartment except for the china cabinet, with the dark-green Thai Celadon dinnerware resting inside; he had bought some of the pieces himself as gifts.
"Yes, Ted puts a lot of work into where he lives; he likes things nice." Cole glanced up at the blond man, having forgotten that he had spoken to him. The stare seemed to make him uncomfortable, and he grabbed his pipe out of his mouth. "Say, I'm Ned Butler, glad to meet you." He stuck out a hand that might have been used in Corn Huskers Lotion ads. But Cole did not rise.
"How do you do? Do you live here with Teddy? Or are you just . . . dropping in for an afternoon?"
Before the man could reply, Teddy swirled into the room in a white terry-cloth robe, rubbing his hair with a huge pink bath towel. Because he was preoccupied with water in one ear, he did not immediately see Cole in the chair. "Where's my drink, big balls of fire! What good are you anyway, except in bed! But there— Wowee!" He looked up sharply when there was

no response, seeing Ned and then Cole. "Oh, it's you!" An abrupt pause followed, no idle chatter able to fill in the moment. "Well, Cole, how are you? How long you been . . . out?" Teddy's wide eyes inadvertently went up to Ned's face, a silent communication of some sort.

"Two days. Nice that you should ask. And how are you—not too lonely, I guess." He smiled meaningfully at Butler.

"Oh, have you two met? Ned, this is Cole Ruffner. Ned Butler."

"I was just introducing myself when you came in." This time Cole agreed to stand, surprised that the man did not overgrip to prove something with his handshake. "You know, our names sort of sound alike, don't they? Ned Butler, Cole Ruffner." He smiled, and Cole no longer feared him in the slightest.

"Why don't we sit down? Or something," Teddy said, all hands. Cole was a bit startled by the sound of his voice—higher-pitched than he recalled, a voice that had no resonance in it, throaty. They drifted into three different seats. "Well, Cole! What can I say! How you been? Everything okay?"

"I didn't escape, if that's what's worrying you. I just got out of jail, Mr. Butler." He nodded.

"Really? How nice for you." Cole looked for sarcasm, but the man was just fumbling for something appropriate to say.

"I suppose you're mad at me for not writing more often, you!" The remark was supposed to make Cole say he understood how it was.

"You still mispronounce 'often' as 'off-ten,' don't you, Teddy?"

"Do I? I hadn't noticed. Ned rarely corrects my pronunciation." But he interrupted himself at once. "How about a drink? I've got just about everything. Some wine? It's only Mogen David, but it's tasty. Really."

"No, you needn't give me anything . . . now." Cole stared at the short man he had lived with intimately for a year and a half—the wasp waist, not an ounce more on his frame, although his face did look different. There were the beginnings of a circle beneath one eye. In addition, he was wearing his reddish-brown hair long, covering half his ear. His skin looked pinkish, but Cole decided that it was from the shower, not from embarrassment. Teddy had gone to a counter near the refrigerator anyway and begun preparing two drinks. "Is Scotch and soda okay?" When there was no answer, he asked Ned: "Want any pop?"

"No, not right now, thanks."

When Teddy returned, he offered the glass to Cole, who did not extend his hand, and so Teddy put the drink on the coffee table nearby. "You're so talkative, Cole!" he said in a little joke.

"Maybe it's because I've had so little practice in the past three years. You can imagine how it was, five minutes here—or there—with assorted convicts, most of them boring as hell. Or unable to say anything beyond elementary things, like 'Gimme some cunt and I'll be happy.' "

Teddy laughed too heartily. "I did send you that letter."

"Oh, yes, thanks for the note. It cheered me up no end."

"Well, I thought maybe you didn't want to be disturbed, or something. You know, like you were best not reminded of the people outside."

"Did you really believe that, Teddy? What did you think I wanted—solitary confinement?"

He patted the arm of the sofa absently. "So I'm a rotten person. You weren't so perfect yourself, and that letter you wrote back to me was not exactly friendly."

"If it's any comfort to you, you were not the only one who left me by myself. I found out that I have no friends I can trust. Not one."

"Perhaps it was your fault for that."

"Thanks."

"Well, it's true; you never were a very sociable person anyway. What did you expect, baskets of fruit?"

"I don't expect anything from anybody. I have learned to be totally self-sufficient in these three years. Unlike you! I can see that you still can't tie your shoelace without somebody to help you."

"Don't be bitchy, Cole."

"If I wanted to be bitchy, you can be sure I wouldn't talk about your shoelace."

"Is this the guy you told me about, Ted?" the other man broke in.

"What did he tell you about me? Not that it matters much."

"Don't tell him, Neddy. He's being a wretch."

"You're more effeminate than I remember, Teddy, or have you just decided to be more your real self?"

"Don't give me that. We know who's *quaint* around here. I don't remember you screwing broads before your big trip Up the River. Big deal. So what did you get caught for? That was dumb, a dumb thing! So stay out of parks. If you get caught in one of them, it's nobody's fault but yours."

"You've gone to parks yourself. Don't give me that holier-than-thou crap."

"I didn't get myself caught, did I?" He patted the sweat from his forehead.

"You could have written to me, even if you wanted to break off permanently. You could have *written* to me."

"I said I was sorry." He stood up, pressing the glass to his neck, to cool himself. "Why don't you drink that drink? You make me feel terrible; I don't want to quarrel with you, Cole. And besides I have to go to work. What I did was done because I thought it would be the easiest way, for both of us. Honestly."

"Up your honesty!"

"Listen, bud, what did you come here for?" Butler moved to the edge of the couch heavily.

"What have we here, a pansy polar bear! Are you going to get your burly friend to beat me up, Teddy? Only I notice it's Ted now. Ted and Ned. Or Teddy and Neddy—how darling! Sit back, Smokey, it's well known that homosexuals are chicken-hearts."

The man stood up, placing his drink on the coffee table. "I

don't like the way you talk." His arms fell to his sides as if he were preparing to form fists.

"We won't need any of that stuff, will we?" Teddy said in what was a combination of relief and gloating. "Look, I'm very sorry that you didn't have any friends, but I wasn't the only person you ever slept with. Why blame me completely?"

"I didn't expect those other men to remember me; I made no demands on their emotions. But you were different."

"You'll find somebody else, I'm sure, Cole."

"Don't give me that patronizing attitude!"

"Why don't you face some facts, Cole. I never did love you, really. You ought to know it. You think you're so smart, but you can't even see the most obvious things that anybody else sees right in a minute. As a matter of fact, why would anybody love you? You're sort of pitted and all, and you do the same things all the time in bed, if you want to know what was wrong. Sorry, but you were never all that interesting to me." He poked out his finger in what was supposed to be a gesture of poise.

"That's a lie, a nelly lie. You used to slobber all over me."

"I never did either. Besides, if I did, which I didn't, you were hardly the only person I made love to. I had to keep telling him," he said to Butler, "that I was faithful to *him* alone. So what were you doing in a park if you were so faithful to me? Huh?"

"It was one time." Cole put his hand across his eyebrows.

Teddy waited for a few seconds before he spoke. "So we live and learn."

"Some of us learn a lot more than we ought to." Cole stood up, brushing his hair back from his forehead. "I'm extremely glad I came today, Teddy; you've cleared me of any real regret, except perhaps the time I wasted in your company."

"Sticks and stones."

"No, I mean it. You are a totally worthless person—vapid, inconsequential, immaterial to the world, and now to me too. I can't imagine what this half-nude blond buffalo gets out of you. How long have you two been together anyway?"

"This is our third time," Teddy said, "and it certainly won't be our last."

"I suppose he mades a good substitute for a woman, doesn't he, Ned? Especially when he gets his vaseline tube."

Teddy grabbed the ends of the towel he had placed around his neck. "Would you leave, please. I do not have to, and I don't want to, be insulted by you."

Cole was momentarily disconcerted by the calm; he had hoped for anger. "You've been taking maturity lessons, I see, Teddy— how to keep the voice low in times of emergency. So butch of you."

"Are you going?" Both Butler and Teddy were standing now.

"No, I'm not going." He likewise stood and then strode at once to the cabinet where the Thai pottery was displayed. "I see you still like your expensive dishes. What's this old thing?" He lifted a light blue jar from behind the glass.

"Put it back, that's a Yuan Dynasty Chun."

"A what? How much did it cost you, several hundred dollars? Imagine all that huffing and puffing over crabby customers to buy this little piece of dirt. It's not even pretty, you know." He held it out straight on the palm of one hand.

"Cole, if you break that, I'll, I'll . . ."

"You'll have to get another one, I suppose. I'm not leaving yet, and if you want your dumb piece of crockery, you'll let me finish my visit." He smiled at both of them and leaned back against the cabinet, running his free hand around the contours of the jar. "I don't suppose you keep vaseline in it, do you?" There was no response. "No? Then probably it's a jelly dish." He pulled off the lid and looked inside. "Must be for K-Y Jelly; it's too small to sit on." He forced a laugh.

"You'd better get out," Butler said in a frown.

"Oh, I'm sorry," Cole answered in as genuine a tone as he could, no edge in it to betray irony. "I suppose that you two haven't screwed yet. I must have interrupted a cozy afternoon of social intercourse. Don't let me stop you, though."

Teddy's hands went out impatiently. "What do you want

from me? Obviously you don't expect to live with me anymore."
"I certainly don't." Cole's mind went blank for a few seconds
as he stared at the wooden floor between the scatter rugs. "I want,
I want—never mind what I want."
"You must be nuts. There are lots of other fish in the sea."
"No, don't come over here, Teddy. You make me nervous,
and I might lose my grip on your—what is it—Chun?" Teddy
stopped after a step.
"You're acting very childish, you know that. To be blunt, I
don't want you around, can't you figure that out? You definitely don't add anything to life, you never did."
"I wonder if we are typical, Teddy? What do you think? Do
we represent the usual homosexual 'marriage'? A brief couple
of years of pseudo-fidelity and lots of cheating and lying about
it, and then the break-up, quarrels and sniveling and backbiting?"
"I really wouldn't know."
"Of course you wouldn't. Maybe we're just typical of a dead
relationship of any sort, what do you think? I mean, the inevitable boredom after all the confidences, the embraces. We
just wore each other out. People are not inexhaustible—that's
the pathetic shame. I saw an old man and his wife a few days
ago; they didn't have much to say to each other either, just 'Give
me a beer' and 'Nice sun today' and crap like that. It's all very
pitiful, if you look at it right. Isn't it?" He watched the other's
eyes go up in a look of exasperation. "I know what you're thinking, Teddy. Exactly! You're saying, 'Oh, he's still being morbid.'
You use the word 'morbid' for anything that you don't like."
"Why don't you go back to your own place?"
"Because I don't have a real place for one thing."
"I'm very sorry for you, really I am, but you can't hold me
responsible for what happened to you."
"You're all heart. You don't give a damn about anyone but
yourself."
"I'm going to be late for work."
"Nice jar you have here, Teddy. How much did it cost
you?" Cole blew a thin stream of breath across the lid.

"Not all that much, as a matter of fact."

"Oh, well, then, you wouldn't mind if I dropped it." He tossed it into the air a few inches and caught it again.

"My God, what are you doing!" Teddy inadvertently moved a few steps closer.

"Stay put, Teddy-Neddy!" Cole moved to the far side of the cabinet. "So it cost you quite a pretty penny—thank you!"

"If you're going to break it, then break it, for God's sake. Don't stand there toying with it. I don't care."

"It's just as well you never tried to go on the stage, Teddy. You're a lousy actor. But let's *talk*. I actually have so much to tell you—well, maybe not all that much. After all, the days in prison are pretty much alike, except for an occasional rape. I worked in the laundry. That's amusing, isn't it? Since I always hated to make my bed even, let alone wash out things. Remember?"

"Yes, I remember."

"And I missed the draft, probably, being in jail. See, everything has its advantages."

"I'm glad."

"So what have you been doing with yourself? Or with anybody else, for that matter?" When there was no answer, Cole spoke again. "I want to know!" Again Teddy simply stared back at him. "Have you seen Bud Smallwood or Angie Fionda or Marilyn?"

"They were your friends more than mine. I think Smallwood is getting married in a few months. Why don't you call him?"

"I may do just that. Maybe he would be less of a bastard than you are."

"Are you ready to leave now?"

"What about Angie?"

"I don't know a word about her, not for years. She called a few weeks after you went to jail."

"What did you tell her—that I'd been picked up?" It was a threat.

"What do you think I told her? I told her you were sick and had to rest up for a while."

"Did she believe you?"

"How do I know? She sounded like she did. I think she was disturbed, but quiet."

"Couldn't you think of something better to lie with?"

"Like what?"

"Do you think either Bud or Angie has found out the real reason why I left?" Cole spoke more to himself than to Teddy.

"You'll just have to find out for yourself, I'm afraid."

"Didn't she think it peculiar that I just up and left?"

"Well, of course she did. She wanted to know what hospital you were in."

"What did you say?"

"I said you were in a private one and couldn't have any visitors. Is that satisfactory, Your Majesty? You know, I didn't have to tell her anything. Or I could have told her the truth if I had wanted to."

"Thank you for your thoughtfulness, but you did it mostly for your own sake. Even you did not want to be associated with a 'homosexual.' "

"Goddamn you, Cole, can't you find any good in anything I do? Or for that matter in anything at all? I think you're warped."

"If I am, I'm not sorry about it. Besides, I've had some help from the rest of the world."

Teddy rubbed his sleeve over his trickling brow. "You can't spend the rest of your life blaming the world for your troubles. You've got to go on living; you have to go on anyway." He said the words as gently as he could.

"Your *Reader's Digest* philosophy makes me ill. Am I supposed to sit back and take the things that happen to me? Be pleased, so pleased, that I was given just three years instead of being guillotined? We're so much more enlightened today in the United States. Why, we haven't hanged a nigger or a queer for over a hundred years! Land sakes, we are ed-u-ca-ted, don't you know!

Why, they can live right next door to me, as long as they don't *carry on* and all that, of course. No, Teddy, I don't have to be overjoyed that I'm not *rooted* out, condescendingly tolerated, only occasionally persecuted. *I* am one of the examples that get persecuted! And I'm not going to bow my head and praise the Lord that I'm a free man at last. What should we call ourselves? Something like an Uncle Tom. An Uncle Mary? Well, I, for one, do not live on welfare and I don't have a natural sense of rhythm!"

"You'll only make people hate us more. Everybody is very tired of the Negroes and their complaints; they'll get tired of gay guys too."

"I don't give a good defecation if they get tired or not. I'm not tired, only angry, right to my guts I'm angry. The rest of the people can go to *Hell* for all I care! A bunch of blubbery-faced old 'decent citizens' is not directing my life any longer."

"They'll just send you back to jail then."

"I'll kill them first."

Teddy snorted and then tried to block his face.

"Laugh if it pleases your vacuous brain. I'm not put off by contempt or merriment anymore. I'm not a 'nice guy' any longer."

"Were you ever?" Teddy folded his arms neatly, as though he had had the final word.

"I'll see how much worse I can be then."

"Then don't be surprised when you wind up alone."

"I'll have friends again, don't worry. I just wonder how much Angie and Bud know about me."

Teddy looked weary. "Why don't you call them up and find out."

"I just may. Maybe she's still at the office, if she hasn't—"

"Why don't you go ahead and call her. Use my phone, if you like. I've got to hurry and get dressed." He went toward the bedroom, a worried expression beneath the encouraging smile.

"I better put a shirt on, shouldn't I?" Butler said, moving toward the bedroom too.

"Why bother?" Cole said. "You had enough showing off of your muscles for one afternoon?" His throat tightened in spite of the bravado.

"It's none of your hacking business what I wear or don't wear." Butler drew himself up with air in the chest.

Teddy stopped at the door to his bedroom. "Ned!"

"Well, it's not my dumb jar; he can't talk that way to me. I never saw the man before in my life."

"You pick such stunning partners to screw, Teddy. What do you do, Mr. Butler? Teach philosophy at the University of Michigan, no doubt? Or could you possibly be an executive with Chrysler?"

Butler knew he was being twitted, but he could not pin down the exact irony. "I model clothes for a store. You want to make something of it?"

"Wouldn't dream of it. I'm merely a curious person, that's all."

"Cole," Teddy broke in, "you've had your little scene, but why don't we continue it some other day?"

Cole turned slowly to face his friend. "Why, Teddy, I'm not going to see you ever again! You don't want to see me and I don't want to see you."

"Well, that's okay by me, but perhaps if you think this over we'll be able to treat one another in a civil manner—"

"You think we can jolly this over somehow? A few stiff drinks and we'll forget all the stiff cocks of the past, forgiving and forgetting, and I'll gradually, painlessly (for you) drift into the sunset."

"I can't even try to be nice to you now; you won't let me."

"That's correct. I won't let you."

They stood staring across the room at each other, no word apropos.

Finally Butler interrupted the silence. "I'm going home."

"Probably have to do your sit-ups, Butler. Or maybe knee-bends? Back-bends, push-ups—all those hyphenated activities must make you dizzy." Before Butler could respond, Cole went on. "Has Teddy—Ted to you—ever mentioned his little problem?"

"What problem?" Teddy asked.

"Hasn't he told you about his *playful* experiences?" He glanced from one to the other with mock amazement.

"He's told me everything I care to know," Butler said.

"Not very flattering what you say. I thought lovers always wanted to know every intimacy about each other. It's in all the best books."

"What problem are you talking about?" Teddy's voice was prickly.

"Far be it from me to rake muck. You two can probably go on for . . . at least a couple of months. What he doesn't know can't hurt him, can it?"

"I haven't got any problem, and you know it." Teddy's calm was gone now, crackling into anger. "Go away! Do you hear me? Go away! Immediately. I despise you. Go on, get out, get out!"

"You can see that he doesn't want you to know about his fondness for little boys. Didn't he ever tell you that he likes to hang around playgrounds, where he takes the little boys into the john and puts their soft, little sexual organs into his soft, little mouth. So glad he's not the murderous type."

Teddy stood at the door with his mouth open. Then: "What *are* you saying?"

"I can understand why you wouldn't want people to know. Being queer is hard enough on the psyche without all this other stuff." Cole looked to see where Butler's eyes were directed. As he had hoped, they were on Teddy.

"Cole, you know that's a lie! What are you staring at *me* for, Ned? You know homosexuals don't want little children—he's making it up, can't you see that!"

"It's not that he hurts them really; they usually like it, in fact. He prefers them under seven. Maybe they taste better."

"I don't know what you hope to accomplish, but by God you're . . . you're crazy."

"People who tell the truth always have to take abuse. I simply thought I'd warn you, Butler, so that you won't be surprised when Teddy misses a few 'appointments' with you. You'll know where he is."

"Will you quit loooking at me, you dumb ape! Why give him the satisfaction!"

"Don't call me names, Emmord. I can stare at you if I like."

"But you can't possibly even begin to think that what he said about me is true?"

"Yes, there are a few things that shock even the perverts these days," Cole said quietly.

"I don't believe what you said," Butler decided.

"No? Well, that's just as well. You can think more highly of Teddy that way, especially when he goes down on you. It was not my intention to hurt his feelings. Or maybe it was. I just thought that telling the facts about him somehow made up for what he did to me."

"You damned liar, get out of here, before I call the police." Teddy's face was a furious pink, the mouth almost knotted.

"I'm afraid I've placed a serious doubt in your friend's mind, Teddy. You'll have to explain to him how you can't help yourself. Butler is a sensitive man; he'll understand how it is. Perhaps the two of you can go out to playgrounds together."

"Get out of here, Cole!" Teddy clenched his hands in his robe's pockets.

"You're absolutely right; it's time to leave. I wouldn't want you to be late for work." He walked quickly to the door he had entered, turning for what he intended to be his curtain line. "It's been so chummy seeing you again, Teddy. Isn't that how the words go? Could be we'll see each other again—you know, around."

"Not if I can help it, we won't." He moved toward the door as well. "And give me back my antique."

Cole made a pretense of having forgotten. "Oh, of course. Your old jar. I'm so pleased that you called it an antique instead of your *pot*. In some way it would have ruined the parting." He turned and nodded crisply at the third man. "Good-bye, Ned. Charming." Then he smiled at Teddy. "Here's for old times' sake, Teddy." He held out the blue jar with both hands. For a few seconds, Teddy hesitated, then moved a few paces to retrieve it. Just as he put out his hands, Cole moved his apart deliberately, spreading them like someone holding yarn. The pottery shattered noisily on the floor, but Cole did not bother to look down at it. "Good-bye, Teddy." He pulled open the door and slammed it after him.

As he was descending the stairs, the door to Teddy's apartment cracked open, and Cole hurried down the steps without looking back. But Teddy was running down, two and three at a time. "You bastard, I'm going to get you," he yelled, and Cole's heart squeezed in a faint fear. Then, from behind, Teddy's knuckles slapped against the neck, stinging across the ear. He turned around, and the hand came down on top of his head. "Who do you think you are! That jar cost me four hundred dollars, and you broke it on purpose. On purpose!" The hand came at him again, hitting the inside of his ear, with a great pinch of pain, like frostbite. Cole reached out and grabbed the wrists of the other man, and somehow caught a glimpse of Butler leaning over the bannister on the third floor, yelling, "Push him down the stairs." Teddy's face was like a blister, the eyes not quite focused. Since he was on the stair above, his weight made it impossible to push him aside, even though he weighed forty pounds less than Cole. One of Teddy's hands got free and struck alongside Cole's nose, sending a trickle of blood over the lips. He grabbed the arm, feeling immensely strong; yet for some reason he could not understand Teddy continued to weave above him, neither of them with the advantage. "I'm going to make you meat!" Teddy said through gritted teeth, banging their arms on the bannister rods. Suddenly he lost his balance and slipped down to the next stair, causing Cole to stumble over him, one of his legs between

Teddy's. But instead of getting up, he started hitting Cole in the thigh, until Cole maneuvered around behind him, holding onto the wrists, slipping into a sitting position behind Teddy, who continued lashing his fists back over his head, unsure of what he was hitting, panting half-groans of helplessness. "What do you want from me? I'm not afraid of you, I'll give you a bleeding, you bastard!"

"You caused it, Teddy," Cole said, fighting off the fists. His injured ear hurt him, and the blood in his mouth made him almost gag. "It was you. You made me, you made me, you made me. But I got you, I got you."

"You never got me, you father-fucker. Never got me." Teddy tried to turn around, but Cole pressed his knees together to prevent the other man from moving any farther. "You're breaking my spine," Teddy shouted.

"I hope so, I hope I rip it in two!" As he shouted the words, he slurred them, unable to articulate, and sliced a piece of his own lip with his teeth. He could feel the ragged skin with his tongue. To breathe, he had to open his mouth, and his arms were wrenched from the effort of holding Teddy. Then, with a sharp twist, Teddy freed himself and lunged on top of Cole, the elbows grazing his stomach, and Cole circled his arms around the man's back and squeezed as hard as he could; yet Teddy's hands were free enough to pound his fists on Cole's collarbone. Although he could lift them only a little, he used his knuckles to hit hard, dull regular beats. When he tired, he tried to use his knees to reach Cole's groin, but Cole stopped him by crossing his own legs over Teddy's legs. They lay there entwined in each other's body, immobile except for the panting that came from them both, hoarse, hot waves of exhaustion. "Do you want to get up?" Cole asked after several minutes.

"I want to get away from your stinking breath."

"My breath doesn't stink."

"All of you stinks."

Teddy's body seemed to grow limper, more of the weight falling on Cole. "I brush my teeth—with blood." Cole smiled at his words; his chin felt wet, the liquid dripping down his throat into his shirt.

"Let me up."

"I can't."

"I'll do—nothing."

"What?"

"I'll do nothing. You can go."

"If you try anything . . ."

Teddy gave one final gasp of rage throughout his entire body. "Leave me! Ohaaa, leave me . . ." The words faded into a sob.

Carefully, Cole loosened his legs, but Teddy had given up, did not move, and Cole therefore stood as best he could, pushing Teddy above him. When the two were standing, the other man fell back against the wall, his slight chest heaving up and down through the opening where his robe had come undone, while Cole backed away from him cautiously. His eyes found Butler still in the same spot, staring down. Slowly, he stepped backwards until he was on the landing and had the doorknob in his hand. "Teddy, I'm . . . Teddy?"

"I don't want to hear," he managed to say, not looking at him.

"Teddy."

"No, no!"

After a long moment, Cole slipped through the door. Outside, he ran a finger over the drying blood on his face. A Negro woman in a checkered head scarf went by, then glanced back over her shoulder and frowned. When he took his first few steps, he stopped. Then he hurried on, bewildered, ashamed of the stickiness he could feel between his legs.

3

Cole let three days go by without leaving his apartment. He didn't shave, and his face became grained and itchy. Now and again he looked at himself in his dresser mirror, but turned away in disgust. He lay in bed half awake, hour after hour, thinking of Teddy, of the policeman in the park. Sometimes he contemplated committing suicide, turning on the gas and lying on his unmade bed and drifting off to death. However, when he actually went into the kitchen to look at the stove, he discovered that it was an electric rather than a gas one. He supposed that there must be something amusing in that fact; yet he could not make the humor rise in him; it lodged within his chest like a bubble of air. *I wish it would go straight to my heart. Can't that happen? An injection from a hypodermic needle, a tiny swoosh of air can terminate my life, all these delicate tissues that have taken years to build, thousands of veins crisscrossing, carrying away the blood, so much effort by my body, so many days of forming me. And for what? So that I can lie here in this dumpy apartment and want to die.*

He rose from the bed and forced himself to get out of his pajamas, which he threw into a corner, as if they were diseased. He struggled into a pair of shorts, first looking at the identification number on the elastic that the prison laundry had stamped on them, and then pulled on a flannel robe.

In the kitchen he opened the refrigerator for something to eat, although only a dull headache told him that he was hungry; his stomach itself gave no sign. He guessed that he had eaten something the day before, but he could not quite remember, groggy from having slept so long. There was a can of spinach, half-empty, inside the refrigerator, which he recalled opening, though not when exactly. *The day before yesterday?* He had always liked spinach, especially cold, even as a child. *That must have been unnatural too,* he thought lethargically. The spinach tasted a bit tainted, and he threw it into the garbage pail next to the sink. Then he went back to the open refrigerator. A dish of Fig Newtons lay on the bottom shelf, but nothing else was inside. He popped one of the cookies into his mouth, and it made him hungry, even though it was dried out. When he reached down to pick up another one, he noticed a dead fly clinging to the side of one of them. Evidently it had flown into the refrigerator and frozen to death. "You ought to have watched where you were going, you little bastard," he said out loud. "It's against the fly-law to seek sweets in forbidden places." For a second he imagined it would revive and fly away, but it did not move. He picked it up with two fingers, gently, and brought it close to his face. *How does it feel to die? Is it slow and excruciating? Did you taste the cookie as you were dying, knowing that it was your last meal? Did you think you could survive somehow on the sugar? Sugar for energy. Maybe you thought the fly rescue team would come and save you, or did you know nothing at all, just that you were getting colder and colder, that you could not move around as much as before? And then you blacked out.* The insect in his fingers began to make him ill, because of its huge eyes, protruding, gigantic eyes. The legs stuck up into the air covered with germs. "You kissed a dead rat before you died, didn't you? Your lover, the rat!" Cole dropped the fly into the garbage can, then eagerly devoured all the other Fig Newtons except the one that had been the insect's deathbed. That he left lying on the sink. Yet the more he ate the hungrier he became. He found a box of Wheaties, which he had forgotten he'd bought on the day he had moved. It was unopened. Although he knew there was no milk, he returned to the refrigerator. Dully, he stared at the empty shelves, then ripped off the box-top and dug his fist into the flakes and scooped out a large handful, stuffing them into his mouth. He took another mouthful—and then another. They were delicious despite the dryness. He upended the package to make more fall out onto his palm, and some spilled onto the linoleum. He took another mouthful, but just before he swallowed he stopped, held the mash in his mouth, then spat it into his hand and stared at it— tiny bits mixed with saliva, caked together. *Why does it have to get gooey like that before we can swallow it, this mess?* He put the cereal back into his mouth, but it made him gag. He forced the food out again, standing over the garbage can. As he looked down at the spinach and the cereal, he felt dizzy. *Why is it so terrible? Why is everything so sickening!* And then he grabbed the pail and ran down the back steps of the apartment, out to the concrete containers where all the refuse was deposited for pick-up. He banged the garbage over the edge furiously, listening to the items fall onto the junk already inside. When the pail was emptied, he stood back a few yards, panting. He smiled at the clean interior of the pail. But then he stopped. *I've only moved the filth, not eliminated it; I just added mine to the huge pile already there. There's garbage everywhere, hiding behind those concrete walls, but still there.* He went over to the bins and flipped the steel lids down on both sides, then stood back, sweating under the arms. The tangy odor of deposited waste floated from the alley; he looked down the rows of houses at the garbage cans throwing their insides out onto the ground: papers, a broken toilet seat, some rusty wire, egg shells. The sun seemed to bring the stench to a peak. Turning away from the alley, he hurried up the stairs to his rooms and locked the door behind him, and went and sat down in the living room, but then got up immediately, going into the kitchen.

He carefully took down an old jelly jar that the landlord provided and filled it with water, drinking without stopping, even though he splashed some of it down the sides of his face. He picked up the discarded cookie from the sink and ran water over it, putting it into his mouth, forcing himself to swallow the drenched sweet.

He went back to the living room and stretched out on the sofa, and since it was too short for his entire length, he had to rest his head on the hard arm, not bothering to get a pillow from the bedroom. He lay inert for fifteen minutes staring at the ceiling. *Was I really happy before I went to jail? I can't keep the past straight. Of course my past wasn't very "straight."* He smiled without mirth. *I used to go to parties, once in a while. I was sociable, despite what Teddy said. I worked and went out. Why can't I remember exactly? Bud and Angie and others used to be my friends, I'm certain of it. They liked me; they invited me to their places for supper. We went to restaurants. Angie liked me, I'm sure, and Bud bought me a shirt one time for my birthday. But why couldn't I write them letters? Of course I know why. Because they'd loathe me—a pervert and a criminal. Or would they understand? Maybe . . . no, they would not want to have anything to do with me after my arrest. I know. Write them off as a bad choice; no doubt that's what they have done with me, if they know. Probably they tell people—no, they wouldn't tell anybody. Maybe I should go to see them.* Immediately the memory of the visit to Teddy sliced through Cole's brain. *No, no more of that! Of course Bud would not be like Teddy. I think he's a little bit gay himself, though he doesn't know it.* Cole glanced at the telephone waiting on the end table. Then he stared back at the ceiling.

Even his cousin Marilyn had not been faithful to him, never wrote. And they had gone to many places together, to movies and a few plays. *She probably knows precisely what I did. She suspected me—the little hints I dropped. Probably she found out through the family gossip-vine. The whole bunch knows what I did.* When he felt his chest begin to stifle him, he tried to erase the pictures of their contemptuous faces from his mind.

He sat up. It came to him once again, icily, that he should kill the man who had sent him to jail. What was his name? Cole's heart jerked. He could not think of the man's name. Officer Something? Of course he had never seen the name written down.

In the car that night one of the other policemen had called him by name. But what? He tried to hear the voice coming from the front of the police car, but the memory made his head throb, so he changed the image to the courtroom. Hadn't the man given his name during the testimony? Yes, although it had been mumbled. Officer what? His face appeared in the back of Cole's eyes, distinctly. *What an oppressive face—wide and thick, florid, probably he drinks too much. Some people would say it is a healthy skin, rich red blood flowing—All-American red blood.* Cole looked across to the telephone once again. *I can call the police station downtown and ask for—who can I ask for? Try to find the vice squad? Though what could I say?* "Hello, I am interested in finding out the name of one of your officers, a man about forty-three or forty-four, with a wide face and a reddish complexion." "And what do you want with him?" *the suspicious voice on the other end would ask.* "I just want to find him, that's all." *No, that would never do.* "I want to talk with him." "We're sorry, such information is confidential. Who's calling, please?" *And then I would have to hang up, terrified.*

Cole leaned back against the cushion. *Why can't I think of the policeman's name? I knew it before, didn't I? Have I repressed it? Yet I can't recall saying the name to myself before. I didn't think of the man as having a name, just a brutal face. Officer Drummond? No. Officer Jones? No, not that. How about Sergeant? Sergeant Lutz? Sergeant Beal.* Cole touched his temples. *That's sort of like it. Beal. The other cop said,* "Cut it out, Beal." *Yes, it was Beal!* Cole pressed hard on the sides of his jaws. *No, I'm not positive.* "Beal, leave the man alone." *Something like that. How could I have forgotten such an important fact?*

He went to the telephone book—a year out of date—but he opened it to the *B*'s. There were seventeen Beals listed. *Should I call each one, to find out which one has a policeman in the family?* He cradled the telephone on his knees as he sat in the chair next to it and put his finger in the hole for the first number. *What should I ask?* "Is Officer Beal at home?" *What if he answers him-*

*self. Or maybe it isn't actually Beal. That doesn't sound right.
And if I call all these numbers, the police might find out some-
how. Someone would report a suspicious man calling up.
Perhaps his name was Steel. It had that sound to it. Steel. Maybe
Field? Maybe the man slurred the word.* "What's the matter with
you, Field?" Cole said aloud. *That was it, or something similar.
I'll think about it, until it comes back to me; I'm sure it will.*

He lay back down on the sofa, letting his hatred diffuse
through the whole of his body, trying to stop his head from
pounding so intensely. He wondered vaguely what time it was,
but he owned no watch, never had, and he had not bothered to set
the clock on the kitchen wall. He was not even aware of what day
it was—Friday or Saturday perhaps. *Maybe it's around eight
o'clock,* he thought. *It's getting dark. What difference does it
make? I'm not going anywhere.*

Groggily, he let one leg slip off the couch, and his robe opened.
A delicate wave of anonymous lust passed through his loins. He
looked at the flap on his shorts. *That never ceases, does it,* he
thought almost angrily. He felt himself stir. "Oh, stop," he
growled. "I'm too tired, too tired." *If I cut it off, would I die?
I can see myself running down the apartment steps, out into the
street, blood streaming down my bare legs, the heart pumping
great gobs of sour blood out through the opening where my penis
was; it would not take long to die—to die and decorate the street.
A quick slash with an ax, perhaps a pair of shrubbery shears.* He
involuntarily shuddered at the picture. And still it was pleasant
as well. *Suppose it healed and I lived in contentment ever after.
There would be no more impulses, no tickles of desire down
there.* "Just a piece of cut-off flesh, a stub!" Cole spoke too
loudly, but he did not move, sinking into the acid of the memory
of his own face buried in the policeman's lap, the smell of talcum
powder.

*Yes, some men have lost their sex organs; they must have. In
wars. And they lived. Yes, they lived. And what about those men
who have operations to change sex, like Christine Jorgensen. How
did he agree to do that? Just to be a woman, he let them cut him*

*up, make his body over, give injections for breasts. Didn't I read
that he also had an artificial vagina inserted? What endurance,
what courage really, to withstand all the thousands of insults, all
those prying questions. But didn't she ask for the publicity in a
way too? "And now about your new box, Miss Jorgensen. How
big is it? Bigger than a bread box?" "Are you enjoying your new
snatch as much as you had hoped? Would you care to dem-
onstrate how it works for the viewing audience? How many children do you intend to have, Miss Jorgensen?" All to be a woman.
I have no wish to be made over like that. Plastic parts, fitted into
place. Made in Hong Kong perhaps. All neatly manufactured and
stitched into position—ready for . . . I'm ready for love.* Restlessly, Cole turned on his side and faced the back of the sofa.

After a while he dozed, and his father's face began talking to
him, only he could not see himself in the picture. They were in
the basement of their house in Toledo; he was ten or so. His father's face was very serious, saying that Cole had done something nasty; he had done something nasty and his father was
ashamed of him. Ashamed. The saddened face of his father
wagged back and forth like a reproving finger. *"That's a sin—a
mortal sin! You must go to confession right away, right today,
and tell God that you are sorry, heartily sorry. You can go to hell
for that. To hell."* There was somebody else in the picture too,
but he could not make out who. Another child? They had been
doing something sexual in the basement, behind the furnace, back
in the corner, and his father had come down to the cellar and
discovered them. But who was the other child? It must have been
another boy, though nothing would close into shape. Only his
father's full, flushed, angry face. He had driven him to church,
to Saturday confession, had sat outside the confessional while
Cole had gone in. There Cole had told the priest something—
that he had committed adultery. The priest had laughed, for the
childish voice must have told him everything. He then made Cole
tell exactly what had happened. With his father sitting outside,
he would not have dared to lie. He remembered crying so hard
that the priest had had to come out of the confessional and open

the door to the darkened cubicle. On the way back home, his
father had kept asking him if the priest had given him absolution.
Absolution. Cole jerked, started himself awake, but lay still, too
weary to move. "I absolve you, father, for you know not what
you did. But I'm not sorry I'm a homosexual; I'm just sorry I
had you for a father!"

More images returned: Above the altar in the church where
he had attended mass before school every morning for twelve
years hung the boney figure of sallow, yellow wood, that great,
drooping, agonized God, nails sticking out of the flesh. Someone
had bothered to carve wooden droplets of blood on the face and
hands. "*Christ have mercy on us; Lord have mercy on us.*" *What
a foolish god to pray to. A god who could not even save himself,
a dying, dopey man, that's all he was. He thought he died for
love.* Cole flipped over on his stomach, stretching his arms. *Yes,
he died for love. It was a lover's quarrel, between Judas and John
—John the Beloved, Judas the rejected, who turned Christ in to
the authorities because he was spurned. A kiss in a park too. Just
a cheap, little affair like anybody else's, and somehow it has gotten all this world-wide attention. Christ hung on the cross and
suffered because he could not tell John how much he loved him,
because all those other people were standing around, because he
could not hurt his mother with such words, not even as he was
dying. But John knew; he could see the feeling in the drooping
eyes, the same look he had seen many times in Christ's strong
arms, before he fell asleep. Only here pain was mingled with it.
The spiteful, plain Judas caused it all. And then he hanged himself because he had destroyed his would-be lover. He watched
Christ put his hand on John's arm at the Last Supper, the intimate
look between the two of them, and Judas' wrath was stirred. He
sold Christ out of jealous lust. Certainly it is as sad as the other
story, and twice as believable as believing in a god who came
down to redeem men. Is there no end to mankind's preposterous
notions of its own worth?*

Cole heard someone slam the door of the next apartment; then
someone was running around in the room next to him. He could

hear giggling—one of the students, probably playing tag with a friend. They were running around the place, tipping over chairs. The night before he had heard them singing songs in a group. At other times they ran back and forth, up and down, visiting between apartments. *When do they ever study?* There was another loud giggle from the next room, and Cole turned his back to the wall. *I can't stay here any longer, I can't sleep another minute, and I'm still hungry. I have to get out—maybe to a movie.* But he knew that he did not want to see a movie. He had never especially liked them, since they seemed to take up so much time; he would rather think his own thoughts. *I could go out for a walk, yes, at least that. For some fresh air. But is it safe around here? I could be knocked on the head.* Then he smiled. *Even the murderers have to worry in Detroit. No, no walking. If I only had someone to talk with. Somebody.* He looked longingly at the telephone. Who could he call? Even Teddy perhaps? No, that was dead, totally dead. He went over to the telephone book. *All these thousands of names and I can't call one of them.* He threw the book on the floor, but at once he retrieved it, thinking, *I'll call the police station; I can't lose anything; I won't identify myself.* He raised the receiver, then waited. Finally he dialed and asked the information operator for the number of the main precinct, on Beaubien. When she seemed to take forever to find it, he half-seriously thought they were tracing the call already. He immediately dialed the number she gave him, without letting himself brood about it; however, when the telephone rang on the other end, his stomach wavered.

"Police department."

"I want the name of a certain officer." His heart swung like a wrecking ball inside his chest.

"Who? What department do you want?"

"I'm not sure . . . vice department!" he added quickly, moving his mouth to one side to disguise his voice.

"One moment."

There were several clickings and then a man's voice: "Yeah?" lazily. "Can I help you?"

"Yes . . . I want the information about a certain police officer who works in the vice squad."

"Are you making a complaint or what?"

"No, not a complaint, nothing like that. I want to get in touch with him; we're old friends and I haven't seen him for a long—some time."

"What's his name?"

"His name?" Cole felt brittle. He had forgotten that he did not know the name. "Is—it's Officer Field, I th— Yes, that's it."

"Aren't you sure?"

"Yes, positive. It's Field, Officer Field."

"I don't know of any Field in this department. What Field?"

"Huh?"

"What's his first name?"

Cole paused, unable to say anything. The other man was waiting, becoming suspicious. "It's John Field."

"Are you sure you know this guy? Where did you say you knew him from?" Cole could see the man lean closer to the telephone, his boredom interrupted. "Who's calling, please?"

Cole put down the receiver delicately, hoping the sound would be soft, making it appear that they had been disconnected. He kept his hand on the receiver for a long while, afraid that something would happen if he lifted it. Unmoving, he sat for five minutes while his insides seemed to quiver in spasms. Just as he finally pulled his hand free and stood up, the telephone rang. He stared at it as though it were a bomb. It rang four times and then he grabbed it. It could not possibly be the police. "Yes?" he said out of breath.

"Is Joline there?" an almost inarticulate Negro voice demanded.

"Who?"

"Is Joline there?"

"No, no, she's not here."

"Where is she?" The man was aggressive.

"I have no idea. You have the wrong number."

"Say, man, you get Joline, where she at?"

"I don't have her. And if I did, I wouldn't give her to you."

There was a pause. "Who's this? Are you that white boy?"

"Yes, I'm that white boy. And Joline's not coming to the phone."

There was a second pause before: "You tell that girl to get her ass over to the telephone."

"She's in bed."

"Who is this?" The voice was more insistent.

"Why don't you learn to dial the right number!"

"What number's this?"

"What number do you want? Didn't you ever learn how to talk on the phone?"

The other side was figuring out something. "I want 931-0710."

"Well, this isn't it." Cole started to slam the receiver down, but he stopped. "Learn the difference between the six and the zero, and you won't make so many stupid mistakes."

"You tell Joline I's going to get her!" The banging at the other end popped into his ear.

Cole laid the telephone down and turned to the sofa. "Joline, somebody wants to talk to you." Then he laughed, harshly, a laugh created in his head, not from the body. He hung up.

In the bedroom he found that he had only one cigarette left. He lit it and took a puff and put it down nervously. He went into the bathroom and turned on the faucet of the bathtub, watching the water spill out in a thin stream. The porcelain was broken off both the handles of the faucets. *Why is everything so tacky?* he thought. *Who painted this room dark gray? Is it to hide the fingerprints?* After he removed his robe and slippers, Cole sat on the edge of the bathtub, which was slowly filling with water. Steam had begun to fog the mirror over the sink, dimming it slightly. He realized what he was going to do and looked down at his naked body. *I'm so white. Like a cadaver. I should be hanging from a crucifix over some altar.* He stood up and watched as he turned from side to side in front of the mirror, noticing the way his back sloped into the thin buttocks with scarcely a ripple. *I'm too skinny in the back.* He turned sideways. The pubic hair protruded, gnarled and stiff-looking. When he ran his forefinger through the snarls, he was stirred, and watched as the blood flowed downward, swelling him. His penis stood out at an angle to the left. *You would think we would get tired of the same old stuff, after all these years,* he thought scientifically. *All this stroking and grunting, week in and week out. And still it always returns.* He ran a finger down the organ. *It really is quite disgusting, considered objectively—all those veins coursing through it, some of them pushed to the outside, like that long blue one. And it's formed into a head, like some vegetable breaking out of the ground, an opening at the end. "Anus" is such an ugly word. This is my "anus," one of my "anuses."* He rubbed his thumb around the tip and sucked in his abdomen with the pleasure. *How can something so unattractive give so much pleasure? It doesn't ask these questions; it simply wants to be thrust back and forth, back and forth, and then it stops its demands for a few days, sometimes a day.* Cole touched himself again, pulling down, and the member sprang up, more aroused. He smiled at himself in the foggy glass. *It's so full, so tight. And red.* A tiny drop appeared. *So I must be ready,* he teased himself. *The lubricant provided by nature. How thoughtful, but I don't need a lubricant, it seems. Nobody here but me. At least it will be over quickly—back and forth, back and forth, ready, aim, fire! And what else comes out of there? Urine. How could that be? The source of life and the source of waste—it must be a mistake. God has fumbled the creation of the body somehow. For why would he make the organ for "love" the same one that carries urine away? Efficiency? It's macabre. "Urine" and "yearn"—they even sound alike. I remember reading in a pathology book once that some people like to be urinated on when they are having sex. I've never met anyone like that.* The idea made him wrinkle his nose. "To each his own, though," he said to his reflection. *Someone told me also of seeing a stag film of a woman sitting on a toilet, with the camera placed inside the bowl to show her urinating. Is that erotic to people? Is that why the sex organ has those two seemingly distinct functions?* He was losing his erection, he noticed. *That doesn't turn me on, it seems.*

He leaned over to adjust the water flow, slowing it, and tested one foot in the tub. As he stood straddling the rim, he looked back at himself in the mirror. *Why do they build bathrooms like this—with the mirror right opposite the bathtub? Is it so that people can see themselves? Are people aroused by their own bodies? Do they do what I am doing? No one has ever mentioned such a thing to me. But the cunning house builders know, for they provide what people want even though no words are ever expressed about the subject.*

Cole could hardly make out his reflection because of the steam on the glass. Stepping out of the bathtub, he wiped his hand across the mirror, which was still unclear, but better. "All the better to see yourself, my dear," he said. He ran his fingernail around the inside of the deepest acne scar, the one near his right eye. Suddenly he remembered the cigarette he had left burning in the bedroom and rushed out of the bathroom. The butt lay on the edge of the dresser still—it had gone out. He crushed the rest of it in the ashtray and started to go back when the small round mirror that he had bought from one of the men in jail caught his eye. He picked it up and went back to the tub.

After a moment he turned the water off, and then held the mirror in front of him below the waist. His testicles looked red, two stones in sagging skin, wrinkled. He moved the mirror closer. There were bumps, tiny eruptions of the flesh all over the underside, chaffed, and the hairs seemed like bristles. *Why does it look like that? Why that? Why isn't the skin smooth, flawless, arranged some other way? Anything but this. What kind of god created this? How can anyone think we are beautiful? What monstrous conceit! This is why people put fig leaves on statues; they're right. It's to hide the bumps on the skin, these sacklike protrusions that descend from the torso like something broken, something full of pus.* He moved the mirror, but could still sense the desire in his body; he could not think himself out of it.

He put the small mirror into the sink and stared down into it and slowly pushed up to the edge. The porcelain was cold against his loins. He began to move his hand rapidly. "What fantasy shall it be this time? Number twenty-four? Or maybe thirty-six?" *The football player in the jock strap or the marine on the desert island!* He tried the first—just he and the football player were in a locker room, the other man flexing his muscles, showing off. Then their eyes met, a long look of mutual understanding. The football player's hand fell to his jock strap . . . "I can't," Cole said, leaning over the basin. "Oh, I can't."

After a minute he straightened upright, and the mirror below him became the policeman's heart. He forced himself to make it throb. The man was kneeling on a platform with his hands behind him, raised up off the grass in a darkened park. And somehow his heart was open, a wound showing all the valves and arteries; yet no blood fell out; it simply whirled and twisted in its natural alleys. The man was shaking his head to and fro, although he could say nothing; the mouth fell open once or twice in inarticulate whispers. And Cole watched the shape that was himself move closer to the kneeling man, hold his shoulders steady, and jab his penis into the man's heart, thrusting hard several times, separating the vessels. The man shouted, but Cole thrust again, and something long and slippery snapped inside as he jabbed once more. The man screamed loudly a second time as Cole withdrew, dripping blood.

"I don't want to," Cole sobbed, the image fading. In the round mirror in the sink he could see the semen dropping out, and he looked away. His body spurted several times, then shuddered, as streaks of white foam ran down the glass. "Oh, please, please," he sobbed to someone. "Please, no."

When his body eased, he turned both taps on full and leaned heavily against the basin; he listened to, but did not look at, the pounding water cleansing, rocking the little mirror.

4

An hour and a half later Cole left his apartment, bathed, various civilized scents convincing him, partly, that he was at ease. He had sat in the bathtub for so long his skin felt prickly, as if thousands of tiny bugs were dancing on it. He had decided to walk to the bar, down Woodward Avenue, but when he got to the intersection at Puritan, he remembered how long a walk that would be, and he would also have to pass dilapidated stores and sinister dives full of black men eyeing him with various degrees of hatred.

In the taxi, he passed a group of blacks standing in front of a sleazy hamburger restaurant called Sweet Daddy's. His throat went dry and he looked away. *I wish I had my own car again,* but it had been sold by his father, who finished up the business affairs, coming to Detroit for that and to pay off the few bills. *So he did me a favor or two. I shouldn't deny him that, I suppose.* Cole tried to think generously of his father, but the sentiment would not linger, slipping into something resentful.

The gay bar was still where it had been. *Well, it's nice to know there are a few reliable things, if not persons,* he thought wryly. It was a darkened building near the General Motors Building; even the neon lights were turned off so as not to attract any of the "wrong" people. The most puritanical citizen could hardly claim that Sin was reaching out its lurid hand for the unsuspecting, because the men who went in knew where they were going. When Cole peered through the small window on the door, he could see a few dim figures sitting at the bar, a few more at tables. However, he did not open the door, instead walked away, down the sidewalk to the corner, where he stood pretending to be waiting for somebody. *This is stupid,* he told himself. *I should go in. I need to think of something else besides myself, besides that cop.* But something undefined kept him from moving. *Is it because I met Teddy here? Or simply lack of practice?* It had been longer than three years, since he had not been to the bar for several months before his arrest.

Eventually he walked back to the front of the building. There was no name on the outside, he noticed, and he couldn't recall if it had ever had one. It was gray brick, water-spotted. As he walked away again, he passed two other young men coming from around a corner, where they had parked. They did not seem to look at him, but he knew they were going into the bar. He followed them back and glanced through the window. After another second of hesitation, he seized the handle, drew a breath, and went inside.

A jukebox was blaring a popular song, something about love of course: "You've made me so *very* happy; you've made me so *very* happy, baby!" The singer's insistence did not persuade Cole, who moved to the far end of the room, where the noise was less powerful. Three men were sitting at a large semibar, seemingly absorbed in their drinks, each one thinking his own thoughts. One of them, a portly man in glasses, about forty, with a nose that bulged at the tip, glanced up at Cole and seemed to want to smile, but he did not. Cole ordered a Vodka tonic at the main bar, then went back and found a stool to sit on, struck anew by the absence of women, except the waitress, who was chatting amiably with a group of three at a table across from him. On the wall was a picture, almost life-size, of a naked man with his hands coyly folded in front of his sex organs. It seemed to Cole that the man had been praying and somehow dropped his hands. As he glanced at some of the others sitting at the tables, he saw that one of them was very handsome, in a T-shirt, to emphasize the physique. After a time, the man lifted his eyes as though he knew he was being watched, and his teeth slipped into sight. But Cole grew nervous when the man kept looking at him, and he dropped his own eyes to his drink.

Somebody laughed wildly at the far end of the room and ran over to the jukebox. The other men at the semibar looked up expectantly, but nothing came of the incident. Another record began playing: "Strangers in the Night." Again the portly man was looking at him, and though Cole gave no response, he didn't immediately look away. Yet when he sensed that the man might get up and come over, he swirled around on the stool and faced in another direction. *I don't want to go to bed with him, why lead him on! I despise the kind who tease, who seem to make advances and never continue their playing into action. And, besides, I'm not that hard up*, he added cruelly.

The rear door opened and four men entered, two of them in suits. They seemed to know most of the others and greeted them, whisking back and forth from the bar to the tables. One of the men in a suit had a loud, very heavy voice, and his head was round and completely bald. He talked with exaggerated gestures, as if performing in an amphitheater, though he was not really effeminate. Rather, he seemed to be doing a bad impression of the stereotype of the homosexual. When someone said something to him, he fell back and stuck his wrist into the air. The gesture made no sense, seemed to have no connection with what he was saying. Then all at once he shouted an obscenity and raised his hands far above his head and let them dangle like those of a malfunctioning puppet. "My dears!" he yelled at a group at the end of the bar near Cole, coming at them, a miniature sea wave. "Gorgeous George, you are looking so well! And so happy! You must be screwing the be-Jesus out of somebody!" The group laughed heartily. A mild Southern accent was evident in the man's speech. To see better, Cole turned his head. "What have I been doing with myself?" the man said, jabbing at someone's shoulder. "You nasty thing, you! You know I never do *myself*. It's too hard on the back muscles for one thing! And besides, honey, I want to share all these glorious pounds of me with other people. I think of myself as one great big Care package for the underprivileged gay folk." Again there were laughs, and the others in the bar began watching the man. Someone said something to him, but Cole did not catch it. "That's not true, that's not true!" He made the words sound as if he were about to sing. "Immoral I am not! I have merely dedicated myself to the practice of concupiscence. Con-cu-pis-cence! Do you all know what that is? Well, it's me, that's what it is. I'm Mr. A. Abraham Concupiscence. I know it and I live it. Indeed, I live *for* it! Take away my automobile, take away my jewels, take away my furs, but leave me my concupiscence. I have never in all my born days asked for anything more. What good is all the wealth in the world if you haven't got love, I ask you, or at least a reasonable facsimile? Take my boss, for example. And I mean you can take him! He don't love anybody; he even hates himself. Why I bet when he gets up in the morning he feels just awful—I mean looking so crabby and grouchy and all and thinking where is the next dollar coming from. And you know what he told me yesterday? I swear to God! He said I was a *frivolous* person. Frivolous! I practically had to go look the word up in the dictionary. What it is, though, is a matter of two different philosophies of life, that's what it is. He must be a Cancer—isn't that the crab? Maybe, for all I know, he's even got cancer—the disease. Well, I told him that it is my considerate philosophy to make the most of what I've got while I've got it. And God knows I ain't got that much!" The man guffawed at the joke on himself. "But I've always maintained that it's not what you got; it's how you use it. And nobody ever yet has accused me of being stingy with what I've got! You know what that old poop did the day before yesterday? Maybe, though, I shouldn't tell you all, since it is sort of personal." The others encouraged the story heartily, and he went on. "Well, I was in the restroom—yes, the men's, don't be funny, honey—and in comes who else but J. Edgar Boss, and he gets in the booth way down at the end. Well, I finished my business and washed my hands—like a good boy—and then I pretends to go out. You know, I opens the door and lets it slam, but I stood right where I was. And that old crab let go with a fart that he must have been saving for the Fourth of July. Lord, it was like to break the toilet! I'm positive he split the inside of it clean in two. And such a god-awful sound he made—I thought it was the Bob-lo boat leaving for Canada, I swear! He was just a-honking and a-tooting like he was preparing to go to the moon. I can't imagine what that man ate, but it must have been dreadful, though—must have been a ton of beans, you know those old navy beans? Well, I can tell you I did *not* stay around for the results of such noises, let me tell you! I just pity the poor beleaguered soul that had to follow him into that john; he must have thought he was caught in one of the ten plagues of Egypt!"

The rest of the men were smiling, and someone offered to buy the man, whose name was Roy, a drink. But he refused. "No, brother, I am on the wagon of the Lord. Not really, I just am cutting down for a few weeks until I lose this." He patted his stomach, which did not seem especially fat to Cole. One of the group jokingly accused him of becoming stodgy. "I may indulge myself in certain sexual ways, but I am pleased to say that I have some willpower for other things. Boys, this is a ruthless business, for the old and the fat, and I don't mean maybe! So as long as I can keep the tummy a vision of delight I may not have to worry about these advancing years." Roy rubbed his palm across his bald head, but Cole thought the man could not have been more than twenty-five, despite the loss of hair. It was so complete that it had to be from some premature cause.

Right then some more young men entered the bar and began ordering drinks. Cole noticed that some of them moved gradually to the edges of the booths opposite the main bar, standing outside with their glasses in their hands, forming a line. Some at the bar had turned around to face in their direction. *It's a gantlet*, Cole thought. They eyed each other noncommittally, afraid to seem overeager, afraid of rejection. It was safer to wait, to watch.

Cole caught the voice of the bald man again. He had gathered two others to himself and was listening to one of them complain about his mother. "That's something you just can't mean, Harry. She's your mother. Think of all those soiled sheets she's washed for you—including the ones recently. And the dirty underwear, not to mention all the ironing and cooking. Everybody forgets those things." There was a mild objection. "So she ruined your goddamn life. Is that all! Well, you ought to be thankful that it wasn't any worse than that. You homosexuals always put the blame on other people. Your mama did this and your daddy did that! Well, everybody's mama does something. You've got to forgive and forget and live! Live! Live!" Roy stuck his arms out as far as they would go and smiled like a sun. Somebody proposed a toast to motherhood, and they all clinked their glasses, and even Roy pretended he had one.

"Say, I'm giving a party in two weeks, I almost forgot! I'm inviting all of you right this minute. Then I won't have to write out all those dratted invitations." Cole wished that he knew the man so that he could go to the party. "It's at my place two weeks from tomorrow, and I'm supplying the liquor. So drink lots of water before you get there." The others offered to buy him a drink, but Roy refused again. "And you, Randolph, you keep your clothes on at this party, you hear me?" The group razzed one man for a few seconds, but Cole could not tell exactly what they meant; they seemed to be kidding him about something he had not really done. "No, it's not going to be a costume party, maybe some other time. Good Lord, Halloween is coming up in no time at all, end of next month already, and if I have to throw another party myself, I'm going to swing on the Eve of All Hallows." Harry asked him what he was going to dress up as. "Well, I haven't decided, though I think perhaps I'll take all my clothes off, pour a can of Pet Milk over my head, and come as a wet dream!" Even Cole grinned, ducking his head down.

The waitress came by and spoke to him. "How are you this evening?" He nodded that he was fine. "Would you care for another drink?"

"Yes, please. Another Vodka tonic."

He was trying to keep Roy within earshot as he paid her, but he had missed some of the conversation. "Oh, gorilla dung! that's not so! She's a very clever person; I don't care what you say, I think she's grand." Cole wondered if they were talking about another man or a real girl. "She went to bat for me more than one time." There seemed to be a shade of true disagreement present, but Roy turned the talk. "And what are you all going to the party as? Randolph?" The shy man said he thought he'd come as a candy bar covered in cellophane. "Be careful you do it right, Randolph, or somebody may mistake you for a contraceptive!" One of the others said that Randolph was indeed something of a prick, but Roy defended him. "Randolph is a handsome, sweet, well-adjusted, hard-working, delightful young man—for a queer." Roy laughed with the others at his joke. The man who had quarreled faintly put in that he was going to come to the party dressed like Adam, with only a fig leaf. He smirked and struck a body-builder's pose, revealing his trim shape. "Well, how wonderful of you! But it would be so much easier if you just left off the fig leaf—and came as Eve!" Roy said it with such gusto and merriment that even the victim joined in the fun.

When Cole looked back at his drink, sipping the tart flavor, out of the corner of his eye he could see that someone had sat down in the stool next to his. Yet he did not move his head because he wanted to continue listening to the bald man. Almost inadvertently he glanced over—at the good-looking man in the T-shirt who had been across the room. "How are you tonight?" the man asked.

Why is he cruising me? He could have his pick. Cole said nothing.

"Nice crowd tonight," the man persisted, a metallic timbre to his voice.

Cole looked at him again. He was handsome up close too. His own voice was husky, but he answered. "Yes, because of the weekend, I guess."

"Some of the boys get out quite a lot. I see them here. Guess they like to have a good time, huh?"

It seemed an odd comment, but Cole granted the convention of light conversation that went with cruising. "I imagine so; I haven't been here much lately."

"I thought I saw you here last week."

"It wasn't me. I've been—out of the country."

"Yeah? Europe?"

"Yes, in Europe."

"Boy, I'd like to go to Europe sometime. Did you get to Copenhagen? I'd love to take in Copenhagen."

"No, I skipped Copenhagen; I had some laundry to do."

The man half-grinned at the cryptic remark, then decided to take a different angle. "There aren't too many gay bars in Detroit, are there?"

"A few that I know of."

"I'm sort of new around town. How do you find them?"

"There are guides. And word of mouth."

"Maybe you could tell me a few, help me out."

There was something in the man's tone that made Cole doubt him, and he spoke slowly. "Try the *Diplomat*; I heard it's good, although I haven't been there for some time."

"Yeah? Where's that?"

"It's on Second, I think. You'll have to check the telephone book to be sure."

"Lots of gay guys go there, huh?"

"I think so."

The conversation seemed to stagnate, until the man found something else to say. "It gets real lonely for a newcomer like me around here. Sort of lonely." He had turned on the stool and stretched out his legs and leaned back against the bar, and Cole felt a wave of lust charge through him. The man was wearing Levi's to draw attention to his good body. Cole stared down into his ice. "I'm from Upper Michigan myself."

"What part?"

"Houghton. Do you know it?" He scratched at his shoulder.

"I've never been there, I'm afraid."

"It's a nice town, but small. I have friends back there. But not around Detroit. Where do you live?"

"I have an apartment."

"Downtown?"

"It's not too far away." Cole could feel his heart speeding up as the conversation centered itself.

"You live alone?"

"Yes, and do you?"

"No, I share with somebody—if you know what I mean." He grinned slyly.

"A lover, as we say in the business."

"Yeah. You have a car?"

"No, I don't."

That made the man hesitate for a moment. "We could go in mine."

"That's an idea." Cole turned his head and looked at the long, well-proportioned body.

"What do you like to do?"

Something tightened within Cole's brain. *Is he some kind of crank? Maybe he wants to beat me or be beaten.* "I'm kind of orthodox myself." He smiled in the man's direction.

"Come on, tell me what you like to do. Do you like to blow?"

He disliked the mixed attraction and annoyance he felt. "It's a possibility."

"You have to be careful these days, with the vice and all," the man said, shaking his head sadly.

"Yes, they're a bunch of bastards."

"Yeah, I know. But they're only doing their job, I guess."

Cole darted his eyes into the man's. "It's a sick job."

"Yeah, gay guys ought to be careful all right." They said nothing more for a while, and Cole could hear Roy's heavy voice from another part of the room, although he could not see him. "So you say you live close by, huh?" the man continued.

"In Highland Park."

"Can we go there?" The man rubbed a finger down between

his eyes and nose, making Cole feel weak with desire. But still he waited, uncertain. *I've waited for three years; a few more minutes won't matter.*

The good-looking man glanced questioningly, and at last Cole said, "I'd like to go."

"Well, let's go then." The man jumped up and stuffed his big hands in his pockets. He smiled broadly and gestured with his head.

Cole felt strange, but he said it anyway. "I don't want to do anything that you don't want to do, is that clear?"

"What do you mean by that?"

"I mean we're going to my place for a drink, and it was your idea."

The man looked at him oddly. "I'm not following."

Cole thought the statement somehow protected him. He grabbed his drink and drained it.

"You going to go?" the man asked expectantly, and Cole stood up, but did not move away. "Something wrong?"

Looking directly at the other, he asked, "Do you mind showing me your wallet?"

"My wallet? What do you want to see that for?"

"I just want to check something. It's not your money."

"You're kidding. Come on, let's go." He walked a few steps toward the door.

But Cole stayed where he was. "I want to see your identification papers."

"But why?"

"Because."

He came back toward Cole. "I didn't ask to see yours."

"I'll show them to you when you let me see yours." Cole hated the foolish opinion of himself that was forming, but he had made up his mind.

"Well, I don't want to show you my wallet." The man was not smiling any longer.

"Okay, good-bye then." He sat down again.

"Come on, come on, let's go to your place. Come on!"

"Open your wallet."

"What do you want to see? I'm over twenty-one." He made an attempt at laughter.

"It's still an offense in this country to do what we're doing."

"You think I'm a cop?" He snorted contemptuously.

"You might be."

"You might be one too."

"I'm not a cop!"

"You already said enough to incriminate yourself."

Cole's stomach constricted at the words. "I've said nothing—and don't forget it!" He was surprised at the loudness of his voice. The man backed away from him, and a few other heads turned momentarily to stare at them.

"Okay, pal, if that's the way you want it."

"Yes, that's the way I want it." Cole's stomach loosened as the man moved farther away. In a second he was gone, disappearing down the gantlet of cruisers. Cole thought that he went out the front door, but people blocked the view. *I can't help it, although I was ridiculous,* he argued with himself. *I can't jump back into this routine in a few days. So I let a good man get away; he won't be the first. He probably wanted me to do all the sexual work anyway. I'm glad he went.* Cole walked to the main bar and ordered another Vodka tonic, looking around at the men facing each other. Nobody seemed to have made any advances—they waited, not even encouraging expressions in their eyes, just waited. "Cowards," he said softly, crushing his ice with his teeth. "Cowards!"

After finishing his drink, he got up and placed a quarter in the jukebox, without bothering to check the buttons he pushed; he merely wanted some music. When a record began to play, however, he went into the men's room, where he looked inside one of the booths for scribblings on the walls, but there were none. He checked the other booth. Nothing. *It's as virginal as a nuns' convent,* he thought.

At the sink he began to comb his hair, even though it did not need grooming. Another man entered, and across the top of his arm Cole could see that it was the portly man he had turned away from earlier. He smiled at Cole this time, and stood at one of the urinals. Cole let his eyes survey the man, who was thick-waisted, but not as fat as he had first thought; it was his face that was round, an unfortunate plump face that made the rest of him seem overweight. The man glanced back over his shoulder with an invitation in the eyes. His reddish hair was in an out-of-date brush cut. He made no pretense of not staring at Cole, who went on combing his hair, unmoved. "Sure is hot out there," the man offered.

"Is it," he said flatly. "I hadn't noticed."

"Yeah, it is." The man zipped up and came up to the wash basins, making an elaborate display of washing his hands. "It's all that smoke, I suppose, and the heat of the bodies." He tried to see if Cole read anything in his words.

"Yes, all that fresh semen churning around out there."

"You aren't going, are you?" Cole had started for the door.

"I may."

"Let me buy you a drink, what do you say?" He started to put his hand on Cole's arm, then thought better of it. Instead he gestured with his open palm at the door. "Why don't you?"

"I'm very tired tonight."

The man read the message. "No obligations. Just let me buy you a drink."

. They went back to the semibar and sat down, and Cole looked for the handsome man, but he was not in sight.

"You waiting for somebody in particular?"

"No more than anybody else."

"What do you like—to drink?"

"A Vodka tonic." The man went to the bar and brought back Cole's drink and a rum and Coke for himself.

"These ought to cool us off."

Cole knew that the man expected a thank you, but he said nothing.

"Say, you're new around here."

"Am I?"

"I didn't mean to bother you." There was a piqued tone.

"You're not bothering me."

"Well, if I am, just say so, and I'll leave you alone."

"I owe you five minutes of conversation for the liquor."

"No, you don't."

Cole pretended he had not heard. "Used to have dancing in here, I thought."

The man smiled unevenly, and eased up to his drink. "They used to, but the cops put a stop to it. About a year ago."

"I guess we're supposed to be grateful they didn't close the place down."

"Wouldn't do that. Too much kickback."

"How much do you think a bar like this has to pay to stay open?"

"I wouldn't know exactly, but I bet it's thousands of dollars."

"And who gets the money?"

"Big cops probably. Maybe some little cops too."

"And I had hoped it was all going to widows and orphans."

The portly man clapped his hands together gently to express his amusement, and Cole noticed the large freckles on the top of them. On his forehead as well were numerous small spots. "So you do have a sense of humor after all?"

"Is that what it is?"

"You certainly ask a lot of questions, though."

"Let's say I'm an inquisitive person."

"Are you from Detroit?"

"No, Chicago. I'm just here for a few days."

"I live in Grosse Pointe."

Cole detected a hint of smugness. "You must make money then."

"I'm a realtor." He paused to see if Cole would volunteer any information about himself.

"I'm—I work in a crematorium."

"Really?" The man was genuinely intrigued.

"Sure, really. I burn corpses." Cole moved both hands as though adjusting knobs. "I set the dials—and snap, crackle, pop!"

"Well, you seem to enjoy the job."

"It keeps me off the streets."

"Say, maybe you can tell me something I've always wondered about. How long does it take to . . . to . . ."

"To dispose of the remains? Oh, not very long—if you set the temperature right. Has to be about eighteen hundred degrees, and it takes about six hours. Though one time I turned it up to twenty-four hundred degrees, just to see what it would be like, you know! There wasn't anything left of the poor old lady when I peeped inside."

The other man looked doubtful. "Why would you do that?"

"Oh, she didn't have any close relatives, so nobody wanted any souvenirs—bones and ashes, you know."

"They aren't exactly *souvenirs!*"

"Of course they are! What else would you call them? People put them on shelves and in little urns."

"I think they'd be called something else, though."

"What's in a name?" He took a long swallow of his drink, keeping his eyes on the red-headed man.

He decided to switch the topic. "A good crowd here tonight."

"You say you've been here often?"

"Fairly regular. Why?"

"Do you know who that brown-haired guy in the T-shirt is? Did you see him—he was sitting next to me a while ago?"

"You mean the guy in the Levi's?"

"Yes, him. Know him?"

"Can't say as I do. Is he a friend of yours?"

"No!"

"Why didn't you go with him?"

"Because I did not choose to." He looked deliberately at the man's face. No, he was certain that *he* was not a police decoy; he was not attractive enough.

"Were you asking him for money?"

Cole chuckled. "Me ask him?"

"You were discussing something."

"Do you know that bald man named Roy? The one who talks a lot."

"Oh, Roy, everybody knows Roy; he's a real funny fellow."

"Why is he so bald?"

"Some deficiency in his diet when he was a kid, he told me, but you never know if he's being serious."

"Do you know him very well?"

"I've been to his house for a picnic once. Do you want to meet him?"

Cole could feel that the man imagined that Cole was interested sexually. "I just found him interesting, that's all."

"Oh, he's a riot, that's for sure."

"He made me laugh," he said quietly.

"Want me to introduce you to him?"

Cole sensed the reluctance. "No, it isn't necessary." Suddenly he felt his stomach twinge with hunger, the various acids bubbling. "I think I had better get some food—before I die."

"You hungry? Well, why don't you come out to my place? I've got a whole refrigerator full of stuff."

"To entice the unsuspecting?"

"Maybe," he said coyly, leaning closer.

"What if I'm a nut? What if I'm dangerous?"

The man frowned at the suggestion. Uncertainty passed in and out of his expression. "You aren't serious. Are you?"

"You have to be careful who you pick up these days."

"You do have rather evil eyes." He was flirting.

"You might be surprised."

"I mean the way your brows stick out—your eyebrows."

"They're the sign of the devil."

The red-headed man squinted uncomfortably, unfamiliar with the way Cole was talking. "You're quite the joker, I can see." It was more of a question than a comment. "Are you a hustler?"

"Is that a compliment or an insult?"

"I just wonder. I don't pay."

"Good for you. I don't charge."

The man smiled tentatively. "Why don't you come to my place then?"

"You probably intend to take my virtue."

"I'll take whatever you want to give, as a matter of fact."

Cole still refused to laugh, would not relent. "Don't you have to work in the morning, sell some houses?"

"I have my own office; I can go in when I like—after special occasions." He winked.

"What would your mother say if she could hear you talking like this?"

"My mother lives with me."

"How cozy. I don't suppose she knows about your sex partners? Hard of hearing maybe?"

The man sputtered into a snicker, but then he stopped, perplexed. "You're . . . You're . . ."

"Am I? You're not the only one who's told me that about myself."

The man leaned closer and spoke with sincerity. "Look, I want you to come out to my house; I'll give you some food, and we can make love."

"Love? Surely this is not love. Let's say 'make lust.' I have no objections to 'making lust,' but don't call it something else."

"I don't ask this of just anybody."

"That still doesn't make it love!"

"Well, it's a reasonable facsimile. It'll do until something better comes along."

Cole swung around to face him directly. "But what if it doesn't work out? What if we can't find happiness together—and divorce is so difficult in Italy too!"

"What?" The man crinkled his nose.

"The children! The in-laws! What will everybody say?"

The man vaguely caught the drift. "I'm not asking you to stay forever, just tonight."

"Ah, you are a man of honesty. I think I'll go with you; I despise men who call their burning crotches 'falling in love.' They have no insight into themselves; they don't realize they are plants. Plants pollinating like a duty. Their little pistils go bang, bang, bang!"

The man backed away from the hand shaped like a gun that Cole aimed. "Well, I'd best be going; I really ought to get up early tomorrow," he half-mumbled.

"But don't leave!" Cole stood up. "I want your large, pink body rolling on top of mine, I do, I do! You're the only one in the world for me; I sensed it when I laid eyes on you."

"Are you putting me on?"

"Of course I'm not. This blinding flash in my breast cannot be mistaken."

"You're the oddest man I ever saw around here. Do you feel all right?"

"I feel super. And if I didn't feel fine, I'd know what to do. I used to have a nun who told us children: 'If you ever feel queer, boys and girls, just put your head between your legs.' Isn't that marvelous advice?"

"I'm sorry, but I can't follow your sense of humor. You'll have to excuse me." The man nodded shortly and started to walk away, but Cole followed him as they passed through the thickening clusters of men, and Cole saluted two of them in rapid succession, not looking for their reaction, however. When they were almost to the door, the portly man turned back. "Where're you going? What do you want?"

"I thought we were going to your place, to visit your mother."

"Let me understand something. Do you or don't you want"—his eyes looked cautiously around him—"what I want."

"I haven't the slightest notion what I want." As he spoke, Cole noticed that the man in Levi's that he had talked to earlier was sitting at the bar with Roy. Cole turned back to the redheaded man. "Introduce me to Roy, will you?"

"He looks occupied!" he answered peevishly.

"I know he's occupied; that's why I want to talk to him."

"I don't exactly owe you any favors."

"I'm sorry I was playing around."

"You are?" The man broke into a broad grin.

"My mother died yesterday."

"Oh, that's a shame. I'm sorry."

Cole glanced over at Roy and the brown-haired man, who were getting up from the bar. The handsome man pointed toward the back door, and Cole heard him say his car was parked in the rear. As they made their way past him, his eyes riveted on the handsome face, and the man avoided the glare and kept moving. In a few seconds they disappeared out the rear exit, and Cole waited in uncertainty, someone's hand placed on his shoulder asking to pass by.

"So," the red-head said, "you're coming out to my house after all?"

"Excuse me, I have to see about something." He threaded his way through the bodies to the rear of the building, glancing over his shoulder, as he went out into the parking lot, at the man with his fists on his hips watching him depart. Cole waved twice sideways with an open palm and let the door slam shut behind him.

There were no people in sight, only about ten cars parked on the deep ruts of the lot that was adjacent to a dingy apartment building. Some other cars were lined up in the alley, leaving only enough space for people to walk through. *The other two must have cut across the lot to a car parked farther away; they could not have driven away that fast.* He turned the corner quickly, but the street was deserted, and he wondered if they had gone around to the front for some reason, but he decided to go in the other direction, a short block. When he rounded the corner, he saw Roy and the man standing close together halfway down the street, the good-looking man with something in his hand, like a card. Roy threw up his hands in a gesture of real or mock despair, and the man went on talking to him, as if explaining. Cole hesitated, then moved closer; then, frightened, he retreated to the corner.

Neither had noticed him. *He's arresting him; that's his identification card. The dirty bastard!* Cole wanted to come up behind the man in Levi's and crush his fists down on his skull. He could see himself kicking the man's face, bloodying and cracking all that well-formed bone and tissue. But he stayed where he was. If he interfered, he might be arrested too, and he couldn't risk that. He felt like shouting at Roy to run, but he let the shout die on his tongue. *Oh, the crummy, slime-eating bastard!* Roy had started talking, and although the sound carried, no words were clear; his gestures were subdued, more controlled. *Give it to him, tell him to go to hell, just walk away, run!* The policeman was shaking his head no and beckoning for Roy to come along with him, but the other lagged. *What can I do for him?* When Roy continued to resist, the decoy took out a small whistle from his hip pocket and blew into it. The shrillness pierced the cool night, and in a moment another man came running around the corner at the other end of the block. Unhesitatingly he came up to the other two and put handcuffs on Roy while pushing him a few times with his fingertips, and he seemed to be cursing, from the tone of the words. After another few seconds, an unmarked car pulled around the same corner and stopped in front of the group. Cole started to take a few steps toward them, and yet once again he froze. *Yes, it is the same man that arrested me. The same heavy body.* He had not recognized it when the policeman was running, but now there was no mistaking him. He had opened the back door of the car and was tugging at Roy. At first Cole believed that his heart had stopped beating, but then he seemed to taste something spilling down inside his throbbing chest, like lye. They had managed to get Roy into the rear seat, and the decoy was crossing behind the automobile to get in on the far side, while the man whose name Cole had forgotten stood guard. Abruptly he looked down the street at Cole and staring for a long time, perhaps thinking he ought to shake his hand at the watcher or walk toward him. However, he merely waited and watched as Cole paced back and forth to the curb.

Eventually the policeman opened the door next to him and slid in beside Roy. When he did, Cole began to walk, then run toward the car. Just as he caught up to it, it moved out from the curb. "You fascist mother-shovers! You goddamned shitholes!" he yelled, but the car did not halt. "Leave us alone, do you hear me? Leave us alone!" The heavy man's face appeared in the rear window, and then the automobile stopped suddenly. The man looked through the glass a second time, and Cole shouted as loudly as he could: "You sick savages! Let him alone, do you hear me! Let him alone! We're not hurting you! Who in the name of hell do you think you are!" At once the car door flew open, and the heavy man's leg jutted out and touched the pavement.

But Cole did not see anything else. He turned and fled up the street as if he were on fire.

5

Cole was awake before his alarm went off; he had set it for seven thirty, to be certain that he would be at Recorder's Court by eight thirty, when Roy's case probably would be tried. He shaved slowly and then dressed in a dark suit so that he would look "respectable." Undetectable. He had not slept more than a few hours after returning from the bar, and he noticed that the eyes looked puffy; they even felt spattered with mud. Slapping cold water in handfuls across his face did not seem to refresh him. He lit three cigarettes in succession and smothered them before they were half finished. When he brushed his teeth, the sharp tang of the fluoride seemed to heat the interior of his mouth and brought back the hunger pangs, for he had not eaten anything since the cereal. He watched the toothpaste's foam and his bloodied spit curl down the drain. Some of it stuck, and he had to take a finger and dislodge it. For some reason it made him nauseous, and he washed the finger for a long while before he was satisfied that it was clean. As he went through the kitchen, he picked up the butcher knife from a drawer; the triangular blade fitted comfortably, though too long, into the inside pocket, as if it belonged there.

He stopped at the grocery store on Woodward where he had shopped previously, to buy something to eat, but it was not open yet. The street was deserted of walkers, although cars were beginning the trek into the inner part of the city. A few pieces of junk—a Dairy Queen cup and parts of a newspaper —were blowing gently against a building. A theater marquee displayed the name of the movie playing: THE EROTIC ITCH. The posters showed a girl in a torn bra with many bodiless arms grasping at her; the girl's face was twisted between fear and sensuality. The advertisement read: "Women in the town called her a no-good slut. Men in town called her . . . anytime." *I bet it pulls them in by the thousands,* Cole said to himself. He turned away abruptly.

He felt weak from the lack of food, but no other store was open. He checked a clock in a drugstore—eight five. He ought to hurry and get a taxi if he was to make the trial on time, although his own had not come up until nine thirty. *I won't miss this one, even if I have to do it in pain.*

At the corner he saw his reflection in a car dealership window. *I wonder if he can recognize me. He may.* Cole went back to his apartment for his sunglasses, unable to find them at once. Then he rushed out to the street again, looking for a taxi; there were none. Even back on Woodward the few that passed were occupied. It was sixteen minutes past eight and the drive to Recorder's Court was at least fifteen minutes long, longer in the morning traffic. He stuck out his thumb for a ride, but nobody paid attention to him. He walked backwards with the traffic for a short distance, and then at last a free cab appeared.

He asked the driver what time it was. Eight thirty. And they were only as far as the Blessed Sacrament Cathedral. *All of us good citizens on our way to work,* Cole thought, trying to fight his nervousness. *Why can't we ride along the sidewalk, the way heroes do in movies, careening, weaving in and out, for some preposterous reason—to save a life, to catch a crook? Well, that's what I'm doing too,* he smiled. *I'm going to catch a criminal and save a man's life.* He eased back into the seat at the concept.

The side of the cathedral caught his eye, the thousands of pounds of enormous stones, the spires, a building that took up a whole city block. *Do people really need that? Would I be planning what I am if I still had my "faith," as the nuns in school called it? Or would I do it anyway? Christians have never cur-*

tailed their killings because of their faith; history is strewn with corpses, the enemies of the "faithful." Sometimes in fact they murdered for God. Yet maybe some have been prevented . . . maybe because of. . . . He let the idea slip out of his mind.

Up ahead there was a minor accident; two men were standing beside their dented automobiles shaking their hands at each other; they seemed oblivious of the cars moving around them, concentrating on their own anger, and Cole hated them with a fierceness that seemed to swell inside him in a fraction of a second. "Get out of my way," he spat through the window as the taxi neared them. But they did not move, if they even heard him.

It was ten to nine when Cole got out in front of Recorder's Court. Long steps led up to the entrance. *They've cleaned it since I was here last. How civic!* In jail he had mailed a dollar to a police campaign called "Buck Up Your Police Force," but he had torn it into a hundred or more pieces. Groups of people were hastening up the steps, through revolving doors. A stray policeman here and there could be seen going in. The thick columns made the building resemble a temple, one about to become a ruin, despite the efforts made to preserve it. *Perhaps if the two columns are close enough together, I could push . . .*

In the large lobby clusters of worried-looking people and a few lawyers were conferring. Everything looked gray, unwashed, and the people appeared to have slept in their clothes. Cole adjusted his sunglasses, lifted them for a second, and then replaced them since the darkness helped cover the reality. He suspected that he called attention to himself in the glasses, but the risk was even greater the other way. *How can I find the proper court without checking each individually?* The roster on the wall near the elevators listed twenty judges' names. *If I ask at the information desk, what should I say precisely? "Where are the morals cases being judged?"* Putting his hands in and out of his coat pockets, he waited a few minutes, and then went up to the woman at the desk. He had to wait for another man who wanted the psychological clinic.

The attendant was a bright-eyed black woman. "Yes?"

"I would like the courtroom of a certain case."

"Which judge?"

"I don't know the name of the judge—"

"Who's your lawyer?"

"I don't have a lawyer."

"Then see the man in that far room—see it? He'll get you one."

"But I want to find the courtroom, right away. I don't need a lawyer."

"Well, you can't be tried until you get a lawyer."

He moved back a step as if slapped. "I'm not the one on trial."

"Well, why didn't you say so? Who do you want?"

He could feel his voice losing its control, but he fought himself. "I want to know where the Lewd and Lascivious Behavior cases are being tried."

"You mean Accosting and Soliciting?"

"I'm not sure." He lowered his eyes, ashamed.

"They're in different places, I'm afraid." She slumped back into her chair and looked in another direction.

"Uh—do you know the name of a heavy man, a policeman, he works on the Vice Squad, something like Field?"

"There are *lots* of policemen around here."

"I know. I want one particular one. Heavy-faced, about two hundred and twenty pounds, highly colored in the face."

"All you can do is look around for him, since you don't know his name." She dismissed him.

Cole almost said thank you, but stopped himself. As he walked to the roster of names again, he could not quite recall if the judge he himself had appeared before was listed. *How could I forget that?* They all seemed to be Irish or Polish, and he glanced around for someone to ask. He went to an empty elevator and spoke to the waiting operator. "Do you know where the Lewd and Lascivious or Accosting and Soliciting Cases are being tried this morning?" He tried to keep his head from sinking from embarrassment, forcing himself to stare into the woman's eyes. "Don't know nothing 'bout it. Try over there." She pointed to the information desk.

He began to ascend the wide marbleized staircase to the second floor. Women with children were seated on benches along the wall, sleepy, haggard. He walked along the corridor looking for a room that might be a courtroom, but they all seemed to be offices. He pulled open one door and three secretaries looked up at him indifferently. He shut the door without speaking.

On the third floor were some courtrooms, some of them locked from the inside. From one, however, voices could be heard as the door opened and closed. Cole grabbed the door when a woman emerged and edged in next to the wall. A lawyer was defending a young girl, obviously a prostitute, who had been picked up the preceding night. He slurred his words, overanxious to say his defense. Cole saw no one he recognized, and moved to the other side of the door to survey the room scrupulously. No one. After a few minutes, he slipped out and then waited to see where a bustling group of five men was headed. They disappeared behind a door marked PRIVATE. Probably lawyers coming from breakfast.

Since no other rooms were open, he started to the next floor. At the top of the stairs his heart jumped. There was the cop! He was standing in the center of the corridor talking to two other men, also policemen. Cole pressed his coat pocket where the knife was concealed. *Can I rush at him and take the chance, slash his throat and run? Maybe they would be too frightened; I could run down again and outside before anyone could stop me.* He became conscious of himself standing at the top of the steps and began to move toward the group. Just as he reached them, the heavy man turned and faced Cole, even sweeping his eyes over him, but they did not register any recognition. He was saying what a bitch it was to have to get up so early. Cole kept on walking without turning his head. The armholes of his suit were dripping with sweat, and his legs felt asleep. At the far end he rested against the wall, his arms suddenly chilled and trembling. He seemed to be attached to the wall, as if hung there on a hook, and he was sure that the cop could feel his eyes burning into the neck, but there was no acknowledgment. In fact, the policeman gave a hearty laugh about something. *So secure, aren't you! You'll laugh when I stick this in your gut.*

The door to a room nearby opened and two people came out, one after the other; one of them was Roy. The first man said something to him and then walked away. For a time Roy stood still, watching the other man disappear into the elevator. Then he sat on a small staircase leading to the fifth floor as Cole quickly moved toward him. "Is that your lawyer?" He nodded in the direction.

Roy looked up at him suspiciously. "Yep, that's him."

"I know why you're here; I saw what happened last night."

"Where—at the bar? Were you there?"

"I also talked with that damned decoy."

"Did he get you too?"

"No, not this time. I was very cautious."

Roy drooped his head. "I guess I wasn't."

"When is your case coming up? Right away?"

"I don't know. My lawyer said it'd maybe be another half an hour."

"Why don't you make a run for it? Just walk out and don't stop."

Roy puffed out his cheeks and shrugged. "What good'd that do? They got my fingerprints and name and everything."

"Leave the city."

"I can't do that; I got my job and other things around here."

"If you go to jail, you won't have any of them."

"But they aren't going to put me in jail!" Roy stood up. "They only want to scare me a little."

"They'll scare you more than a little; I know."

"My lawyer said we'd plead innocent."

"You might as well plead guilty for all the good that will do you. A queer's word is worthless here."

Roy wrinkled his forehead at that. "He said they'd probably

give me a suspended sentence at most, being it's my first time and all."

"You'd better run for it, that's my advice."

"Then they'd really be after me."

"They have no right to arrest you in the first place."

"Well, they did anyway."

"Fight them! Fight them like hell."

"You know what that old pretty cop said to me when he pulls out his ID? He says, 'It was good trolling weather.' You get that! 'Good trolling weather.'"

"He's a scream."

"Well, it is sort of funny, if you look at it right."

"Just stand here and laugh while they toss you in prison!"

Roy's eyes darkened and lingered on Cole's hardened face. "What can I do, I ask you?"

"Do you know the name of that other officer, the heavy one, over there?"

"Yeah, he was there last night; he's a cuss, you know that!"

"What's his name?"

"I'm not rightly sure, something like Officer Wheeler, I think."

"You aren't sure?"

"No, he didn't exactly *introduce* himself to me. Why do you want to know?"

"I want—" He thought better of telling the truth. "I want to know him, that's all."

"Did he get you too?"

"He's a cunt-chewing coward."

Roy stared at Cole and then at the officer, trying to understand the vehemence. "Who are you anyway?"

"Hamlet."

"Oh, you're putting me on; that's an old play."

"I'm a knight killing dragons."

Roy grinned, and Cole noticed that Roy's face was ill-proportioned; the ears and nose were too large, calling attention to themselves.

"If he were dead," Cole continued, looking over at the policeman, "then maybe there would be an investigation and the entrapments would cease."

"If who were dead?"

Cole barely heard the question because he had begun to wonder if he were simply expressing what every assassin thinks: *This killing will rectify events, change life for the better. But this case is different! Certainly nothing will change if we let the police continue doing it. But I'll have to let them catch me in order to explain the reasons. But they might shoot me to death before I can utter a syllable. There would be nothing more than two lumps of riddled meat on the floor that might make a minor headline in the newspapers: "Maniac Stabs Officer for No Reason."*

"Are you listening to me?" Roy asked.

"What did you say?"

"I said you're going to get into more trouble than I'm in if you're not careful."

"I will be careful. Count on it."

"My lawyer thinks—"

"Where did you get this lawyer? Was he appointed?"

"No, he's a friend of the bondsman who got me out last night."

"They let you out on bond?"

"Yep, though it took a couple of hours."

"Consider yourself lucky."

"He seems like a good guy."

"He's exploiting homosexuals just like the rest of them; he makes his fat living from the fees he picks up around here from terrified little pipsqueaks."

"Here now, I'm no 'pipsqueak.' "

"No, of course not. Sorry. You're bold and brave and already convicted!"

"You talk big, but I don't see you doing anything."

Cole's eyes narrowed. "I'm telling you what to do. Deny everything, don't admit that you were even at the bar. Make them *prove* it."

"But I am guilty, really."

Cole set his mouth in a hard line. "As long as you accept the insane standards by which you're judged, you'll be a slave, a stupid, sneak-in-the-dark fairy."

"So fuck you, buckeroo!" Roy leaned back against the railing, insulted.

"God, you turn *against me!* Instead of against them! No wonder we get nowhere. No wonder we get kicked in the head."

Out of the edge of his eye Cole saw the police officer start to move away, nodding good-bye to the men he had been conversing with. Uncertainly Cole moved a few steps in that direction, but came back to Roy, who said nothing. "As long as you think of yourself as unnatural or 'diseased,' you'll go on standing in courtrooms with your tail between your legs."

"Well, it *is* unnatural, what we do."

"It's none of the goddamn police's business what we do! They have no right to touch us. If I want to go to a park, where I can't be seen, they should keep their hands to themselves. They can't, they won't tell me how my sex is supposed to be had!" He noticed that his knuckles were white from squeezing.

"Well, they can and they do."

"I thought you were smarter last night."

"Being smart ain't got nothing to do with it. So I'll get a fine or something."

"You'll have a criminal record. That will follow you around for the rest of your life. But it's more than that—it's being spit on, being considered deformed!"

"It's just something you got to live with, that's all."

"Christ in hell! You want to be gelded!"

"I just want to live my life, nothing else."

"You want to crawl in where you think you're safe—in some hole or under some rock, like all the other cowardly queers!"

"Shhh." Roy gestured that he was talking too loudly.

"All right," he whispered furiously. "But if the cops who arrested you were dead, then no charges could be placed."

Roy's eyes opened gradually as the thought sank in. "But I'm not about to kill anybody!"

"Yet you'll let them murder you. That's what they're doing, and you're just watching them do it."

"Am I supposed to throttle them with my bare hands?" He smiled contemptuously.

Cole wanted to open his suit coat and show the knife, but he considered it melodramatic. "There are many ways." He stopped as a policeman in uniform carrying a folder emerged from the courtroom where they were waiting; he briefly smiled at them and walked away.

"Should I go jump on his back and kick him to death?" Roy asked, pointing after the policeman. "He's just a man doing his job; probably has a family and bills to pay."

"So did the Nazi executioners. Christ, you're a sentimental boob! What's so virtuous about having a family? So he keeps the human rat race running along, so what? Is that the only reason for life, to keep reproducing ourselves? Use your mind instead of your gonads!"

"Well, if somebody didn't, then there would be nobody left at all."

"The danger hardly lies in that direction. Men keep swarming out of their cradles. There isn't room enough for all of us as it is."

"They're not mean people."

"The best men in the world are vicious!"

"I don't like talking like this." He folded his arms nervously.

"It's guys like you who keep the system operating. Don't you realize that the lawyers make a fortune from us and other yellow nobodies. And the judges get a kickback too—for most of the cases they try. And the cops take bribes. They keep arresting us because if they didn't they wouldn't have enough to occupy them—it's easier to capture a homosexual than a real criminal, safer too, because most of us are as scared and pansy as you."

"I'm not a pansy and don't you tell me I am." He rubbed his hand across his perspiring bald head and looked away.

"Blessed are the meek, for they shall suck ass."

Roy did not answer, but kept looking to the side of Cole, his fingers jiggling on his crossed arms.

After a few silent minutes, Cole spoke. "Is that cop who plays the decoy inside there?"

"I haven't seen him."

"Who's your judge?"

"The lawyer said it would most likely be Fitzpatrick." He continued to pretend interest in something on the other side of the corridor.

"If you jump out that window over there and break both legs, they might feel more sorry for you. Be sure to make certain the bones protrude, however—and they'll only give you two months in jail instead of six."

"Will you stop!" Roy snapped his head toward Cole, a flush on his cheeks.

"I'm trying to save you from what happened to me."

"Well, you can't save me. Only . . ."

"What?"

"Have you got any money with you?"

"Why?"

"The lawyer said maybe if I gave him five hundred or so he could see somebody, you know, in the back."

"And you don't have that much?"

"I don't have it because I just bought a car."

"I don't have that much with me, but I can get it."

"He said I'd need it right this morning."

"Get him to postpone the case."

"He said they're cracking down on postponements. Too many cases drag on and on."

"It seems that you are up the river without a paddle."

"You're a big comfort."

A gray-haired man strode out of the elevator; his clothes looked tailor-made. "Your 'attorney' is returning."

He approached them briskly. "Get ready; the judge is in; it'll be only a few minutes now." He put his arm around Roy's shoulders to aid him toward the courtroom. "Fitzpatrick is not a bad fellow."

After they let the door close behind them, Cole sat on the steps, feeling the cold stone with both hands, then pressing them to his forehead. He got up and walked to the end of the hall. Through an open door he could barely make out some middle-aged men lounging in a rear room; someone had just finished a funny anecdote, because they were all laughing. He walked back and entered the courtroom.

Roy was sitting alone on one of the benches; the lawyer had disappeared. Across the way policemen were filling up what looked like a jury box. A robust woman was adjusting the chair on the raised platform where the judge was to sit. Cole sat down about a quarter of the distance from the front, and waited. Then he moved to the second bench, behind Roy, near the aisle, so that he would be able to hear. When he pressed his hand inside on the knife, he felt it tearing through the lining of the pocket, the point lost in the material.

It took another twenty minutes for the court to assemble. Groups of relatives and friends of the defendants bustled in; other lawyers and clients began filling up the room and the noises grew louder. Roy made no attempt to talk, and so Cole waited in silence. At last the judge appeared, bulky in the black robe, a washed-out man wearing thick glasses; he was helped up the high step by two policemen, both with guns at their hips. Roy's lawyer was discussing details with another couple that he was defending when the clerk called for order. The sounds died away into the talkers' throats and the first names began to be called.

A file of defendants was rounded up by the various attorneys and positioned behind the brass guardrail. Cole stiffened when the police decoy and the florid-faced officer came out of a door at the side of the judge's chambers, the officer holding their report in one fist. For a few seconds he surveyed the people, and when his eyes fell on Cole, they seemed to hesitate. *Can he recognize me through the sunglasses?* But he sat still, his eyes on the man's. The eyes moved on. *It would be better with an ice pick,* Cole thought quietly. *It would penetrate his clothing more easily.*

The cases began almost unnoticed: The first was a man who had chased his fifteen-year-old son with a hammer because the boy had come home from a date later than he was allowed to. The son and father traded insults until the judge told them both to close their mouths. The case was settled by mutual promises to try to understand each other's side better, and they left, still muttering at each other.

The second case concerned a husband and wife, the woman with a bandage on her ear, who had come to blows because the husband did not want to come home until after midnight, even though he got off work at three thirty. The wife accused him of seeing other women, and he retaliated that he did not want to go home because all she did was bitch at him. The judge settled it by telling them to keep their arguments within their own house or next time they would get fifteen days, a fine, or both.

Roy came up third; he seemed to be the first of about five morals cases. At least, five other men stood sheepishly awaiting their turns. Cole leaned forward to hear the names as the clerk read the complaint of the citizens of the city of Detroit against Roy Dalby, but no names of the officers were given. The police decoy did the speaking, maintaining that while checking a bar he and his fellow officer had discovered the defendant acting in a lewd, disorderly way, even making immoral suggestions to the policeman himself. The tone was somber, matter-of-fact, as if he were reading a list of numbers. Roy's lawyer put in a plea of not guilty to the nodding judge.

"What is your defense?" the judge asked Roy, switching papers around on the huge mahogany desk.

"I don't know rightly what to say, Judge, except that I'm not guilty as charged. I was minding my own business. There must have been a misunderstanding or something."

"You are accused of making indecent proposals to this officer. Didn't you?" The thick glasses came forward to see better.

"I don't think I did. We were only talking, and then he ups and arrests me."

"What do you say to that?" the judge asked the decoy.

"The defendant was quite overt about his proposition, Your Honor. The officer here was sitting near me at the bar and overheard the conversation."

At the judge's acknowledgment, the heavy man spoke up, excessive respect coating the words. "That's true, Your Honor; the defendant said that he wanted to make an illegal sexual contact."

Cole slammed his back against the bench in a fury; the words in his chest struggled to get out, but he put his wrist on his mouth, pressing up hard.

"What did you say precisely to the officer?" the judge asked Roy.

"Well, I think I said I had a new car and would he like to see it, and he was going to show me his car too."

"Did you say it or do you just *think* you said that?"

"That's what I said, Judge, and that's all I said too." Roy sort of bowed at the two men standing on the other side of the desk, but they gave no reaction.

"You know that it is the responsibility of the police department to see to it that ordinary citizens are not annoyed and molested. What if people started grabbing just anyone they felt like grabbing? Sex maniacs and child molesters would run amuck if we didn't put some checks on them. You knew that bar was a well-known homosexuals' meeting place." The judge leaned forward accusingly.

Roy smiled. "It seems that the police officers knew it too, Your Honor." No one else smiled.

"Suppose some man just happened in there for a drink and you made an indecent proposal? Or some youngster!"

Roy hesitated, then went on. "Youngsters wouldn't be in a bar, I don't think."

The judge was piqued slightly at being caught out. "You people have got to do something to help yourselves. Like any other disease, it can't be cured overnight. You'll just wind up a lonely old man with nobody."

"Lots of people wind up old and lonely, Your Honor. You can't prevent it by being lonely when you're young."

The words seemed to touch the judge, for he paused and looked thoughtfully at the man before him. "Have you ever thought of getting psychiatric help?"

You're so brainwashed you can't think of anything but sickness, Cole shouted in his mind. *You legislate your own sex drives into laws!*

"I have considered it, but it costs a lot of money to do that."

The judge began to grow fatherly, and Cole noticed the two policemen become restless. "You can be helped, you know. There are many good doctors around. That is, if you really *want* to be cured. It takes a good long while, but you can go to the Lafayette Clinic, through the court here, and it will help you get over your affliction."

The lawyer broke in. "The defendant will be glad to seek psychiatric help, Your Honor. He's a hard-working citizen."

"Do you want to be helped, young man?" The judge peered at Roy through the thick glasses.

"Yes, sir, I do!"

"Blast you!" Cole said under his breath. *Put your tail between your legs and lie on your back, you sniveling appeaser! Tell him what he wants to hear, the blind old moron, elected because he has an Irish name. Tell him you want to have electrodes placed into your neck and have the "nastiness" jolted out of you. Tell him you can't wait to fuck your wife under the Christmas tree.*

The judge motioned for the lawyer and they conferred inaudibly for several minutes, while the rest waited. Once, Roy glanced back at Cole, though he gave no sign. Finally the judge announced, when the lawyer returned to his place, that the defendant would be given a suspended sentence with the stipulation that he make arrangements with a properly authorized clinic for psychiatric treatment. *How much kickback do the doctors pay?* Cole wondered.

The group began to break up, but the judge had an afterthought. "Just a minute. There's something else I wish to say." He had raised his voice to public-speaking volume, expecting the whole room to hear him. "I want to commend these police officers for their work; they are doing these homosexuals a service. First of all, they protect such men from exploitation by the ruthless. Second, they give them the opportunity to rehabilitate themselves and make themselves over into thoroughly adjusted, upright members of the community. Some critics say that we're too lenient these days, letting the sexually misfit free to commit these acts again. However, I stand by the advice of the experts, who tell us that homosexuality is not a crime. It is only a misfortune."

"Shut up!" Cole said in a murmur, and a man nearby shifted to stare at him.

"These unfortunate men are not to be persecuted; they are to be pitied, for they have had the ill luck to be born different from the rest of the world. The enlightened person does not turn away in disgust; his sympathy should go out to these unhappily misshapen personalities, just as it does to the insane. Only with such tolerance can some of them be altered for the better."

"Altered, like a cat!"

The man next to him shushed Cole.

"Society has come a long, long way in its understanding of such perversions. Time was when people were hanged, or worse, for such acts. Today we are much more educated, and I am hopeful that in time we will eliminate this problem altogether."

With the completion of his speech, the judge flipped some more papers on his desk and the men before him dispersed, the lawyer leading Roy off to the back room. The man he had come to kill moved away toward the jury box for another case. Already the next case was beginning as Cole sat rigid on the bench, nothing focused; the sounds seemed to pour down from above him as though he lay at the bottom of a deep tunnel. He closed his eyes.

Why do I sit here? Why can't I move? What would my Italian killer ancestors say? They'd laugh me to scorn, because the revengeful Italian blood has been drowned by the English in me. I might as well be chained where I am for all I can accomplish. I'm a fool, a blatant, cringing fool, who imagined that he could change events, the manipulator of not only his own fortune but other men's. Cole heard himself choke into a laugh, a series of weak noises that fell back upon themselves. The man sitting near him bent over closer and said, "Will you kindly behave yourself; court is in session."

Cole got up heavily, and he could feel eyes crawl over him as he moved away from the judge's bench, toward the exit. He turned as he came to the door and looked briefly at the florid-faced officer, who sat with his hands primly folded across his stomach. Cole reached into his coat pocket and ran his fingers down the edge of the blade; he pulled the sliced, not-yet-bleeding fingers out and closed his fist. A policeman in uniform at the door stepped aside to let him out, and Cole whispered, "Do you know the name of that man over there?"

"Which one?"

"The one in front, the second over."

"Sort of hefty man?"

"That's him."

"That's Officer Keel, Lieutenant Keel."

"That's John Keel, right?"

"No, Andrew." The policeman frowned him into being quiet.

"Just tell him he's won Round One."

"Huh?"

But Cole said no more. He closed the door behind him softly, aware of his own hunger—he was starving, and the red liquid was seeping across his palm. He thought that he might faint from the razors whirling inside him before he could escape.

6

~~~~~~~~~~

As Cole descended the steps to the outside, he forced himself to drink in breaths of air. He took out his handkerchief and wrapped it around his stinging fingers. A numbness ran down from his neck to his spine. The sidewalk felt unbreakable: gray, pitted slabs laid side by side, stretching off everywhere he could see. How could there be any earth beneath those concrete droppings that some gigantic, filthy flying creature had deposited? He could stamp against the hardness, try to sink into the ground, but the shocks would merely reverberate up through his body, jangle and shake his heart until it scattered in fragments, pieces sticking through the flesh from within.

He crossed the street toward a parking lot, and in the middle waited, not looking at traffic, hopeful for a moment that a car would hit him, flip him gracefully into the air and blot out his consciousness. But then, from habit alone, he kept on until he reached the safety of the curb. Once there, he did not know where to go. *I must eat*, he thought. *I must eat or I will die*. But the sharp pangs had dissipated. Only his brain told him that he must have food.

He glanced up to the sun, a drab, mildewed September sun that created a strange warmth. After a few moments, he lowered his head, eased the neck; he did not know what to do with the sun.

Taking the butcher knife from his pocket, he moved toward the fence around the parking lot, where some weeds were growing in a corner. But he saw the attendant squinting at him when he leaned over to drop the knife. A black, black Negro. He seemed about to shout if Cole let it drop, and he put it back inside his coat and turned up the next street.

A few blocks away, people were beginning to shop, the early bargain-hunters. Stopping outside a bakery, he watched the crisp salesgirls in their frilly, polkadotted dresses stuff hearth bread and yellow-iced donuts, the day's specials, into bags for the customers. How beautiful the stacks of baked goods looked, sugary, plump, cellophaned—his mouth watered—but he did not go inside. He knew that if he did, he would buy a roll with a spider inside it; it would be lying there in the raspberry jam and stick to the flesh of his mouth. When one of the salesgirls saw him and smiled, he moved away.

At Kennedy Square—various levels of somber monuments—he sat down on one of the benches, an ugly brownish material, functional public. *It was made to withstand the onslaughts of people like me*, he realized. *Smudged people who soil everything they touch.* A beer can and a smashed whiskey bottle lay at the bottom of the fountain's pool. Shortly, a withered man about sixty in baggy pants sat down on a bench opposite him, eyeing him. *Only thirty years to that. I'll be sitting here in thirty years watching for somebody. You sad old creep, what can I give you? What do you want? I ought to talk to you, make you less lonely for an hour. But I will not. No, I will not.* The old man was trying to dislodge a particle of food from a back tooth.

When Cole rose, the man's gaze alighted on him again, and this time Cole smiled. He walked to the back of the square, up some steps, and then down to the lavatory. Although one of the fluorescent lights was burned out, darkening the place, Cole could tell that no one else was present. As he expected, the old man followed him, and Cole smiled at him again when he entered the room. Cole opened one of the booths and sat down on the toilet, leaving the door ajar; he could see the legs of the old man as he stood at the urinal opposite. He was turning back to look, and Cole pulled open the door with his bandaged hand and felt a delicate sting in the cuts. The man's eyes were wide with hope, although he gave no other sign. "Come in," Cole said. But the old man shook his head. "Come inside for sex." The man looked around to the entrance, then half-turned so that his erection showed. "Come on, what do people care what goes on inside here? If men can crap, they can at least do this." Still the old man would not move. So Cole got up and stepped up to him, taking his arm and drawing him to the stall. "I'll be gentle with you, don't worry," he said.

He locked them in. Immediately the man went on his knees and began to fumble at Cole's zipper. "No, not that," he told him, clamping his hand down on the other's. "This is for you. Stand up." As the man slowly got up, Cole grasped the belt and unfastened it; the trousers fell to the tiled floor. The man wore no undershorts. "Face the toilet," Cole whispered. Very hesitantly, frightened, the old man obeyed. Then Cole slipped one arm around the man's chest and with his free hand reached for the man's penis; it was thick, uncircumcised; the end looked like a sausage that had burst open. Nevertheless he began to masturbate the man deliberately, making a tunnel with his uninjured hand. After a few seconds the man leaned back against Cole's body. Although he smelled of tobacco and dried sweat, Cole did not flinch. Soon the man started to breathe heavily, a muted whimper emerging from his lips. "Feel good, eh?" Cole asked, and, as he did, he remembered the knife in his pocket. It would be so easy to take it out with one hand and thrust it into the old man's side. He could see the limp body tumbling across the toilet, an arm dangling in the water. He touched his chest where the knife rested, feeling its outline. The old man moaned more loudly and Cole speeded up the rhythm—the sweat began to bead his face. The body next to his writhed, pumped, fell back next to the blade in the coat, and Cole closed his eyes and pressed his arm firmly around the other's chest. "Make it come, fella, make it come!" In another minute, he sobbed and ejaculated; the little drops of semen spilled into the water, except for some that spattered on the seat. After the last spasm, the man cleaned himself and kept looking up at Cole as if he expected to be hit. Then he drew up his pants, unsnapped the lock, and hurried from the lavatory. Sadly, Cole examined the liquid on his fingers. He unwrapped the handkerchief and held the thin, red slashes next to the jelly. "Semen and pain—I could start a universe," he noticed. It took him but a brief while to remove the traces of blood and sperm from himself and the seat. Then he walked over to the basin and ran hot water on his hands, wincing. To his image in the mirror he remarked, amused, "You know what? He didn't even say thank you."

Back up in the square, Cole felt exhilarated, thinking, *I ought to devote my life to good works like that.* He sat down and watched people riding by in their automobiles and busy mothers with children clinging to their hands. *It's good to see all these things; yes, I'll sit here for hours absorbing everything.*

But after twenty minutes his back began to ache; the pedestrians and drivers looked the same, and there were so many of them, hundreds and hundreds of them moving past him. He felt himself sinking in spirit. *What difference would it make if one of these buildings toppled over, even the biggest, the Penobscot? So a thousand or five thousand would die; it would make the evening's news, and the human race would supply the gap in abundance in a week—less than that. Billions and billions of us crawling around, over each other.*

Above his head some jets zoomed by, their roars dumped on the pedestrians like boulders. *Where are they going? Training? A mission? Yes, a mission—they are flying with their cargoes of mercy:*

A copilot spoke into his headset. "Four minutes to target."

"Roger." The pilot raised his hand to the man behind him.

"I hope we're in time."

"We will be—if the stuff works."

"It's got to, that's all."

"Only enough food and space left for a year. After that—" He made a cutting noise.

"I hope the other guys have good aim."

"Just worry about us for a moment. Belle Isle, here we come!"

The plane swerved in the sky and headed for the park; it was Sunday, so many would be outside during the attack; the antifertility spray would catch them unawares. It had to be done by surprise because people were unwilling, despite the pleas of scientists and the government, to submit themselves for treatment individually, even though the population was smothering. Already people fought to get into the parks, the stores, the movie houses. A week before a million cars had jammed the freeways; fistfights and murders for jobs, even for a place in a line, were everyday occurrences. Nobody seemed to mind very much, for one less person meant that much more room and attention for himself. Desperate, the government had decided to use the Air Force to stop the population increase. Even then, the situation would be horrendous until more died. The experts predicted it would be at least fifty years before the number balanced itself into a manageable figure. The squadron selected for the mission was made up of single men, one of the toughest outfits in the service. They were nicknamed the Spartans.

"Bombs away!" the copilot yelled.

The airplane swooped low and the orange smoke spilled across the startled faces of the picnickers. No pain. But there would be no reproduction by these people for twenty years, and by then, some of them would be too old.

"We got 'em, boy! We got 'em!"

The jet sped away into a cloud, and Cole opened his eyes. *Yes, the best squadron in the Air Force, the Flying 69th.* He wondered if passersby could read the humor he felt tickling his lips.

He walked down Griswold toward the river, where the newer buildings of Detroit were located. Along the way, he passed a burlesque house, with faded, curled pictures in the display windows. Open-mouthed, busty women with tape across their bodies in strategic areas gave their siren call to the viewer. Miss Linda S. Natch was the name of one of them. Hedy Heaven was another, a woman who looked fifty even in the old photograph. Cole thought of one himself: *Miss Outrageous Fortune and her slings and arrows. But, no, she wouldn't sell.* He stared at the pictures, trying to form a reaction, but he felt nothing. *Why is this any worse, any more "pathetic" than anything else in life? They're just earning a living, that's all, just living.*

At the river he strolled along the quai. Canada lay a mile away, its smokestacks and dock buildings and storage tanks rudely turned toward him. *Is that the view one is supposed to see? Or is that blocking the view? Is there something marvelous on the other side, something compelling, unforgettable?* He chuckled, when a memory appeared. *True, there is a steambath across the river. Yes, that is something compelling, unforgettable. Yet the land seems so far removed, billions of tiny waves between me and it. How did anyone ever have the energy to build a tunnel under all those tons of water?* He looked to his right, at the Ambassador Bridge. *How many men worked for how long, all that straining labor, to raise that bridge? What kept them moving? It seems incredible.*

He took the knife out of his pocket and dangled it by the tip, letting it slip, until gravity pulled it free, but then he snapped his hand through the air and seized it by the handle before it fell into the river. It seemed somehow that he had performed a miracle, and he looked around to see if anyone had seen it. But he was alone, except for a solitary woman who sat far down the quai staring at the waves. Dark-headed and fat.

Like my mother. A woman sitting quietly, thinking of her dead son in prison. A mother. How did my own mother ever marry my father? He tried to recall—had they met at a dance sponsored by the Knights of Columbus in Toledo? It could have been that. Or a church party. She had come to America when she was fourteen, already a woman really. Because it was time for his father at twenty-six to marry and because her relatives wanted to settle her down, as a woman must, at eighteen, he had come into existence. It was strange, but everything was strange. . . . His mother talking him to sleep, in her heavy English, stories he could hardly comprehend, just her voice lapping over his body. His mother bathing his acne with steaming towels when he was thirteen.

Cole looked away from the woman. With his back to the water, he stared at the huge skyscrapers in the distance. *All those rooms full of people, adding and subtracting, and I used to be among them; I might still be getting ready to go to lunch. I contributed to society like a good little worker. All those maps of Michigan—not even real maps, just preliminary ones, not even my name as an acknowledgment, people tracing their fingers along those lines I drew so carefully, and yet never once aware of me. Well, so what!* he scoffed at his idea. *Who am I to make anyone aware of me? The world is constructed so that most people are never known. Somehow they find their predictable loves, have children, make their few friends—too busy or too distracted to want something else. Even if they want more, they cannot get it. Only the few. Maybe nobody.*

He recognized the Federal Building, where he had worked, among the towers stabbing at the sky, and he headed in that direction. Nothing had changed; it was still massive and bleak, with people hurrying into the post office on the first floor to mail their packages and letters—so busy, so much to do. *Have I been aiming for this ever since I left the court? Do I want to see someone I know, a tiny mechanism in a crevice of my brain directing me here?* Inside, the wall clock read eleven eleven. *What do I hope to find here?*

The directory listed the Public Documents Office as still on the seventh floor. *Three years mean nothing, except to human beings.*

In the elevator he felt taut; the silence of the other occupants seemed sinister. *Why should I go up to the office? Am I going to rush into the boss' office and scream vile words at him, like a cartoon character! They would all come out X's and asterisks and percentage marks. If I walked into the rooms, the faces would*

*look up embarrassed, though maybe someone would smile falsely
and clap me on the back and say, "How you been, Cole? Long
time, no see!" The rest would just nod awkwardly and try to
get away. Annoyed whispers and turned heads—and then I would
have to turn and leave, slip out in disgrace.* The doors of the
elevator split open in front of him like the blades of a torture
device.

The corridor was faintly disagreeable with paint fumes. Down
at one end some painters were rolling a brighter green onto the
walls. The windows had been opened, and Cole went over to one
and leaned out. There was an alley below, with a few cars parked
illegally. Something, a cat or a rat, was rummaging in a refuse
barrel. He wondered how long it would take to reach the cement.

"Ladies and gentlemen!" the circus ringmaster intoned. "The
Great Homo will perform for your delectation and amazement! Watch while the young man tumbles to his death from the
high platform above you. See this once-in-a-lifetime treat right
now. Only twenty-five cents extra. Only twenty-five cents." Cole
could see some disgruntled patrons rising to leave—a quarter was
too much. And what if he did not die when he smashed onto the
alley? Would they want their money back? Of course they could
then come to see the Crippled Man, who sat in his bed with his
spindly legs folded under him, the shards of his bones rattling
with each breath. Cole drew in his head and shoulders.

From the window he could make out the door to his former
office. He walked by without looking at it. At the end he turned
around and walked back. There was a scratch in the frosted
glass that had been there when he had started to work. He put
his eye up as close as he dared. Though he was not certain, he
thought he saw his boss' back. He leaned closer, and the door
flew open. A startled young woman with a thin nose, whom he
did not know, stuck her purse into the air in front of her as if
he might attack her. "Excuse me," he said. The girl hurried
away to the ladies' restroom, glancing back twice. When she
disappeared, he put his eye to the glass again; on the left he could

see a woman's legs. Then, nervous, he walked down to the painters and pretended to watch them work. A short time later, the girl returned from the restroom. She hesitated outside the door, turning her head toward him. *She'll probably call the police.* She took a couple of steps in his direction, then stopped, then a few more. She called from halfway. "Is there somebody you wanted?"

His throat constricted, but he managed, "No, it's all right."

"Are you sure?" She advanced several more steps.

"No, I—I had the wrong office."

The girl considered that momentarily, then turned away.

But he hurried up to her on an impulse. "Does Angie Fionda still work there?"

"Who? Angie? Oh, sure. She's inside. Why don't you come on in?" She beamed at him like an old friend.

"No, I don't want to do that. I just wanted to know. Don't mention that anyone asked."

"Why not? We're not busy today." She reached for the door.

"No, I'd rather not. Thank you, but I have to leave."

"Well, would you want me to tell her a message?"

"Tell her—" He let the words hang.

"Yes?"

"Tell her that the diamond needs polishing."

"The diamond needs polishing? Is that what you said?"

"She'll know." He had no idea what he meant.

"Okay, I'll tell her."

"No, don't! Tell her nothing. Good-bye."

"Say, what's wrong here?" Her pink lips parted in exasperation.

"Please, don't say anything to her." He walked to the elevators and pushed the button as the girl gave a final look, confused, and then entered the office.

When the elevator did not come, he pressed the button furiously, but because of the noon traffic in the building, the lighted number overhead appeared frozen at two. He heard the door down the hall open, and he turned his back, the shoulders hunched. Then a voice, questioning, sweet, struck him from behind. "Cole?" She walked around to face him, and his eyes lifted to Angie's.

She had let her black hair grow long, a spiral at the back, making her seem Oriental, supple, as her harsh-green eyes sought his. "Cole, it is you!" He did not know what to say, and for seconds she stood before him with her arm outstretched. "Are you all right? What's the matter?" She grasped his forearm gently. Still he could not quite make his eyes look at her worried face. "Can't you speak?" He glimpsed the concern lining her forehead. "Say something! Cole!"

"My elevator's arrived." He pointed at the box of passengers staring out at them. Then the box closed and disappeared.

"Your hand is injured, isn't it?"

"It's not painful."

"What happened to it?"

"Mountain climbing."

She considered that. "Why didn't you come into the office? When Madeline said a man was out here, I wondered who in the world it could be. I'm so glad to see you, Cole!"

He looked at her steadily. Where was the sarcasm? But she appeared to be genuine. Her skin was lovely, and she was more of a woman than when he had last seen her—twenty-eight now, a year older than he, and just developing into full maturity as a woman.

"Are you working downtown?" Her eyes did not leave his face.

"No, I was just passing by." He could not keep his fingers off his lips, which itched maddeningly.

"Why did you pass us by? You ought to have come inside."

"Why, do you need a few laughs today?"

She crinkled her eyes, uncertain of his meaning. "Yes, we could have used some."

His head jerked up, the mouth angry. "Oh, you could have? Well, it won't be from me that you get them." He pulled his sleeve free of her grip.

"What's wrong? All I meant was that we could have used your sense of humor." Her lips fell open slightly in wonder.

He glared into her perplexed eyes. Was she telling the truth? He relented. "I should not have bothered you."

"Bother? What bother? I'm delighted to see you." She paused, as if trying to be polite about where he had been, forming a suitable question.

He waited too. Then: "Nice weather we're having."

Angie did not catch the irony, but was relieved that he was talking. "Yes, it's been so pleasant these past few days, not hot at all."

He smiled at her simplicity. Others were always leading her on, and she seldom minded even when she knew they were. "You look fine, Angie."

She put her hand to her cheek in mild embarrassment. "I think I'm getting fat." She brushed her fingers vaguely over her flowered yellow dress. He noticed that she did not say that he was looking well. "Are you living in Detroit again?"

"I'm in Detroit at least."

She smiled politely because she thought he might be making a joke. "Oh, Cole, it's really so good to see you! Have you eaten lunch yet? Why don't you come out with me? It's practically time—just half-day today. I'll go tell the boss I want to leave now. Okay?" She started away. "You won't leave, will you?" She came back.

He bit into his lip. "I'll be here."

And he did wait. In a minute she returned with her purse. "It's all set. He didn't even object."

"Sounds like he's eased up in the past three years."

"Actually he's not so bad. A tyrant, but a person can learn to live with just about anything."

"Who else is working in there still?"

"Lots of new people. We have had so many vacancies filled . . ." She became aware that she had spoken thoughtlessly. "I mean, Betty and Albert are still here. And Maxine Watkins. You know her, don't you?"

"I want you to know I appreciate the way you're treating me," he said just as the elevator opened for them. During the slow ride down, neither spoke because of the others present. Once, she looked up at him and smiled with her mouth closed. He felt like crying at her kindness.

"Is Howard Johnson's all right? Or do you want something fancier?" she suggested in the lobby.

"Whatever you like."

"It's just a few minutes' walk from here. The girls and I go there about every day. But then you—was it here before you left?"

"I don't really know."

As they strolled along—Angie brisk and forthright—he caught a glimmer of them as a pair in various store windows. He thought that they looked good together.

"Watch your step!" he clutched her shoulder before she stepped near the automobile she had not seen.

"Thank you, sir. I owe you my life."

"Be careful, or I'll hold you to it."

"Maybe I ought to sue you instead," she said playfully. "I could have been knocked down and collected two hundred thousand dollars for a few scratches."

"You're an incurable optimist."

"No, I'm a jaywalker!" she called, running happily across the street right after a car; he was left behind on the other side. She waved from the far curb.

As he waited for a clearing, he examined her carefully, critically. A pretty girl, she appeared to be cut out definitively from the background of streets and buildings. He wondered why she was not married. Why had no man found her? She was thoughtful, happy, normal, and, yes, pretty. Why were there some people who did not fit in?

"If you break the law, you pay, my dear," he said sternly when he approached her.

"They have to catch me first!"

"Yes, they have to catch you first," he echoed. But she did not seem to pay attention.

"Up ahead—the Maxim's of Detroit." She laughed at her little joke. Cole did too, and their eyes met again.

They had to wait for a table. "How's Bud Smallwood—do you see him often?"

"Once in a while. I'm going to see him next week. He's getting married, did you know?"

"I heard that."

"Haven't you called him?" When Cole was silent, she began to chatter amiably. "I hope you don't mind coming to this place; it is rather ordinary. But *I* actually like the décor. Look at how thick that rug is!" She pointed.

He smiled at her, thinking how sweet she was.

"You know, some of the girls are always saying that this place is so bourgeois, but I don't mind it. Maybe I'm bourgeois!" she bubbled. "It just seems to me that the decorations in here are better than the things most of the kings in the past would have died to have. We're really lucky to be alive now."

"I would like to believe that." The line moved closer to the velvet chain.

"I've always wanted to get through all twenty-eight of their flavors, but somehow I never do. When I was about sixteen I ate straight through sixteen of them, but I kept relapsing and going back to chocolate almond. I guess I just have no stamina." She checked to see if he was amused. "Actually, these Howard Johnson people are a fraud. More than one time I have asked for certain flavors and been turned down because they were out. If they advertise licorice sherbet, then it's only right that they carry it. Right?"

"Right! The world is immoral enough without that."

"They had one here a month or two ago; it was fabulous— Purple Popcorn, it was named. I ate a whole pint for lunch, can you imagine."

"That one seems interesting—Baseball Nut."

"Oh, that's because the Tigers are almost winning the pennant, or something."

"Is baseball still going on? Yes, I suppose so."

Angie cocked her head, and then chatted on: "I went to a baseball game earlier this summer. I tried and tried to like it, but it seemed so useless. I mean, those grown men shaking sticks at each other and running around because of a little ball. Not that I mind that they do it, but why do people get so excited about it?" She wrinkled her fine, straight nose. "It's beyond me."

When he said, "It keeps them off the streets," she laughed heartily, with more energy than he knew the remark warranted. But something unlocked inside his heart at the sound she made.

The hostess, a silver-rinsed woman with too much make-up, greeted them. "How many?"

"For two," Cole requested, pleased at the way it sounded. She led them to a small table in the rear, only one other table close by.

"Frankly, I'm starved. Are you hungry?" Angie asked, grabbing a menu.

"You might say that." His stomach felt hollow, but there was no sensation.

"The french fries here are delicious!" She held her menu for him to see. "Look, at the grilled cheese—only thirty cents today."

"Must have been overstocked on cheese."

Her eyes flitted up to see if he was moody again. "Try a soda. Or one of those strawberry shortcakes. I dare you."

"Do I dare to be so dangerous?" he asked slyly. "Double-dare you."

"Double-darers go first!" she teased.

"You're leading me astray, Angie."

"Stay away from me, or I'll make you fat. My mother says that I am going to turn into a sloppy old peasant woman if I'm not careful."

He held the food list lower. "How is your mother?"

"A little under the weather of late. Rheumatism, she thinks."

"Your father?"

"Just fine."

He looked back at the menu. He had liked her mother and father the two times he had met them, when he had stopped by their home to pick up Angie.

A waitress came and took their orders—grilled cheese and vanilla sodas for both, with a side order of french fries for Angie. When the woman collected the menus and departed, he felt strange, vulnerable, for there was no more busyness to keep them from talking. "Well, Cole, so you're back?"

He clenched his knuckles before him. "So it seems."

"Are you coming back to work?"

His eyes bored through her, back into her brain, searching for cruelty. She tilted her head, waiting. "No, I'm a free spirit."

"I certainly wish I were; I'm getting tired of my job a bit." She sighed—comically.

"You've worked there for how long?"

"Since college—six years. It's not that I don't like what I'm doing. It's just that—oh, I don't know. I have a month off in December. I think I'll go to Mexico. That might help."

"Why don't you live off your parents' money?" He could tell from their house that her father was rich, probably a millionaire—that huge colonial in Bloomfield Hills.

"Oh, I couldn't do that! I'd be bored stupid. Work gets monotonous, but doing nothing is worse. Besides, Americans don't live off their parents."

"Do you still live at home?"

"No, I moved out over a year ago, though I visit them about every other weekend. I've got this gorgeous apartment with Beverly—did you ever meet her?" He shook his head. "She's at the Dime Building; I met her through Sandy in the office. We get along pretty well; she makes fabulous dishes—you'll have to come over and try some one night."

At the invitation, he felt his chest ache, a misty, sad hurt. "Why are you so nice, Angie? You have nothing to gain."

She blushed delicately. "I'm not being nice. How often do you get to meet old friends again?"

"You aren't ashamed to be seen with me?"

"Ashamed? Don't be crazy!" She put her hand up to her mouth at the word she had selected, but she did not apologize.

"I didn't intend to stand you up at that party."

"I understand." She plunged on over their discomfort. "Say, that reminds me—I'm giving another party next weekend, on Friday. Do you think you can make it to that one?"

"Seriously?"

"Quite seriously—say you'll make it, okay?"

"I'd like to. Can it be that people in the Midwest are becoming as broad-minded as some New Yorkers?" He lowered his eyes at his words.

"Well, everyone certainly ought to be broad-minded. It could happen to anyone."

Cole stopped with his cigarette package in midair. What did she mean? "Anyone?" he asked huskily.

"I don't want to pry; maybe you'd rather not discuss it; that's perfectly understandable, though with the pressures everyone has to live with nowadays, it really is a wonder that more people don't have problems."

The match shook in his throbbing hand, but he completed the lighting of his cigarette. "What exactly did you hear happened to me?"

"That fellow you used to share your apartment—what's his name?"

"Teddy."

"Yes, he said that you had had a nervous collapse." She paused. "It must have been an ordeal."

"You might say that."

"It must have been so sudden; you seemed all right that afternoon when you left work."

"Didn't the boss at the office ever mention my sudden 'absence'?"

"He just said that you were leaving."

"No reason offered?" The smoke felt like sulfur on his tongue.

"He said something sort of mean—that you had brought it on yourself." She frowned, centering her gaze on Cole. "I think it's awful the way some people can be so heartless toward illness even today. I mean, in the twentieth century."

He stared at her as the waitress placed their lunches in front of them. *So she does not know after all.* The blubbery arms weaved back and forth depositing dishes and glasses. *What would she say if I told her the truth? Would she still be as kind?*

"Oh, these french fries are greasy today." She touched the dish. "Well, I'll fix that." She took several napkins from the dispenser and began wrapping them around the potatoes. "Don't mind me, but too much grease bothers me." She blotted the french fries thoroughly, pressing down to let the paper absorb the moisture. "They'll have to kill me some other way, I guess." She looked up brightly.

"Angie, what if I told you that I did bring it on myself, as the boss told you?"

She was about to bite into the sandwich, but stopped. "Cole, don't be cruel to yourself."

"I don't have to be," he answered wryly.

"You have to start over again."

"There's no starting over for some things; they just march on to their conclusions."

"But people can, and do, make their own lives." She stared at him earnestly, and he was touched by her concern for him.

"That's a comforting thought— I wish it were true."

"Of course it's true! If you *don't* believe so, then you *won't* have any control over your life."

"The leper can wish away his sores; the spastic can skip away to Tahiti . . ."

"Oh, eat your sandwich," she said half-angrily, half-mockingly.

He picked up the pieces of bread; the golden color of the toast was beautiful, he saw, beautiful and warm.

"Try it; it's wonderful, really." She talked through a bite of her own.

"Somebody had to burn this—just a little—to make it so beautiful. See, all these tiny burns." He held the sandwich with both palms, and someone at the nearby table glanced at him.

"It's going to get cold," she answered gently.

"Perhaps people have to be burned too, eh? Only the danger is that it will be more than a little." He lowered the sandwich to his plate.

She let her food rest untouched for a moment. "You had a very bad time, didn't you, Cole? I'm so sorry."

He looked into her saddened eyes. He wanted to reach over and touch her face, her hair, and he felt that he might cry, because of her sympathy—and because there was a crumb stuck to her chin, a fleck of bread that she was unaware of.

"How long did you stay there?" she went on.

Should I tell her the truth? She may still sympathize—but then she may draw back, carry on falsely, hoping to get away.

"I've been gone all this time—three years."

"Weren't you treated well?"

"Reasonably, considering that I was locked up." He noticed that the man at the other table looked at him a second time.

"You don't have to say it that way, you know."

"Why not? Calling it something else doesn't change the fact."

"You should have tried to get in touch with me. Couldn't you?"

"Let's say it was . . . inconvenient."

"I might have been able to help you, somehow."

"Like the man who had fallen among thieves?"

She smiled. "Perhaps. I could have at least sent you some balm."

"To bind up my wounds . . ." He tipped his cut hand toward her.

"You ought to see to that, Cole; it might get infected."

He drew the fist back. "Aren't you embarrassed to be seen with the 'unstable'?"

"I know you—you're as stable a man as anyone else I know."

"Maybe I was born in a stable, huh?" he said, aware of the bitterness of the joke.

"It takes a while to settle back into old habits."

"Aren't you afraid—just a little—of somebody who's mal-adjusted? Might I not attack you with a knife?" He thought of the blade resting against his chest.

"You are a bit different," she said cautiously. "But that just makes you you, that's all."

His face relaxed. He wanted so much to touch her cheek, stroke it. "You have another side to you, don't you? A temper, great seething hatreds buried someplace?"

"I may have." She moved her head coyly.

"Doesn't everyone have the demonic in him?"

"I'm afraid I'm about as demonic as a pansy."

He sputtered involuntarily because she did not realize what the word meant.

"What's so funny? Is that funny?" She tried to catch the full joke.

"I'm not laughing at you, believe me, certainly not at you." He sucked in his breath abruptly.

"Does your hand hurt you? Let me see it."

"As they say in the movies, 'It's just a scratch, m'am.'"

"Let me see." She held out her slender fingers.

Would you be as sympathetic to internal cuts? Or does it take something as visible, as ordinary as these? He rested the elbow on the table, holding up the bandaged fist.

"How did you get those?"

"Which ones?"

She answered softly, "Any ones you want to talk about, Cole."

"Would you want your sister to marry a necrophiliac?"

She waited for a long moment, and then replied: "I don't care who my sister marries."

"You can help me, can't you?" He seemed almost to be plead-ing.

"I can, if you want me to, Cole. I can try."

He raised his eyes, then dropped them. "Your grilled cheese is getting cold."

"You take a bite first; then I will. I eat too fast anyhow." When he did not immediately respond, she coaxed again. "Come on, eat 'em up. You're too thin."

"Will you beat me to death if I refuse?"

"I'll cram it down your throat, buster," she taunted, pushing the plate closer to him; then she giggled melodically at her own game.

"Feed it to me," he said, dropping the smile.

Their eyes caught, held, and she moved hers slowly off to the side.

"Please," he asked almost inaudibly. "Just one bite."

She stirred, uncomfortable. "But why?"

"For me. Let's say that I'm starving."

"But people are likely to think . . ."

"Never mind them. Please do it for me."

"Oh, you aren't ser—"

"Please—just one bite."

She looked at him to detect the humor, but she could not find any. He pushed the sandwich toward her. She put out her hand, then halted, and her eyes came up to his black ones again. She hesitated, then broke the end off, split that in two. As she carefully lifted the piece, he bent forward, the cigarette smoke curling between them. The man at the other table was staring openly at them now, had tapped his companion on the wrist. Yet Cole opened his mouth anyway, conscious of the jagged edges his teeth made. Angie placed the piece of food on his tongue with care, not smiling. Her hand fell away faintly, as if melting, into her lap.

He chewed and swallowed—he had forgotten how exquisite the sensation of taste could be. "Thank you, priestess."

"Of course."

"You saved a man from dying." He found her eyes again, and this time she did not look away.

"Is it so easy to do? I thought it would take more effort than that."

"You taught me the way. See!" He picked up the rest of the sandwich and bit into it. "It doesn't seem to be a nasty function now. In fact, I want another one. Maybe two more." He sipped from the soda, and she raised her lips. "Can I see you tonight—right now—the rest of the day?"

She protested, weakly, laughing, "But I've got a dental appointment this afternoon."

"Don't go; he'll just inflict pain."

"Oh, I have to, Cole. I've been having occasional twinges and it's so difficult to make an appointment."

"We can run through a woods someplace. Isn't that what's done? It isn't every day that people have someone they can . . . especially over a grilled cheese sandwich." They both laughed, full-throated.

"Perhaps tomorrow evening, if you'd like," Angie said.

"Wonderful! Although it's too long to wait."

"It will seem all that much better then," she teased.

He became serious once more. "You do . . . care about me —don't you? I'm not making this up?"

She held her head down, then looked up matter-of-factly. "No," she replied, "you're not making it up."

His eyes brimmed, impressing her fresh skin, the warmth of her green eyes into his brain. "We should have admitted our feelings long ago. I love you, Angie. I do, I promise."

"Don't say too much," she whispered, pleased, so that the eavesdroppers could not hear.

"Here, let me begin with this," he said, reaching out for the speck on her chin.

She drew back momentarily, startled. "What is it?"

"Only a little piece of something. Here." He pressed his finger against her skin. "There, it's gone." He smiled.

"Are you sure it's gone?" She was embarrassed.

"Positive."

"What was it?"

"It's gone."

Angie felt at the place he had pressed, and then they both began to eat in silence, and Cole felt as if his hunger would never be satisfied.

7

After he left Angie, an hour later, at the door of the David Stott Building, he wanted to leap, grab a pole with a no-parking sign, and glide through the air. He contented himself with sipping at the vitality he sensed within himself. What a marvelous girl —a woman! The three years of absence had only defined what he had felt for her all along. *Church bells should be ringing,* he thought, pleased with his own silliness. And how was he to pass the day until tomorrow at seven o'clock, when she was to come to his apartment in her car? He had not liked that, but she was so sensible—why should he take a taxi all the way to her apartment? They would talk, go for a drive. All of it was so incredibly, beautifully simple. No wonder the idea never wore out, despite the endless songs, the poems throughout the centuries.

He fleetingly thought of going to the downtown library, but he did not want to read—not today. He would make too much noise just sitting in that chilly, vaulted room; some prim, middle-aged man would wiggle an epicene forefinger at him in warning. No, not libraries! He wanted to expand; his legs demanded movement. *I was in a tomb and I have come to life.* But where should he go? For an instant the steambath in Canada slipped into his mind, but he erased the notion. *And there is one right downtown, I think. No, I don't need that anymore. It was a substitution, a habit, a bad habit.* Then a gay bar crossed his mind. But he did not want to drink—and certainly not to meet a man. *I'll have to begin thinking like a married man, proper, thrifty thoughts about car payments and cribs.* He smiled at two little girls their mother was pushing in a twin-stroller. He would have two of his own and guide them around a park near their house, and love them, love them, oh, yes, he would love them! *I'm no longer free, but I don't want to be free. That's what's so amazing. I was wrong believing that I would resent the trap; it was simply sour grapes. Because I couldn't have it, I said it was a trap. And even if it is a trap, I want it; it is a fine, perfect, beautiful trap!* He stopped and watched the babies until they were too tiny to be seen any longer.

Walking along, he saw a movie theater across Grand Circus Park. A huge cardboard advertisement stood on top of the marquee—with two figures, one a white woman, the other a black man, embracing. Cole was not quite sure, but he thought the title read: THE WOMAN STEALER. But he did not want to see a picture either, especially not in the middle of the day; he thought that only useless, lonely persons went then.

But of course—the zoo! It's still open at this time of the year, and I haven't been there for nine or ten years. I can take a bus right up Woodward to Ten Mile Road; I ought to begin to save some of my money.

It took him an hour to get there. The bus was crowded, but he was impressed by the politeness. No one shoved. Rather, people stepped out of each other's way; a man offered his seat to a woman with packages. Cole watched the jiggling bodies sway with the bus, which stopped every two blocks to let passengers off. *They endure the staleness and the rattles because they are going home to their families. That lady with the bony jaw is loved by somebody; all her packages are full of groceries that she wants to prepare for their dinner. If they did not have that, they might as well stop living.*

Later the bus passed a few blocks from his own apartment, and he could see how commonplace the neighborhood was, seedy. But eventually the street got broader as they left the run-down sections. Woodward became a wide boulevard with a park running alongside it. Expensive, tailored houses appeared. *We'll have*

*one of those; I'll mow the lawn, and complain about it and get
excited about a sale on grass seed; we'll spend long hours talking
over the kitchen table, making new friends, growing old gradually; we'll laugh at the first gray hair one of us finds, and the
children will ride around on my shoulder; we'll have arguments
full of love, then make up, and continue on, just living, wondering where all the time disappears to.* He pressed his cheek
against the coldness of the window glass, and let the rippling
images move before him.

He had dozed, from his tiredness, until he saw the tower that
jarred him awake, the tower with ZOOLOGICAL GARDEN written
on it in gigantic white letters.

The zoo was free. That fact made him convinced that the day
was turning perfect. Something in the world was actually free!
Many people were visiting; the parking lot was full. He fell in behind a group of six children and a man as they passed through the
gates.

The grass was trimmed neatly; clusters of flowers in exor-
bitant colors stood straight in their plots, a sharp break, made of
stones, keeping them in their black earth, apart from the grass.
A winding path led toward the various animals, and he wanted
to see them all. *Like Adam in his Garden. Yes, all!* He hastened
his step to keep up with the six children who were scurrying
despite the pleas of the man with them.

LION HOUSE—the sign read. *I wonder if it was ever called the
Cat House. Public taste must be served,* he smiled. *Even if all
the cats in there are not really lions.* He was struck by the stench,
salty, perhaps the scent of raw meat mingled with it. A zoo
worker was hosing down one of the cages; he kept flipping his
long hair out of his eyes with a weariness that indicated he had
done the cleaning task too many times. Cole walked to look at
two lions lolling in a cage at the far end. All the other cages were
empty, and he imagined that more cats might be outside. The
lioness lay back in the corner, gnawing at a stick of wood. Every
once in a while she stopped and looked to see if the lion was
interested. He lay facing her, blinking in indifference. The lioness

picked up the stick in her mouth and then dropped it; it bounced a few inches away and she leaped up and growled over it. The lion yawned, and she chewed on it again, waiting for the lion to try for the stick. But he dropped his head onto his paws and closed his big eyes. After a few seconds, the lioness walked behind him and snarled, but he did not respond. "He's not having any," Cole told her. She then walked over to the stick and bit at it furiously. "Maybe they put too much saltpeter in his food," Cole joked with her. He remembered reading that animals in captivity do not reproduce very much, and the idea lingered for a second that it might be because it is too easy. *The spice is all taken out of it. Or is it something else? Not much desire to continue life in such a state? Oh, well, some scientist is working on an explanation now, complete with decimal points.*

When others came into the lion house, Cole went outside, where the other lions were lounging in bushes, on rock ledges, barely noticing the children calling to them. Some of the manes were scruffy, and the brown bodies sagged underneath. *The good life, eh, boys?* he said, nodding his head as if they could hear him. He wished that he owned a camera to shoot the big one closest to him. Cole rested his arms between the spikes of the fence, glad of the uninterrupted view. The empty moat that separated the animals' area seemed so narrow. *So lions don't leap very far.* As he watched, a feeling of joy filled him, a cool freshness creeping into his brain. It was so fine to be there, to see the lazy cats, to have the iron of the fence supporting his weight, with the people wandering by, taking pictures, munching on ice cream cones. *It's the way it should be. Yes, it's the way it should be.*

One of the shaggy males lumbered down from a jutting rock; for a minute he stretched full length, rippling the skin. "Here, kitty; here, kitty," a child about seven was coaxing. But the lion merely looked away. An ear twitched at an insect, and after a moment of hesitation, it walked up to the big lion closest to the moat. It put a paw on the other's rib and pushed until the other opened its mouth lazily, a half-hearted bite, but the shaggy one persisted, trying to get the other one to move somehow. Even-

tually, the one on the ground fell over on its side, and the first one
nuzzled its nose in the stomach fur. He succeeded in getting the
lion to stick all fours into the air, making the children beside Cole
giggle with delight. "Look, Mama; they're playing!" a tiny
voice called out, and Cole grinned at the child. When he looked
again, the shaggy lion had moved his muzzle farther down the
other's body, and was smelling the genitals. The one on the
ground waved its legs lethargically as the other rooted in the
groin. "Look like a couple of queers," a man's voice said, coming
over Cole's shoulder. *Why are they doing that?* he said to himself, his joy turning to anger. *Why that!* He found himself cursing at the lions, the words rebounding again and again in his mind.
When the lions continued, Cole yanked his hands free from the
iron fence and cut his way through the crowd behind him.

His cut fingers were aching, and he wondered if they were infected. Maybe the man in the lavatory was syphilitic and somehow the germs had infiltrated the bloodstream, cunning, crooked
little monsters that went about their tasks. He squeezed his fist
tightly, to stop them, to crush them. What were such germs for?
What god created them? One jealous of sexual pleasure, it had to
be, some spiteful, spurned, insane goddess in a frenzy of revulsion.

He wanted to get rid of the knife, still in his coat pocket, and
looked for a waste barrel to throw it into, but the one nearby was
overflowing already. However, he went up to it although too
many visitors were passing. When he turned back toward the
lion house, his eyes flickered across the face of a man who was
turned in his direction. He thought that the other was staring at
him; yet the man shifted his gaze. He was a light-skinned black,
his hair growing in a subdued Afro style, no paste holding it
down; he wore a black raincoat and high shoes that were almost
boots. Subtly he swept his eyes back across Cole's, as if interested
in the swans swimming in a small pond behind him. Cole became
conscious of his own breathing, and followed the path to the reptile house.

The architect had designed the building so that echoes clam-
bered up the walls to the uneven ceiling, hiding in crevices and

then streaking down in double force. At that moment all the sounds were human ones; the snakes lay in their glass prisons. A dead mouse lay in a pan beside a blue racer that seemed to be asleep. Something slithered from under a tree stump in the next cage, and Cole involuntarily watched its movements. It was a python, a small one, oozing through the gravel; it reached another stump and entwined itself around it, slowly, the delicate muscles quivering as it settled into place. Could it kill him? Could it embrace him until he smothered, drowning in all the surrounding air? He saw why people hated snakes; this one had a slash for a mouth; its forked tongue flickered twice before it rested.

As he moved on, he came to a larger cage, with cobras inside. One of them was raised almost to Cole's waist-level, the hood slightly distended. What eyes it had! As if they might be blind. Yet it could easily dart its fangs forward and inject the poison into his body in a fraction of a second, the droplets blistering his veins, while he waited for them to stop the heart. He moved to the left, and the snake moved toward him. He tapped on the glass in front of its head. As he did, he noticed a reflection; someone was standing behind him, watching him. When he looked over his shoulder, there was the Negro who had been outside, leaning against the railing above the crocodiles and tilting his head a few inches. *What does he want from me!* Cole spat. *I've given him no encouragement. Maybe he's a thief? But, no, he would not give himself away like that.* Cole knew what the man wanted, but he still argued with himself. *I've done nothing to lead him on. Nothing!*

A particularly grotesque lizard was chasing a fly around its cage on the opposite side of the building, where Cole retreated. Its skin was a series of multicolored bumps and black-and-green scales. *I suppose its mother told it not to worry about its looks, because beauty is only scale deep.* Cole laughed to himself, trying to forget the Negro. The lizard jumped into the air, but missed the fly, which flew up to the top of the cage. A quick glance told Cole that the other man had not followed him; he remained looking down at the crocodiles. The lizard sat on the sand, the throat pulsing rhythmically. Cole could not stop himself from turning back once more to the Negro, who this time smiled, a wan, careful smile that made Cole's guts constrict, and he whirled around to the cage and hunched his shoulders, recognizing the trickle of desire in his thighs. But he would not let it grow, he swore to himself. If he had to take out the knife and jab it into his own groin, it would not grow. The lizard leaped into the air as the fly buzzed by it and swallowed the insect before it hit the ground again. Then it twisted its head around, the bright eyes gleaming, as if it expected applause. Leaning forward, Cole felt himself become faint, flushed. Some children had entered the reptile house and were screaming in imitation fear.

"Are you sick?" the voice inquired.

"It's nothing," he heard his own voice respond.

"Do you want me to get you something? Some water?"

Cole closed his eyes and refused to raise his head. "It'll go away."

"You don't look good. I'd better call the guard."

"I said I was all right!" His eyes slapped against those of the black. He was attractive, lithe.

"Are you certain? It's no trouble."

"You're too kind!" Cole mocked. "Just a slight indisposition, you might say."

"I thought I'd offer, since so many nowadays seem indifferent to . . ."

"Is that why you did it? Your virtue is to be commended. So many nowadays have ulterior motives for everything they do."

The black man stared at the flushed face. "I didn't mean to interfere; I'm sorry." He backed away a step.

"Why did you have to follow me?" Cole said, lifting his anguished face.

The man blinked. "I didn't know I was."

"You knew! You were lusting after me like a dog in heat."

The Negro started at the accusation. "I did not know it was a crime to look at anybody." There was a hardness in the tone, and his expression became defiant.

"Am I so obvious? Do I look aberrant?" He wiped the sweat from his brow with the bandaged hand.

"Man, I'm not asking you for nothing."

"But what did you see? What did I do? Somehow you realized—I don't wiggle, do I? I can't be that flagrant!"

The Negro twisted his head around, embarrassed, as a man and wife went by. "Pardon me, forget it." He started to go.

"No, wait! I want to know what you saw."

"I tell you, man, I didn't see nothing."

"Why pick *me* out?"

"What makes you keep saying I picked you out? I don't know you."

"I'm engaged—almost. Why do you annoy me? Why don't your kind keep out of parks like this. Sneak off someplace where the sun hides and do your business where we don't have to know about it."

The black man's lips moved with silent words, and he stood upright. "Listen, mister, I made no demands on you. I was just watching the animals, that's all, just the animals. If you saw something else, then that's your business, not mine. But I'm not taking any crap from you." He gulped despite his words.

"I offered you not one ounce of encouragement, I didn't!"

"Nobody forced you into anything. You look at yourself, man."

"I've got a knife in my coat, do you know that!" Cole's voice rose; he could not restrain the pitch, though he restrained it to a whisper. "If you don't leave me alone, I'll stab you to death. Do you understand? I will stick it in your black neck."

As Cole placed his hand under the lapel, the Negro took two quick strides to the door and then began to run, weaving in and out of the walkers on the path, and disappeared. Cole stumbled outside, with his heart jumping underneath his fingers; it seemed trying to break loose. To block his face, he put his wrapped fist up to his eyes as people went by looking over at him. There were whispers, but he could not make out the exact words. He waited, holding his body in check, waited for the calm to return, thinking, *I won, by God; I drove the tempter out of the garden.*

A few minutes later he sat on a bench farther along the path, near some antelope, exhausted, although he also felt lighter. There was no sign of the black man. Cole massaged the bridge of his nose methodically. He suddenly wondered if perhaps he had mistaken the man's attention. Perhaps he was simply interested in Cole's face, nothing sexual, merely a man who happened to catch his eye. The idea made him frown. *Yes, maybe I misread the whole episode.* Cole stood so as to watch the antelope down in their grassy pit. A young one was suckling at its mother's swollen udder, and Cole found himself relaxing. Then across the pit he noticed a group of people coming closer, about twenty of them. A large woman in a print dress was guiding them, it seemed. As they came up to the other side, Cole could tell that most of them were children, but some were adults. Yet, two by two, they were all holding hands. They had rounded heads, not quite properly formed, as if they might be filled with gas, and their bodies were misshapen and their clothes seemed too big. Because some of them swung their locked hands out over the concrete fence, the woman told them all to place their hands along the edge; then she walked up and down to supervise. Two of them giggled as she arranged their hands for them, and their heads seemed to bob, to loll from side to side as if detachable. One of them, who must have been in his thirties, jabbed his finger toward the baby antelope and laughed until he drooled. In a clear voice the leader began to speak to them, pointing at the animals, telling them the names, Cole thought, although he could hear only some of her words. Some of the group began to jump up and down, and the woman reprimanded them. "Yes, explain to them the miracle of birth, lady. Tell them how wonderful it is," he said quietly, looking for a long while at their retarded faces, feeling what might have been tears burning inside his nose. "Oh, God!" he said aloud. "Oh, God!"

He deliberately made his way to another exhibit, vowing that he would not be chased out of the park. *I am in control.* The polar bears were ahead. *Yes, they are what I need.* He quickened his steps to where people were throwing peanuts to the bears, although a large sign forbade feeding the animals. The yellowed bears sat on the uneven stones around their pool like mammoth toys, their fringed arms held out, appealing. Every once in a while one of them would catch a prize in its mouth and the shells would crackle between their teeth, falling to the slabs of shale. Then they would sit and beg for more.

Cole took out his wallet and held a dollar toward the vendor. He could not quite focus on the freckled boy, though he managed to say, "Give me something for the bears." With the bag of peanuts he worked his way among the squealing children. A little boy about eight was attempting to feed one of the polar bears, but his arm was not strong enough; the father had to do it for him. All the people watching the bears and throwing tidbits were smiling, giggling at their bad aim, delighted when one of the creatures selected something they had thrown. Cole cocked his own arm and threw with all his strength, and the nuts sailed over the moat, over the heads of the bears. Two of them craned their necks but did not move after them. He flung some others, but a wind caught them and blew them into the shallow water. He tried again, determined, and this time a bear caught one in his teeth. "He got it, daddy!" the boy near Cole exclaimed. And Cole stared down at the child, flicking sweat from his eyes. He threw again. And again. And again. He was part of the line of busy arms, just like the others. Just like the others, he was certain.

8

He bathed at five thirty, shaved a second time, then fixed himself a meal with the groceries that he had purchased earlier in the day. He took two porkchops out of the bag he had left in the refrigerator and dropped them into a frying pan. Then he thought better of it and added some water so that they would not stick. Next he placed the lemon tarts on a plate and covered them with wax paper before putting them in the refrigerator. Angie would like those. He tried to recall precisely—was it lemon that she had so often asked for? He put the can of coffee near the percolator, and opened a can of carrots. In a minute they too were beginning to cook beside the porkchops. The clock said fourteen after six. Perhaps she was already eating at her apartment, telling her roommate that she had to hurry because she had a date. Maybe she was whistling as she fixed her hair in front of her mirror. He stopped. Did girls whistle when they were happy? He couldn't be sure. *I'll learn, become an expert.*

But what if she does not come? What if she returned to the office somehow and mentioned my name to the boss and Franklin told her about the arrest. He could see her face shatter at the revelation. *And so now she is not getting ready at all, is sitting watching television, drowning me out of her memory with a news program. No, I'm just torturing myself. She's in her car right now, backing out of a parking space, and she looks happy.* He watched her drive toward him. Twice she leaned forward to check her appearance in the rearview mirror. *She wants to look nice for me. And I will make her happy. Such a pretty girl, sweet and considerate.* He remembered a time before the jail sentence when they had driven together into the country on a Sunday afternoon, out to Rochester. At a mill on a brilliantly lit yet cool day, they had bought cider and donuts. She had wanted him to kiss her, he had known, from a certain quietness in her, a delicate lilt in her voice when she spoke to him. But he had not done it, zigzagging the car back and forth on the country road, making them both breathless, altering the other mood quite consciously. *And she has been waiting for me, perhaps, all this time, believing that I've been recuperating and would return.* Cole flipped the porkchops over, dismissing the idea. *I'm probably only flattering myself. Why would she wait for me? Who am I?* But a smile broke out even so. Yes, it was fine to be loved by someone. He thrust his fork into the air above the stove like a fencer. "For my lady, sir!" The fork stopped, extended. *Should I love a woman with such poor taste?* He laughed. *And do I really love her? There's this tightness in my chest—should it be more intense, or is that just Hollywood junk? Anything that bright will burn out in a month.*

"Actually we need not have children. The most intelligent people do not have very many anyway, many have none at all," he said to no one. *And no one denies them the right to make love. If children were the rule, then barren couples would not be allowed to come together. But I imagine her parents will want grandchildren to spoil, and so will my father. And, yes, I want a child too, although I can see that a child will merely take away my time, and Angie's. My brain can see that the baby will only interfere, and still I have this desire for it. I can see myself cuddling it in the hospital, imagining that I performed a miracle, that I did something unique—just me and three billion more! We're all dandelions blowing our seeds in any wind.* However, the thought would not linger in Cole's mind, for the tiny, toothless baby's face intruded.

He speared the porkchops out of the frying pan and switched off the flames under the two burners, then put the carrots, still in the pan, on top of a potholder on the kitchen table. He sliced into the meat as he sat down; it did not look entirely cooked, but he ate it anyway. *Suppose I get trichinosis! Don't worms pop out of your skin, something hideous like that? There are so many ways to suffer in the world. So let me relish the few happy moments!* He swallowed the piece he had cut off. The fresh Band-Aids on his hand crinkled when he flexed them as he drew the steak knife through the meat a second time. *Somebody sliced you too, didn't he?* He thought of the dead mouse lying in the pan in the snake's cage. He stared down at the pieces of dead pig on the plate. *Someone bashed its skull or ripped at its jugular vein in order to put it there. Why does it taste so good*—he felt the juices in his mouth swirl around the bite—*so good and yet it is a dead animal, slaughtered in a smelly factory devoted to murder?* He chewed faster and swallowed, and then cut another fragment. *Is this the way it's supposed to be? Is this natural? Or is this not some despicable distortion of what is right!* He stared at the bone running down the center. *How ordinary it is, and yet how grotesque! Someone has trimmed away portions of the fat and left this neat, symmetrical bit of a creature's flesh. People do this every day, year after year. It must be right, it must be. And if it is not, then you must live with life the way it is. You have to.* Cole took another bite, mixing it with some carrots, and tried to think of something different.

He turned on the radio in the living room before he washed up the dishes, trying to sing along with the vocalist on the record, but he could not match the rhythm. It was an ugly noise actually, a great stretching of a scratchy voice, mumbling something about love, he guessed. It was impossible to tell. Just a throbbing screech that rose and fell. *Maybe like that slaughtered pig. Yes, that is what it must sound like when it watches its blood gushing out on the butcher's apron.* Cole hoped the record would be over soon and a different kind would be played.

Some soap stung his cuts, and when he examined them he thought of the policeman who had caused them. "I wanted to slaughter you, didn't I, Officer Sir? Your face looks like a pig's." *Is that why the slang term is used? The pigs! What is the good pig doing right now? Preparing to go out and round up some other men? Back to Rouge Park to entrap a few cocksuckers? Or perhaps tonight he's raiding a stag movie for a change of pace. The citizens pay to keep their minds and bodies clean. It must be tiresome to be so devoted to wholesomeness.* "*Good Officer Pig! Here is a medal for your thick, white chest—for meritorious service in rounding up and branding social offenders, a man unselfish in his fervor for the Protection of the Moral Order. God save the King!*" Trumpets sounded and Officer Keel let the medal —in the form of a golden porkchop—be pinned on his breast.

In his bedroom Cole changed from his robe into gray slacks and a shirt. It was ten to seven when he was ready. He sat down in the living room, then got up at once to brush a smudge from one of the chairs, then moved the couch a few inches. Nothing seemed good enough. He went to the kitchen and opened the refrigerator, to see if the tarts were chilled; they looked lonesome on the wires that made up the shelves. For a time he stood biting his thumbnail. Suddenly he remembered that the butcher knife was still in his suit pocket. He got it from the closet, returned to the kitchen, and threw it into the garbage pail near the sink. He looked down at it, relieved, then walked over to the door and went out into the hallway, peering down the long flight of darkening steps toward the front door. He hurried down them and looked outside in both directions. It might be better if he waited there, he realized, because it might not be safe for Angie. A dog, part Doberman Pinscher, sauntered past the door, leaning to the side, the way some dogs walk. It appeared to know where it was headed, and did not even acknowledge Cole. "You cocky son of a bitch!" he called after it, but it merely turned into the alley.

He tried to control his nervousness, but he could not; his knuckles kept scraping themselves on the rough bricks of the apartment building. Then, a few minutes later, a big car slowed down in front of him. Angie was in it, waving, and he ran up to it, delighted. "Hi, did you have any trouble finding it?"

"Not really, but it's hard to park." She looked expectantly at him.

"We could go for a drive now," he suggested. "Would you like to?"

"Fine with me. How's your hand?"

"Healing."

"Did you put something on it?"

"Wait, I'll be back in a jiffy." He raced back up the apartment steps and turned out the lights before starting to close the door. For an instant he stood patting his pockets, checking to see if everything was in order. *I have only this one key. Only this one.* Somehow that seemed wrong. *Nothing belongs to me; even this one key is borrowed.*

Angie was still in front when he emerged. "Would you like me to drive?" He leaned in from the passenger side.

"Oh, I might as well. I like to drive."

He nodded, thinking that perhaps she did not trust him completely. He slid into the seat.

"I almost had an accident getting here," Angie said.

"What happened?"

"Some nut swerved coming onto the Lodge Freeway. Another few inches and he would have killed me, probably."

He sat crooked so that he could see her profile. It would be so terrible if she were dead, he thought. A picture of her head crashing through the windshield splattered through his brain. He blinked his eyes to blot it out.

She took a glimpse in his direction. "What's the matter?"

"I was thinking how awful it would be if you died."

Angie smiled back at him, and he became aware of her perfume, the fragrance of lilacs. "It's nice to know that I'd be missed."

"I'm glad that you're not dead."

She expelled breath, saying, "What an odd compliment! Why didn't you say you're glad I'm alive?"

"I'm glad of that too," he answered slyly. "Actually—no, never mind."

"What?"

"Where do you want to go? Not that we have to go anywhere."

"I haven't been bowling in a long time." She had obviously prepared an evening.

"Bowling is for people when they don't have much to say to each other. I want to talk."

"Brrr! So sorry," she teased. Her chin crinkled a bit when she moved it.

"Did I seem gruff? I'll have to get back into the habit of speaking more softly."

"I'm just joking. Where did you go after lunch yesterday?"

"To the zoo."

"Really? I'd love to see the zoo again."

"It wasn't as much fun as it should have been."

"What did you see—monkeys? Say, by the way, which way should I aim this vehicle?"

"Why don't we drive out toward Ann Arbor; it's country, sort of."

"Where all those girl-murders took place?" She looked at him solemnly.

"Don't look at me. Remember, I've been away." They laughed in unison.

"Why do you suppose men would kill like that? Am I going right?"

"This is fine. Just keep on Six Mile for a while, until we come to the freeway. Why would they kill? That's easy—because of hatred."

"I've never hated anybody enough for that. Do you think the murderer knew those girls?"

"He may have. I read that murderers usually kill their friends."

She seemed to ponder that. "It's so awful—those poor girls."

He hesitated for a moment, but then said what he thought. "They must have wanted to die."

"How can you say that?" Angie's voice was severe.

"They would not have gone with a man if they didn't want to."

"It's possible to go with a man without wanting to be killed."

"Didn't they know of the danger, when the car stopped near them? Certainly the ones after the first must have been aware of what they were doing."

"Well, I think they just weren't thinking."

"They were flirting with death, and they got it."

"Cole! You sound like you want them to die."

"On the contrary. I think it's terrible that anybody should get pleasure out of inflicting pain. I'm just saying that those girls must have been conscious of the risk."

"I still say that they were probably tired of walking and just hitchhiked a ride, that simple."

"Nothing is that simple."

They both paused, disturbed by the mild friction between them. Finally Angie returned to the former topic. "What else did you see at the zoo?"

"People."

"Oh? Were they in cages or just walking around?"

"Both." He laughed as if in merriment.

"They must have been funny." The car stopped at a red light. The ball of sunfire was sinking beneath the horizon ahead of them "Isn't that a pretty sight?" She pointed.

"Gorgeous."

"For some reason sunsets make me happy—almost want to cry sometimes."

"Be my guest." He extended his palm in an invitation.

"Not this one. Some other one." She half-glanced at him.

He noticed her white fingers wrapped around the steering wheel, efficient, sturdy fingers that knew how to manipulate the Oldsmobile, all two tons of it. She appeared so strong with her back straight against the seat; her soft, white dress emphasized how strong the body was inside it.

Cole directed her onto the freeway that led toward the downtown area, to the interchange to the west. They were silent until the tension of merging with traffic was over. Then he heard her quiet voice. "Do you really think those girls wanted to die?"

He decided to compromise. "I don't know. I guess maybe they

were just lonely and wanted someone to love them. Only they picked the wrong partner."

"I hitchhiked one time," she said cautiously.

He was very surprised. "You? When was that?"

"Oh, when I was about twenty."

"Way back then?"

She turned and faked a scowl at him. "It was the only time I ever did anything like that." He sensed that she was ashamed.

"And what happened?" He waited, puzzled at this aspect of her.

"Nothing—a nice old man gave me a ride."

"Where was it, around here?"

"In Birmingham—during a summer home from college. He was quite a friendly old man, really."

"Do you still get Christmas cards from him?"

"What is that supposed to mean?"

"I don't know. Nothing."

"I wonder why I did it, though; I never told my folks. I don't think I wanted to die. Yet I could have been killed, couldn't I?"

"You picked your driver with fortune's blessing, the way I picked mine." He reached over and tapped her wrist.

"If I didn't know you better, Mister, I'd say you're handing me a line."

Strangely Cole found himself fighting off a blush; he thought he had forgotten how to do that. He looked away toward the metal railing between the expressway lanes whizzing past, as if they in the car were fleeing something in terror. And yet they were just barely keeping up with the other cars.

"Maybe it would be better if we smashed into that abutment there, right this minute, while we are happy. Reasonably happy. Wouldn't this be the best time to die, before everything sours!"

A slight fear was tugging at her words. "Cole, you don't mean that. Things can get happier still."

"I wonder how many so-called accidents—men running off the road at night—are really suicides?"

She did not like the way he sounded. "Besides, what makes you think I'm all that happy right this minute?"

When he turned to her, they searched each other's eyes, something yielded in the air, and they smiled. He made himself stare straight out the windshield and said in a monotonous chant: "I will not be morbid. I will not be morbid. Twenty-five times on the blackboard—I will not be morbid."

"Most people think about committing suicide, once or twice. All right, all right," she said to a driver who wanted her to move over so that he could pass.

"How does one learn to want to live?"

"By being needed."

"But who's needed—truly needed? What for? To change diapers and type reports. *Anybody* can do what anybody else does."

"You have to want to live for somebody *else*."

"You would think the system would work differently—that it wouldn't have to be so roundabout." He meant it seriously, but felt that it sounded comic when he spoke it aloud.

"Each man must learn that he is needed by somebody. When he sees that, then he sees how valuable he is."

"What if nobody ever needs him—or what if he is without any value?"

She was tender. "People ought not to be so hard on themselves."

He turned. "Often they don't have to be—the world does it for them."

"But people can discover their talents. Everyone can do something—something fine too, not just change diapers." She nodded her head in a mock reprimand.

"What if one learns that he is disgusting and freakish?"

She waited for a moment. "Then he has to look through another's eyes at himself, and he won't be so disappointed."

He was touched. "Angie, you are delightful. I don't find it easy to say some things, but you are . . . you're medicinal." He had retreated from a more sentimental word at the last second.

"Medicinal? Thank you very much!"

He did not believe that she was perturbed, only pretending. "Anybody can say 'marvelous' or 'wonderful.' "

"Clichés can be comforting, at times. If I'm so medicinal, maybe I ought to charge you for a prescription."

"I'll pay, even if it's scribbled and in Latin—I'll get a translator."

"It might be a bitter pill," she teased.

"How many times a day?"

She lifted her eyebrows ever so carefully at the double entendre. "That depends."

"On what? The doctor's orders?"

"The nurse may have something to say about it."

"She's not licensed to practice medicine, is she?"

"She can at least—" She halted.

"What? Tell me!"

Angie seemed embarrassed, but she replied, "At least she knows how to keep the body's circulation going."

"Oh, I bet she does!" he smirked.

"And how to stop it too," she added coyly.

He sat sideways again. "I haven't laughed this hard in a long time, Angie."

"Just practice is all."

"I think all the gears inside are rusty."

"Where were you exactly—I mean, while you were away?"

The question made him clutch his hands in his lap, rubbing them on each other. He tried to create a believable story. "It's called the Haven, do you know it?" She shook her head. "It's a sanatorium out I-75."

"What's it like there—but if you'd rather not discuss it . . ."

"No, I don't mind. It's only right for you to be curious. It's very attractive actually; the trim grass stretches everywhere for acres and acres; it's something like a castle. You are like a mad monarch and all those people are employed to wait on you. Psychiatrists and feeders, brushers, cage-cleaners—all of them." He felt rolls of something coming off his skin where the fingers

rubbed, but he would not look at them. "I'm coming apart."
He held the hands in front of him on the dashboard.

She looked over nervously. "What do you mean?" Her eyes
were wide.

"I mean the skin or dirt comes off when I rub my finger along
my hand."

"Is it hurting you?"

"No, not that. It's just strange that people are so soiled."

She seemed to relax, then her voice dipped ironically. "Of
course you might try washing once in a while."

"It comes back—from inside, I guess."

When he turned, she dared, after giving a smile as a clue, to
say, "Are you positive they *let* you out?"

He sputtered. "Touché, lady!"

"Oh, I'm sorry, Cole; I didn't mean that." She was sincere.

"It was beautiful! I take myself too seriously anyhow."

"I shouldn't have said it. I don't want you to be moody, that's
all."

"You know what the psychiatrist at the Haven told me? That
I'm torn between admiring myself and hating myself. Wasn't he
wise?" Cole was really thinking of the prison psychiatrist, whom
he had had to see after the rape in the laundry room. The doctor,
a graduate student from Wayne State University, had told him
that he probably had an anal fixation and paranoia mixed with
masochism.

"And what did he advise?" he heard her saying.

"To stay out of the laundry room, as a start." Cole laughed at
his joke. "And he likewise suggested that I throw away the vaseline, and next that I refrain from accusing him of persecuting
me. But I told him that society really did hate me; I wasn't making it up."

"I'm afraid I don't follow all that," Angie said quietly, and
he awoke to her presence, startled, because he had forgotten she
was listening.

"Well, he released me; I should shout hallelujah, should I not?"

"Do you have to visit him ever?"

He twisted his neck. "Do you think I ought to?" Her concern made him vaguely annoyed, amused—it was that simple to convince somebody that you were crazy. "Yes, I have to visit him periodically, for a conference." The scene flashed before him: The psychiatrist grinned professionally, as he unzipped his own trousers. "Yes, Mr. Ruffner, these treatments seem to be helping you immensely. About a dozen or so more and you ought to be right back on schedule. All right, you may proceed now."

"Are the sessions expensive, Cole?"

"Not too bad—the knees of my pants get worn, though."

She wrinkled her face in uncertainty.

"I'm just fooling."

"Oh."

The image of the probation officer that he was supposed to see in a week bothered him for several seconds.

"Is he good?"

"Oh, indeed! The worst part is the nasty names he calls me."

"Oh, he wouldn't do that. You're fibbing."

He enjoyed her childish word. "No, it's true."

"What sort of names?"

"Are you calling my bluff?" She nodded, but indecisively. "Names like 'Oddball' and 'Weirdo.' 'Freak' is a common one. And sometimes there's 'Deviate' for variety." He checked to see if she could read behind the words.

"But that can't be right—the psychiatrist?"

"Oh, of course the names are changed to protect the guilty. He uses other terms, but they amount to the same thing. I don't play the social game properly, and hence I must be punished, shamed into wanting what he wants for me."

"Doesn't he want to make you well—fully well?"

"I suppose you can say it that way—only he defines what it means to be well."

"He has nothing to gain by not helping you, does he?"

"He gains a sense of his own sexual sanctity. Besides, I provide him with a job; he needs me as much as I need him. More!"

She looked puzzled. "You don't seem to like him very much."

"Not true. He's a grand person, really. He has these warm blue eyes that sort of *cherish* me when I come in his door."

"How often do you see him?"

"Every so often." The likely face of his probation officer lodged in his mind again.

"Perhaps I shouldn't say something . . ." Angie paused significantly.

"Say what? Go ahead."

"You know I like you, Cole, and I don't want to hurt you the least bit." She waited once more.

"Sounds like it's going to devastate me."

"Oh, let's talk about something else, what do you say?"

"No, tell me. Please."

"All right, I will. Perhaps if you were a little more thoughtful —no, *kinder*—you wouldn't be as unhappy as . . ."

Although he tried to withstand the sensation, he felt hurt; the feeling surprised him because he thought he had surpassed that stage. "Angie, I know I should be, but I can't learn how to do it overnight. Or is that just another excuse on my part?"

"I don't mean that you aren't kind. Merely that you seem a lot less gay than you were before."

He wanted to grab his face and howl, but he restrained the impulse. He subdued his voice. "Was I very gay before?"

"You were jollier. Please don't let me hurt you—but you *are* moodier now."

"Guilty as charged, Your Honor! Yet what can I do to change? I really don't want to be this way, really I don't. What should I do?" He left his emotions bared for the first time in three years.

After a long moment, she answered, "I guess I don't know. We could start by just having a good time, just ordinary fun, something trivial."

"Why don't we get off at one of the next exits and go play miniature golf—do they still have those?"

His enthusiasm spilled out and touched her. "I think so. I think there's one in Dearborn. Shall we go there?"

"Fine, I'm game. No sarcasm, no cynicism."

"It's agreed then."

"Agreed."

After a few minutes, they silently drove off an exit ramp onto Michigan Avenue, two endless rows of tacky furniture shops, refrigerator resales, grocery stores—on and on, no break in the monotonous variety.

"I should have asked you to dinner!" Cole said suddenly. She turned her head. "What's the matter with me? It never crossed my mind. We could have gone to some place fancy. Are you hungry?"

"I ate before I left—but maybe a snack."

"You *do* like lemon, am I right?"

"Yes?"

He felt relieved. At least he had not forgotten that. "We can go back to my apartment for something later." As an afterthought, he added, "If you would like to."

"I'd love to. How nice of you."

"It's nothing much. But I am trying, Angie, I'm trying."

She wanted the moment of confidence to last and so she said, "Remember that picnic we went on with Bud Smallwood and that awful woman several years ago? She tried to help carry the basket of food and dropped her side, and all that poorly wrapped stuff fell on the ground!"

He chuckled with her. "We were all so hungry, and had to settle for potato chips."

"And she—what was her name?—she said it wasn't her fault because Bud made her trip."

Cole's eyes began to water at the remembered scene. "Wasn't funny then. Why is it so funny now?"

"I don't know." Her shoulders were shaking.

"Maybe everything becomes a scream if enough time passes. Probably tragedy is only the short view."

She sensed the humor evaporating from his voice. "Everyone needs a good laugh every day, like an apple."

"That's good. A laugh a day keeps the shrink away."

She gestured. "Look, Cole, there's a place for archery. Want to stop there?"

He looked toward the wide windows with people standing at the shooting lanes. "I've only done it once before."

"Come on, let's try it, it might be fun. No, it *will* be fun!"

"I'm willing."

"Okay then. Agreed to change plans?"

"Agreed."

"What do they call a place like that—an archery gallery? It sounds so clumsy."

"We are going to 'arch.' I do so enjoy 'arching,' don't you?"

"No, we're going bow-and-arrowing," she corrected, mockingly.

"Words do get in the way, sometimes. The bows and arrows of outrageous fortune."

"I hope we can park nearby," she said, maneuvering the automobile through an opening in the median of the street. She drove up to the back of the building and bumped into the retaining curb slightly. "Excuse me; I don't drive all that well." She laughed. She twisted the ignition key and the motor stopped with a few gasps. "I ought to get that fixed." She pointed at the hood.

"It sounds like it has TB."

"Could be choking from the air pollution."

"Wait!" Cole insisted, getting out of the car and going to open the door for her.

"My! Chivalry is not dead after all."

"Merely sleeping, like the princess. Or should I say like the frog, who needs just a little affection to be transformed into the handsome prince." Their eyes grazed as he helped her out of the car, and they both looked down at the ground shyly.

"Thank you, kind sir, for the use of your fingers."

Cole felt the heat of her blood where their hands touched, and he wanted to raise hers to his lips, kiss the wrist. Instead he bowed to her. "I'm at your command."

"Well, then," she went on majestically, "I command you to open the door to my sporting field." She gestured grandly in the direction of the back door.

"Your highness!" he responded, drawing back the scuffed door. "To the field of sport."

At the counter inside, they rented the equipment—elaborate leather arm guards and semigloves to protect them in the game. They were instructed how to wear them, and the long, willowy arrows were placed in their quivers by the attendant, a very short, chubby-faced boy. They had to select their own bows from the racks along the rear of the alleys. For a minute Cole watched the advanced shooters who stood separated at the left side of the building. Their equipment was even more elaborate—thick, custom-made bows that allowed them to shoot their arrows with great power into the targets many yards away. Even some women were among them, drawing back their strings and letting loose with incredible accuracy and speed. Cole's stomach twitched at their skill.

Angie met him at Lane 13, their lane, with a lighter, green woman's bow in her hand. In her white dress she looked like some huntress-goddess he had seen in a book one time. They had to help fasten the arm-guards on each other, their skin stroked and patted indirectly. It took him a long time to fit her glove because of his injured hand. "Are you sure you can use your hand, Cole?"

"It's fine. See!" He moved it, lying about the pain.

When they were ready, he went over to the scoreboard and pushed the button. The target far down the alley started to move toward them, a tall mat of straw advancing to where they waited, connected to the controls, which could be set for ten, twenty, forty, and sixty yards. When the target stopped in front of them, they noticed that the circles in the black paper attached to the straw had several holes in them, one of them almost a bull's-eye. "What distance should we try, Angie?"

"I don't know. What do you think?" She went up to the mat and felt the texture. "It's soft."

"To keep the arrows from bouncing off and flying all over the place."

She jumped up onto the platform and faced Cole, her back against the target. "Shall you shoot an apple off my head?"

"How about a cherry?" he answered before he could stop himself. He felt sure that she did not catch the meaning.

She seemed small with the target stretching above and around her, stiff yellow reeds drooping here and there. She pressed back into it. "Sir Knight, I place my life in thy hands. Aim carefully; shoot with care."

"And what is the prize, my lady? A dukedom?"

"A thousand crowns if I live."

"A true test of mettle. But of course only this trial can free you from the curse of the wicked sorcerer."

"Avoid my heart," Angie replied, pointing to where the arrow should stick next to her chest.

"I want your heart intact, my lady," he said. "And that will be my only prize." She smiled at the compliment.

"Quickly—while the sorcerer sleeps!" She leaned back and closed her eyes.

"I slip the swift shaft into the sturdy, strong string!" He lifted the bow at her and pretended to draw back as far as he could, and Angie's eyes widened in fear. A second later Cole broke the game by lowering the bow. She stepped from the platform, brushing her wrist across her forehead. "For a moment there I thought you were actually going to shoot me." She looked reproachfully at him.

"But the arrow wasn't in the string."

"You frightened me."

"I wouldn't hurt you for all the kingdoms in the world."

He stared at her for a long time; she attempted at first to meet his gaze, but eventually went to the controls and began to flick them. "Let's start at forty yards, okay? That seems safe."

"Ladies first," he said, sitting down.

"But I don't know what to do." She turned to him in his chair, helplessly.

"You hold the string with these two. Like this." He stood beside her and placed her hands in the proper position, feeling the glow of her body near his. "Now, draw back and open your hand quickly, to release the arrow. Keep your left arm perfectly straight or you may get a burn."

"It sounds dangerous."

"Don't panic, and it'll be all right."

"I don't think I'm strong enough." She made a pretense of great strain in pulling back the string, and he sensed that she liked him standing with his arms around hers. However, he felt perspiration leaking down his ribs, and he stepped over to push the button that sent the target rumbling down the lane, then sat back down.

"Don't hit that man over there." He thrust a finger at a solitary Negro three alleys distant, who seemed as unskillful as they were.

"Thanks a lot, Galahad." Angie raised her arms, adjusting the equipment. "Oh, I can't do it!" She frowned and let the bow rest on the floor.

"Sure you can." He helped her raise the bow again, made her draw back, his hand forcing hers to stretch the string.

"It hurts," she cried. His fingers were pinching hers, the tension running in a tiny spasm up their arms.

"Let go!" he told her.

"I can't—you're holding too tightly." He opened his hand and the arrow flew down the alley, skimming the top of the target and clattering over to the far side.

"Let's try again," he commanded, his tone crueler than he realized.

He placed another arrow in her bow and they bent it a second time. The shaft whizzed down to the black paper, but slithered off to one side. The stick of wood lay in an adjoining lane like a twig. "We're doing better, I think," Angie said uncertainly.

"Again!" He knew he was pressing too hard against her hands, and his own hand muscles ached from the effort, but he drew back a third time. "When I count to three, open your hand with mine. Okay?" She nodded while he pushed his body closer to hers, even though he felt he must be soaking her with his perspiration. "One. Two. Three!" Their hands opened simultaneously, and the arrow thudded into the mat, just below the piece of black paper, and they turned in triumph to each other.

"We did it, Cole!" She blew a gust of warm breath across his face in her excitement.

"We're practically experts; Robin Hood's a piker next to us. We can split the arrow that he used to split the first arrow."

"Where did you learn to shoot so well?"

"You're more than kind, Your Majesty. I picked up a little here and a little there." He waved his arm in an ironic cockiness.

"Shoot one by yourself," she said, stepping aside.

He glanced at her, and joked with himself aloud. "I've done that many a time."

"Go ahead then."

He smiled to himself and lifted his own bow. Just as he was ready to shoot, the arrow they had shot together fell out of the straw mat and clattered to the floor. Shaking his head, he looked at the tiny sliver of wood lying inert. How could such a small thing be so powerful? It could kill a man. And how could such a small thing matter so much? He did not turn around to Angie to see what her reaction was—he simply released the arrow and watched it ram into the piece of paper, quivering, defiant.

"Bravo!" Angie's voice said from behind. "That's almost a bull's-eye."

"I'm a very good team, by myself." He saw her face darken, somewhat injured by the remark. "Why don't you shoot?"

After a second encouragement, she came up to the line. "I hope they have insurance. What should I aim at?"

"Think of something you want to kill."

She shook her head thoughtfully. "I don't want to kill anything."

"No? Not some bright bird? Think there's a ferocious bear down there, reared up."

"I think it's terrible to kill things."

"But men love to murder; it's only natural."

"Cole!"

"It's true. Murder is as common as apple pie. It must be good because it's so everyday. That's what normality means—I'm sorry," he said immediately. "Aim at the center of the black paper, a little higher, since the arrow might fall."

"All right, here goes." She stood sideways and pulled, the arms shaking. Finally she let the arrow slip out; it hit the mat near the bottom, but managed to pierce the straw. "I did it!"

"Wonderful! You know what—we're not too bad by ourselves."

"In archery anyways." She said it with a trace of melancholy. "You try now, Cole."

He sited the target that was halfway down the alley. Then he reset the dial and pushed the button. "Let's try it all the way."

"So soon? We're just started."

"Nothing ventured, nothing gained. Right?"

"I suppose."

The target appeared immeasurably farther, and he wondered if he would embarrass himself by not having strength enough to reach it. "Any bets?" he said over his shoulder.

"Not just now," she teased.

As he stared back down the shooting lane, a picture of Keel appeared, his coat buttons glimmering invitingly. Although Cole shut the image out, even shook his head to dismiss it, when he glanced up again, the policeman was still there, wiggling back and forth, flicking his suit coat open, daring Cole to shoot at him. It would be so easy to let the shaft slice through his gut, or perhaps through the throat. Cole turned around toward the girl. "Is something the matter, Cole?"

"It's nothing important. A sort of indigestion."

"Are you sick?"

"No, that's too simple a diagnosis." He wheeled around and shot the arrow without looking carefully; it skidded on the floor, short of the target. He felt himself trembling, chills racing across the back of his neck. He sat down near Angie. "Let's leave this place, all right?"

"What's the matter?" She bent to him, anxious, wrinkles formed about the eyes.

"This is the wrong time and the wrong sport. Oh, Angie, I need something, I don't know what it is . . . it's something I can't explain. Why? . . . Why?"

She was startled at his anguished expression, and reached out to soothe him somehow. "What can I do? Shall I call somebody? A doctor? The attendant?"

"It's not that easy. Yes, if it only were." He could feel his reserve draining away; he feared he might collapse on the seat, sob until a crowd of starers came and formed a circle, amazement on their mouths. It would be like an epileptic seizure, his body writhing and jerking, and the watchers would point and snicker.

"Let's leave," she said, taking control. "Of course!" She even helped him take off the archery equipment, guided him to the counter, where he managed to pay the attendant. They said nothing until they were in the car, and then Angie spoke gently. "Do you want to go home?"

He felt her pity; it filled the inside of the automobile like a saturating mist. *Not that!* He defied her with a glare, saying nothing.

"Cole? Where do you want me to take you?"

"Don't *take* me anywhere." He put his forehead on the dashboard.

"What should I do?"

He put his hands on his cheeks and brought them together over the eyes. "Save me. Save me. Save me." The insides were wet, a trickle moistening the Band-Aids. He was sure that in a moment the sharpness of the salt would burn the lacerations.

"Cole, please don't cry. Please don't!" She moved closer to him, patting his upper arm, her misery for him as intense as his own. "Please, for me."

The tears sweated down his face, and he felt bitterly ashamed;

yet he could not stop himself, could not end the boiling waves that poured out. Angie's eyes were brimming as well, streaks of soft water at the edges. "Let me help you, Cole. Let me."

"No one can help me." He turned aside so that she could not see his face.

"I can try, remember?" She pressed down on his shoulder gently and leaned her head against his back. He turned around and forced his arms to circle her, pulling her body to his. "I want you—I love you." He squeezed her tightly, the confinement of the car making him awkward.

"I want you too," she whispered, surrendering to the embrace.

He kissed her mouth, tasting his own tears mingled with hers; he wanted to crush her into himself. "Save me, Angie!" His hot body seemed like a lump of metal, impermeable; the two of them were objects joined together, but essentially ununited. He kissed her eyelids, aching.

Her arms closed around his body. "Yes, Cole. Yes."

He fumbled at her clothes, but she pushed his hand away gently. "Please, not here."

"Angie." He leaned against her, desperately, aware of himself swollen, his trousers pulled tightly against his body.

"No, at your apartment." She drew back behind the wheel, and Cole moved closer to the door. He nodded.

For a few blocks they drove in silence. Then she asked, "Are you all right?"

"The moment is passing. I'll be fine. The nuns told us to avoid the near occasions of sin: I can see now what they meant."

She did not answer, and drove on.

When they stopped at his building, Angie looked over at Cole, still at the far side of the car, his eyes gleaming in the darkness.

"What should we do?" he wondered, both to her and to himself.

"We can go upstairs, if you like."

"Yes, I would like you to—the lemon tarts, remember?" He tried to grin.

"Is that the surprise?"

"Didn't I tell you?"

She shook her head; she did not mention that he forgot to help her out of the automobile. Rather, she took his arm as they walked up the street. At the door to his apartment she gave an affectionate little squeeze to his forearm. After a struggle through his pockets, he found the key and forced it into the unwilling lock. "Abandon hope, all ye who enter here," he said. He had to search the wall for the light switch, unable to find it, while she stood waiting in the dark. "Excuse me, I don't know my way around here very well yet." He smiled to himself at the remark and wondered if Angie did as well.

"Your apartment is very nice," she said at once when the light came on, as though she had prepared it in advance.

"It keeps the rain off."

They faced each other awkwardly in the middle of the living room, trying to think of words to exchange, but neither could summon anything. Finally, he said, "Please, be my guest. All this luxury is yours." He swept his hand across the drab furnishings, and she sat down on the sofa. "Would you like something to drink? Some food?"

"A glass of pop?"

He rubbed his lips, uncomfortable. "I don't have any pop. How about some milk?"

"Just some water would be fine."

"Would you like the tarts now?"

"Maybe after a while."

Cole stared at her strangely. How had they become so formal? They were talking like persons who scarcely knew each other. He took the opportunity to hide, and went into the kitchen and let the water run. He listened for sounds from the living room —nothing but stillness.

When he returned, she looked up. "Thank you, Cole."

"It's nothing. Any time." He sat down on a chair opposite the couch, watching Angie drink the water carefully, slowly. Now and then their eyes hit and glanced away. Eventually the glass was dry, and she set it on the end table next to her.

What should I say to her? "*Shall we proceed?*" *Can I say I love her again, just pick up and continue?* "Angie," he said aloud, "do you think this is what we ought to do?"

She dropped her chin modestly. "I don't know, really."

He wondered if she believed that they would be married shortly, married at all. "How do you do? My name is Cole Ruffner."

She laughed. "I'm Angela Fionda."

He lowered his hands, which were formed against his lips as if for prayer. "Nice to know you."

"Nice to know you."

Suddenly he made himself walk over to her and take her wrist, making her stand up. "I don't want to hurt you, Angie."

"I won't be hurt."

"Come with me." He led her into the bedroom, where he turned on the lamp on the night table, and shadows swarmed over the walls; then he turned back to her, cold. She waited, her arms crossed before her, in the middle of the room. He placed his arms, full length, on her shoulders and stared into her green eyes. "Two virgins and no place to go."

She touched his hands with her palms. "I don't know if I ought to tell you . . . Cole, I've been with two other men." She blushed red at her confession. "I only tell you because it might make . . ." She broke free and moved away.

"Oh, Angie!" He followed her and slid his fingers down her cheek from behind. Then he kissed the nape of her neck, the way he had seen some lover in a motion picture do it. He began to unbutton her dress, reaching around her waist. The buttons fought to stay fastened, slipping out of his fingertips, the white cloth resisting. But at last they were undone to the waist, and he cupped his hand around one of her breasts. Like a melon, he noticed, firm and full. The fingers clung there like a growth until he closed his eyes and tried to imagine that they were somewhere else, in a gorgeous room, on an island. Still no passion raced through him. In fact, he felt he was watching them both from a height, each move transcribed into a record book. He pulled her back against himself, and she sighed, relaxed, as he kissed her shoulder, the soft skin, and she shuddered involuntarily. "Erogenous zone number two," he said so quietly that only he could hear.

She moved from him to the edge of the bed and began to undress, first her shoes. He watched her, like a scientist—the white dress falling to the small rug, then the half-slip delicately laid on the nightstand. She was full in the waist, though not fat; the white underpants clung to her buttocks, and the idea that her sweat made them stick flashed through his brain. She reached back to loosen the brassiere hooks, and, as she did, she looked at Cole, seeming to tell him to come closer to help.

His fingers chilled her back, and she winced, retreated slightly, then leaned around to kiss him. When the bra dropped between them, he could see the streaks from the elastic imbedded into her flesh, red indentations leading to the breasts, which were small hills with protrusions on them, brown nipples sticking out. Cole stepped back from her body, and she reached for his chest, running her finger inside his shirt, across the hairs. He slowly undid his shirt as she watched, dropped it on the floor beside him. On his skin were a few pimples. He tore at them, blotching the skin further. "Don't!" she told him.

"They're ugly."

"No, they aren't."

"They're ugly, like a rash, little bumps of disease."

"Hush!" She slapped her hand against his lips, but too hard, making his teeth sting. "Did I hurt you?"

"Nothing. A knight always receives a blow." They stood unmoving. Then she grasped his belt and yanked until he had to follow her to the bed. She lay down on the pillow, above the covers, and rested her free hand on her stomach, the other still entwined in his belt. "Lie down with me," she whispered.

"Two consenting adults." He smiled and stared down at Angie's body. How white it was, like the Christ's on the crucifix. Turning his back, he loosened his buckle and slipped out of his trousers, afraid to turn to her, ashamed that he was not aroused. She waited for him to turn back and then pulled at her pants, arching her back to get them off; it was a voluptuous movement, and at the same time clumsy, he thought. Her pubic hair was black, sparse. She lifted her arms in an invitation, but he could not move, could merely look down at the figure. "Cole?" He bent over to remove his shoes. When he stood above her again, he looked directly at the space between her legs, the slit. Really a wound, he saw. A great wound that needed to be healed. "Cole?" Angie said again. "Come to me." He did not answer. "What's wrong?"

"Nothing. Everything."

"Don't you want to?"

"Maybe wanting is not enough."

She put her hand on his thigh and stroked softly.

"Yes, turn the machine on," he said too loudly, as he felt himself grow slightly excited. Then he pulled his shorts off and stood naked before the girl. "See, I'm fine," he said, his face aflame. "Perhaps you thought it wasn't there, eh? It is. All the parts are here." The phallus rose abruptly. "All I needed was the right current. A.C. or D.C.—I forget which," he went on, his voice breaking. He lay down on top of her immediately and kissed her neck, the declivity beneath it. *Now I put it inside and pump up and down, like a steam engine, a good piston. Chug, chug, chug.* He tried to enter her, but the organ grew limper as he did. *Come on, Cole, boy, you know how to do it. Tab A goes into Slot A-prime. It takes no previous training, no skill. Mother Nature, the Old Procuress, makes it all so simple. Up, down—a merry go-round! Ride her, boy! Stick and jab, Sir Knight! A joust, a joust! My kingdom for a joust!* He felt his flesh weaken and Angie stir beneath his weight; he reached down and grabbed his penis, massaging it. *Keep her up, my lad! Don't disappoint the lady in distress.* He began to enter the vagina, and Angie's heart stammered furiously against his chest. *Come on, Cole,* he went on tormenting himself. *You've got work to do—a duty. And immortality awaits you, just beyond these doors. All it takes is a little work, a little effort, that's all.* Again he became flaccid. He kept rising up above their figures on the bed, scrutinizing their movements, analyzing, kept seeing their attempts at a rocking motion. *How ridiculous we are! This bumping of our sweaty, grotesque limbs on each other! All these hairs all over us. Hair down there between us, for lice to nurse in. This is not me doing this. It is not me; it's some animal performing a function, something it cannot avoid. It's not me! No, no, not me!*

He fell to one side, his stomach heaving, and saw Angie's face watching him, bright, pained eyes that held his own like pincers. "What's the matter, Cole? Have I done something wrong?"

"Forgive me," he choked.

"What happened?"

"Forgive me."

She touched his cheek. "There's nothing to forgive. The time was all wrong, that's all."

"It's more than that—or less." He wanted to weep, or to shout, but he simply lay on the bed panting.

Angie ran her index finger down his hip. "If at first you don't succeed, they say . . ." She smiled at him.

"Angie, it's no good; I can't."

"Let me guide you."

He shook his head, but let her direct his body over hers once more. She rubbed his sex organ across the opening as he held himself on his arms. He thrust twice, the phallus shrunken in her hand. He looked down at her face, caught between a smile and the exertion. *It's like being lowered into a grave!* She glanced up at his eyes examining her and began to manipulate her hand faster. His arms started to ache, and she changed to her other hand. When she did, he gritted his teeth. "It's useless, Angie."

"Wait!"

"It's obscene!" He flung himself to the side of her, shaking. "It's no good; I won't fool myself any longer."

"You're tired. I ought to have helped you more." She moved closer to him, touching his spine.

"There are some things in being alive that wishes won't change."

"Oh, what's a little impotence, between friends!"

He almost laughed with her, but he could not. Into the covers he said, "Between lovers it's deadly."

"The first time is usually not the best. I know!"

He put his head on the pillow and glanced at the ceiling, which he had watched alone for so many hours, saddened by Angie's kindness.

"Maybe if we wait a while . . ." She rested her palm on his neck.

"A hundred years?"

"I'm not in a hurry."

"We'll get bed sores."

"Oh, something will happen before then." She scooted her hand down his chest.

He looked the other way. "No, it won't."

"Maybe with the lights out . . ."

"Maybe with the lights out, maybe with dirty pictures on the ceiling, mirrors, maybe with a leering dwarf, maybe with fantasies of other people . . ."

"Don't be so hard on yourself; it's happened to lots of men before. Lots of them."

He knew that he was going to tell her the truth, but the words stuck inside his mouth like burrs. "Angie?"

"Yes?"

"I'm going to tell you something. Please don't be hurt. It has nothing to do with you, not really, but I can't let you think that . . ." He waited.

"So ominous."

He would not let her joke him out of what he had to say. "I love you. It happens to be with considerable ineptitude, but I do love you. In my fashion."

"Cole, you are, without a doubt, the world's worst complimenter!"

He went on, the words falling out of his mouth like rocks. "Angie, the trouble is . . . is I'm a homosexual." She seemed to stop breathing. "I'm not saying it as a 'confession.' Why should it have to be that? But I doubt that we can ever work together, not this way."

She lay very still for a long moment before she said anything. "I don't think you are."

"I was trying not to be, but I have to face the facts." He leaned on his elbow to watch her. "I have been for a long time."

"But that can be cured nowadays." He felt her body seem to inch away.

He drew an imaginary line between them. "See how we cured it."

"Were you just using me?" The voice was falsely light.

"I hope not. God, not in the usual way, I hope not." The idea disturbed him.

Her voice was tiny, faraway. "We could have been so happy, Cole. Couldn't we?"

He held his forehead. "I shouldn't have wanted what I'm not supposed to have. I'm sorry I misled you."

"You know, Cole, I sort of suspected."

He was surprised at her smug tone. "Why? Who told you?"

"Nobody told me; I'm not as naïve as I may lead you to think. You dropped clues."

"Then why did you agree to . . . this?"

"I don't know exactly. Maybe I thought I could . . ."

"I see. Charity. You imagined that you could redeem the black sheep. The love of a good woman and all that. Tea and sympathy."

"Couldn't you still change, if you want to?"

In answer he let his breath expel in a long gust.

She let his sigh die into the air before she went on. "Wouldn't you like to be married?"

"I already was married."

"What?" She rose on both arms. "I don't understand."

"To Teddy. We were lovers for a year and a half." She wrinkled her nose. "I'm sorry if it offends your wholesome instincts. Not everybody should be married, not everybody must increase and multiply—and I'm one of them."

She leaned over, her sorrow filling her voice. "People get so much happiness out of being in love, being married."

"I know." He tried to resist the anger he felt overwhelming him. "But I don't fit into the pattern. Square pegs and round holes, remember? Why should we all have to fit either? Why?"

"It's so sad, so sad," she answered.

"It's not sad—it's not!" He felt ridiculous denying her feelings.

She sat on the edge of the bed, where he could see her spinal column, the chain of bones, through the luminous skin. "I'm very sorry for you, Cole. Really I am."

"Please, not that! Stop pitying me! Accept me—that's all I ask. I can—why must I feel guilty?"

She rose and when she glanced back, slipping into her underclothes, he noticed her wet lashes. She began to slide her dress over her head. "You won't have anybody, will you?" she said, avoiding his stare.

"Stop it, do you hear me?" He wanted to slap her, to make the tears disappear. "That isn't all there is to life. Don't be such a woman—stop making me hate myself for not being what you want. You must! You'd use me too!"

Her eyes dwelt on his for a lingering, quiet moment, and he felt that a weight was being pressed onto his skull. "I loved you, Cole—against my will, and yet I loved you."

"Don't leave, this way." His throat was parched.

"What should we do?" She gestured at him with a useless hand that scored him like a lash.

He sank his throbbing head into the bedcovers. "You can't leave—and you can't stay! How silly I am! I don't know what to say." He tried to cry, but the sobs formed into icy, sputtered laughs. "You ought to hate me—that would be better. Much better."

"But I don't hate you, Cole. Never that." She was trying to hide her glistening eyes from him, averting her body.

"Oh, Angie—my God!"

The tears falling out in full force, she tried to joke, "Too bad we couldn't have had the lemon tarts." He started to rise, but she shook her head violently. "No, Cole!"

"I'll go downstairs with you."

"No!"

"But the knight is responsible for his lady, remember?"

She let her gaze deliberately settle into his. "The lady forgives the knight his vow," she replied flatly.

He said nothing more, just listened to her retreating steps as she left the room, waited for the lock that snapped back into place, like a mechanism inside him, as she quietly closed the door to the outside, as though she were afraid she might break something.

9

~~~~~~~~~~

After dreaming angrily, in pieces, through the night, Cole awoke covered with sweat. The sheets were musky and wrinkled, but he was too tired to change them, unable to make the effort to go to a store to select them, although he had no fresh ones. Little hooks seemed to pull at the edges of his eyes, and he was afraid to look into a mirror, lest he see something frightening staring out at him. He flipped on the radio, startled to learn that it was afternoon. The same records he had heard the day before were being played by a glib disc jockey, and he snapped the radio off.

He wanted something—but what? He wondered if he might be hungry; yet when he looked at the tarts in the refrigerator, he did not want them, puckered, tiny puddles of water on the top of them. He drank some milk from the carton, and sat in the kitchen chair. The sunlight was mocking him with its intensity, creeping in around the window shades. He felt that he might sit there forever, until the skin dropped away, until the skeleton gracelessly fell against the plastic tabletop.

After he finished the carton, he walked to the door, afraid at first to touch the doorknob—fingerprints, Angie's fingerprints. What if she were still in the hall outside, ready to say "Boo!" when he opened the door, a hideous prank. Then she would giggle and spit on him. He grabbed the doorknob and rattled the door open. The hall was empty, except for a newspaper that had been left in front of the other apartment. He wished he had a newspaper too, had something to read. He went over to the roll and bent down and seized it, hurrying back into his apartment at once.

Cole spread the paper open on the table, excited by the theft. The Detroit *Free Press*, it read. On the first page was a column of minor pleas from citizens: someone wanted assistance on tax forms; another begged for help in collecting a highchair that a store refused to surrender; a more serious one asked someone to send word about her brother whom she had left in Poland years before. He read them all carefully, amazed at the ease with which the solutions were given; some godlike man made telephone calls and ended the longings; it took only two or three sentences of black ink to erase such worries. How easy it was! The tax instructions were in the mail, the highchair was in the mail, maybe even the Polish brother was in the mail. *If only all human problems could be eliminated so efficiently. Yes, even mine. Why not write a letter asking for a solution. What should I say?* He puzzled over the column, seeing that he didn't even begin to know how to put into words what he wanted. He was not even positive he wanted someone to smooth the snarls out of his life. There was something inhuman in such simplicity.

At the bottom of the page there was a scandal about a millionaire and his wife, who had run away with another man. Both of their blasé faces, in separate photographs, stood out stark and deliberate. *No, even the rich and married are not satisfied,* Cole decided. *Not even they.* Inside a cluster of crime stories spilled across several pages. One of them was about a grocery owner who had been stabbed with an ice pick—tortured by the thieves—and then shot through the ear. The killers were still at large, probably squandering the fifty-seven dollars they had taken from the cash register. A second story told of a girl who had been raped downtown in a parking lot. It was just a tiny square on the newspage, as though the episode were of little moment. The editors wished to rush forward with all of the other horrors of the past day—two neighbors who had shot each other to death in their backyards, over a tree limb that raked the roof of one of them; a man who had been shot at a traffic light, assailant unknown, just a person who had murdered a man waiting patiently at a red light; shootings at bars, quarrels, arguments—the stories went on and on—killings over women, over money, over tree limbs, alcoholic, enraged, indifferent, mistaken, frivolous deaths huddled up against one another on the cheap newsprint, each clamoring for attention, each taking a few seconds to digest and then to be passed by. Cole pushed the newspaper away. *Are these real? Or are they fabrications made up to titillate the public? Is the world falling to slivers, the crimes trampling upon one another in a frenzy of destruction, or is this the way it has always been, only here the concentration of horrors makes doom seem inevitable? And even I was tempted to contribute my crime to this holocaust.* "Policeman Slain!" *Yet it might actually go unnoticed, would be squeezed in among thousands of other words, hidden between the advertisements for a clothing sale, for denture cream. All my choking hate would be wrapped around someone's garbage.*

He read on for hours, absorbing every article. Everything was a crisis—a shipwreck, no funds for the beginning of the school year, a labor strike, corruption in the state senate, pollution, soil erosion, student demonstrations—he wondered how the world could contain all of it without exploding, and this was but one day's worth. He felt numbed, but he read further. Turning each page was like careening around a dangerous curve. He found the horoscope near the comic pages, at the back. His read: "Scorpio—Make tentative plans. The unexpected can be expected. Romantic trends favored, but not until late in the evening." He scratched at the words idly. "This must apply to last night," he said to the wall. The irony hung before him, unsavored. At last he glanced back down at the page.

When he finished reading, his back ached, but he continued to sit there, rubbing his nose. *Which direction is my life to go in now—toward a job somewhere, maybe away from Detroit, or perhaps suicide? Or toward murder?* He felt that the least knock from anywhere would send him in one direction rather than another. Everything would be different depending on the next few seconds. *Is this how lives are formed, by whims, by boredom?* He waited for a signal from something. Where were the voices that lunatics and saints heard, with all their explicit admonitions? Save France! Save France! Not one wispy angel to tell him how to run his life!

Then, without thinking much about it, he rose from the table and went to the bedroom, where he searched through the clothes he had tossed into the closet, and found the pair of Levi's that he wanted—faded, low on the hips. He looked at himself in the dresser mirror; they were almost too loose; he held them tighter against the crotch. Yes, that was better. But he did not have the energy to sew them. "I'll just have to commit my crime poorly dressed," he told himself. Next he selected a white knit shirt from a drawer and drew it over his head, then put on his brown loafers. He stuck his thumbs into the rear pockets and turned sideways. "You're a man of considerable cock. You'll do. Damn right, you'll do!"

Because it was only late afternoon, he stopped for dinner at a restaurant in the neighborhood. Except for the waitress, he was the only one there. She gave him a big motherly smile when he entered. All he wanted was scrambled eggs and toast, and the waitress was disappointed. "Nothing to drink? No coffee or nothing?" She made it an accusation, but he persisted. When she sauntered away to tell the cook, he rested his head on one fist. *Why does it take so long to get dark when you want night, and so long to get light when you want day?* And he wanted the dark fiercely now. *Where is the best place? Near the gay bar on Woodward? Will the cops be patrolling? In a park perhaps—Palmer Park? Is it dangerous? So it's difficult after all. Men know where to go to find women.* Cole had seen them around the YMCA downtown, Negro girls with blond or red hair and huge eyelashes, strutting up and down the sidewalks in splashy gowns, no doubt about their services. *They make them pay for it; why shouldn't I? There must be a thousand men in Detroit.* He twisted his lips into what he considered an indifferent smile—for practice. *You should let the eyes be languid, not*

too knowing, the fingers hung over the hip pockets. He nodded
agreeably when the waitress brought his food. "Nice day today," she said.

"Yes, isn't it?"

It was still early when he got to Six Mile Road, and he decided to walk to Palmer Park, over two miles, he was sure, but
in the meantime the sun would set. But after a quarter of a
mile, he felt exhausted; he sat down at a bench used by bus
patrons, watching the cars whipping past on Woodward. He
got up and stood alongside the curb and stuck out his thumb.
He wondered if a cigarette dangling would help, but he had forgotten his. He moved into the street and jerked the thumb. Several cars went by without acknowledging him.

Farther along the broad boulevard, after stopping here and
there to hitchhike again, he came to a cemetery, a gorgeously
green park on the other side of a high wrought-iron fence. Cole
seized the bars and peered into the serenity. Large slabs of
marble stuck up in various pious shapes, crosses usually. One
grave was marked by a huge angel with a full wingspread. "Are
you my guardian angel, behind bars?" he called out to the figure.
He half expected it to reply, but when it did not, he let his
eyes scan the slopes of manicured grass. *It must be peaceful to
be dead, only the occasional sound of a lawn mower rolling
above your corpse.* "Are you peaceful, all you dead people?"
he shouted. Silence. "I want to know!" He looked around him
quickly to see if anyone could overhear, but the street stretched
for blocks without a person in sight. "You don't know any
more than I do, do you! You'd probably lie anyway—just to
get me in there with you. Well, I'm not coming in." He released
the iron bars as if they were sizzling. "You're dead and I'm not
—and I'm going to prove it. No one wants your stinking carcasses, but somebody wants mine, because there's a heart in here.
In here! And it's thumping gallons of live blood—how do you
like that, dead people? I'm alive and you're not!" Cole ran from
the graves, aware of the heaviness of his legs, refusing to halt

until he reached the end of the long block, where the cemetery ended.

It was at least a mile farther to Palmer Park, and he began, breathing wildly, to hitchhike again, glancing at the descending sun to his right, a passionate globe. His clothes seemed to cling to him with each backward stride. He frowned at the automobiles that ignored him. "What do I have to do to get a ride—unzip my pants?" he spat at a car that sped by. A second later, another car slowed down as it approached; the driver, a man, looked at the hitchhiker uncertainly, and, when Cole waved, he applied the brake. At the car, which waited off to the side, Cole saw that the man looked nervous. "Where are you going?" he asked, a hint of a quiver in the voice.

"Just up to Palmer Park, okay?"

"Sure, okay," he answered anxiously, and then unlocked the car from inside.

Cole was uncertain himself, briefly, but then he got in next to the driver. Up close, he could see that the man, in his late thirties, had terrible skin, acne that was like boils, dark, encrusted knots that covered the face, even part of the neck. Yet the man was carefully dressed, in a gray suit that looked expensive. In a hesitant second-thought, Cole worried that the man might be a madman, one of those berserk killers who prey on hitchhikers. What if he took out a revolver and shot him in the mouth?

"Live in Detroit?" the driver asked, raking his eyes up and down Cole's body.

"Just a transient."

The man snapped his eyes at him, suspiciously, at the word. "What are you going to do in the park?"

At first Cole almost said it was none of the man's business, but the man gave hints that he was interested sexually. "I might sort of look around."

"Go there much?"

"Only when the mood hits."

"What mood is that?" The man grinned slyly; he had nice teeth.

"I get itchy."

"Why don't you scratch it then?" The man jiggled oddly as he chuckled.

Cole thought the man might reach over and grab him at any moment. What should he say? He really did not know how much to ask for—twenty dollars?

"Do you have to go to the park?" the driver said, dropping one hand on the seat between them.

Cole stared at it; it was just an ordinary hand, thick. "I want money."

"Are you a hustler?"

"Twenty dollars."

"I don't like to pay." The hand rose from the seat to his blemished face and stroked several of the pimples.

Cole tensed—what if the man was a policeman? Or what if he refused to pay?

"How about ten dollars?" the man suggested.

"Fifteen. I need the money," Cole lied.

"You got to agree to do what I like." He sort of bounced against the steering wheel at the words, and Cole realized that he was effeminate.

"And what is that?"

"I want to be screwed. Can you screw good?"

He slid the words toward the man softly: "Absolutely professional."

"Maybe I'll screw you too, eh?" he said jovially.

"Maybe you won't."

He looked injured. "Why not? I'm paying for it."

"Not all of me is for sale."

"Which parts?" The throat was slippery with lust.

"You guess."

"I guess—your cock. You got a good cock?"

Cole squirmed slightly; this was not what he had anticipated. He remained quiet.

"I bet you got a big, hard one, haven't you? I like big, hard ones. Let me see it."

The salaciousness aroused Cole, but made him queasy. "What if it fails to come up to your specifications?"

"I saw one last week that was big around as a little tree. Like this." He demonstrated.

"Congratulations!"

"Niggers got the biggest ones, though. Nothing like a yard-long black prick."

Cole felt his loins grow heavy, filling with dead desire. "I'm sorry I'm not black."

"Why don't you get it out; let me suck on it. Have you got good cream, huh?"

"Right here?"

"You ashamed?" His fingers clutched Cole's knee and began a massage. "You ought to be proud of what you got." The fingers moved higher.

"I want the money. First!"

The man's hand ceased its groping. The pathetic face slackened. "I'll give it to you. I promise."

"I want twenty."

"You said fifteen before."

"Twenty or nothing." The harshness is his own voice scared him, but he had to have the money; he did not know why, but it mattered to him as much as anything ever had.

The driver pulled his wallet out of his pocket and flipped it into Cole's lap. "There. I trust you to take out a twenty."

"I need it—that's all," he explained, almost a murmur. He opened the wallet and grabbed a bill, not seeing what it actually was, and stuffed it into his shirt pocket and handed back the wallet.

"You ever do this before?" the driver asked, doubtful.

"Sure, lots of times."

"You sure know how to turn a guy off."

"Do we have to do it here, in the car? Why not stop someplace?"

"So you can run away?"

Cole caught the strong note of anguish mixed with resentment; obviously this had happened to the man before. "I won't run away. That's my promise."

"You won't?"

"There's Palmer Park. We're going to pass it." The night was falling over the trees, although some late tennis players were still active, playing by artificial light. The car swerved too abruptly into a space, the tires scraping along the curb until the car came to rest. The man turned off the ignition. "Are you trying to kill us?" Cole said.

"Sorry. You said to stop."

"I didn't mean all at once."

"Well, you made me nervous."

After that, they sat unmoving for several minutes. "Do you want to go into the woods?" Cole finally inquired.

"No. Here's good enough." Again they sat without moving.

"Would you like your money back?"

"You aren't going to leave!" There was disappointment in the tone.

"We both made a mistake," Cole sighed.

"Look, all I want is some hot cock; I don't need any of your sympathy. Why don't you do something?"

"All right, I'll try to be more pornographic for you. What would you like me to do first? Should I flex my masculine muscles and smile my masculine smile? Unbuttoning my shirt, I stroked the burning flesh inside my briefs, as my ten inches expanded to their full masculine length. The paratrooper bent down on both knees, masculinely, and began to ease the gigantic member into the fiery masculine furnace. How's that?"

The man leaned over, caressing Cole's thighs. "I want it, baby, that's all." He ran his hands excitedly over the blue cloth, and then pinched at the zipper, which gradually slid open. He gripped the penis greedily. "No shorts on, eh?" he said grinning upward. He smothered his face against the warmth, and his mouth closed on Cole. The man made grunting noises, slurping enthusiastically. "Don't come yet, baby, okay?" And he continued, thrilling Cole, who sat watching the man's head writhe back and forth. Briefly the notion that the man might bite him flitted over his mind, sink the teeth into the pulsing organ and make him scream in agony. But a mounting flood of pleasure drowned out the idea. The man worked intensely for several minutes. "Oh, it's great, fella, give it to me. Come! Come!" It had been so long since Cole had felt such sensations he thought that he might faint, his head thrown back, the breath forced out of his mouth in rapid spurts. He felt the ripples coming from every direction toward his genitals, millions of little sparks, tingling, almost stinging. Nothing mattered but this! Nothing! "Give it all to me, fella. All!" Cole climaxed with shudders, his body throbbed again and again. *Oh, why does it have to end!* he thought, quivering, feeling the pleasure evaporating. "No, no, no, no!" But it had already ended, except for a spasm produced by the withdrawing lips. The driver sat back behind the steering wheel, his cheeks reddened from the exertions. "That was fine, though you almost made me choke. What a load!"

"I'm sorry." He hated the diminishing organ.

"What for? I enjoyed every drop. Can you come again?"

"But you ate my children—it's some sort of cannibalism, isn't it?" He asked the question sincerely, but the man's eyes narrowed in fright in the near darkness.

"I gotta go, fella. All right? You all right? It was real good, don't think nothing about the twenty dollars; it was worth every penny. Yes, sir." He leaned tentatively across Cole to open the car door. "See you again some time. Real good." He waited cautiously as Cole zipped up his pants and then nearly stumbled getting out. He slammed the door behind him and looked toward the woods of the park while the man started the motor. Instantly the engine ignited, and the man waved as he aimed the automobile into traffic.

"What's wrong with me?" he said weakly, stepping onto some crackling leaves that had fallen so soon in the season. *I envy that man, acne and all. I could make him happy, but not myself.*

He enjoyed the sex, didn't think it was nasty or disgusting—and I charged him for it! Cole drew the crumpled bill out of his shirt pocket and turned back to the street, as if to return the money. A gleam from the streetlight revealed that it was just a dollar bill. A couple of saddened chuckles rose into Cole's throat and seemed to ease the shaking of his arm.

Already muted figures were moving through the inner sections of the park, circling in elaborate patterns about each other, around the picnic tables that dotted the grounds, abandoned now by the daytime users. Cole noticed somebody hiding, crouching, in a clump of bushes near a shack used to store playground equipment; the man's face was swallowed up by the dark, probably a black, Cole thought. A man and a woman emerged from a tangle of trees, intruders now, lovers who had allowed their rightful time to disappear into the evening, making love behind a screen of flowers and weeds. "It's our park now," Cole told them, but so that they would not hear. They held each other's waists and headed toward the parking lot.

The restroom lay within view, near the duck pond. *What a shame,* Cole reflected, *that we always must congregate around excrement, like flies buzzing hungrily around manure. No wonder it seems crude; the stench contaminates us.* He saw a man wander into the doorway of the building nonchalantly, the very casualness a clue that he was cruising. Cole sat down on top of one of the picnic tables, where he touched a few cake crumbs that someone had neglected to clear away. He waited. Another man went into the lavatory. *It's like a dance, a huge dance with many intricate steps, played without a melody. First one partner, then the next. They are standing side by side now at the urinals, disinterested; now a faint bob of the head, perhaps a polite smile; now possibly they are uniting; soon they will move on to other partners.*

As one of the wood-rovers approached, Cole stood up on the bench, legs spread apart, the thumbs jammed into the front pockets. This too was part of the dance. Shyly, the man passed

by, looking over his shoulder; he was young and attractive. He
would not want to pay, Cole knew at once, and he sat down
again. The young man peered back, paused, but Cole looked
away. When he checked, the boy had gone on.

After a while, Cole walked to the far side of the lavatory, into
the black bushes near a large stone monument, which stood
rampant. Like a wreck of a temple. Going up one of the two stone
stairways on either side, he waited on the top in the shadows.
Ultimately another man picked his way to the top, eyed Cole,
then dawdled at the other side. The expectation exhilarated
him—dangerous, thrilling, the weaving in and out of the silhouettes, the rustle of the concealing trees. Cole felt himself
fully aroused again, and leaned back against the sandstone
monument. When the man neared him, Cole rested his hand on
the front of his Levi's, kneading. The man, who looked Oriental,
stood closer, watching the movements. He came nearer, the
longing struggling with fear. Cole unzipped the zipper and slid
his damaged hand part way in; the man bit at his thumbnail and
moved to the other side of Cole. "Okay?" the man muttered, his
hands in his pockets.

"I want ten dollars."

The short man blinked and stepped back. "Ten?"

In answer Cole exposed himself, even though a third man
was approaching the bottom of the stone stairs. "Not here," the
Oriental whispered.

Cole did not move when the third man reached the top, seeing
the eyes fix on his flesh. The man waited, licking his lips sug-
gestively, and Cole beckoned to him. The man's thin face came
up to Cole's, half-lighted; he was squeezing himself through
the cloth, staring bluntly at Cole's sex. "I need five dollars from
each of you. What do you say?" Both of them came closer.
"Not here," the Oriental insisted.

"Yes, here. There's nobody."

The thinner man took five dollars from his billfold and slapped
it into Cole's hand, and then encircled the chest with his arms;
excitedly he started to rub his hands underneath the knit shirt,

baring the torso. The other man reached out for the sex organ, but Cole stopped his hand. "Five dollars!"

"Why?"

"Five dollars!"

"All right," he answered, and reached into his pockets for the money. Then he knelt immediately in front of Cole and began to undo his belt.

Standing with one bill in each outstretched fist, feeling the men's fingers and mouths caressing him, Cole rested his shoulders on the monument rising above him; he squeezed the paper as if to make his skin absorb it and shivered with the delicious pleasure. The pressing of the other two against his flesh, sometimes getting in each other's way—he was desired. Yes, desire was equal to love. It was wonderful, just that way, with their gropings, their passions centered on him! When he exploded into one of them, he closed his eyes and gritted his teeth, and sighed . . . long.

For a time the others lingered, and Cole let them touch him. After several minutes, their hands withdrew, patting his legs affectionately in farewell, before they disappeared down the stairs into the shadowy trees. He remained, watching the dancers.

Night had fallen totally now; it chilled Cole, but still he did not want to leave, go back to the apartment. Walking along the bricked path, he wound between the shrubbery. Near him were solitary men loitering at the edge of the path, their eyes flickering like candles. Sometimes they stepped deeper into the recesses and waited, expectant, motionless, for someone to soothe their feverish bodies. Cole shoved the money into his shirt pocket, conscious of his hard breathing. Dimly he could see two forms close together as he passed a curve where a row of evergreens formed a hedge. The forms started and looked up, but he motioned for them to continue. *They're entitled to this— their birthright. Our birthright. Whoever decries this sex— just like this—is blind; they do not know the excitement. Anonymity increases it, no matter what others imagine. Let them lie in their soft love beds, their lust ringed with oaths and lies; passion needs no excuse. It is what it is—strong, devoid of sanctity, devoid of names. We make no demands except the flesh. There is purity in the desire. No other way than this— only this!* He felt his body aroused again. Alive! He was thoroughly alive, a delectable, welling joy. How could anyone not understand? Yet perhaps they did understand—that was why Keel and the other policemen went beating through the blackened parks with their chains, flailing the exposed flesh, to subdue, to chastise, to destroy!

His jaws ached from the image of Keel racing behind his eyes, a club in his hands, coming toward them in the dark, hate lining the brow. *"Male and female only! Only! In bed! Only! In love! Only! Only!"* Cole slammed his hand up to his forehead to stop Keel, and the two men in back of the evergreens heard the slap and moved apart as if they had been shot. No, he would not let the law crush this hour; it was wrong, and he was right. Cole went through the shrubs, up to the other men. "Wait!" He stood against a tree and began to unfasten his fly. He shivered as the Levi's slid down his skin; still he went on, pulling them off, until he stood partly nude, the men holding their breath as they watched his movements. Then he held out his hands to them. They waited, not brave. He signaled again, and yet they held back, like dogs that had been kicked too many times. "Come unto me," he said more loudly, and, hesitantly, they inched nearer, still frightened. "It's good!" he whispered. "It's godlike." At last, when they stood silently next to him, he reached out and touched first one, then the other, drawing them to him, gently. As he fumbled with their clothing, two other men slowly approached. Even Cole's heart lurched until he realized they were not enemies. He stretched out his wounded hand to them too, cupping the fingers to communicate. As they all surrounded him, the huskiness of their bodies overwhelming his senses, he stroked them, each in turn. And their fingers rippled and swirled over his shoulders, across the stomach, the thighs. They covered him, descending, rising, warming him.

Their breath filled the air about him, as the hands undulated, squeezed. Someone seized him with his mouth, the hands continuing to rub, to heat his flesh, and he felt as if he were being slowly torn apart—but gently, unbearably, magnificently. He threw his head back and panted in ecstasy, and then grasped the dollars from his shirt pocket and let them fly from his hand as he climaxed—splendid, hot and wild, as if he were dying.

10

He was sketching, sitting on the sofa, two days later. From somewhere he had summoned the energy to go to an art store and purchase some India ink, pens, and heavy paper. With the sun streaming through the windows, Cole scarcely let his mind come to rest on any of its bruises; he was trying to recapture the faces in the gay bar, blending them on the paper, a shared eye linking one with the next. He wondered if the faces were any good. They seemed adequately drawn, but were they merely competent? It saddened him, although he forbade the idea to penetrate very far, that most likely he would never be an artist, always merely a competent draftsman. *And nobody cares about competent draftsmen.* He held the drawing away from him, at arm's length, to study its proportions. How strange, he noticed—none of the faces was smiling, a ring of ciphers with quiet, noncommittal features. Even Roy's bald head showed nothing of the humor associated with it in his mind. He considered adding a laughing face, perhaps in the middle, but something inside told him that it did not belong. *There is something trivial about happy people anyway.*

When the telephone rang, Cole stared at it without surprise. It probably was a wrong number. Who would be calling him? Something strident resounded in the ringing. After the fifth ring, he went to it. "Yes?"

"Hello? Is that you, Cole?"

"Angie?" He felt himself flush.

"Yes, it's me. I'm calling from work. How are you?" The false lightness belied her nervousness.

"It was very nice of you to call."

"Oh, I just wanted to see . . . how you are?"

"I'm well, thank you."

"That's good to hear."

There was a long interval because neither could think of another sentence.

"So you're well. I'm so glad, Cole."

He caught himself entwining his fingers in the telephone cord. "And how are you? All right, I hope."

A counterfeit laugh tinkled into his ear. "Just fine. Just fine."

He felt the silence taking over again. "How did you know my number?"

"Oh, that was easy. I asked for the list of new numbers from directory assistance."

"Did you?"

"You were easy to get—on the phone."

He pictured her twisting the cord on her side. "It's nice to know I'm not utterly cut off from the rest of the world. I'll have to memorize my number now. What is it anyway?" He bent down to check.

"Oh, yes, the telephone people were very efficient."

"That's because they know where all the plugs go."

"Yes, I suppose that's why, isn't it?" She paused. "I wish I owned stock in the Bell Company."

Again they waited for thought.

"You were extremely kind to call me, Angie. I wish I knew a magic charm to chase away the other night."

"Oh, that! It was nothing." She sounded unconvincing.

"Very aptly described."

"I'm sorry; I sometimes say silly things, inadvertently."

"People always seem to be apologizing for one offense or another, don't they?"

"Have you looked for a job, Cole?"

"Not yet, but you needn't worry. I haven't stuck my head in the oven even once."

"I'm very glad that you sound . . . fine. I wouldn't want you to be hurt in any way."

"Men like me don't always kill themselves. Only in books for the 'straight' market. Like Ol' Man River, we just keep rolling along."

"Cole . . . I just want you to know that we can continue to be friends. There's no reason why we can't, is there!" Her effort in saying the words showed through.

He puffed out a gasp of air. "Of course not! You and I will become jolly good pals, very good pals, no doubt. How civilized of us. We're even denied tragedy."

She did not reply, and he pictured her reddened eyes as they had been that night. "Worse things have happened, Cole."

"We can probably go to parties together. Nothing quite like a safe date."

"It doesn't bother me, Cole . . . not as much as it bothers you."

"I guess that means I inspired a truly deep affection in you— gone in three days without a scar."

"I didn't mean that. I definitely feel this. Other people have feelings too. But we don't have to run from each other as though we have a . . . a disease."

"Couldn't you at least pull out a handful of hair—for my sake? Maybe a simple little 'Woe is me'?"

"See, there is a sense of humor somewhere in that moody brain of yours."

"Angie, I appreciate your call, I really do. I know this was not at all easy for you to do."

She laughed. "My face is still burning, if you want to know. And the boss is probably going to fire me for making social calls."

"My clothes are drenched too."

"It's good that we can tell each other such things. That will save us."

"Yes, if anything will."

"Cole, another reason I called is—"

"Wait! Don't tell me. You left your coat here? And that's the real reason for your call."

"No, I didn't! But I am throwing a party, and I want you to come."

"Come at the party? That would be putting me on the spot."

"It's a party I planned a long time ago. I think I told you about it when we had lunch downtown that day. Some people you know will be there, like Bud Smallwood and Maxine."

"They can come and throw darts at my face."

"They are interested in you as a person first of all. Secondly, they don't know anything about . . . But seeing some old friends, and making some new ones, will be invigorating for you. We're just going to talk and maybe play some party games."

"Kissing games?"

"Not this time."

"Pity. I'm quite good at kissing games."

"Maybe you'll be better at charades."

"Touché!"

"I think you read meanings into my words that I don't put there—but if it makes you happy . . ."

"Excuse me. I talk to myself sometimes."

"I've noticed. So will you come to the party? It should begin about eight or eight thirty. Remember, it's at my father's house. They agreed to let me use it because there's more room. Please say you'll come."

He waited only momentarily, thirsty for the generosity. "You don't even have to coax. How formal should I dress?"

"Quite casual. As you like." An image of Angie's naked body lying on his bed glimmered.

"Friday night?"

"Right. Do you remember how to get to our place?"

"Seven-eleven Burning Bush Drive, second house on the left. Don't forget to lower the drawbridge."

She laughed politely at his old jest. "We'll be looking forward to seeing you, Cole. Do come!"

"Word of honor."

"That's enough for me."

"Good-bye, Angie."

"See you Friday." They lingered, unspeaking, for a few seconds longer, and then hung up.

And that is how life's agonies are resolved, Cole marveled. *Removed more effortlessly than a spot on a rug.*

But of course he would not go to the party.

Friday arrived, the days having evaporated like bubbles; the sun had popped out of the East each morning, shimmering, and then had burst when pricked by the twilight. His sketches lay around the apartment at random, to give the illusion, he realized fully, that "genius" was at work. If he were to pile them neatly on a shelf, they would seem to be less worthwhile, though as shelf paper probably they would find their true position in the world.

Yet he knew that he needed a change; his sex drive had returned, as virulent as ever, filling him with restlessness, and he wanted to talk to someone, anyone. How terrible to crave the drivel of everyday conversation—and yet he did. So at seven thirty he dressed in gray slacks and yellow cardigan. He even gargled with mouthwash, thinking that he must be getting more social if he cared how he smelled. That had to be a good sign. Looking into the mirror, he noticed a long hair growing out of one ear; he pulled at it, surprised at its length. *The barber at the jail must have kept me neat and tidy. Would I be some sort of monster if I just let nature take its course? Baying at the moon, tufts of bristly hair spouting from me. A wolf-man.* He smirked at his reflection. How odd that even wolf-men had become comic figures. He snipped the hair with the scissors and trimmed his heavy eyebrows. Then he looked at himself sideways. "It's my night to howl." *Do you suppose there are any gay wolf-men? They cruise by the light of the moon. Or perhaps they've sent all the gay ones to rest homes, so they can readjust to the real wolf-world and get back to the proper business of devouring people—or making arrests—all those normal duties the wolf-world loves so much.* He was surprised at the way the corners of his mouth curved downwards when he was not forcing a grin. *In a few years I'll look like one of those old, broken men who sit eating by themselves at counters in run-down restaurants.*

The long taxi ride made him nervous, and he kept fidgeting on the hard seat, as the city of Detroit faded. Increasingly suburbanized fields and houses drifted by, until eventually he arrived in Bloomfield Hills, amid sloping lawns, spacious homes. Some of them had brick fronts that had been rubbed by hand to give the appearance of age—scrubbed, lovely houses that sat smugly in their places like earls and dukes, each confident of its domain.

Angie's house sat on the top of a small hill, a white colonial, complete with swimming pool. Cole stood in admiration near the perfect grass that stretched leisurely in green slopes. *Ah, I should have married for wealth.* As he started up the path, he halted. *Maybe Angie will open the door, invite me in, and then a net will fall around me. Two men in masks will appear and bind me with cords. Then she'll order me taken to the basement, a dungeon, where her father will be bricking up a wall—leaving only enough space for my body. Or perhaps she will offer me some wine or cheese, and the poison will slink through my bloodstream, dulling me, as her green eyes grow fiercer and fiercer. As I stagger, she will abruptly lash out, with venom in her voice, accusing me of humiliating her, and her father and mother will nod in the sinister fuzziness to the rear of her, then help carry my unresisting corpse into the garden, to bury it under one of their expensive, well-cared-for trees. They will spit on the dead body, revenged upon it for the insult to their family.*

Cole rang the doorbell without pausing; then he peeked

through the window. A few people were already there. Angie's father answered the door. "Come in, Cole. Nice to see you again." He was a tall, lean man of great dignity. Cole had never seen him without a suit on. "We're happy you could come tonight. Angie's out in the game room, in the back, mixing some drinks, if you want to join them."

"Thank you. How are you, Mr. Fionda?"

"Not bad, for an old man." He grinned.

"You're looking well."

"I'm feeling well, actually. Tonight I beat Angie at ping-pong —first time in months. It's these little victories in life that matter most." He clapped an affectionate arm around Cole's shoulder and directed him through the rooms. "Angie tells me that you're looking for a job. Any luck?"

"Not really. I . . . I've just started."

"If you're interested, I'm in need of some young men on my staff. You draw, I understand?"

"A bit, yes."

"Drop around one day soon, at your convenience, and ask for Mr. Kramer in my commercial department. Of course, you may not be interested in that sort of work." He gave the shoulder another squeeze. *He is a nice man, even if he is planning to throw me into a vat of lye. Maybe one more hug like the last one and I'll marry the boss instead of the boss' daughter!*

"The offer is very generous of you."

"I mean it. You just drop by this week. We can talk about it. Kramer will help you a lot."

"You're extremely kind, Mr. Fionda." Cole felt silly being steered by the big man's arm. *Angie has told him nothing,* he concluded, relieved, yet disturbed as well.

"Look what I dragged in!" he said loudly to Angie, whose face formed into a pale welcome at the sight of Cole. If she noticed her father's arm around him, she did not acknowledge it.

"Hello." Cole was too conscious that they were both fully dressed, their bodies hidden.

"Good evening. I'm pleased you're here." Their hands clasped ever so lightly.

"Cole's coming to work for me, how about that?" her father said brightly.

"Really? How nice." Cole thought he read in Angie's expression his own feeling: that her father considered him his potential son-in-law, and he thought Angie's face blushed a little.

"I'd better see how your mamma's doing. You two talk." As he moved away, Mr. Fionda winked at Cole, surreptitiously, but Angie could not miss the obviousness of his departure.

The two stared at each other. "Well," she said, "any trouble getting here?"

"None."

"That's good." She smiled fully at him, her lavender dress bringing out the luminous qualities of her eyes. *How brave she was to invite me here!*

"You're looking very pretty tonight," he complimented.

"Oh!" She waved a hand to dismiss the flattery. Something in her movement told him more, told him that their relationship could never be restored; there was too much exasperation in it, nothing of the coquette. Clearly she did not think of him as a man anymore. "Come, let me introduce you." She did not take his hand, which he was certain she would have done a few days before, as she led him across the large room to a group of people. "Everybody, this is Cole Ruffner. I'll let you introduce yourselves; it's more efficient." The names of the two couples were spoken, each immediately forgotten. The group tried to think of something appropriate to say. "You know, Cole used to work in our office," Angie said to one of the women.

"Yes? What did you do?" a woman with a sharp nose inquired, while the others' heads turned in semi-interest to Cole.

"I made maps."

"Really? . . . How dull!"

When the group laughed, Cole broke into a sweat; the noises

of their amusement felt like switches across his eyes. He could say nothing, could not even force himself to grin.

"Madeline's just joking," Angie's words came from somewhere.

He blinked. "Of course. I see that."

"Don't mind me," Madeline said. "I'm never serious. That's my problem!"

"I'm always serious. That's mine."

The people in the group exchanged looks when he said that.

"Didn't I see you outside our office—weren't you the one?"

"Guilty," he answered.

"I knew I recognized you. I—At first I thought you were acting so weirdly."

"I didn't mean to frighten you."

"I thought you might be some kind of nut!"

"What would you like to drink, Cole?" Angie asked.

"Vodka tonic—please."

"Anybody else?"

"I'll go one more—Scotch and milk, remember," said a snub-nosed, goateed man whose clothes looked too tight for him, as though he might be fat underneath. He had a deep voice that he threw at his listeners like an actor. When Angie left them, they glanced down into their drinks or at the thick rug. "Not a bad little place they have here—for fourteen-nine," the bearded man joked.

"Isn't it fabulous! I had no idea Angie was from the *hoi polloi*."

The other girl corrected Madeline. "The *hoi polloi* means the poor, not the rich."

"Is it? Well, you learn something every day."

"What do you do now, Cole?" The big voice seemed to seize his head with its muscles.

"Nothing at the moment. Just a man of the idle class, I guess."

"I wish I could say that. I've just started another year of teaching. Sigh!"

"What do you teach?"

"Creeps. High school creeps. I teach speech and English to American youth!"

"You sound fed up."

"Oh, it's not as bad as I make out—it's worse." He laughed loudly.

"Oh, Guy, are you complaining again, as usual!" The girl patted Guy's knuckles, revealing their casual intimacy. Cole noticed that he made a fifth in the group—a fifth wheel? He wondered.

"Haven't I met you somewhere before, Cole?" the man asked suddenly.

He wanted to ask, "Do you hang out in parks?" But he thought better of it. "I don't think so."

"You're very familiar to me." He scrutinized Cole's features, making him uncomfortable, as though at any moment Guy might remember seeing him in a bar or in court.

"I really doubt that we have met before."

"You didn't go to the University of Detroit ever?"

"Not as a student, no."

"I can almost place you."

"Most likely you have me confused with someone else."

"Could be I just saw your kisser on a Wanted poster, eh?" He opened a wide, toothy mouth.

"Not yet," Cole replied, trying to restrain his hands from crawling up to his face.

"How are you doing, honey?" the man asked the girl next to him.

"Fine, darling. You?"

"I feel good."

"Where do you teach?" Cole asked him.

"Henry Ford High."

"I'm afraid I don't know it."

"It's not a bad school—as schools in the States go. A friend of mine was telling me that at his school they caught six kids having a gang bang in the gym. The day before, two teachers had been tied up in a closet while the kids went on a rampage up and down the halls. Aren't you sorry you don't teach?"

"It sounds like misery—why does anyone put up with it?"

"The spirit of the times, the spirit of the times! They were only doing their thing, man! We wouldn't want to warp the psyches of the dear students."

"Somebody has to do it," his companion commented. "You have to know how to handle them right."

"All right, tell me then what I should have done the other day when one of my darlings told me—this was in class, mind you—an honors section—that Shakespeare was full of shit!"

"Did he actually?" Cole said.

"I kid you not. I probably brought it on, though, because I was making jokes about *The Tempest*, saying things like Ariel shows latent homosexual tendencies. But what a nerve these kids have now! You try to joke and kid with them, as I was, and they take advantage of the situation."

Cole said, "Maybe they didn't think the joke was funny."

"I don't know why—I read some of those speeches with a lisp."

The women giggled at the way Guy moved his eyebrows rapidly up and down.

"Where the bee sucks, there suck I. Tra la, tra la!"

He began to cough because of his own intense amusement, and the other three were enjoying the performance greatly, but Cole merely stared at Guy.

"What's the matter?" Guy asked, wiping water from the edge of his eye. "Does that offend you—fooling around with Shakespeare like that?"

"I suppose such jokes are funny," Cole replied. "You all seem to think so."

"Oh, it was really a scream, if I have to say so myself."

"Excuse me," Cole said, turning away from them. He had to get free of their laughter. He walked to another section of the room, trying to quell the mixed fear and wrath rising in him. *So I've forgotten how to mingle socially, how to accept jests at my expense, all the while remaining silent, dumb—affable and so eager to fit in. I've forgotten, and I want to keep on forgetting. I'd rather be damned to solitude than beg crumbs of approval.*

Angie at that moment came by him with the drinks. "Where are you going, Cole?"

"I haven't decided."

"Something the matter? Here's your drink."

"Just a pain, a minor one." He took the glass.

"Wait for me a second." Angie hurried over to the group of four to give Guy his glass, and then came back. "Aren't you socializing?"

"I didn't realize how out of practice I am."

"Are you sure you're trying?" The reprimand was clear even though she spoke delicately.

Just then two other people entered the room, Bud Smallwood and the girl who was his fiancée, and Angie went to greet them, and the three came over to Cole.

"Cole! Why you ditch-digger you! I hardly recognized you —you're thinner. How are you? Long, long time, no see."

"Hello, Bud." Cole's voice sounded hollow.

"What a sight for sore eyes!"

Cole warmed under the greeting, tingling at Bud's evident satisfaction in seeing him. *I must have been alive once, mustn't I—if he remembers me with fondness?*

"Say, Cathy-Lynn, this is Cole Ruffner. Cole, Cathy-Lynn Morisette." They nodded to each other. "Wait now! Before anything else, you give me your phone number. I'm not going to lose you again."

Cole grinned and told him the number, and Bud wrote it down in a notebook. "How have you been, Bud?"

"Fine. Hey, we're engaged, Cathy and I."

"Are you?" He noticed that the girl was conventionally pretty, with her fluffy hair chemically streaked with gray.

"I'm a lucky man." He squeezed the girl's hand lovingly.

"Congratulations. Taking the big plunge?"

"Right. The big day is coming up in a couple of months. There're too many bachelors like me running around. Say, when're you joining the club, fella?"

Cole caught Angie's eye. "When I get a special invitation, I guess."

"Well, don't you wait too long. Time's running out. Of course, not everyone has to get married," he added as if he remembered something.

How much do you know about me? Just how much? Is it more than I think you do? Out loud he said, "The difficulty is in finding the proper partner."

"Have you looked in the right places?" Bud said with a touch of irony in the question.

"Perhaps not." He looked into Bud's eyes, trying to decipher the expression. Was Bud telling him that he knew about his sex life? Cole let his mind sink into a fragment of the past— the time at a beach when Bud had brushed against him in the shower, when he had smiled at Cole with such brimming eyes while they had dressed. *What modesty I showed; I was afraid to touch you.*

"You could use some sun; you're so pale."

"You look healthy, Bud. Like an advertisement." He actually looked handsome, Cole thought; he had filled out since he had seen him last, though he still had that boyish, vulnerable look that made his features charming. Occasionally he would bite his tongue near the tip to emphasize a point, making the silly mannerism ingratiating.

"I feel healthy. In fact, never better in my whole life. It must be love." He nodded toward the girl, who waited confidently for her man to greet a friend. "Cole and I used to be real good buddies, Cathy. A few years ago."

"Yes, you told me all about him, remember?" She gave Cole a frozen stare, and she and Bud seemed to share a secret for an uncomfortable second.

"You're a fortunate girl, to get Bud," Cole said.

"I know so. Nobody has to tell me."

Cole caught Angie's eye again, suspecting the reason for the girl's coldness.

"Though we haven't communicated for some time, have we?" Bud said, putting too much joviality into the statement.

"Not nearly enough, no."

Cathy-Lynn gave him an appraising look as if to see what Bud had seen in him. "It's amazing how friendships die off."

"Sometimes they can be recovered."

But the girl cut him by turning to Angie. "That's such a pretty dress, Angie."

When Cole met Bud's face, he could read the embarrassment.

"I'm dying to meet some of these other people!"

You bitch! Cole thought to himself.

"Come on, Bud; let's mingle."

But before she could move, Cole asked, "Did Bud ever tell you about the time we slept together, Cathy?" He was surprised at his own daring, but her rudeness infuriated him.

"Now, you'll give her the wrong impression. Where was that? Some cottage, right? Where was that, Cole?"

"So you do recall it? It was up in the Thumb—Jimmy Trosper's cottage."

"That's right. All of those people stayed there that weekend."

"Not so many." Cole almost enjoyed the grim, little pretense of a smile on the girl's face. "How are Bob and John and Jimmy, all the fellows?"

"Gee, I haven't seen them for ages. Not ages."

"So you have a past you haven't told me about, honey." Saying it, the girl refused to acknowledge Cole.

"What past!" He chuckled more awkwardly than Cole would have suspected.

"Wives shouldn't always know all their husbands' secrets," Cole said with calculation. "Can only spoil things."

"Would you two care for a drink?" Angie asked, trying to interrupt.

"No, thank you. I'm so lucky that I trust Bud completely, aren't I?" She defied him with a glare.

Cole was astonished at how much he detested the girl, after just those few moments. Her proprietary air, the sense of possession of Bud. "Yes, blind faith can be such a comfort."

He felt Bud and Angie grow fretful, but he was not going to grovel any longer for anyone.

"Gosh, dear," Cathy-Lynn said, "I'm so tired. Could we sit down, please?"

"Sure, darling."

"You will excuse us, won't you, Mr.—?"

"My pleasure." *Go to hell, dearest, lamby, sweetum-ickums!*

"Sure I can't get you two something?" Angie asked.

Bud said, "How about two martinis, okay, honey?"

Angie jiggled a bracelet when the other two moved away. "I'm sorry, Cole."

"Not your fault. I suppose it's not even her fault. I'm an enemy."

"You did bait her, in a way."

"I'm a master at baiting people. Most of all, I'm tired of being apologetic for existing."

"Don't spoil the party, okay?" She gave him a wispy look as she started to the bar.

"I promise. I don't want to be thrown out because I don't have on a wedding garment."

Angie met some other people who had come into the room, led by Mr. Fionda, who then disappeared. All of them appeared to be in couples, and Cole wondered if Angie had invited him to provide herself with a partner. He watched her as she listened meditatively to one of the newcomers. No, she was simply being kind. Or was she so dependent on social approval that . . . ? She avoided his eye, he thought, when she glanced up.

Keeping his gaze averted from Bud and Cathy-Lynn, whom he felt certain were discussing him, he moved to the hors d'oeuvre tray and picked up a wedge of cheese cut out in a heart shape; he bit into it, holding the fragment away from himself. Such a small heart and such a big chunk out of it, he noticed. Angie carried drinks over to Bud and Cathy while he stood alone; then he went to the bar to fix himself a second drink, uncomfortable.

"Cole!" Bud's voice said from behind. "Cathy-Lynn's resting for a minute; she's a little tired." He looked ill at ease telling the lie.

"She doesn't approve of me."

"No, that's not it."

"The gentleman doth protest too much."

"You two will have to give it another try."

"Everyone I know seems determined to give it a second try!" Cole said bitterly, looking at Angie.

"It can only help."

"It was hate at first sight."

"Come on, now; it's not all that bad."

"She's probably going to give you hell because you left her to come over to me."

"I'd like to see her try."

Cole examined Bud's eyes. *Has he ever thought of me as something besides a pal? If we could only read minds.* "So you're getting married, Bud!"

"Will wonders never cease, huh?"

"People start to talk about a man when he gets into his late twenties and still hasn't made the expected overtures." Cole looked closely to see if Bud read his meaning.

"True, all my relatives kept after me and after me to get married."

"And you're doing your best to please the relatives?"

"Not quite." Bud let a shadow of a frown appear. "I think I've found the best girl at last."

"Are you certain?"

"Why wouldn't I be?" Bud's humor was forced.

Cole felt his tongue yearn to say more, to ask him directly if he was not doing it chiefly out of conventionality. "Oh, I don't know. I wouldn't want you to marry the wrong person."

"She's really a fine, bright girl, Cole."

"I can tell she is. What did she say about me, just now?"

Bud tried to pretend he had not heard. "I've missed you, fella—"

"No, really, I'd like to know what she thinks."

"Oh, she hardly knows you!"

"I know it wasn't good. But tell me."

"She didn't say anything. What makes you think that?"

"Did she say I was a bad influence on you?"

Bud snorted slightly to cover the discomfort. "All she said is that you are not her type of friend."

"Nothing more? Or less?"

"You're so suspicious."

"Did you tell her something about me?" Cole drew back inside his eyes, steeling himself for a blow.

"Like what?" he asked, drawing out the words, very embarrassed.

Cole realized for certain then that Bud knew about him. "Like I'm one of the 'warped' people, more warped than most, perhaps, because I'm not a good Joe who accepts his place in the shadows."

"I told her that we were friends . . . and that you acted differently sometimes."

"I suppose I passed away an evening for you."

"I've always been glad I had you for a friend."

"You mean, even though there's something wrong with me?"

"I liked you because of what was right with you, not the wrong."

"But still you told your fiancée that you knew somebody who was strange, true?"

"I said that I had known a lot of different types of people, and one of them was you."

"And what type is that?" Cole said evenly.

Slowly: "What do you want me to say, Cole?"

"I don't know actually." He looked at the floor.

"I've always considered you my closest friend."

"How long have you known?"

Bud looked startled. "It doesn't make all that much difference when you come right down to it." He tried to sound light-hearted.

"Maybe you even hoped to gain something?"

"What do you mean by that?"

Cole stared him full in the face, letting the import settle. "Nothing, I suppose."

"What did I hope to gain?"

"Nothing."

"I thought of you as a friend, a good friend." Bud jerked his body around as he spoke.

"Of course! I wouldn't want you to lower your opinion of yourself."

"What are you implying?"

"Not a thing. You're about to become a married man." Cole could not help himself and looked over at the girl on the couch, who was deliberately not looking at them.

"I felt very close to you, Cole, but it was not . . ."

"Don't drop your drink. No one's accusing you of anything."

"Sometimes men do things that—when they're young—that have no real connection with their later lives."

"You sound ashamed of something in your past."

"I confess I was attracted . . . you know, I liked you . . . as a person."

"And I liked you as well, Bud."

Bud turned crimson, switching his glass from hand to hand. "We were quite a bit younger, weren't we!"

"Yes, I suppose it was simply a young man's friendship. A pity so much time has passed."

Still embarrassed, But nodded agreeably. "A lot of blood under the bridge."

"I suppose there's no going back either?" Cole's voice dipped until it was all but inaudible.

"No doubt . . . no doubt." Bud was pulling at his jaw, not meeting Cole's eyes. *What should I say to you now? Should I dare to start a different relationship with you? Should I try to "corrupt" you, to bring out what you won't fully admit in yourself, or should I be a "nice guy" and let you go? But to whom— to that girl over there, that frivolous spawner of endless babies? Someone named Cathy-Lynn! She'll put fifty pounds on you in a few months, make your brain soften with the tedium of her passive little Catholic body—so tidy under the covers. No, she's not what you want; she's not good enough for you. Maybe you only think you want any woman because you're afraid to think anything else.*

"When Cathy gets to know you better, all that will change," Bud went on before Cole could seize the moment.

"Optimist still, I see. Some people like each other less the more they know of each other."

"She doesn't think of you with all the memories that I do."

"She just wants you entirely to herself, I suppose."

"She'll like you when she knows you as I do."

"That pleases me very much, Bud—to hear that."

"But why didn't you get in touch with me during all this time? I never heard a word, nary a peep out of you," he said, trying to lighten the situation.

"Do you know the whole story?"

"Do you want to talk about . . . these past several years? We don't have to if you'd rather not."

"What were you told about me?"

"I learned it from Franklin, your old boss—ran into him in the lobby at work, and he told me that you had been picked up by the police. Why didn't you get in touch, telephone or something? I would have helped you."

"*Would* you? It's good to hear it, even if it is a little post-mature. I guess I didn't tell you because I was too humiliated."

"And you went to jail all this time?"

"It was sort of like stealing a loaf of bread—I only got six months for that—but because I protested the basic injustice I was sentenced to two more years. And then something else happened while I was in. And that is how the cookie of life crumbles."

"If I had known, I could have helped you—my father knows many lawyers."

"I don't mean to sound ungrateful, Bud, but would you really have helped me? Once you found out, did you write to me?"

"I was uncertain of what to do—and you didn't get in contact with me, so I thought . . ."

"I see."

"You don't think much of my friendship, do you?"

"It isn't that; I didn't think much of my reputation. I couldn't stand the idea of losing my friends—it would have been too much on top of too much."

"But why didn't you write at least?"

"Let's say I'm a poor correspondent."

"Rotten, I'd say."

"I wrote you a letter once, but I never mailed it."

"Why not? I worried about you."

"The letter said all sorts of preposterous things; I guess I was out of my head."

"Jail must have been terrible."

"Pretty much. But now of course I've learned from my 'crime' and I'm on the straight and narrow—well, almost."

"How did you get arrested, though?"

"I'll spare you the ghastly details. Suffice it to say that I was bold enough to take my sex to the great out-of-doors, when every decent citizen knows that God created bedrooms and roofs to do the dirty business in and under."

"Were they cruel to you?"

"No, after the first spike in the fingernail, one can get used to almost anything. I *would* like to settle a score with one of the cops."

"Just one?"

"You can't kill everybody."

"You sound extremely bitter."

"I am extremely bitter."

"Maybe we can talk more about it when we get together next." Bud looked over at Cathy-Lynn, who was still chatting with Angie.

"With your marriage, though, probably you won't have much time—all those obligations, places to go."

"Nonsense. I've got time for you—if I have to squeeze you in."

Cole felt melancholy at the remark. "Can we meet on dark corners at midnight—when the moon is full? Is Cathy-Lynn much interested in the moon?"

"The moon?"

"It's not important. We always think we're important—are you still working for the government?"

Bud decided not to pursue the other issue. "Still plugging away. I'm a GS-8 now."

"That's fine, Bud. You're filling in your life with the appropriate responsibilities, good."

"Not completely. You know, though, that's somewhat true! I haven't read a book just for pleasure in about six months."

"You're dwindling into a husband."

"God, it sounds awful—like a disease!"

"Symptoms are: fever, that is, hot flashes of the forehead—as well as other parts of the body; second, you break out in a rash —rash actions, like getting married. Followed by pains—labor pains as well as pains in the neck and the rear end."

Bud was amused, as his beaming eyes revealed. "Perfect description, except for one thing—most of the time I like being sick." He waved to Cathy-Lynn as he spoke.

"True, being healthy is so boring anyway. People love their illnesses because they break up the daily monotony."

"Maybe you and Angie can team up too? Huh?" Bud poked him familiarly on the elbow, inclining his head in her direction.

Cole watched the other's blue, festive eyes. *You're as whole-*

some as an apple. "Who knows! Perhaps we'll make it a four-some at your wedding."

"We can do it, buddy. Really! And we can have lots of wonderful times together, the four of us."

Cole simply let his lips spread into an imitation of a smile.

"You'd enjoy being married, Cole. I'm positive. Put some meat on those bones of yours—and there are other physical advantages, right?" He winked obscenely, or what he considered such; however, he was too innocent a person to make anything he said seem dirty.

"Is it so easy as all that?" He felt a tickle in his throat as he glimpsed Angie talking to more new guests. *No use crying over spilled semen,* he told himself, *not even unspilled semen.* He looked back at Bud.

"Something wrong?"

"No. Why?"

"You're staring a hole through me, that's all."

"Do you mind if I ask you a very personal question?"

"That sounds provocative." The blue eyes did a little dance. "What is it?"

"Are you a virgin?"

Bud sputtered, "Is that an insult?"

"Should it be? I'm not certain. I've forgotten how to talk to people." He shifted his glass to the free hand, clinking the melting ice cubes.

"It's a rather loaded question—I stand condemned whichever way I answer; either I'm impure or else I'm a dope."

"Don't answer it then; I was just curious; it shouldn't matter very much. It's simply one of the hoops you have to jump through so that you can perform in the Big Ring with the Big People."

"I'm not sure I'll tell you. Are *you?*" He gave Cole a look meant to be humorous; yet his discomfort showed through.

"That depends on how you define the term."

"Well, to give the honest-to-God truth, no, I'm not—wait, yes, I am!"

"Which?"

"I'd rather not say."

"Why is abstinence from sex considered such a virtue? I've never understood that—although I practiced it." *But not as long as you have,* he continued in his mind.

"The body is sacred, and it has to be saved for those special, holy occasions."

"What holy occasions—your marriage night? It could turn out to be quite a letdown." He laughed, really at himself.

"If you cheapen it, you spoil it."

"People who make too much of it likewise suffer, because they expect bliss, which they almost never get."

"It's too easy for people to just use each other."

"No it isn't—but why shouldn't they—if it's mutual? Why do people acknowledge the necessity of food, but deny the necessity of sex?"

"It's more than just a meal or something to pass the time—it is!"

"It can be. But it also can be something to relieve the day-by-day anguish, *without* the bonds that people want to put on themselves."

"Isn't that what those who don't have anybody say?"

Cole felt the sting of the words. "Maybe. Maybe too we've been brainwashed into believing that we have to want exactly what produces the greatest number of offspring. Perhaps love is merely a trap, a pleasant trap sometimes, I grant you, but still a biological trap."

"If you could find somebody, Cole, I think your attitude would change." Bud tried not to sound smug.

Cole waited, weighing his words. "I'd rather not be in love; it hurts too much."

"And I want to be in love; it gives me a reason to be alive."

"Could it be that we 'fall in love' not out of any miraculous combination of two unique individuals, but only because we *want* to give meaning to our driveling lives. We deceive ourselves into love."

"If so, then it's a needed deception."

"I'd rather live with nobody than think that I lied to myself."

"Isn't it better to be happily deceived than miserably clear-headed?"

"Is that why you're marrying Cathy?"

"That's not fair, Cole!"

"Or is it so that you can reap the social privileges that come from sticking your apparatus in the acceptable orifice?"

"I suspect that your view is biased, Cole," he said, maintaining control.

"I suspect that you are not facing the reality in yourself."

Bud paused. "I don't believe that's true."

"Are you *convinced* it's not?" The blush had returned to Bud's skin, but before he could reply, a scowling Cathy-Lynn got up from the sofa and came toward them.

"Are you going to leave me alone all night long?" she challenged Bud.

"I've only been away a few minutes, honey."

"Well, I think you're being thoughtless if you want to know."

"We're thinking of you every minute, Cathy-Lynn, if that's a comfort," Cole said.

"It was very nice meeting you, Mr.—. But really, honey, I'd like to get to know some of the other people."

"Some of the real people, the good, wholesome folk?" Cole could not restrain the sarcasm.

"Please, darling!" Cathy-Lynn reached out for his hand, and Bud shrugged at Cole in an exaggerated comic gesture.

"I understand, Bud. Captain's orders."

The girl turned toward him with a furious expression. "Will you kindly stop interfering, Mr. What's-your-name! Bud can choose whatever freakish acquaintances he sees fit to, but I don't have to subject myself to them."

"I'll see you later," Bud interrupted, and took her away by the arm. Their contesting voices rose as they crossed the room, and the girl petulantly pulled her arm from Bud's grasp.

To quiet his anger, Cole walked over to the bar and poured

himself half a glass of Vodka, then swallowed a large gulp, waiting for the liquor to stun the brain.

"How are you managing?" Angie asked him from the rear.

"Fine, Doctor," he answered loudly, turning to face her.

"Is something the matter with Bud's fiancée?"

"Her—that sweet thing? Rather high-strung girl. I almost tripped over her in fact. She'll make some man a good husband."

"Come over with me. We're about to play charades."

"I'm not very good at games."

"Come on, be a good sport. Come on!" she encouraged with a wave of her fingers.

"Oh, what the hell. Why not!" he responded. "What have I got to lose?" He followed her to where the others, fifteen he thought, were gathering. Madeline was arranging some chairs on one side of the recreation room to face the long second couch. More introductions had to be given, until all had been formally presented to each other. *So that hereafter we can play games together. How strange!* A man passed out slips of paper with X's and O's to determine teams, and Cole and Bud turned out to be partners, with Cathy-Lynn and Angie on the other side. Once Cole looked at Bud's fiancée, who gave him a brittle, superior smile. He pretended he had a hat on and tipped it toward her.

"I'm sorry, Cole," Bud said, unable to meet his eye as he came near.

"Forget it. Let's be merry. Why not even gay, eh? Their hearts were young and gay, a fine old phrase."

"Come on, teammates," Guy called out to Cole's team, and the group gathered at one side of the large room.

"I'd rather play the game where you pass the orange from person to person with your head and shoulders," one of the men suggested.

"Maybe later," Guy said, and some of the others nodded.

"Now let's get some good titles," one of the girls said.

"How about *Principles of Psychology* by William James?"

They agreed with Guy's suggestion, and he wrote it down on a slip of paper.

"How about *The Pooh Perplex?*" Madeline offered.

"That's got a proper name in it." Guy shouted to the other team across the room. "Hey, no proper names, okay?"

"Right!"

He returned to their confidential whisper, and Cole watched Bud, who seemed to refuse to look at him. "How are you doing?" he asked gently.

The answer was a wan grin.

What should I say to you? Do you possibly want me, or am I merely flattering my ego?

"How about *The Sound of Music?*"

Guy wrote that one down too; Cole was surprised at the energy expended in getting ready. Other titles were suggested and written down, but neither Cole nor Bud participated, standing silently next to each other.

"Come on, Bud, what's wrong? Give us one," someone encouraged.

"I can't think—how about *Love Is a Many-Splendored Thing?*"

"Good!" Guy put it down without consulting the rest.

"Let's get a few sexy ones, what do you say?" a man put in. "Like *Seduced and Abandoned.*" The name was put on the list.

"How about *Naked Came the Stranger?*" Cole added, thinking that it would be good if Cathy-Lynn had to act out that one.

"Fine with me!" Guy responded, and the others seemed to agree.

"Are you set yet?" someone from the other team yelled.

"Hey, that makes eight," Guy said to his group and called back, "We're ready whenever you are."

After more whispers, they dispersed to their seats, and Bud went over to Cathy-Lynn, telling her something. She shook her head no, and he reluctantly returned to a seat, next to Cole. "Why don't you say something?" Cole asked.

"What should I say, buddy?"

I should have left you alone, shouldn't I? I should have let your mind stay where it was. But I'll lose you entirely, I know that, if you marry that girl; she'll never consent to having me as a friend; she'll always suspect you with me. And why should I have to step aside and surrender you? Why shouldn't I fight for what I want just like anybody else?

"All set?" Angie, who had agreed to be the timekeeper, inquired. Because her team preferred to go first, Maxine, whom he had known slightly, selected a piece of paper from the bowl that Cole's team had filled.

When she had the title in mind, Cole's team wanted to see the slip, to enjoy her contortions fully, and passed it down the line. But the girl was bad at the game, throwing her arms out in inappropriate and imperceptive attempts to communicate *The Tempest*. Once she started to make a wind noise, but the opponents hooted her into silence. Her awkwardness made Cole squirm, and he was struck by the ineffectiveness of everything she tried. She was too self-conscious and dropped her hands in front of her from time to time, giving up, letting the seconds run out while she tried to think of something to do. *No, I won't be the same*, Cole insisted to himself. *I won't wave my arms about and let my time add up to nothing. Here I am halfway to my death—all of us are—and I sit passively waiting, hoping that Bud will read my mind. Why? Why do I have to?* The woman leaped into the air foolishly, to convey wildness, he imagined, and he thought of her body. *Filled with half-digested food, sustenance, nourishment—for what reason? The body converting all of it into energy to move us around—and to where? In a few hours it turns into excrement. How bizarre that all of us are carrying excrement around with us, even at this moment; in fact, we're never free of it. Even lovers throwing their impassioned bodies upon each other cannot escape the refuse inside them.* Cole felt no disgust at the reflection, only a delicate, vapory melancholy. *Yes, I'm dying; the hopeless fact of life—I'm dying.* He turned and stared at Bud's profile chiseled out of the heat of the room. *I don't want to die alone*, he thought in a panic. *No, not alone!*

"You should have done something else, Maxine," one of her

teammates called out when the time ran out without their getting either word of the title.

"Well, I didn't know!"

The man with the goatee, sitting on the other side of Cole, leaned over to say, "But she knows how to shake those boobs, though, doesn't she?"

"Our team's next," one of the girls said, grabbing the bowl. "You go, honey," she said to the man next to her, but he did not want to. "Bud? How about it?"

"Sure, I'll go." He threw himself into the game with gusto, pantomiming the operation of a movie camera.

"It's a movie."

At first he tried a sound-alike, by flexing his muscles, but when no one gave the right response, he made a circle with a finger and thumb and ran his other index finger in and out of it, provoking lots of sputters and noisy laughs.

"Hole?" Guy asked, leering.

Bud shook his head no.

"Intercourse!" tittered one of the girls.

"Sex," Cole said flatly, and Bud was forced to point to him.

"Sex, huh!—well, that's a good start," Guy joked.

Holding up five fingers, Bud began to stride across the room, swaying his hips.

The crowd snorted, and someone shouted: "Queer!"

"Queer sex!" Cathy-Lynn called out, even though it was not her team's turn, and when Cole made himself look into her eyes, he saw her contempt for him. For an instant he caught Angie riveting her gaze on him, but she looked down when she saw him notice.

"No, no," Bud replied.

"You're not supposed to talk—just go about your charade. Give us that walk again; it's a lulu." But he refused, losing his nerve, and instead pointed at three girls around the room.

"Women?"

"Is it *Sex, Women, and Wine*? Wasn't that a movie?" a man asked, almost giddy.

"Is that supposed to be women or girls?" someone asked.

"Girl," Cole said, and Bud came toward him nodding.

"*Sex Girl?*" Guy said doubtfully. "Never heard of her, although I'm all for it."

Bud held up five fingers again.

"*Five Sex Girls—Five Sexy Girls?* Bring 'em on!" Guy jumped up pretending to look for them.

"Oh, Guy!" his date exclaimed.

"*Sex and Five Girls*—is that what we've got so far? Well, what more do we need, eh, fellows!" he said to the room.

"Your time's running out," Angie said, holding up her watch.

Bud tried one more word—the fourth one—by gesturing that he wore a wedding ring and then pretending to take it off.

"Married?" someone suggested.

"Not married," Cole said, and Bud nodded to him.

"Single, Divorced, Single—I see," Guy said. "*Sex and the Single Girl?* Hey, I got it!" he thundered.

"How long, Angie?" Bud asked.

"One minute and thirty-one seconds." The players buzzed amiably, chatting about the things they had almost thought of, while Bud took his seat again.

"You had no trouble with '*Single*' did you?" Cole said softly.

"Not much, no."

"It was the '*Sex*' that gave you the problem, right?"

Bud looked directly at Cole. "A bit."

Cathy-Lynn agreed to be next, and Cole smirked when he saw the piece of paper, for she had actually selected *Naked Came the Stranger*. But she did not seem to be perturbed. Instead, as soon as she was given the signal, she began to pantomime a strip-tease, discarding her imaginary clothes in all directions, several times moving in front of Bud and winking.

"*Nude Descending a Staircase!*"

She shook her head, and then pretended to step out of her panties, affecting modesty by placing her arms over her breasts and loins.

"Who cares what the title is," Guy said. "Kiss me!"

Everyone laughed, and the girl casually lifted first one arm above her head, then the other. Contrary to what Cole had hoped, he, not Cathy-Lynn, was embarrassed.

"*The Naked and the Dead,*" someone yelled, and she nodded that he was partially correct. For the word "*Came*" the girl beckoned to Bud with a crooked finger, seductively.

"Pregnancy," Cole said aloud, and was jarred by the amusement it inspired.

She ignored him completely.

"*Come Naked,*" a voice contributed. "Now that's an idea!"

For "*Stranger*" she did a sound-alike, extending her hands in fright.

"Danger, granger, manger, stranger—" Cathy-Lynn grabbed the shoulder of the girl in her excitement. "*The Naked Stranger!*"

"No," Cathy said and held up four fingers.

"*The Danger of Nakedness,*" Cole heard himself say.

"Are you on this team or that one?" Cathy-Lynn spat at him. "You're interrupting me!" She turned her head and stabbed him with her eyes.

"Hurry, Cathy," Angie said, apprehensive. "The time."

She went into her strip a second time, more violently.

"Way to go, Cathy-Lynn!" Guy said, beginning to clap in a rhythm. The girl did a few bumps and grinds, smiling back at Bud.

"All she needs is a drum," Cole muttered to Bud, whose neck was covered with a blush.

"How about *Naked Came the Stranger*, the book?" somebody called out.

"That's it!" Looking very pleased with herself, she sat down on the couch among her teammates, blowing a kiss to her fiancé.

"You go next," a blond girl said to Cole, offering the bowl.

"I'm willing, although I can't promise burlesque." He meant the remark for Bud, but it carried to everyone, and there were a few uncomfortable giggles, and when he stood up slowly, the eyes examined him, particularly Cathy-Lynn's, which were like those of a viper poised to strike. He felt warm and dizzy as he faced his group. On his slip of paper *The Odd Couple* was written, and he glanced bitterly at Cathy-Lynn, wondering if she could have suggested the title. "I can play too," he said to her, not caring if she heard or not.

"Good luck," he heard her throw at his back.

"I'm ready."

Angie hesitated for several moments as if she were considering stopping the game, and the others sensed the friction in the air. "Angie?" he asked, and she finally signaled him to start.

He held up his hand. "Three-word title." He nodded.

"First word."

Cole formed a *T* with both index fingers.

"The!" Then, ignoring the rest, he directed all of his movements to Bud, pointing back and forth to himself and to the other man, drawing a bold, imaginary line between them.

"Men?" a girl asked.

"Is this the second or third word?"

Cole held up three fingers, and then drew the line again.

"*The Blank Men?*"

For a time he could not make himself move, but at last he took Bud's hand and closed it in his fist. There were loud guffaws and a barrage of jokes, everyone chattering at the same time. But Cole ignored the noise, leaning forward to Bud, who had begun to perspire, looking into his face. "You and me?" Bud asked.

"Yes, you and me."

"You're not supposed to talk!"

"What's the second word?" the bearded man insisted.

Cole reached out toward Bud, and then slapped his own hand with the free one.

"I don't get it."

"Forbidden?" Bud said quietly.

"*The Forbidden Planet?*"

"What's the last word again?"

"What have we got so far?"

Cole walked closer to Bud and kissed his own fingertips and then slowly held them toward the other man's cheek.

"I don't get it," one of the men said in exasperation.

"Cole, please!" Angie called, but he ignored her.

"Is this the second or the third word?"

"Is my time running out?" Cole asked, not bothering to check for an answer.

"*The Lovers?*" Cathy-Lynn's sarcastic voice sank into his back.

"How about *The Weirdos?*" Guy said.

"Or *The Degenerates,* huh?" someone else added.

"Right!" Cole said, angry and hurt. "*The Perverted Ones! The Son-of-a-Bitching Displaced Persons. The Sneaks!*" His words rose, quieting the others, who looked astounded.

"Cole, you're spoiling the game," Angie said, rising.

"Am I? Why should I do that?"

"Perhaps you ought to sit down for a while—your time was about gone anyway."

"I want all my time, every second of it!" He noticed the eyes sticking in him like arrows, and his shirt began to blotch with sweat.

"It wasn't *The Beautiful Couple,* was it?" Cathy-Lynn asked the crowd.

"What the hell do you know about it anyway?" he said directly to her, his mouth parched.

"I don't believe I was addressing you."

"Well, address me now—or I'll address you. Why am I not entitled to just as much as you! I'm sick of being punished and made to shut up. And, by God, I'll be damned if I'll take it anymore!"

"Cole!" Bud stuck out his arm to quiet him.

"You're acting stupid!" Cathy-Lynn accused.

"Yes, how odd of me to want someone. How depraved! How shamefully distorted and queer—Queer! Queer! Queer! I confess to it, you normal fucking bastards. How dare I express my feelings! Well, I refuse to grovel for you, and I swear to God I'm going to go on refusing!"

He stopped, surveying the alarmed faces. Bud's was violently colored, the eyes down. "I'm sorry, Bud. I'm sorry, Angie. I'll leave." With his legs shaking beneath him, he headed for the front door, then turned back. "Now you can all play that game where you pass the obscene orange between your bodies. Why not use your legs this time! Why all the pretense? Have a happy, normal time, I beg you!"

Cole slammed the door behind him, and halfway down the block he looked back, to see Angie and Bud staring motionless at him from the partly opened door.

11

Despite the rain, the next morning Cole presented himself at Recorder's Court as he had been ordered to do when he left jail, but he was fifteen minutes late for the nine o'clock appointment. He was required to go to Room 208, to see a certain Mr. Schultz, who had been designated as his probation officer. He had never seen or heard of the man before, although he had been appointed for the "readjustment interview" that released prisoners were warned not to miss. The lobby was bustling, and when Cole ascended to the second floor, the same crowd of mothers and children that he had seen when he had come to Roy's trial was sitting in the identical places—at least the people seemed the same. *No wonder that lawyers and cops become blasé, with day after day of the same complaints, the same disordered lives, the same dumb tragedies. How can anyone care when the monotony is so overwhelming?* He hurried down the corridor to get free from their dull, sullen faces.

"Yes?" the secretary asked when he entered the proper room.

"I'm to see a Mr. Schultz."

"Have you an appointment with him?" She did not appear to care if he did.

"Yes, I do."

"Ruffner? For nine o'clock? Well, you're late, you realize!"

He stood staring at her, deciding to make no excuses.

"Why are you so late?" The secretary became domineering.

"Is Mr. Schultz able to see me now?"

"Mr. Schultz is a very busy man, who's not used to being kept waiting by people whose responsibility it is to be where they are supposed to be at the appointed time. You can't just walk in here when it pleases you."

"If Mr. Schultz is available now, I'd like to see him."

"By all rights, I ought to report you as delinquent." The woman looked up at him, plain, fifty, holding a pen in her fingers, as if she might drop it to some form and send him back to prison with her signature.

Cole waited briefly, then spoke, hating himself. "I'm very sorry I'm late. It's raining out."

The woman accepted her victory and put the pen back into its holder. "Well, have a seat, please. Over there." She pointed at three metal chairs against the wall.

"When may I see Mr. Schultz?"

"He'll be in shortly."

"He's out?"

"He doesn't sit around waiting for you to come wandering in when you please."

She dismissed him by shuffling through some papers, and he sat down in one of the metal chairs, wondering, *Have I made a serious mistake in coming late? Can the man really send in an unfavorable report? What can they do to me?* His chest pained him as he tried to breathe. To distract himself, he picked up a copy of the *Reader's Digest* and flipped the pages, but nothing focused. He looked again at the secretary, who was typing a letter, apparently unaware of his presence. He wanted to hate the woman, but he could not rouse any emotion, having expended himself the previous night, raging even in his dreams, he suspected, from the way his body felt cramped, exhausted. A flicker of the faces at the party invaded his mind. *I've lost everybody*, he thought. *Poor Angie! And Bud probably despises me now.* The realization that he was just a few blocks away from where they both worked slipped into his consciousness.

"Good morning, Eva," a burly man with a brush cut entered the room.

"Good morning, Mr. Schultz."

Because of the greeting and the fact that the man wore his raincoat, Cole was positive that he had just arrived, and he gave the secretary a brutal glance, but she ignored him, going into the next room after her boss. Not for several minutes did she return, and even then she said nothing to Cole, who flipped impatiently through the *Reader's Digest* again, his eye lighting on an article about how to make one's sex life more meaningful.

After a few more minutes, the secretary came a few steps closer and said, "Mr. Schultz will see you now." Cole decided not to flatter her with a sneer, and merely went into the office, which was small and cluttered with dusty books. A bowling trophy sat on top of a bookcase.

"How do you do, Cole?" the man said, extending his hand. "Sit down, won't you?"

He wore a bow tie, a bright green one, with his checkered suit, and there were some gray hairs in the brush cut. "So how have you been getting along since your release? All right?"

"Fine." Cole spoke with an animation that he did not feel because he knew that was what the probation officer wanted to hear.

"Do you have a job yet?"

"I have a good chance for one; I'm going to see about it quite soon."

"Where is it? Cigarette?" He held out a pack.

"No, thanks. It's as an artist with a commercial firm."

"Well, that sounds excellent, Cole. By the way, I'm Will Schultz." He shook Cole's hand with a firm grip. "How strong is this job?"

"Pretty good," Cole lied.

"I'm certainly pleased to hear about it. How are other things? Any problems?" He lit himself a cigarette and took a long drag.

"Not really."

"You should have notified the police department of your new address, you know! Did you forget?"

"Yes, I forgot."

"Well, we can settle that right now." He pulled a form out of his desk and placed it in front of him. "Where is your apartment, or whatever?" He poised the pen.

"My whatever is on Geneva—457 Geneva—in Highland Park."

The man grinned broadly, and Cole asked himself how he could hate this man, who was trying to be friendly; he was controlling his life, but he was trying to be friendly. He put the paper aside. "Has the readjustment to ordinary life been hard on you?"

"Not as hard as the adjustment to being in jail was."

The man let the remark sink in without committing himself. "Sometimes fellows like you find the going a bit rough at first, but they settle down eventually."

"Are they happy when they settle down?"

The man looked surprised for a moment. "Yes, I believe so. They very seldom are repeaters—I mean here in court."

"That must be easier for the records-keepers."

"They see that being discreet pays off in the long-run." The voice was meant to press down on the listener.

"Are you happy, Mr. Schultz?" Cole asked suddenly, truly curious.

"Happy? I certainly am."

"Why?"

"Why?" He began a laugh, but thought better of it. "Because I have everything I ever hoped for—a lovely family, a fine wife, a respectable position, friends."

"And I'm supposed to want those things as well, is that the point of all this?"

"We here only want you to fit into society as a whole, not to butt your head against a stone wall. The greatest rewards in living no doubt come from such things."

"No doubt."

The other man caught the muted irony in Cole's voice. "Have you some relatives of your own, Cole?"

"I have a father and a brother."

"Do you see them often?"

"No, not often."

"You ought to. They can make this transition period less of an ordeal. The warmth of a family just can't be duplicated in any other way." He looked sincerely at Cole.

"I'll think about it, Mr. Schultz."

"Here's a picture of my family, Cole," he said, turning a large photograph around so that he could see it. "That's my wife." He put his finger near a woman about forty-five wearing glasses, a woman with regular features, dark hair, typical of thousands of women Cole had seen in supermarkets and stores doing their shopping. "And this is my oldest girl, Melody. She's starting junior college at the end of this month. She plays the piano, has had some recitals in fact." Cole's attention fell on the girl, who was a younger version of her mother, neither ugly nor beautiful, a crowd-filling face. Melody Schultz. He nodded at the man. "And that's Will, Jr., and Bobby, he's ten, and Kim, who is twelve. I couldn't ask for a nicer family." He smiled fondly at the photograph.

"And you're really happy?"

"Yes, Cole, I really am."

"Or do you just call having what you have being happy?"

"I don't understand."

"Isn't there more than one form of happiness?"

"Don't you want to have a family, Cole, people who love you, love you because you are *you?*"

"I suppose—but are the members of a family the ones who love you for *yourself?* It seems to me they love you because you fit into a certain category, Son B loves Father B because it is part of the pattern. Is that so personal?"

"You've intellectualized it far too much, I'm sure. It doesn't work like that."

"Wouldn't you love your Melody just as intensely as you do now even if she were an entirely different being?"

"Yes, I love her because she is mine—out of my own flesh and blood."

"That seems an impersonal, tainted sort of love, I'm sorry."

"You homosexuals ought not to make such value judgments," Schultz said with a tinge of pique. "Your perspectives tend to be distorted."

"I'm sorry about that too," Cole stopped himself from going further lest he say too much.

"I'm certain, Mr.—" Schultz glanced down at a paper on his desk. "Mr. Ruffer, that you would be much better off if you found someone and settled down."

"With a man or a woman?"

"I realize your tastes are different, though you ought to at least try it with a nice, young girl. Who knows, maybe you'd enjoy it more!"

"Who knows."

"Your life is in danger of morally running downhill otherwise."

"Is there a moral obligation to be ordinary? What if some of us don't fit our square pegs into the round holes. Are we condemned to weep and gnash our teeth?"

"You should learn one lesson, Cole." The man bent forward confidentially. "The blade of grass that sticks out is the one that gets cut down first. I'm telling you only for your own good." He tapped his cigarette at Cole for emphasis.

"Am I a threat to society? I'm hardly likely to perpetuate my species."

"By spreading your sexual activities around indiscriminately, you run the grave risk of nullifying all feeling."

"Which textbook did you read that in, Mr. Schultz?"

The probation officer flicked an ash methodically, determining the right phrase to use. "You can't mean to tell me that you think promiscuous sex is better than sex in love."

"Not better necessarily. Only different—with rewards of its own."

"But if you could find someone to love, you would learn how much *more* the experience was meant to be."

"Mr. Schultz, to fall in love on cue is more difficult than some people suspect, as I've had occasion to discover."

"Are you looking in the proper areas?"

"Like what—dances, young people's clubs? I don't relish butting in where I don't belong."

"A sound society stands or falls on its family structure, Mr. Ruffer. When that is destroyed, the rest of the civilization collapses."

"Is there a danger that the occasional drop-outs, like me, will destroy the system? Why can't society leave *us* alone?"

"You're under the mistaken notion that you're persecuted. On the contrary, society has become remarkably tolerant of deviant behaviors. But when you flaunt contemporary notions of decency by frequenting parks and the like—well, what can you expect?"

"I can expect the police to protect people, not for them to stick their puritanical noses into my 'deviant' sex life." Cole knew he was growing too angry, that he was not speaking deferentially enough, but he could not restrain the words.

"Even if you could settle down with a man of your own persuasion, you would be making a reasonably healthy adjustment. Society is not unreasonable."

"I see—the secret is to learn to curtail one's passions, to center them, to let them explode in a small space. Or suffer the consequences."

"Lots of men like you have found great satisfaction in the mutual respect and attraction of a partner."

"Even if I found somebody, Mr. Schultz, I wouldn't want to devote my sex life to him exclusively; I'm not made that way."

He paused. "Perhaps you lack a certain essential maturity."

"That's only a word used to frighten us into behaving. I think it's likely that your so-called maturity is merely lack of opportunity."

"Could you not be refusing to admit your inability to form a permanent relationship?" He puffed smoke at Cole as though to punctuate his point.

"Permanence is overrated."

"Homosexuals are promiscuous because they can't tolerate the responsibilities of a truly intimate union."

"Heterosexuals have to marry in order to get it regular."

Schultz swallowed a smile, pushing himself back in his swivel chair. "I wonder if you have ever considered taking measures to control this excessive self-indulgence, Cole? There are procedures nowadays that have helped a great many men such as yourself."

Cole sat up straight, believing for a second that the secretary was about to run in and bore a hole through his ear and insert an identification tag. "What sort of procedures?"

"Some doctors have worked out some very sensible means for restraining the sexual appetites when they get out of hand—so to speak." He laughed at his little obscenity. "Seriously, they have discovered how to snip a few tubes and things—or give injections—I'm not certain of all the details—so that one's desires —that way—are not so overpowering. One doesn't even miss the . . . indeed men are grateful at the new sense of relaxation they feel."

Cole stared for a long while at the man, unbelieving. "How thoughtful," he said at last.

"And they've been very successful with positive and negative reinforcements to insure acceptable behaviors. There have been some amazing transformations and suitable realignments of aberrant patterns." The man crushed his cigarette deftly in the ashtray, squinting from the acrid smoke in the small room.

"Is that a threat?" Cole listened to his own voice as if he were an observer.

"Of course not. But two- and three-time offenders indicate to the court that no progress is being made. Our duty is rehabilitation, not just punishment."

Cole forced the words out one by one. "I don't want to be changed—altered; I want *society* to change its attitude."

"Well, Mr. Ruffer," came the brief, amused retort, "that

hardly appears likely, does it? After all, it's Johnny who's out of step."

"And all this means—that you'll use electric shocks to get me to do what you want?"

"Oh, no, no, no, Cole, nothing painful. They simply reward you for social behaviors and refuse to reward you for antisocial ones."

"I see . . . I'll get a piece of sugar if I'm obedient, if I love in tempo—one, two, three—screw—one, two, three—screw. Do I get a special bonus if I spawn?"

"Of course you're twisting the significance of the whole thing; the treatment is meant entirely for the good, the well-being of the individual. No one's trying to ruin any lives, only remedy them."

"Did it ever occur to you that maybe homosexuals are necessary as they are? There are artists and writers in the thousands who wouldn't be creative if they were 'processed' by your scientists. What the fucking world needs is more mixture of the masculine and the feminine in each person! Who says that your neat, separate divisions are better! Better for what, for whom?"

"Exactly what art have you produced, Mr. Ruffer?"

"As much as you have, Mr. Schultz. As much as you have! I'll call my second-rate drawings my 'Melody Schultz,' my beautiful 'Melody Schultz.'"

"I don't see what my daughter has to do with this."

"If we have to justify ourselves for being alive, God help us all."

"Some men have willingly agreed to the reinforcement treatment, in an effort to help themselves. As a matter of fact, I don't see why someone would object, since behaviors are determined by early training anyway. It's really just a matter of learning newer, normal roles."

Cole realized that he must restrain himself. "Since I'm just a bundle of behaviors anyway, why not let me cling to the ones I know?"

"But, Cole, what if everybody started to feel that way? Suppose everybody wished to go off in his or her own particular direction? Where would it lead?"

"Of course to chaos. If a single one escapes the patterns of the rest, then he endangers the whole; it's mathematically clear-minded."

"What if some want to molest children, or inflict pain on others? Should society let them?"

"Stop confusing me with all of the others. Homosexuals are not child-molesters. And if someone wants to inflict pain, what concern is it of society as long as the other party doesn't object?"

"Ah, but there's the rub, my friend. Aberrant individuals do not always choose the suitable partners, even within their particular perversions."

"Well, then bother those that don't. Leave the rest of us alone."

Schultz shook his head rapidly in disgust, lighting another cigarette. "Obstinacy never accomplishes what you think."

"Well, I won't give up my soul without a fight, no matter what shape you think it's in."

"My advice—in all sincerity—to you is *not* to get picked up again by the vice squad." The threat hung between them like a spear.

"I'm not planning to."

"Good, very sensible." The man grinned, revealing his regular, white teeth, probably false, Cole imagined.

He squinted harshly—a long glazed stare—at Schultz:

Cole rose from his seat and went over to the probation officer, who looked up in alarm. "What do you want?" he asked.

"Why don't you admit your true feelings?" Cole said, stroking the man's cheek. "You've repressed yourself for too long." He ran his fingers inside the man's shirt, rippling the chest hair.

"What are you doing to me?" the man protested feebly, beginning to perspire.

"Just bringing you out, that's all. How do you know you won't like men better than women?"

"Leave me alone." The man jumped up from the desk and backed away, up to the bookcase, seizing his bowling trophy to hold before him. "What would people say—my secretary!"

"Forget them. Be your true self." Cole put his hands around the man's waist and slid them up and down. "Think of it as learning a new behavior."

"Stop it, please." But his breath was growing heavier.

"Just turn around; you'll like it. I promise. It's a positive reinforcement, that's all."

"No, no, not that!" But Cole already had unfastened the belt and had begun to penetrate the rectum, slowly.

"How is it? You like it, don't you?"

"Oh, yes, it's marvelous. Give it to me." The probation officer thrust his body back against Cole's, sighing with pleasure.

"It's not such a bad kind of behavioral pattern, is it?"

"I never knew," Schultz breathed. "It's wonderful!"

Cole thrust several times, thinking of the syphilis germs that he was inserting into the probation officer, drawing out the intercourse, deliberately, rhythmically, making sure that the devastating little spirochetes had time to spiral into the other's skin, spread their domain into the dark, moist recesses where they would not be noticed, or perhaps only after it was too late.

"Don't you?" Schultz's voice was saying.

Cole startled himself into concentrating on the man's puzzled expression across the desk. "Don't I?"

"Don't you think you ought to schedule another meeting with me?"

"If you want me to."

"It'd be for your benefit, I believe."

"By all means let's do what's for my benefit."

"You seem distracted? Don't you feel well?"

"I guess my visit here has been upsetting."

"Would you like something—a glass of water or something?"

"A glass of water? Your kindness is limitless, Mr. Schultz. But no thank you. I'll be fine."

"You're sure?"

"When do you want me to come again?"

"What about two weeks from today; your job should be firmed up by then and . . ."

"True. Maybe I'll even be married by then. If I am, I'll try to bring a photograph."

Schultz decided to treat it as a jest. "Well, you needn't rush it that much." He stood up behind the desk and extended his hand. "I hope our little get-together proves useful. After all, as a public servant, I'm just here to aid you."

"Naturally," Cole replied, letting go of the handshake.

"Oh, yes! I almost forgot!" Schultz went to a file and slid open a drawer, pulling out an envelope. "You received this letter about a week ago. We would have forwarded it to you, but, you see, you didn't send us your address."

"My loss," Cole took the letter and turned it over, reading his brother's return address across the flap. *Why would Edwin write to me?* "Do you mind if I open it here?"

"Go ahead, although I do have another appointment shortly."

"I'll read it in the next room."

As Cole started to leave, Schultz grabbed the form. "Let's see now—is everything set? I did get your new address—right? And you're coming to see me two weeks from today, same time?"

Cole nodded, feeling the weight of the letter in his hand.

"I do hope you will be prudent, Mr. Ruffer—for your own sake."

"My name is *Ruffner*, incidentally. Not that it matters, much."

"Sorry, Mr. Ruffner, of course; it's written down here right in front of me. Good-bye, Mr. Ruffner."

"Good-bye. Tell your daughter Melody that I wish her well at her next recital."

"Why, thank you. I will."

Cole almost smiled, but simply nodded once, turning toward the door.

"Just a final word," he said, coming closer to see him out.

"Remember that the seashell that lies flat doesn't get pounded by the sea."

"Yes, you've made your point, sir." And with that, Cole walked to the next room, where another young man was sitting in one of the metal chairs.

"Come in, Bob, won't you?" Schultz said heartily to the young man as Cole went out into the hall before the secretary could say anything. He tried to find a spot under a stairwell. Distressed, he unsealed the envelope and slid out the letter, which read:

> Dear Cole,
>
> Hope this finds you well. I didn't know as I should write to you on account of everything that's happened. But since Pa is your Pa to, I figure you ought to know. Pa is terrible sick and in bed. We tried to get him to the hospital, but you know him—so stubborn. He won't budge. A few days ago he had a real bad spell. Doctor says its his lungs, but maybe its cancer and he's not telling us. I don't know. I asked him if he wanted me to write you so you could visit him, but Pa never answered me. I can't read his mind, so could be he would like to see you again. He's in bed at home, but Eunice and me go over at least once a day. If you are out of jail and you want to, maybe you could come and visit him, cheer him up—I don't know. I just don't want Pa to die and you not to know.
>
> Your brother,
> Edwin
>
> P.S. Eunice, me, and the kids is eating regular and hope you are to.

The letter was ten days old, Cole noticed, and he felt his hand quiver as he read through the message again. *So my father is ill or maybe dead by this time. So why should that concern me; I hardly know the man. Or perhaps he's recovered and I would be an embarrassment if I came now. Didn't answer even. What am I to make of that? Why do I have to be involved with people at all? It's nothing but pain, nothing but stupid pain.* Cole crumpled the letter in his fist and threw it into an ashtray filled with sand. Then he walked down the corridor between the waiting, tired-looking families, trying not to see them.

12

~~~~~~~~~~

However, the image of his father would not vanish, and Cole sat down when he arrived home, to write a letter to Edwin, to find out if his father was still sick, if possibly he might want to see him. While licking the envelope, he cut his tongue, a sharp, swift slice that he knew would last for a long time. He put the letter on the kitchen table, uncertain whether he would mail it. After staring at it for several minutes, he went to the bedroom and started to pack his suitcase. He would take a Greyhound bus and be in Toledo in several hours. *And what will happen then?* His heart quickened at the prospect, but he was unable to untangle his feelings. *Should I call? What if he hung up on me? If I go there, he wouldn't chase me out. Maybe his sickness has made him softer.* Cole went back to the kitchen table, picking up the envelope. *I ought to send a telegram*, he suddenly realized. *My cut was for no reason*, he thought, touching it with a fingertip.

As he was working out the telegram's message, his telephone rang. He leaped to it, certain it was his brother calling to say that his father was dead. "Hello?"

"Cole?"

"Edwin, is that you?"

"No," the unfamiliar voice answered.

"Who is it?"

"It's Bud." Before Cole could respond, he hurried on. "I

thought I ought to get in touch with you—you know, check you out, so to speak. How are you?"

Cole's breath caught in his throat, but he managed to imitate calm. "I'm well, Bud . . . I'm sorry about the party."

"Oh, that . . ."

"Perhaps, though, you all continued anyway."

"We stayed around a little longer, but then Cathy and I left. I think the others stayed."

"How is Angie?"

"She's a strong girl."

"I know. I guess that's what I wanted from her. So you're still speaking to me?"

"Yes . . . certainly." Bud made some blustering noises at the other end.

"You're braver than I am."

"In fact I'd like to meet with you, Cole. I've been thinking a lot, all night in fact. I called earlier, but there was no answer."

"I had to see my probation officer; we criminals have so many commitments."

"Would you be free this afternoon anytime? Perhaps we could play tennis, you know—and talk."

Cole wanted to ask what the call really meant, was Bud telling him something else? "You can't tell me on the phone?"

"I just . . . it would be better if we met."

"Will Cathy-Lynn be there too?"

Bud waited a second. "She and I had a rather lengthy fight last night, as a matter of fact."

"About the way I made a fool of myself?"

"Oh, a lot of different things."

"And what conclusions did you arrive at?"

"Actually, I'm not at all clear. We agreed not to see each other for a week or ten days, to let things settle."

"Am I to fill in the interim?" Cole attempted to make it a joke.

"No, it's just . . . I think we should talk about some mat-

ters, if you really meant . . . what you said at the party. If you
don't want to . . ."

"Where do you want to meet? What time?"

"Is an hour too soon?"

"That's fine. I don't have a tennis racket, though."

"I've got two. I'll come by with my car; we can go to Palmer
Park. The exercise will be good for us anyway. Is it a deal?"

"It's a deal."

"Where do you live?"

"Four fifty-seven Geneva, in Highland Park. Turn off on
Puritan if you take Woodward."

"I'll find it."

"I guess we're set."

"Okay, then. See you in an hour. I'll honk."

Not knowing how to react, Cole put the receiver down, and
sat down trying to analyze Bud's meaning. How had Bud
sounded—not angry? No, it was more like concern, a tinge of
pensiveness perhaps.

After a time, he called the Western Union office and placed
his message to his brother: "Just got your news about Pa. Is
he still sick? Should I come there? Wire collect. Cole." He went
back into the bedroom to complete the packing, although the
operator had assured him that he would not be able to get a
return telegram for about four hours. Enough time to talk with
Bud.

As the hour came to its end, Cole reminded himself for the
twentieth time, *I must not want too much,* and ran his ragged
thumbnail over the upholstery of the chair near the window,
frowning at the dismal sky, but it had stopped raining. Even if
the tennis courts were wet, it wouldn't make the least difference to the two of them. Uneasy, with the slightest throb of a
headache, he nevertheless felt expectant, almost happy. *Yes, we
can play some tennis, then talk; we might even be like we were
before. That's sufficient. Of course I must not expect too much.
Well, what am I imagining anyway?* he smiled. *Bud is a happily*

engaged man, and I am just a friend of his, a mere intruding, minor friend.

A startled noise emerged from his mouth when he heard the honk of the car horn, even though he had opened the door to let the sound penetrate. He surveyed the apartment, feeling that he had forgotten something; he checked the gas and then stuffed the bag of apples he had taken out for lunch back in to the refrigerator, and tossed an apple core into the waste pail, remembering that the lemon tarts and butcher knife still lay inside.

Descending the steps to Bud's waiting car, he felt a tremor of panic race through him. Maybe he ought to go back upstairs, forget Bud, pretend that he was not at home. Life would be so much less complicated if it could be lived unensnared in the lives of others. Bud would be better off with a wife. Schultz was no doubt correct. He could simply turn around and go back, stay in his apartment and draw. Yet he knew that he could not do that, for he would grow fretful, his body pulling him out of the sanctuary, or if not that, then he might sink into despair, until the landlady or the police had to clean up his stubborn, spilled blood from the bathroom and lug away the cumbersome corpse. "See, I'm saving the landlady a lot of trouble," he said aloud, closing the door.

"Going my way, sir?" he asked into the car window.

"Howdy! How's Old King Cole this afternoon?"

"Rarin' to go." Cole sat next to Bud, amazed at how easily they both were pretending that they were as casual as the conversation.

"Good! Hope your tennis game is ready for a sound trouncing."

"I've heard worse threats before."

"Wait till you see my backhand. Then you'll be sorry you ever agreed to this match."

"Are you going to give me the back of your hand?"

Bud grinned with his mouth closed. "I promise not to, Cole."

"Of course I haven't played in a long time."

"Excuses already?" Bud said, teasing.

"Maybe the courts will be slippery too."

"They're likely dry by this time."

"You can turn up here, to the left."

"Here's your racket," he said, pointing to the back seat.

Cole picked it up, feeling the strings. "It's a pretty good one."

"The best that money can buy."

"Does Cathy-Lynn usually use it?" They exchanged a glance.

"Cathy-Lynn has her own, something like that, a Tensor."

"So she's a tennis player, eh?"

"Better than me actually."

"Must be hard on the male ego."

"We have some excellent matches at times."

"Like last night's?"

"No, that was not one of the better ones."

"You should have invited Cathy along with us this afternoon, just the three of us."

Bud looked over. "I'll tell her next time I see her."

"When will that be, Bud?"

"I'm not certain."

"Are you interested in having dinner later?"

"Oh, I'm sorry, Cole; I made plans to see my dad and mom tonight."

Cole pressed back into the seat quietly, disappointed. "That's too bad."

"Maybe another day, eh?"

"Certainly. Besides, I'll be waiting for a telegram anyway. My father's very sick."

"That's too bad."

"Yes. Well, we still have all this tennis-time, don't forget."

"You forgot your tennis togs," Bud teased. He pointed at the khaki pants.

"You look quite nice in yours."

The man moved uncomfortably. "Brand-new, practically. If

clothes make the man, I'm all set." Cole ran his eyes down the hairy legs of the other man—muscled, reliable-looking legs.

They drove along for several minutes saying nothing; Bud read two store signs to have something to say. Then he said, "It's a shame the season's going to be over soon."

"We'll have to make the most of what we've got left, right?"

Bud nodded vaguely. "I suppose so. Yes, I suppose so."

Cole looked at Bud's face and sturdy neck, and felt light—and surprised, for why should this particular man make him feel happy? "How old are you, Bud?"

"Twenty-six."

"Twenty-six. And where will we all be when we are thirty-six? Or sixty-six?"

"I'll probably still be working at the goddamn Federal Building."

"True. And I'll be going to Mr. Schultz's office for my four-thousandth reinforcement treatment."

"Your what?"

"Are you—were you very much in love with Cathy-Lynn?"

Bud snapped his head. "I think so. Didn't I seem to be?"

"You like a certain kind of girl, don't you?"

"What type is that?"

"Oh, what should I say—strong-minded, perhaps a bit dominant."

"Dominant? That's an odd description."

"What do you two talk about when you're alone? What do real lovers say to each other?"

"We make plans. I don't know—just talk. Cole—"

"Is it sort of like the way we're talking now?"

Bud answered, embarrassed. "Sort of. But not quite."

Cole nodded. "No, not quite."

"We discuss lots of things, sure."

"A family?"

"At times. Cathy-Lynn wants to wait, though."

"Really? Do you discuss birth control?"

"We've brought it up a few times."

"You seem ashamed. Why should you be—it'll affect the rest of your entire life. If you have children, you can't decide to change your mind."

"We've considered the problem."

"Isn't Cathy-Lynn Catholic?"

"She's converting—for me."

"How many insurers of immortality do you want?"

"What do you mean?"

"How many kids?"

"Four."

"And what if she wants two?"

"Then I'll just have to worry about that when I get there."

"And you'll practice birth control even though you're a Catholic?"

"Yes, nosey. Some things have to be guided by individual conscience."

"Isn't your individual conscience created by a host of outside influences? Nobody does only what he himself wants."

Bud was serious. "I can at least control the number of children I have."

"But can you control the *wanting* of children in the first place? You'll wind up a victim of your offspring. You father them and then surrender your life in order to feed and rear them; you have to learn to care for them and then let them go; you even have to let them rebel against you so that they in turn can become fathers. Somewhere in the changeless pattern you —and your individual conscience—get lost."

Bud stared for a long time out the window before saying: "Isn't that the purpose of living, when all is said and done?"

"If it is, then there's something unbearably sad about being natural."

"What would happen to the human race if people didn't consent to have children?"

"Ay, there's the rub! But, no—they could have the children,

until a better method comes along, and let professional nurses raise them."

"But how can I carry my boy around on my shoulders if I don't raise him myself?"

"Could be he's only weighting down your shoulders, Bud."

"But the weight—he's not heavy, Father—he's my son!" Both made believe that the jest amused them.

Then Cole continued. "There's something so sorrowful in the whole process—the courting, the mating, the fertilization, the burping, the teaching, the reprimanding, the hours of caring and loving, and the chances are high that you will not produce anybody worth all the effort anyway. And then the aging, the shriveling up, the short-temper of your children at your forgetfulness, your growing senility, at last the dying, in pain, making them hate you because you require money, time, and, most of all, sympathy from them."

"You're telescoping the years rather fast."

Cole looked down into his own lap. "It's just so certain, that's all."

"Isn't it sadder yet to be alone all one's life?"

"Not necessarily *sadder*, just a different kind of sad."

"There're plenty of bright moments in those years."

"That's true of my kind of life too." He slapped one hand into the other. "I don't believe I'm typical."

"Nobody can think of all those bad aspects when he's beginning—the way I am."

"Would anybody ever begin if he could see what lies ahead?"

"When you find the right person, you'll sing a different tune, my boy."

"I don't carry a tune very well, I've found. How do people manage to get a lover and a friend and a parent all in one individual? They can only fail."

"If you love somebody completely, that makes a hell of a difference."

"Sentimentalist!"

"No, not at all. Before I fell in love with Cathy-Lynn, most days sort of dragged by. And now they go—or were going at least—too fast."

"And does she love you as much?"

"This traffic is a bitch. I think she does."

"Do you believe that out of all the possibilities in the world, just two people are meant to be together?"

"I can't say that. But love gives life a meaning, a completeness."

Cole tapped the tennis racket between his shoes, looking sideways at Bud. "Do you suppose a person can *make* another love him?"

He turned an ironic expression to Cole. "How? With a secret potion?"

"Why do we have to be in love at all! If we didn't expect it all the time, we might not care so much. You can't escape if you want to. Look!" Cole switched on the radio, which emitted a vocalist's husky song: ". . . is just despair, but I don't care. When he takes me in his arms, the world is right—all right." Cole shut it off. "See what I mean!"

Bud lowered his voice after thinking for a moment. "What you need, Cole, is someone to love you."

Cole felt his skin burst with warmth and looked directly into the blue eyes. "What I need most is to love somebody else. I'm dying to be sentimental."

Bud averted his eyes, and he pointed. "Look, there's the park. Do you see a free court?"

There were many empty ones, actually, and plenty of parking spaces. Bud parked, and then Cole stood watching him get his own racket out of the trunk. He moved steadily, as if each movement were planned: the back bent, exposing the top of the underwear, while he searched for the tennis balls. Cole wanted to reach out and straighten the shirt, a simple, familiar gesture, but his arm remained at his side.

"My balls are in here somewhere," Bud said, deliberately emphasizing the bawdiness.

"What are they doing in the trunk?"

"I keep my spares back here—in case of an emergency." He

looked up over the trunk door. "You've heard of heart transplants? Well—" He lifted a can and waved it at Cole before slamming the door closed.

"What'd you do with the old ones? Throw them out?"

"No, no, they make perfect fertilizer. Make things grow big!"

"How you Catholics talk!" Cole teased.

"You think I ought to lock my car? Lots of bad kids hang around this park."

"You decide."

Bud locked it, and they walked toward the courts across the lawn. In the daylight, Cole could see all the way to the stone monument behind the distant trees where he had been with the other men. He thought of their spilled seed on the ground and wondered, wryly, if that was why the trees grew so tall.

The courts were half-filled with many tanned, skillful players, many couples, but they found a free one easily on the far side. "Are you prepared for your humiliation?" Bud asked.

"Those who are about to die salute you."

"Well said, well said!"

Cole went to the distant court, glancing back as Bud removed his jacket; he had strong arms that knotted when he whipped the racket through the air several times like a weapon. *How brutal even this so-called sport is. Even Bud wants to crush me, to triumph over me. All the talk of conquering isn't really a jest.*

"Let's rally a little first," Bud shouted.

Cole bowed low in mockery, but then thought to himself, *No, I shouldn't have done that. The knight, remember, has been released from his vow.*

"Watch it!" Bud said, as the ball came hurtling across the net. Cole chased it to the back. How strange he felt on the court, confined to his small square, just like all of the other players scurrying around within their limiting lines. "Sorry!"

"It's all right," Cole answered. When he returned the ball, mild shocks ran up his arm, but good ones, ones that made the buried tendons and muscles come to life. It felt fine to lob the ball back and forth—it gave one the impression that he controlled things.

After about five minutes, Bud called, "Are you ready?"

"If you are!" he shouted back. "If you are," he said under his breath.

"Go ahead and serve."

Cole took his place next to the white line and raised the racket as Bud crouched forward to receive. His first serve was outside, but the second smashed past Bud. "Nice one, you son of a bitch!"

"Just a sample," he yelled back.

Bud returned the next serve, and Cole had to rush in to play the ball, sending it to the far outside, where Bud ran furiously, although too late.

"I thought you said you hadn't played," Bud complimented.

"A bit of luck." Cole himself saw that he was playing well; he had never been much competition for Bud when they had played previously.

He won the game easily, and as they passed each other to exchange sides, Bud said, "Cheater!"

"Hard loser," he answered, and they both grinned and moved on.

"Skunk game."

"Love game," Cole corrected.

As he waited for the service, he wondered if he ought to lose, on purpose, to make Bud happy, or would that make him lose respect? *Does Cathy-Lynn plan such losses?* The ball popped off the racket toward him—such violence in them, all for a game! He hit it back and watched the other man's perspiring face, the exertion evident already, determination set into the brow. When Bud rushed the ball, his body came at Cole as if to swamp him, and he pushed the shot deftly out of Cole's reach. "Got you!"

"Deep," Cole replied to Bud's questioning look after his next serve.

"Very deep?"

"Not so very."

Bud won the second game by running hard at the net, almost falling over it in fact, to score the last point, and he waved his racket in triumph above his head.

During their third game, which Cole was winning, a thin Negro man came out of the woods to his right, stopping outside the fence to watch them. Cole glanced over and bent to tie his shoelace, hoping that the man would go away. The man, in a rumpled suit, tieless, ran his finger along the wires as he edged further to the rear of the court, where he stopped, almost behind Cole. "Something wrong?" Bud asked.

Cole shook his head and threw the tennis ball into the air, but he hit it awkwardly, and Bud smashed it back, taking the point. For a few minutes, Cole tried to ignore the black man standing behind him, but there was something oppressive about the eyes staring through the openings in the fence, something forlorn. "Go away, go away," he muttered under his breath. When he missed an easy shot, he let his racket fly out of his hand toward the fence where the black man stood; he jerked his face away in fear, even though the racket had not come close to him. Up close, Cole could see that the man looked ill, from alcohol or drugs, because his eyes were bloodshot and spiritless. "What do you want?" Cole said coldly.

The man did not respond, just stared back.

"Do you want some money?"

The man merely stood in silence.

"What are you watching me for? You don't belong here."

"What's up?" Bud asked, coming closer to the net.

After a moment of hesitation, Cole turned back to his partner, approaching him. "Why don't we take a rest. After all, I haven't played in a long time. We can come back later, okay?"

"Sure, if you want. Did that guy say something to you?"

"No, he's just a drunk, I think."

"Did he bother you?"

"Very much."

"Why—because he was staring at the game?"

"He reminded me of . . . somebody."

"Maybe he just wanted to play."

"Well, he's not supposed to. Outsiders have to stay outside, don't they know that?"

Bud smiled tentatively, although Cole's tone did not encourage it. "Why don't we walk around then," he said, wiping his handkerchief across his sweating forehead. "Give me a chance to cool off and catch my breath."

As they opened the gate and stopped at the water fountain, Cole glimpsed the Negro, who had not moved from the fence. "He'll probably die there—looking from the outside in!"

"Pathetic old guy," Bud said, leaning down to the bubbling fountain.

"He needs some positive reinforcement. Why don't we walk this way?" Cole pointed in the direction of the monument.

"Okay by me. It's pleasant here, isn't it? With the trees and the ducks."

"Practically the Garden of Eden."

"Though I've read recently that kids have been roaming around here, especially after dark, beating up people and robbing them."

"Really? Even in Paradise?"

"It's getting impossible all over."

"Why would people be out here at night anyway, in the park? Sounds suspicious to me. Don't they deserve to be beaten? They should be home with their families watching television."

"Hey, that's almost what Cathy-Lynn said when I mentioned it to her."

"Cathy-Lynn is the salt of the earth."

"Yeah, she can be a sweet girl." He seemed to picture her fondly in his mind.

"You know, though, I've always wondered—how does anything ever grow in salty earth?"

Bud laughed heartily. "It's a shame you two don't get along. It's going to make it harder after we're married."

Cole turned to the other. "Don't get married then."

"Maybe I won't," Bud said, biting the tip of his tongue, causing Cole to press his own sliced tongue to the roof of his mouth and wince.

I must not say too much, Cole warned himself. *Not a second time.* "It's not easy to remove yourself from entanglements."

"There's nothing I can't get out of."

"Haven't you heard of breach-of-promise suits?"

"You're right! I'm trapped. I promised!" Bud lowered the arms that he had raised in mock surrender. "But I *am* looking forward to it."

"Sex, sex, everything is sex!"

"Yeah, isn't it great!"

"I thought we agreed you were a virgin last night."

"Maybe I was a virgin last night."

"Oh?"

"Well, I can dream, can't I?"

They followed the winding path toward the monument, passing a few old men playing cards at a picnic table, and Bud moved his tennis racket from one arm to the other nervously. "Something the matter?" Cole asked.

"We did come here to talk, didn't we?"

"If you'd like to."

He adjusted the racket again. "Some things are hard to bring up, you know?"

"I know. Like what, though?"

Bud touched his hair. "Oh, just . . . do you suppose there are such things as . . . bisexuals?"

Cole at first started to make a joke about "such things" but stopped himself. "I've heard there are."

"You . . . you don't know any?"

"No, I don't." Cole realized that Bud was asking him about himself.

"It seems strange; you don't hear much about it."

"You don't hear about a lot of things, even though they exist."

"With both men and women, it's . . . it's . . ."

"No, it's not what the good priests told you in your boyhood."

"Do you think such people are happy?"

"Happiness is a luxury."

"Do you suppose they can adjust to a mixed life like that?"

"They never know until they try." Cole did not look to see if Bud read his meaning, afraid.

"They might make a terrible mistake."

"Yes, that's a possibility."

"It must be a hard decision to come to."

Cole let his eyes slide up to Bud's face, his own feelings wrenched, longing to soothe him, but undecided about what to do. "Sooner or later they have to come to the decision," he said finally.

"But when a man has not even had sex once—not all the way —oh, this is so awful, talking like this!" Bud swung his tennis racket through the air as if practicing. "My swing's a little stiff today."

Cole would not let him change the subject. "You need other kinds of practice perhaps."

"Where do I get it, um? Look at that brat over there throwing rocks at the ducks. Somebody ought to stop him."

"He's just one of the Schultz boys, merely growing up to be properly masculine."

"The little bastard!"

"No, he's quite legitimate. The world's hope and perpetuator."

"Where's his mother?"

"He's just being perfectly normal, just a regular kid."

Bud did not reply, but pulled a leaf from one of the trees they were passing. "It's still wet. Rain gives a good smell, doesn't it?"

Cole knew the man wanted to avoid the topic; he himself was too disquieted to return to it, because he knew that he must not risk his emotions again.

"It's important how one is introduced to sex, don't you think?" Bud asked abruptly, catching him by surprise.

"Indeed."

"How did you begin, Cole?" He ran his racket across some bushes, sprinkling the waterdrops free, pretending he was only incidentally interested in the talk.

"I was sodomized by my father."

"What? You're kidding."

Cole smiled grimly. "Only half. He helped. No, actually, I let myself be picked up in the university john when I was a freshman."

"That way? And what happened?"

"It turned out to be wonderful. He was a faculty member, in chemistry, I think."

"You haven't been with a woman?"

"Only half."

"Half? Who was she?"

Cole knew that he would never tell anyone about the episode with Angie. "I forget her name."

"I haven't been with a woman either. I've always had the misfortune to know 'nice' girls."

"It *is* important how you lose your virginity. Seriously."

"You don't say, Dr. Freud! Just how should it be done?"

"I have a couple of suggestions."

"Tell me more, Doctor."

Because they were bantering, Cole could not say what he felt; moreover, he wanted to be positive about Bud. "Well, as a starter, for practice this is, you might send away for something I saw advertised in a magazine."

"What's that?" Bud grinned.

"Her name is Judy."

"What is she—dirty pictures?"

"Judy? Certainly not. She's an inflatable doll, one you blow up, actually life-size. You can take her for drives in your car, go swimming with her, take her to bed."

"Oh, you're making this up!"

"I swear I'm not. I saw it in black and white."

"What magazine?"

"I forget the name—though it wasn't the *Reader's Digest*. Some man's magazine. I saw it in the jail's library."

"Inflatable? What would anybody want with a—with a doll?"

"Probably she comes equipped with a suitable indentation, hopefully with disposable fillers."

"You mean somebody would . . . ?"

"Your crinkling nose indicates a man who has never known true loneliness. Better a Judy than nothing."

"Well, I suppose that's necessary, although rather disgusting. Maybe for really ugly people and perverts, I mean, and people like that." Bud remembered himself. "I'm sorry, Cole."

"Thanks." He even smiled.

"I didn't mean it that way, really."

"It's all right. I'm almost getting used to it."

"Would someone truly buy one of those dolls?"

"Yes," Cole went on with fake animation. "For those perverts, wherever they may be, lest they sully our dear children. For God's sake let them rut up and down on their washable, unbreakable, mateable, inflatable Judies! Heaven knows what they may do to our young ones otherwise."

"I said I was sorry," Bud said quietly.

"Don't be *sorry!* Everybody's so *sorry* all the time."

"Well, what does this thing look like?"

"Why? Thinking twice about it?"

"Come on now." His hand flew up in dismissal.

"Never know, might come in handy during those quarrels when Cathy-Lynn kicks you out of the bedroom."

"Very amusing!"

"You could come over to my apartment of course—I mean to look at my Judy. She's a real swinger. I keep her a little below 'Full.' Get better action that way."

"Will she whisper sweet things in my ear, like, 'I Wuv You'?"

"Come now, be modern, up to date. You can get different styles. Some say genteel things like, 'I like your prick inside me.' But others have a vocabulary of up to eighteen money-back dirty words, including a ten-second combination groan and orgasm."

"Yeah?" Bud said with a wide smile. "What dimensions is this babe?"

"Suit yourself. But a fifty bust is about tops."

"That'll do. Different colors of hair—redheads, blondes, and so on?"

"Certainly—with modern plastics! On the head, elsewhere too. And even the skin—Negroes, Orientals, Indians. You can buy two or three for orgies."

"Or in case she breaks?"

"Or in case she breaks! Don't have to worry about getting carried away some night, because Judy's only twelve ninety-five, not including the air pump."

Bud gave him a long, incredulous-amused look. "You're making all this up."

"I saw it with these eyes."

"It's so grotesque."

"Why call it that?" Cole dropped the joking. "I think it's honest. You never have to promise Judy you'll marry her to get her to go to bed with you. And she never says no."

Bud said meaningfully, "I don't suppose the rewards are as good either."

"Perhaps not. But probably someone is working to refine the model, getting the kinks out. Next year's model will be a wonder."

"With safety belts?"

"Sure. Padded . . . dashboard."

"Maybe with a flexible mouth too?"

Cole raised his eyebrows. "It's a real possibility."

"Do you believe a thing like that actually sells?" Bud said marveling.

"You Catholics are so old-fashioned. Why shouldn't it sell?"

"Well, it's against nature, for one thing."

"If all the semen in the world got into all the so-called proper receptacles, there wouldn't be an inch of space left on this natural planet!"

"But screwing a doll?"

"The body isn't as choosy as the mind, you know."

"Well, I'd be damned before I'd buy one of those!"

"Would you accept one as a present?"

"It's creepy."

Cole shook his head wearily. "Ah, how cruel the young are, how intolerant the healthy."

"Don't make me into a villain. I wouldn't stop anybody else from riding his babydoll, if he really wants to. But, God!"

They were walking near the evergreens, and Cole swung his racket languidly back and forth. "Well, then, let me ask you this—would you be willing to supply the doll's place for somebody who has no choice but his Judy? Would you do that?" Cole watched the path beneath him, afraid to raise his eyes.

"But I'm committed already . . . I think."

"See! People get their own Judies and they don't give an inflatable damn about what happens to others afterward."

"Am I obliged to love all the left-overs in the world?"

Cole glanced at the man's robust chest, the easy walk. "No, I suppose not."

Bud apologized with his eyes, as if he knew that he had been cruel. "After all, I don't exactly think I'd fit as well as a Judy. We're made different."

"Not so very different."

"Thanks a whole lot!"

"Is it an insult to be compared to a woman? How strange."

"Well, when you're a man!"

"Categories, categories."

"People place too much stress on sex nowadays anyway."

Cole could feel Bud pulling away mentally from him. "I'd say they don't *think* enough about it."

"I was never so confused before in my life."

"Do you want to go, leave?"

"I don't know."

"Why don't we sit down over there." Cole gestured toward a wooden bench in the midst of some trees and bushes, only a few yards away from where he had been with the others a few nights earlier. Most likely one of them had pulled the bench into the trees to wait in the obscurity of the high foliage. A person sitting there even in the daytime could see if anyone passed, but the bench could not be seen fully unless someone ventured off the path.

Bud found Cole's face when they stopped; the eyes dropped. "All right," he agreed. Cole led the way. "It's quiet in here, isn't it?" Inside the thicket the light was subdued.

"I bet it's even better at night."

Bud sat down on the bench. "Alone at last," he chuckled, letting it die.

"Welcome to my lair." Cole made his hands into claws, baring his bottom teeth.

"Shriek! Gasp! The monster has me!" Bud shrank back against the bench and lifted his arms before him like a person begging for mercy.

"Don't be afraid. This monster won't harm you—if you don't scream."

"But I feel a scream rising in my throat."

"Please! I'm just a plain, ordinary monster. People always run away from me."

Bud lowered his arms. "What do you want with me?"

"I'm not a real monster, you must understand. On the inside I'm a simple likely lad. Only I've been enchanted—by a witch."

"And what can I do to help you, likely lad?"

Cole pressed his forefinger into the center of his forehead in an exaggeration of thinking. "I don't know for sure. How *are* curses removed?" He stared deliberately into the blue eyes. "Can you help me?"

Bud lowered his head. "I read in a book one time that it's done with a kiss."

Cole felt his blood bolt, but he spoke evenly. "But wasn't that merely a fairy tale? Everybody knows *they* don't count."

Bud made himself look up. "And what happens . . . after the kiss?"

"Don't they live happily ever after?"

"It's not always so easy, I would suspect."

"Perhaps not. Yet how do you know unless you . . . try?" Cole's throat was dry.

"Isn't it possible that the kiss will turn the kisser into a monster too?"

"Monsters, even monsters, get used to each other."

"I don't know what to do, Cole. Excuse me if I'm botching this, but it's something I've never handled before, and I'm trying my hardest to be level-headed."

"Don't be so level-headed. Do you believe that you like men —no, do you like me?"

Bud rubbed his jaw, pulling at the skin. "The idea sort of singes me—inside."

"Have you never been with a man?"

He hesitated. "Yes, in college one time—but it was just kind of an accident; I didn't see him again."

"And you worry that we might be the same sort of accident?"

"My religion says that I'm in grave danger of losing my immortal soul. I don't want to do something I'll regret."

"How did you feel after that other . . . accident?"

"Disgusted with myself."

"Doesn't sound very encouraging." Cole smiled.

"But I'm attracted to you, Cole. It's hard for me to say this." He was tugging at the hair hanging over his eyes.

"And how are we to resolve the problem?"

"I don't know. I just don't know."

Cole moved a step forward, dropping his racket onto the ground. "Would you?" he said, holding out his arm. His heart seemed to open and close, once, like a fist, as he took another step. He looked around him in all directions to see if anyone was near, but there was no one. He took another step, and Bud waited, motionless. "I just want to hold you," he said at last, putting his fingers on Bud's sleeve.

"Maybe we—"

Before he finished the sentence, Cole drew him close to his body and kissed him on the mouth, hearing the rustle of their sweaters as they pressed together, Bud's arms encircling him tightly. His breath seemed to grow hotter inside his mouth, spilling forth as he squeezed Bud, who relaxed. Cole's body filled with heat, and he darted his tongue into the other's lips, but Bud drew back, turning his head away. "Not that," he said. He grabbed Cole again and pushed his body against his, but after a few moments he drew back again.

"What?"

"I can't do it. It makes me . . ."

"Let's go to my apartment."

Bud moved farther from him. "I can't! It's too awful, I can't!" His face was white, and he refused to let himself look at Cole.

"Why? What's the matter?"

"I don't feel well. This was an awful mistake. I'm not queer— I know I'm not."

Cole went nearer. "Are you frightened of being called a name?"

"This just isn't right. I tried to be blasé about it, but it's ripping me up."

"Are you certain you're not ashamed of the truth?"

"I really don't know, Cole!" he almost shouted.

"Admit it! That's all you have to do."

"I can't." He put his wrists over his face.

"What should I say? What do you want me to say? I want you, Bud. There, I spread my grubby little heart in front of you. I do want you!"

"Cole," Bud whispered, "it was a mistake."

"No, it wasn't! Don't say that! It wasn't a mistake. This is the mistake! Now! I'm not going to surrender so easily. You felt something for me, goddamn it, or you wouldn't have gone this far. And you're not going to back out because you're afraid. You want to see me groveling on my knees, is that it? Well, here!" He threw himself on the ground, grabbing Bud's thighs. "Whatever it is you feel for me, accept it. Even if it's lust, don't deny me. You're aroused, I can see that." Cole ran his palm down the front of Bud's pants. "I'll settle for affection—or lust. You don't have to love me even." His voice broke, and he put his cheek against Bud, rubbing until the cloth began to chafe his skin. When he felt Bud attempt to move, he grabbed him harder.

"No, don't go! Please! Don't leave me now!" He stared up at Bud, who was pressing the hands slowly away.

"I shouldn't have, I shouldn't have." He disengaged the clutching fingers.

"Please don't go, Bud!"

"It's wrong, it's wrong!" He broke the grasp and hurried out of sight, breaking leaves underfoot as he disappeared.

Cole bent forward onto the bench, resting his head on his cupped hands. He thought he was crying, but when he wiped his lashes, there was no moisture. "I don't even cry anymore," he said aloud. "Bud?" He believed he heard someone. "Bud?" He stood up and brushed his knees clean. But it was not Bud; it was the thin black man who had been watching him at the tennis court; he stumbled along the path, looking terrified when Cole spoke. "Have I been a good laugh? Huh?" He grabbed a handful of evergreen and yanked it loose. "I'm such a clown. What a laugh!" He took a few steps and called after the Negro hurrying from him. "Shall I meet you here tonight? How about it, huh?" He tore another handful of evergreen. "I wonder," he said to no one in particular, "I wonder if they sell an inflatable Rudy." He wanted to laugh very hard, but somehow the joke did not seem funny anymore.

13

Up behind the driver, in the first seat, Cole could watch the fields roll by, mediocre fields, he felt, that were neither colorless nor distinctive. Rather they rippled into inoffensive hillocks here and there, a tame, faint green. The Sunday passengers dozed on the bus as if they had stayed awake the previous night worrying about their journey—lolling heads bumping gently with the movement over the expressway. A mother was trying to hush her crying baby somewhere in the back, and occasional coughs spotted the silence. Through the window he noticed late-summer butterflies straggling along the sides of the road. Two gaily colored ones chased each other into the path of the Greyhound bus and were smashed against the windshield. When the driver turned on the wipers, the corpses resisted momentarily, but then were scraped free. He pushed a button to dispose of the liquid that had been their blood. *That'll teach 'em to stay in their place,* Cole said to himself. In no time there was no trace.

The man on the aisle next to him looked foreign, about thirty, with a skinny body covered with an obviously new suit. He held a paper bag on his lap with a quart bottle of beer inside, which he took swigs of, wiping the rim each time before he drank. "You want some beer?" he asked Cole fuzzily, lifting the bag. "I've got some more down here." He reached down and patted another bag.

"No thanks."

"Sure? You look pretty glum."

"No thanks."

"Lifts my spirits," he continued, taking a long swallow. "You from Detroit?" He took Cole's nod as a sign to converse. "Me, I'm from the East Side, Lycaste, but I'm going to Toledo, on account of my sister. She's real bad sick, with emphysema. You know what that is?"

"It's a disease, I believe."

"Makes the lungs get all sort of congested and grimey. She's been in the hospital six times with it already."

"That's too bad."

"She's only thirty-nine years old too. Ain't that a shame? She smokes like a chimney, though. Always has, ever since we was kids, little bitty kids. She was doing four and five packs a day until she got so bad they had to put her in an oxygen tent. Nurse caught her smoking a cigarette while she was sitting in the oxygen tent one day—how about that!"

"She seems to enjoy it."

"She knows it's killing her, but she can't break the habit. The liquor'll get you too, but at least it takes a hell of a lot longer." He toasted Cole and drank another swallow. "You headed for Toledo or someplace else?"

"Yes, Toledo." Cole paused, deciding, then added, "My father is ill; I'm going to visit him."

"That's a real pity. What's wrong with him—cancer?"

"I'm not certain. He's not a young man anymore."

"Cancer's eating up just about everybody these days. I think it's in the food we get, all them carbohydrates and stuff they put in stuff nowadays."

"I haven't seen my father in some time."

"Yeah. I ain't seen my sister in about a year. I just got over being laid up myself."

"What happened to you?"

"Got hurt in a vat at work, a brewery. Fell into about a thousand gallons of yeast, almost drowned, and wrenched my back something fierce."

Cole sensed the slight hesitation, for the expected condolence. "That's too bad."

"Yeah. I guess I gotta find a new job. I just can't haul things around no more."

"What do you plan to do?"

"Sure you won't have a drink?" He shook the bottle. "No?" He drank some himself. "Maybe I'll get a job at Ford's; I hear they're hiring."

"It must be difficult to switch jobs."

"When you got three kids especially, let me tell you! My wife, she says I ought to go back to school, and I been thinking about it. You think that's a good idea?"

"What sort of school?"

"College. I graduated high school. Maybe I could get a degree in engineering or something. I hear them engineers make real good money. I've seen some of them highfalutin college graduates working at the brewery; they ain't much, let me tell you. Half of 'em can't tell shit from Shinola. Pardon my French. Maybe, though, if I was to go back to school I could get an education and make something of myself. I ain't doing no good now. What do you think?"

Cole was sorry he had let the conversation continue, but he replied, "I don't know what to say. How long has it been since you went to school?"

"Well, I'm thirty-four now. That makes it—what?" He tried to calculate in his head, but could not arrive at a definite number. "Still, I never was much for school. Them prissy-faced teachers yakking about poetry and crap like that; I was real glad when I got out. I took all my schoolbooks the last day and ripped 'em up into little bitty pieces and threw 'em in the toilet in the john at school. Hooey, what a mess that made, water spilling everywhere; it was the most fun I ever had at school anyway."

Cole twisted his neck to see the smiling face better. He decided to be kind. "Perhaps if you brushed up on a few things, you might be able to go to college."

"Them niggers is getting all the advantages these days." He looked around cautiously after he spoke, then lowered his voice. "They'll knife you for looking the wrong way at 'em anymore. They get everything handed to 'em—just like that, you know that! My kids ain't getting no special treatment, why should the niggers? I got one's a supervisor over me now; he ain't no damn good. Only got the job because he's black. Farts around most of the time, and we're supposed to be happy for 'em. Shit!"

"I guess there isn't enough room for everybody at the top."

"Yeah, they keep guys like me squelched down where we can't get up. The politicians and the niggers work together at it."

"Is that so?" He felt more and more depressed listening to the man.

"If the people get riled up enough, then there's gonna be hell to pay, let me tell you. They ain't gonna stand for all this shittin' around."

"What'll they do?"

"They'll fix things—like tear down a few buildings, get a few of them fat-assed executives living in Bloomfield Hills and Grosse Pointe. Why ain't I living there instead?" He curled his upper lip, showing discolored teeth.

"And you'll take over their jobs?"

"Damn right! I can sit in them swivel-back chairs and sign papers. It's the man sweating over the line that does the work as it is."

Cole thought of Angie's father dragged out of his office and decapitated in the street by a bunch of men who looked like the one next to him.

"My oldest boy's got a right to some of the advantages, like I never had," the man went on, talking to himself really. "You know, I got a boy sixteen years old; he's a junior in high school. Smart as a whip. Only trouble is he's got sort of a withered arm, since he was a baby. But he reads all the time; gets real fine grades in school. It's only a real shame about that arm of his."

"Maybe he wouldn't be as good a student if he were like the others."

"Before he was born I always kind of hoped he'd make a football tackle, but he was too small and he had that withered arm of his." The man took a swig of the beer. After a brief pause, he went on. "Yeah, but I'm sure worried about my sister; her husband's no good. Left her."

"With how many children?" Cole asked.

"Five. I'm the godfather of one of them."

"Only five?"

"Yeah, one died. She could of done better than that guy she married, let me tell you. He worked only three months all the time they was together."

"I hope she gets better."

"She's had a rough life, let me tell you."

"So it seems."

"Nobody gets out of this life as easy as they get in, that's for sure. Some are lucky to leave it early, when it comes their time. Like my father. You know how he died?"

"No," Cole muttered, wanting to turn aside completely.

"It was in all the papers. Struck by a car on Kercheval. Threw him straight up in the air and he landed in the back seat—it was a convertible. Sitting up he was! He was dead, but that crazy driver was so confused he just drove around with my father in the back seat for about two hours. Let's see now, that must be about ten years ago next month." The man stared ahead, trying to remember the date more precisely.

"Excuse me," Cole said, getting up. "My legs." He pretended to stretch and walked down the aisle to get away. As he moved between the seats, he wondered if each one of the passengers was going to some dying relative or to some other horror in an everyday whirlwind. He almost wanted to laugh.

When he grew weary of standing, he returned to the seat. Fortunately, the man was dozing, the beer bottle still between his legs. Cole slipped into the seat easily and closed his own eyes at once. Against his will a picture of Bud flashed below the lids. He sucked in his lower lip, flicking the laceration on his tongue with his teeth. *Maybe he'll get in some tennis with Cathy-Lynn today. Just a fine, normal couple. Mr. Schultz would be proud of them, particularly in their white clothes. White for purity.* Cole let the image of Bud linger inside his brain, like a ball of lead—a bullet—but he could feel no emotion. He was surprised, then concluded that all of his bitterness had drained out of the opening where the ball of lead had entered, oozing away into a sink or into the ground or into his bedclothes. Falling into a semisleep himself, he was dimly grateful that the body had some way of saving the mind.

The bus drove into the terminal about noon, and Cole decided not to call first, even though Edwin had included his telephone number in the return telegram. His father would know that he was coming for the visit. He might be able to take care of him for a few weeks, relieve Edwin somehow, perhaps relieve his own frayed mind. He stepped off the bus in front of the man who had been sitting next to him. He tapped Cole. "I hope your mother gets better real quick," he said.

"Thank you." Cole hurried away from the man before he could continue.

He went into the men's room, setting his suitcase down, and at the urinals three heads turned to watch him. He looked down at some gum someone had spat into the bottom and concentrated on urinating. "We're only permitted to piss in this room," he said out loud to the other men, who look startled. "You wouldn't wish to violate the law, now." Cole walked over to wash his hands, while the three disappeared, intimidated.

Outside he hailed a taxi, keeping his suitcase beside him on the seat, for security, he guessed, and gave the address of the house he had grown up in. Toledo was an unattractive city, totally drab, even though the sun was shining. He wondered if it had always been that ugly, or had he only realized it because of comparisons with other places? Maybe there were magnificent interiors somewhere, but not one cent appeared to have been spent on reducing the dullness and the dirt.

It took fifteen minutes to arrive at his old street, which seemed about the same as the last time he had seen it, three and a half years before, except that construction work was being done at the far end of the block, a new sewer, causing a drone to rise from some machine. He sat in the cab for a few extra moments, unable to get out, staring at the dry yard with the patches of crab grass and spiked weeds. Somehow they had never been able to grow good grass there. The house needed painting, he saw. Maybe he could do that for his father while he was here. Because the cab driver became restless, at last he forced his body out of the vehicle and stepped up on the curb. The house's white paint had blistered, and in some places large segments had fallen off. Even the steps needed repair, and the forsythia bushes were threatening to block passage up to the porch. The neighbor houses waited close by for the coming winter rains and snows to attack them, as they had for all those years he had lived in this house, waited for summer and then for autumn, for change that was no change at all. He stared across the street at the Sampsons' house, where the son, nutty Jimmy, as they had called him, used to come out on the porch and stand on the swing and throw eggs at passersby. *Perhaps he still lives in that house. Or maybe Jimmy has married and started a family of his own. After all, anything is possible.*

Cole hesitated on the porch, trying to peer into a window, but the shade was drawn. He rapped on the screen door. There was no answer, and he knocked harder. He tried the knob, and the unlocked door opened a fraction. He drew his hand back, shaken, as if he were a thief caught in the act. He checked the numbers on the wall again to make certain he had the right address. Then, carefully, he pushed his way inside. "Pa?" he called out, softly, moving into the hallway. The stairs led up to the second floor, where the bedrooms were located. He touched the faded brown carpet in the center of the steps before he ascended, wondering how many times he had been up and down that carpet.

For a minute he examined his old bedroom. It looked as if no one had been in it for months—swirls of dust under the tucked-in bed. Edwin's high school graduation picture hung over the dresser, where he had placed it, years before, but there was just an oblong white mark where his own had been.

Entering the next bedroom, he stopped as if he had crashed into a wall. His father was sitting in his bed, propped up with pillows, looking directly at Cole, unmoving. "Pa?" He felt positive that he was dead, the arms loose in the lap. He moved a bit nearer, trembling, "Pa!"

"What?" the voice came out at last.

"Oh, God, I thought you were dead."

"Not yet. Maybe next week."

Cole stayed at the door, clutching at the frame. "How are you? Better?"

The man waited and then faintly shook his head, as though he knew he would never be well again.

"Can I come in?" Cole asked.

"Nobody's stopping you."

Cole tentatively moved. "I took a bus down, because Edwin thought . . ."

"So you're out of jail?"

"Yes, for over a week now."

"I'm glad. Come on in." The naturally full face had thickened grossly; the skin was glistening and unwashed and too red; the eyes had a brightness betrayed by the despair that showed in the stooped shoulders, the rumpled hair, in the sagging white flesh that was exposed through the open robe he wore. A knotted, soiled handkerchief was tied limply around his neck. Boxes of Kleenex, with used tissues scattered on the bed and floor, lay where he could reach them without having to move. Some bottles of medicine sat on a nearby night table, with more on the dresser. The television set faced the bed.

Cole put his suitcase down, and went over to his father. "Can I get you something?"

"No, you don't have to bother. Edwin and Eunice, or one of them, comes over twice a day; they know what I need."

"Well, I can get it for you, if you like." His palms were moist, and he wiped them on his pants.

The old man said nothing.

"I'll get it, Pa. What is it?"

The man refused to answer, but then he said, "I need to go to the toilet, but I'm supposed to get help."

"Well, I'll help you, Pa. I will." He came up to the edge of the bed.

"I don't need help, but the doctor thinks I might fall. I didn't need no help before. Not me!" Suddenly his father started to cry, his face twisting as he tried to stop himself. "I go all over myself sometimes, Cole. I can't help myself. Just like a baby, and I can't even stop myself." He brought his big hands up to hide his tears and sobbed.

"Pa!" Cole reached out, feeling his own eyes become wet. "What should I do? Can you lean on my shoulder? Or what?" He came close, uncomfortable, never having seen his father weep before.

"There's a pot under the bed, but I can't reach it, on account of I shoved it way from me. I'm supposed to use that when no-body's here. But I can't stand it—like hearing Eunice dump it into the toilet every day. It's awful."

"Can you walk at all?"

"Sometimes. I think I can today. Let me get my slippers." He wiped his eyes with the sheet, then threw his legs over the side of the bed and managed to put on the slippers. Cole bent down and waited for him to put his arm around his neck. It was the first time his father had touched him since he could remember. The man slapped away some more of his tears, and struggled upright. "I'm forgetting how to walk."

"I'll help you, that's all right." Cole felt the weight pull at his neck, but he guided his father from the room, helping him to the bathroom. He was afraid to ask if he should stay in the bathroom with him, but his father motioned that he could stay by himself, and Cole closed the door. In a moment, the urine splashed heavily into the bowl, and Cole blocked his ears.

The strain of standing showed in the man's face when he drew open the door. "Let me get back to the morgue," he said, without humor, leaning on his son again. He led him to the bed, where he fell awkwardly onto the sheets. "Are you okay, Pa? Did you hurt yourself?"

"No, it's nothing. Can't hurt me." He flung his body around and got under the covers, while Cole moved his hands uncertainly, not knowing how to help.

"Sit down!" his father said after a moment, sweat beading his hairline.

Cole pulled a chair closer to the bed and sat in it. "Why don't you go to a hospital, Pa?"

"Now, don't start that. Is that why Edwin got you to come down here? I'm not going to no hospital, and that's final."

"I just thought it would be better—"

"You die faster in a hospital. Every day you read about how some stupid nurse or intern left a knife or tube or something inside a patient. Well, it won't happen to me."

"But that doesn't happen all the time."

His father gave him a look that said to be quiet, the look he had almost forgotten. Ruffner grabbed the dirty handkerchief tied around him and blotted his dripping neck, adjusting a pillow at his back. "You're thinner, aren't you?"

"Somewhat."

"Well, I'm fatter, aren't I? The doctor finally took the candy away from me. Easy to do too. Like taking candy from a baby. That's all I am now, a big baby with his bib on." He yanked at the handkerchief.

"What does the doctor say about your health?"

"He don't say nothing to me. I hear him whispering to Eddie outside the room. It's my lungs mostly. Probably all that damn sawdust I've inhaled at the yard all these years."

"How *is* the lumber yard?"

"Prosperous, finally. A lot of good it does me now." He indicated his body.

"Don't you have something to read, Pa? I could get you some magazines or books."

"What do I want to learn, and what for? You can't read them in the grave."

Cole could think of nothing comforting to say, so he said nothing.

"What have you been doing with yourself since you got out?"

Cole looked up. "Not much."

"Staying out of trouble?"

"Pretty much, Pa."

The man straightened a rumple in the bedclothes.

"Do you ever hear from Marilyn?" Cole asked.

"Don't hear nothing from those anymore."

"Oh."

"You get a job yet?"

"Yes—almost."

"What kind of job?"

"Sort of in advertising. Drawing."

"Drawing? What do you mean *drawing?* Pictures?"

"Illustrations."

"I guess they call that a job nowadays. Why don't you find one where you can do some work?"

"There are different sorts of work, Pa."

"If a man isn't earning his living by lifting or moving something, he can't call it work, to my mind."

"There isn't a need for that back-breaking work anymore," Cole quarreled quietly.

"No, not for most of these punks I hire. Their idea of a good job is to do nothing for eight hours and get overtime for what they didn't do when they should have."

Cole let his father's anger die down. "How long have you been sick?"

"In bed for about a month, but I haven't been feeling right for about six or seven months."

"Do you think you'll get better here in the house?"

"If I don't, I don't, that's all! Your mother died here in this room, and I guess I can too."

Cole looked around the room, seeing a portrait of his mother and father on the dresser. "I never did know what Ma died of exactly."

"I sent you a card, didn't I?"

"Yes, but it didn't say very much." He began to pull at his fingernails.

"A coronary is what it was; she had three attacks in two days, and that was all there was to it."

"Did she suffer much?"

"No more than most." His father frowned to himself and looked away.

"I'm glad it wasn't too painful."

"She's in heaven. More than the rest of us can say."

"I hope that what happened to me . . . didn't . . ."

"You did. Broke her heart, and would have broke mine too, if I hadn't been strong."

"I'm sorry it happened."

Ruffner squinted at his son. "I'll never understand what you did, boy. Never!"

Softening the tone, he replied, "I'm not asking you to."

"I really don't want to talk about it either. I'm still ashamed to show my face to most of the family. How could you do such a nasty thing, Cole? I just don't fathom it!"

Cole dropped his gaze to the rug. "It's a long story."

"If you'd gone to church, you would have never gotten into all this trouble. But, no, you had to prove something! Had to turn away from the church because you think you know better."

"Pa, we probably shouldn't talk about it."

"Of course not; it hurts your conscience."

"No, it doesn't hurt my conscience."

"I was the reader at the mass the next Sunday after you was arrested. How do you think I felt getting up there in front of those people, reading prayers to them—me with a son in jail for . . . for God knows what!"

"I'm sorry, Pa. But you could have asked someone else to read for you."

"No, I wouldn't. *I* hadn't done nothing to be ashamed of. I went ahead because it was my responsibility. I did it too."

"We all do what we think is best for us."

"Then Wallace Billingsley comes up after mass and compliments me real fulsomelike on how well I done, and then he says it was a pity that my other boy—you—couldn't be there to hear me. I bet he had a big laugh over that; his own boy is doing so well. In fact, he won the prize for the biggest rabbit in the hunt the church sponsored. And he isn't seventeen yet."

"Good for him. Nothing like good Catholic slaughter to make a man of him."

His father looked sharply at him. "See, and all you do is make jokes about it!"

"If it's any satisfaction to you, Pa, I'm not laughing at them."

Downstairs, there was the sound of the front door opening, and someone entered. Cole swung around, then turned questioningly to his father. "It's only Eddie coming from church. He stops by on Sundays about this time. Is that you, Eddie?"

From a distance came the voice. "Are you all right?"

"Well enough."

Edwin came into the bedroom, dressed in a black suit, his hair combed with water. He had become a broad, slow-moving man, with his father's florid complexion. He stuck out his hand and approached Cole almost shyly. "Hello, how are you?"

"Not too bad. And yourself?" They shook hands as if benumbed.

"Fine." He immediately turned toward the man in the bed. "I dropped Eunice and the kids off at home before I came over, Pa. We're having some people over for dinner and she wanted to get to it."

"It's all right. Can't expect her to visit me all the time. It isn't like I was her folks."

Edwin half-nodded and looked over at Cole beside him. "So

how are you and Pa getting on?" he asked with pretended jol-
lity.

"Sit down!" the father directed. "Get a chair—that one."

Edwin dutifully carried the chair from across the room and
placed it near Cole's and sat down, trying to smile.

There was an ugly stillness in which all three were unable to
look at one another. At length, Cole said, "How's your family,
Edwin?"

He seized the opportunity gladly. "Fat and sassy. Real good!
Yeah, doing real good. Saw Reba this morning after mass," he
said to his father.

"What's she doing at our church?"

"She said she dropped by because she likes Father Schayb's
sermons better than her priest's." Cole was attentive, though not
knowing whom they were talking about.

"How was the collection this morning?"

Edwin patted his hands up and down on his knees out of nervousness. "More than a couple of thousand today."

"I wish I could have been there. Maybe I'll go next Sunday."

"Sure, Pa, if you want to."

"Maybe Cole'll go with me." He waited then for his younger
son to meet his eye.

"I'll go, Pa, if that's what you'd like."

"Can you stay the week?"

"Yes; I'd like to."

"Well, let's say it's all set then. Edwin, you won't have to
bother with me for a whole week. That ought to be a rest."

Edwin looked uncomfortable. "We don't find you a bother,
Pa."

"Not too much, I hope. No more'n *you* two were all them
years I was raising you."

Edwin's response was to pucker his lips faintly; he spied the
bottles of medicine on the dresser. "Did you take your green
medicine yet?" He rose to get the container.

"Oh, that crap! I swear the doctor's trying to poison me with that stuff. Only I know he wants to have me linger on to make his bill that much bigger."

Edwin uncapped the bottle and filled the lid and held it out to the sick man.

"Want me to get a spoon?" Cole offered, standing.

"Naw, naw, none of that!" his father protested, and for a moment Edwin looked at Cole to communicate something, and he felt a burst of warmth at the possible closeness.

"No, you don't have to take it in a spoon, Pa," he agreed, with a hint of weariness.

"Well, let's get it over with," Ruffner said, grabbing the lid and drinking the medicine. "Blagh! It still tastes like scum, I don't care what the damn doctor says."

"You're making more of a fuss than Jenny does." Edwin pretended amusement.

For a minute, Cole could not remember who Jenny was; he thought she must be one of Edwin's children.

"I know it's no fun taking care of a sick man. But I'll be dead in a year anyway."

"Oh, Pa, don't say things like that," Edwin said automatically.

"Truth's truth."

"Cole maybe can talk you into getting out of this house and into a hospital, if you really want to be cured." Edwin stood on one side of the bed, glancing at times at Cole on the other side.

"I only would like to see your mother's grave one more time, that's all. I haven't been there in months and months." He started to sigh slightly.

"We could go sometime, Pa, if you feel up to it. I'd like to," Cole offered.

"We'll do that, son," the man replied gently, affected.

"Where's your pan, Pa?" Edwin asked suddenly.

"Oh, forget about it!" Ruffner waved the back of his hand through the stale air.

"Well, you'll need it."

"No, I won't. Cole here's going to help me." He smiled at his son.

"Okay, but in case of an emergency," Edwin continued, "is it under the bed?" He bent over to see, then knelt on one knee to retrieve the bedpan. "Really, Pa!" He put it on the night table. "Somebody just has to pick it up."

"How'd you like to have one of those old piss-pots sitting next to you all day long! By the way, Eddie, I need some more Ex-lax. If you think of it, pick me up some at the drugstore."

"Are you clogged up again? If you'd tell the doctor, he'd give you something to straighten you out."

"No doctor's going to go poking around inside me."

Cole sensed that the two had had this dialogue many times previously because they uttered the words as if tired.

The words faded into a clumsy pause, and they all looked down until Ruffner asked, "So who you having over for dinner tonight?"

"Somebody and his wife from work."

"Yeah? What's Eunice fixing for supper? Something good?"

"Beef, got a nice roast at the store yesterday—three pounds. And she's making some new-fangled jello salad or some such."

"At least I haven't lost my appetite, Cole. Eddie brings me over what they have for supper in this warmer they bought. Keeps stuff real nice."

Cole realized what a nuisance that must be. "Maybe I could cook you something tonight, Pa. How would that be?"

"Well, I don't want to hurt Eunice's feelings about her cooking."

Cole could see Edwin's relief at the suggestion. "It wouldn't be any trouble; in fact, I'd like to."

"Okay, if Eddie don't mind."

"I can fix a special meal—you name it. I can go to a store and buy whatever you want. It's all right, isn't it, Edwin?"

"Maybe a change would be real good for you, Pa," he agreed.

Ruffner seemed to ponder the idea for a second before saying, "Good idea; I get kind of fed up with leftovers anyhow."

Edwin caught Cole's eye and almost shrugged. He looked back at the bedridden man. "Well, it's set then. I've got some money I'll leave to buy the things." He reached into his back pocket and slipped out his wallet.

"No, I can afford it," Cole said, gesturing away the money held out.

"Take some money out of my pants over there," their father commanded. "The blue ones."

"Really, Pa, I can pay for the food. Besides, I'll be eating here myself."

"I'll leave it here, just in case," Edwin objected, putting down a twenty on the night table.

"You're both being silly," their father protested. "I'll pay for it! Get my pants, Cole. Over there."

"I want to, Pa. Let me, okay?"

"You save your money; I can take care of it," Edwin said.

"Nobody ever said I couldn't afford to buy groceries," Ruffner continued.

"It's no hardship on me," Cole said, taking Edwin's twenty and holding it out to him.

"No, no, you keep it; you might need it."

"I'm paying, and that's settled!" the father ordered.

"Please let me do it." Something in Cole's insistence struck the other two, and they relented.

"Well, this once," Ruffner said as Edwin put the money back in his wallet. Cole smiled in relief, having won the minor battle.

"Is there anything else you want, Pa?" Edwin inquired. "Except the Ex-lax?"

"You going already?"

"I've got to be getting home. Bobby wants me to fix his bike."

"Can't he fix it himself? I think you're spoiling that boy, Eddie."

"He's a good kid, Pa."

"He's practically getting big enough to go out with the girls." His father winked at Cole.

"He's only twelve," Edwin explained to his brother.

"Twelve is plenty old enough these days. Though these kids

aren't so fast as they like to think. In my day we knew just about all there is to know about some things when we was ten—or less than that!"

"So I better go help him with that bike."

"When we was raised on the farm, we watched the roosters and the bulls, and we pretty soon caught on."

"Eunice has had a bad cold and she wants me to get her prescription refilled before I go back to the house."

"I remember one time," Ruffner went on, "when me and this neighbor girl was sitting on a fence watching the bull trying to mount one of the cows. He was having some trouble—mostly on account of size; he was just too damn big. So up he gets—"

"Maybe I should also pick up some candles for Jenny's birthday cake next week. We're out, I checked."

"—and the neighbor girl, she pokes me, wondering what the bull was trying to do to that cow, and I says as how I could learn her a whole lot down at the barn if she'd come down there with me—"

"I hate to have the kids disappointed with no candles. They get a kick out of it."

"Well, this neighbor girl looks down at my pants, and got off that fence and run like the dickens—with me right after her—"

"Billy's party wasn't as much fun as it could have been since we didn't have enough candles . . ."

Cole stared at the two men. And then they looked at each other, becoming aware that they were talking to themselves.

"So I'll drop by tomorrow after work, Pa, same as usual."

"Sure enough, Eddie. After work."

Edwin nodded. "You want the TV on before I leave?"

"Naw, me and Cole'll talk for a while."

Edwin nodded again, and moved away from the bed. "Well, so long for now," he added uncertainly at the door, and then he went out. Cole had started to rise to shake hands, but stopped, catching the awkwardness.

When they heard Edwin close the downstairs door, they settled back to talk, and Cole searched his brain for some remark.

His father broke the silence. "Eddie's been pretty good to me."

"He seems healthy and . . ."

"He's got a lovely family. Couldn't ask for nicer grandchildren."

Cole detected a tinge of a reprimand to himself in the compliment. "I'm glad you have them."

"Wouldn't mind having a few more, though."

"You'd better discuss it with Edwin then."

His father sought his eyes. "How about you, Cole? Aren't you thinking of settling down and raising a family?"

"No, Pa."

"Sure you are, one of these days. Sure!"

"There are other forms of self-expression."

"You're still young," Ruffner said.

Cole said what the other wanted to hear. "Maybe some day, sure."

"You can start fresh. Probably the time in jail washed all that other stuff out of your mind. Some men don't marry till late in life."

"And some never marry."

"It hurt me bad, Cole, when I heard you had done that. It was like a ton of bricks dropped on my heart."

"It was . . . just one of those things."

"Don't you ever think of finding somebody?"

"You can't always get what you want."

"You don't want to die and leave nobody to carry on your name, do you?"

"Most of all, Pa, I want my life while I'm living it to be my own; I want to make the most of what I am—for me now, not merely for somebody who comes after me."

"Maybe if you went to see the priest."

"I've already been to the priestess," Cole answered.

"The priest could straighten you out, I'm positive."

"The priestess almost *straightened* me out, but my spirit—or flesh—was too weak, I guess."

"What do you mean?"

"It's not important."

"Well, you've got to try at least."

"You can try just so much, and then your heart gives out. I'm going to take a rest, no emotional commitments—except to you, how's that sound? Just to you."

His father grinned. "I'm very pleased you came down to see me, son, really I am. You can move into your old bedroom, and we can get to know each other a whole lot better, because I know we never did say much to each other when you was growing up."

Cole rose, nearing the bed. "I hope we can, Pa, I hope so."

The sentiment embarrassed them both, and Ruffner stuck out his mallet of a hand. "Let's shake on it, what d'you say?"

Cole surrendered his hand to the grip. "I say it's a deal!" They laughed, but then his father turned Cole's palm over to look at it. "What are all these scars?"

Cole tried to clench his fist to hide them. "They're nothing; they don't hurt anymore."

"Who did that to you? In the jail?"

"No."

"Who then?"

"I've forgotten, Pa."

"You've forgot?" His father wrinkled his face.

"Yes, and let me go on forgetting, okay? Let me go on forgetting." He pressed his cut tongue against the roof of his mouth. "You see, you see, Pa," he said, smiling to himself, his hand within his father's hot grasp, "I won Round Two."

14

〰〰〰〰〰〰

Dear Angie,

I hope you don't hate me. I don't believe that I hurt people so much before. It is a skill I have picked up only recently. But I am trying to forget that I learned it. I seem to have bad luck, or fate or something, in connection with your parties. Perhaps I'm not the party type.

But this letter is supposed to be about you, because you deserve something infinitely better than all the trouble I have caused you. Kind and thoughtful people like you should be happy, all the time, and not saddled with selfish and moody would-be friends. I just want you to know that I apologize, fully, for everything that has occurred. Maybe someday, in a few years, we'll meet and laugh about it. Didn't we say once that all it takes is time? You are the finest woman no doubt I will ever know. I count on your generosity to accept this note in the spirit in which I send it. I wish you well; I wish you the world.

Cole

He put the letter into the envelope and addressed it to the office in the Federal Building, sealing it cautiously, using his moistened finger, to avoid another cut on his tongue. He laid the envelope to one side of his desk and read through the letter he had written to Bud.

Dear Bud,

   We are adults. At least we have the potentiality. Therefore I'm writing to tell you that I apologize for the anxiety
I caused you. Because I planted an impossible notion in
your head, I am truly sorry. I don't find these words easy
to put down, perhaps from lack of practice. But there is
no chance that I mean what I say insincerely. I was stupid
and ridiculous to try to interfere in your marriage. I hope
that by this time you and Cathy have reconciled. You will
have the happiness that you have earned. My great sadness
is that I have lost your friendship. But of course it is best
if we don't meet again. Just take this note as a feeble sign
that I apologize for bothering your life. Strangely enough,
people can manage to make something worthwhile out of
even the misfortunes.

He signed it and placed it in a second envelope, mailing it to
Bud at his office, since he did not know his home address. He
decided not to put his return address on the letters. No need to
force a reply from either Angie or Bud. He leaned back in his
chair, his shoulders heavy with tenseness. *I'll put my house in
order, I will!* he vowed. He started writing to his landlady in
Detroit, to tell her that he would be up to vacate his apartment in
a few weeks. *I'll see Mr. Schultz the same day and tell him that
I am taking care of my ailing father who needs me. And he does
need me. These three and a half days have been good for both
of us. Pa is glad for some company and talks about getting into
the sunshine before autumn ends. I'll get some work around here
and take care of him, until he recovers.*
   Finishing the third note, he rose from the desk and went over
to his bed and began to adjust the covers. Formerly he had hated
to make a bed, but today there was something comfortable in
the stretching and tugging and tucking of the cloths; he had
cleaned the dust from under it and put up his college graduation picture on the wall over the white square, having found it
in the attic in a cardboard box full of photographs. He had

spent the morning in fact looking at the pictures: hundreds of moments saved out of the past, usually stiffly posed bodies squinting into the camera, photographs of dead people and forgotten people sitting around Thanksgiving and Christmas dinner tables; picnics, with relatives holding beer bottles out toward the viewer; children having their hands waved by a mother or father or grandparent; and so many animals. Cole had displaced from his mind all of the pets that he had owned—and yet there he was squeezing a collie to his chest; a plump boy holding a stick for the spotted dog, the one that had been hit by a car; washing another, which had been stolen or run away, in a metal tub in the backyard; and cradling a kitten in his arms without even acknowledging the camera; pictures of his mother when she was a girl in Italy, a round, jolly-seeming girl with her hands caressing the forehead of the little boy, perhaps her brother, standing before her; and one of his own father sitting in a tractor, a sunburned, energetic-looking man with a wad of tobacco distending the jaw. All of them had made Cole's chest heavy until he had had to stop and put the box back into his corner.

He glanced at the graduation picture, five years old already. It was a grave, stark young man who peered from the wall, the pits of his skin flatteringly hidden by the retouching, the eyebrows subdued somehow so that they appeared trim. Cole saw that the exaggerated coloring of the lips and cheeks made him look like a painted corpse, for display. But there was a certain mockery about the mouth that made him like the image nevertheless; it made him feel the sense of anticipation that the college boy had possessed, the sense that life was just beginning, waiting to be used.

He went into his father's room to see if he wanted anything; he found him reading the *Newsweek* he had purchased for him. "Can I get you something?"

His father glanced up. "No, thanks. Say, I'm glad you bought the magazine."

"Do you feel like going out into the backyard today?"

"Tomorrow for sure."

"Promise?"

"It's a promise."

"Well, I think I'll sit on the porch for a while. Sure you don't want to?"

"You got me so interested in this magazine, I ought to stay with that for now."

"Okay, I'm just going to sketch a little."

"Why don't you show me some of them pictures you make?"

Cole smiled secretively. "The Midwest is not ready for them yet."

"What do you mean by that?"

"I'll do one today that I'll show you, Pa, all right?"

"Make it a good one!"

"I promise."

Cole carried his paper down to the back porch. The day before he had, with a ballpoint, drawn some nude figures and torn them up, not because they seemed as average as his previous work, but because his father might come across them by accident. *I think I'll go downtown for some materials after a while.*

He sat on the rear steps with his back to the screen-door, and tried to think of something his father would like. A summer rose was invading the yard from next door, and he tried a few lines, trying to capture the hesitancy of its creeping over the wooden fence. *Maybe he'll like something sentimental like that.* He finished the drawing and examined the flower. Although it was well done, it looked like a thousand pictures of roses, and he wondered if it mattered. It was to give his father pleasure, and perhaps that was what counted most, pleasing someone.

He put the sketch on the step and began to draw another, a wild dog, its muzzle baring savage rows of fangs. He worked at it for half an hour, roughening the coat of fur, trying to perfect the eyes, a particular expression of dazzled rage, as though the animal were surrounded by a pack of its own kind, about to cannibalize it. Cole transferred the image to several new pages, until a string of wild beasts lay beside him. In the sixth drawing, he felt that he had captured the mood that he had been trying for, and he was surprised, chilled at the way the practice had resulted in something satisfying. Yes, he decided, he would go later and buy some ink and do the animal again, only larger, then maybe frame it and submit it to a gallery someplace. If he was lucky, a person might be interested; he would even give it away if the new owner really desired it. There was an odd beauty, he felt, in the anguish—actual madness—in the animal's expression, but made bearable, somehow enjoyable by the composite of strokes and spaces.

Cole dropped his head onto the ham of his hand, contented, and yet itching faintly inside. Perhaps he ought to enroll in a course in an art school, or at the university. There he could improve his craftsmanship, devote himself to turning out better work. A teacher might be able to point out areas where he needed more practice, maybe in perspective or something that he himself could not see. He had nothing to lose, that was certain, and maybe he would uncover untapped ability. If he could sell some drawings, that would be more than anyone had the right to expect—and a great deal more than he deserved. The idea quivered in his mind for several minutes, a fuzzy scene of viewers standing around and admiring his sketches while he lingered in a corner eavesdropping on their appreciation. He squeezed at his cheeks to make the image disappear, lest it last too long and thus in some way be destroyed.

Suddenly there was the sound of running in the alley behind the house, and when Cole looked up he saw three Negro boys speed by the back gate; they looked about thirteen or fourteen, dressed in Levi's and cotton jackets. A few houses distant they appeared to stop running, and a man's voice called out, but not loudly. Cole sat still, unable to tell what was happening exactly. Were they playing a game of some kind? He listened, and could make out muffled noises, maybe scuffling. He got up from the steps and walked to the fence at the rear of the yard.

Down the alley the three boys were wrestling with a man

about sixty years old; two of the boys held his legs and were trying to turn him over onto his stomach, while the third boy tried to get the man's billfold from the back pocket. Cole glanced around for a weapon, for a stick, but saw nothing. He unlatched the gate and yelled at the boys, who stopped momentarily to stare at him, but when he did not advance, they continued pounding the old man. Cole picked up the lid from one of the garbage cans, and, holding it in front of him, he ran toward the sprawling group. The old man was out of breath, his face dirtied by the gravel and dust. "Get away from that man," Cole shouted at one of the teen-agers.

"You go to hell."

"Leave him alone."

"It's none of your damn business," the boy said, keeping his eyes on Cole's movements. "Get out of here and you won't get hurt."

"I'll call the police!"

"You do and we'll beat your ass."

The old man started to get up on one arm, saying, "Help me! They're stealing my money."

Cole moved closer, waving the lid back and forth, afraid that they might have knives or even guns. One of the boys stood up to face him with his arms outstretched. He leaped at Cole, who stepped aside, slamming the lid down on the boy's hip. The face winced with pain and then turned into a scowl.

"Come on," one of the others said. "We got it!"

The boy fighting Cole inched backward, and then he came hard at Cole and kicked him in the side of the leg. Cole waved the weapon through the air despite the severe pain but only grazed the boy's jacket. The other two were halfway down the alley, and finally the third raced away as well, calling back, "You white cocksucker!"

Cole's throat was on fire, and his chest heaved up and down; the old man lay on the ground, unmoving, his eyes shut. When he knelt beside him, wondering if they had stabbed him or if he had suffered a heart attack, abruptly the old man smashed his fist into Cole's ear, scooting himself across the pebbles to get away. But, looking up, he recognized Cole as the one who had assisted him. "Did I hit you?"

Cole massaged his deadened ear. "I'm trying to help you."

The old man got up feebly. "I didn't mean it. I thought you was one of them other punks coming back." He glanced fearfully down the alley in the direction they had vanished.

Cole began to rub his leg, then his ear again, both throbbing. "Did they get your wallet?"

"Yeah, I knew they would. Little bastards." The man looked dazzled, his breath still coming hard.

"Not so little. Why did they chase you?"

"I don't know. I think they must have saw me in the grocery store, over there a few blocks."

"And they followed you?"

"I guess so. I didn't see them until I cut through this alley."

"Are you hurt very badly?"

"I don't think it's too bad; I'll be stiff for a month, though. And they got my money, that's the worst part. I need it. I had my whole Social Security check cashed."

"Do you know those boys?"

"Them niggers? I don't know them. The black sons-of-bitches."

"You ought to call the police."

Cole helped the man back to his father's house and called the police. While they were waiting, he got the old man a glass of ice water and a wet washcloth for his forehead. When he came back into the living room, the man lifted his head from the sofa, where he was lying. "Thanks."

Cole sat down opposite him. "You sure you don't know who those kids are?"

"Black trash, that's all I know. A woman was killed around here not too long ago. Trying to get her purse."

"Can't anything be done?"

"Done? They don't send nobody to jail no more. Let 'em loose to run anywhere they please, rob who they please. My wife's afraid to go out in the daytime anymore, never mind the nighttime."

"Maybe they need the money badly."

"Sure they do—to buy a lot of nothing. They don't care how they get it, just so long as they get it. They have no respect, no idea that you're supposed to *earn* what you have."

"It's terrible, I agree."

"They skip school and lie in wait for the likes of me, older men and women who can't defend themselves very well, and then they pounce on us. Well, I gave one of them a sound whack, I know that! He's likely to remember that."

Cole rubbed his ear. "I'm likely to remember it too."

"I'm sorry I did that to you, but I didn't know who you was."

"I'll recover." He felt the coming bruise on his leg.

"Good thing you had that garbage lid. That scared them away."

"That was my trusty shield. Unfortunately I couldn't find a lance."

"You gave that one kid a good lick with it."

"I'm an old knight from way back. Even when I'm dehorsed, I hang onto my garbage can lid." He snorted at the joke on himself.

"Well, I'm very happy that you did."

"Just call me Sir Galahad."

The old man grinned. "I heard of him."

"My strength is as the strength of ten, because my heart is pure."

The man looked doubtful about the meaning. "I don't know what to do next, though." He shook his head wearily.

"The police will be able to help you."

"Well, that's what they get paid for anyway."

"The man who answered said it wouldn't be long."

"My head is killing me."

Cole reached for his own wallet, to check if it was still in his pocket, believing for a moment that it had been stolen too. But it was there. He took it out and counted the several hundred dollars. "Why don't you take this," he said, taking out two twenties and offering them to the man.

"I couldn't do that!"

"Of course you could—and you will." He thrust the bills into the other's hand and sat back down.

"Won't you need it yourself?"

"When I'm beaten up, next time, you can help me."

"I may not be around."

"Take it. It benefits me as much as you."

The man looked dumbfounded, as if he might cry. "I can't say . . ." He stopped.

"I'm only sorry that you had to suffer in order for me to be generous."

"I'll pay you back."

"No, don't. Just pretend that you found it in the alley."

"You're a fine young man; your family can be mighty proud of you."

"Do you have some way of getting enough to live on for the next month?"

"I can write my son; he might help. I really don't know what to say about this."

"Just say that the good fairy gave it to you."

The man smiled, and then sat up when the sound of a knock was heard.

Cole let the policeman in, his partner remaining in the car in front. "What's the trouble?" he asked.

"This man was knocked down and robbed in the alley behind here." Cole pointed.

"Are you hurt?" he said to the old man.

The man sat upright. "Just a headache. But they got my money."

"How old were they? Teen-agers?"

"There were three of them, about fourteen." Cole was surprised that the policeman made no notes.

"Do you want to be taken to a hospital?" he asked the old man.

"I want my money."

"I can describe them to you, if you like," Cole offered.

"Yeah, yeah—Negroes?"

"Yes. They—"

"Never mind. They're gone by now anyway."

"You might see them around if you drove," Cole suggested.

"Only get in trouble if we go picking up suspects. I was almost hit by a brick a couple of weeks ago."

"But you can't let them get away with this."

"We'll get 'em; they do anything else? Property damage?"

"No, just the assault."

"You didn't know them, did you?"

"No, but I'd recognize them."

"No use prosecuting unless they do something major, because they just let them free since they're kids.

"Come on, sir, we'll take you to the hospital for a check." The policeman helped the old man out to the car, and Cole, amazed, watched them drive away, feeling as if the wall he rested his hand on were made of papier-mâché.

15

After the police and the old man left, Cole heard his father's uneasy voice call from upstairs. "Cole? Are you down there? What's the matter?"

"It's all right, Pa," he called back, going up the steps to the second floor. In the bedroom he saw at once the worried face. "I wasn't going to bother you with it—it's nothing about us, Pa!" he interrupted himself when he saw the doubt on his father's face. "Some man was robbed out back in the alley, and I called the police."

"The police?" The man's mouth fell ajar.

"They took the man to the hospital, just to see that he's okay."

"I could hear voices; I thought something had happened."

Cole realized that his father had said nothing all the while the others had been there. "It was about somebody else, Pa. Some kids stole his wallet."

"I wish you had come up and told me sooner; I was worried out of my head."

"I didn't want you to know about it."

"That was a police car parked out in front of our house."

Cole noticed the apprehension in the eyes. "Yes, it was."

"The neighbors'll get a lot of talk out of that, I bet."

"They'll forget about it, Pa."

"I saw it out the window."

"They got the man's money, but he wasn't hurt too much."

"Did anybody come out on their porch to watch?"

"I really don't know; I didn't look. They weren't here very long."

"I bet I hear about it, though. Did you have to get involved in all that?"

Cole examined the frown. "The man was in trouble," he answered gently.

"That's a shame, but people ought to look out for themselves. You might have got killed."

"Well, I didn't. It came out fine."

"You've got a red mark on the side of your cheek." He gestured.

"It's unimportant." He decided not to mention his bruised leg, knowing it would further upset his father.

"Did they beat you up?"

"They ran away—three of them."

His father suddenly smiled. "Three of them? And they ran away?"

"Unfortunately with the man's money."

"But really—three? What were they, punks?"

"Teen-agers."

"That's wonderful, son. Can't let these punks push us around. I hope you gave 'em a hard time."

Cole felt embarrassed. "It wasn't very heroic, I'm afraid."

"The point is you scared them off. That's how a *man* treats them; he don't let nobody shove him around. I'm proud of you, very much."

"I didn't think about it fully. It just sort of happened."

"I hope you beat their balls good. They got a nerve—right in broad daylight!"

"The police seemed to think it was nothing extraordinary."

"Did you hit them with your fists?"

"No, not quite that. But I got in a few whacks," Cole chuckled.

"God damn! That's wonderful, Cole!"

Cole beamed, his eyes almost watering. "I got another bruise on my leg," he said, rolling up the pants leg.

"Let me see." Cole hobbled over to the bed. "Why those sons-of-bitches! Who do they think they are? I hope to God you cracked them good!"

"Well, I tried." They smiled warmly at each other.

"You were always sort of afraid to fight when you was a little boy."

"I'm sorry. I guess I was a disappointment to you in most ways."

"You'd never fight 'em back; they'd chase you right up here on the front porch, and you wouldn't fight 'em back." His father stared straight at him.

"I didn't see the purpose, I imagine. Or something."

"But you got in a few good whacks today, huh?" His father slammed a fist into his palm. "God damn, I'm glad! I wish I could have seen you do it."

Cole started to say it had been nothing dramatic, but let the words die on his tongue. "I'd better make you some dinner, what d' you say?"

"I'm not real hungry, but maybe a steak or something like that, with a salad."

"I think I'll go downtown later, to buy some things. Is it all right if I borrow the car?"

"Sure! The keys are in my pants."

Cole went over to the pants on the closet doorknob and took the keys. "You want your steak well done, Pa?"

"Yeah. Could you put some tabasco sauce right on it when you cook it; I like it that way."

"Happy to oblige."

"So you got in a few good whacks, did you!" his father repeated happily. "Wait'll I tell Eddie this. Maybe I'll call him up."

Cole felt he should tell him not to make too much of the episode, but perhaps it would help his father, he thought; he was so obviously enjoying the story. "Is there anything you want me to get you when I'm downtown?"

"Get some more Kleenex, will you. I'm about out. And how about another magazine?"

"Your wish is my command, sire."

"And, say, do you have any French dressing for my salad? I'm getting tired of that other kind."

"I'll look. I think there's some in a cupboard in the kitchen."

"I hope I'm not being a nuisance."

"Not a whit. When you get to be one, I'll let you know."

"Why don't you bring your dinner up here and eat it with me? There's no use in you and me both eating alone."

Cole stopped at the door, touched. He knew how difficult it was for his father to say something as tender as that, and he replied, "I'll do that, Pa. I'd be glad to."

"You can tell me more about the fracas in the alley."

"I won't be too long. You want the TV on?"

"Please."

Cole went and turned on the machine, waiting to adjust the picture. "I'll go fix supper now."

His father nodded, and Cole went down to the kitchen and began to rummage through the refrigerator. He took out two steaks that he had not frozen and placed them under the broiler in the stove; next he opened a can of corn and emptied it into a sauce pan. While that was simmering, he fixed a salad for each of them, searching for the French dressing and putting the salad in the freezer so that it would be a little chilled, the way his father preferred it. He made a pot of coffee for his father and later poured himself a glass of milk. He turned the steaks and stirred the corn and felt contented. When the steaks were brown, he scooped tabasco sauce onto his father's, spreading it, letting it soak through. Some of it fell to the bottom of the stove and popped and sizzled like something alive. When everything was prepared, he put the dishes on a tray and carried them upstairs. "Ready or not, here I come," he said, entering the room.

"Shhh! I want to hear this." His father indicated the television.

Cole felt his feelings hurt for a moment, but he shrugged it off, arranging the food on the tray for his father's lap and clearing a small table for himself. He glanced at the program, where a sociologist was giving her opinion on something to do with rearing children in an Indian tribe in South America, saying that superstitions were taught as part of puberty rites. Cole sat down beside the food to listen, but the woman's time was up and a commercial came on. "What's she saying?"

"Oh, a bunch of stuff, about them primitive people in Peru."

"Sounds interesting."

"There was a missionary from one of them places at church the last time I was able to go; he told some real strange things about the way they behave."

"Are you ready for your dinner now?"

"Bring her here." He slapped his thighs. "It looks good," he complimented when Cole set it on his lap.

"I could have been a chef. Or a waiter." A glint of a picture of Teddy passed through his brain.

"This is good!" Ruffner said with a bite in his jaw.

"It'll go to my head." He grinned.

"Eunice is a pretty good cook, but she fries everything, or puts too much pepper or salt or something on the food."

"I'll tell her," Cole teased.

"No, you won't! I'll have to rely on her when you leave . . ." The man looked up. "That's if you have to leave."

"I guess I'll have to leave sometime . . . but not right away. When you get well!"

"You know what—I think I am getting well. I haven't felt this strong in weeks."

"You need to get up and around, that's what. Tomorrow for certain, what d' you say?"

"All right, it's a deal. The backyard or bust."

Cole wagged a finger. "Remember now, you made a solemn promise."

"Why don't you turn that set off, so we can talk."

When it was off, Cole and Ruffner began to eat, occasionally looking over at each other and smiling shyly.

"Are the stores downtown open Thursdays like they used to be?"

"So far as I know they are."

"I'm going to do some shopping then. I'm going to draw a lot from now on."

"Do you think you might sell some of them pictures you make?"

"Probably. I heard a Picasso went for forty thousand last week. A Ruffner will go for . . . let's say at least forty-seven cents."

"Some of them artists make a fortune."

"I can't count on that, Pa."

"Weren't you going to show me some of your stuff?"

Cole paused between bites. "I've got one down in the living room; I did it this afternoon, between dragons."

"Why didn't you bring it up so as I could see it?"

"What would you like me to draw for you, Pa?"

The man meditated for a while. "Can you do a picture of your ma, do you think?"

"I'm not very good at portraits," he began, but because of the look of disappointment, he changed. "But I can try. I'll use that photograph as a model."

"I'm sure that would make something real nice." He held his fork on his plate, reminiscing.

"You miss Ma a lot, don't you?"

"Life was pretty lonely the last few years."

"I guess we all have our share of it, sooner or later."

"I made her life pretty miserable, at times."

Cole was struck by the confession. "I remember the fights you used to have; we cowered under the steps in the basement sometimes."

"I've learned to control my temper better in these last few years . . . But too late for your ma."

"Your food's getting cold," Cole pointed. "The cook'll get distressed."

"Tell the cook he did a real fine job with this meal."

Cole smiled back. "I'll tell him, but he may want a raise."

When they finished eating, Cole collected the dishes on the tray. "Do you want some dessert, Pa?"

"Naw, maybe later tonight. You might bring back some cookies or something."

"Do you want to brush your teeth?"

"Might as well." In the three and a half days, they had come to that euphemism for helping the older man to the bathroom after each meal; it seemed to satisfy them both.

At the bathroom, he helped his father to support himself on the sink while he squeezed toothpaste onto the brush. As he handed it to his father, he noticed the bathtub. "Would you like to take a bath, Pa?"

"Do I stink?"

Cole had not meant to insult him. "I just thought you might like to wash off completely."

"Well, as a matter of fact I wouldn't mind one; it's been weeks."

"Do you feel up to it right now?"

"I thought you was going downtown."

"I can go tomorrow."

Ruffner looked at the tub. "Not right now, thanks; I can last another day."

"I'll take these things back downstairs, okay?" Cole said, inching out of the bathroom, closing the door. "Just call out when you're ready."

He washed the dishes and put away the items he had used for the dinner, taking his time, knowing that his father would be at least twenty minutes. Yet there was something pleasing in the way the two actions overlapped. There was no escaping them, and the idea that he was using his time well made Cole hum as he moved around the kitchen. Life was a series of blocks of time that had to be endured or enjoyed, and any sort of symmetry made even the dull minutes better.

When he returned to the bathroom, he listened outside and was going to speak when he heard his father grunt. Cole knew that he was constipated, but neither one would discuss the subject. He moved from the door, uncomfortable at the sounds of straining from within. For an instant he imagined himself giving his father an enema, even saw the thin black tube in his hand, saw himself shove the nozzle into his father's rectum. He recoiled from the scene, and shivered involuntarily, stepping farther across the hall, into his bedroom, where he sat on the bed, waiting.

Several minutes later the toilet flushed, and then the voice: "Cole?"

He stood up, weak. "Yes, Pa?"

"I'm ready to come out now."

Pushing in the door, Cole asked, "All set?"

"I suppose."

"How long has it been since you saw the doctor last?"

"Couple of weeks."

Cole paused, hoping his father would suggest another visit.

"Maybe I ought to call him tomorrow, have him look at me again."

"I think that might be a good idea."

"We'll do it then." His father reached out for Cole's arm, but then lowered his hand. "Wait! Let me see if I can get back to the bedroom by myself. I don't want to get too much like a baby. I used to come and go by myself."

"You sure?"

"You walk along with me."

The two of them proceeded, slowly, toward the master bedroom, where Ruffner got under the covers without assistance, beaming into Cole's face at the triumph. "How was that, son?"

Cole nodded. "See, tomorrow you walk around the backyard —that's settled."

"Could be I'll get over this yet."

"You will, Pa." They found each other's eyes, unembarrassed. Then Cole moved away. "I guess, I'd best be going."

"Why don't you catch a show tonight, Cole? You need some entertainment, staying around here all day."

"Perhaps I will, if there's something good. You want the television on?"

"Yeah."

"I'll bring some cookies or something. I don't think I should be too late."

"Well, I can turn the TV off if I get sleepy. No need for you to hurry back. Enjoy yourself."

"Your white medicine should be taken at nine, don't forget."

"I'll be a good boy," his father answered, with a touch of bitterness.

Cole switched on the television to a program his father liked, and adjusted the volume. As he left the room, he waved in silence, but his father did not notice, already absorbed by the dancers.

The automobile seemed gigantic when he backed it out of the garage, for the three years had expanded the strips of metal, his sense of smallness. For a few moments he considered not driving, frightened that he might have an accident. But once he was in the street, he was in greater control.

A few blocks distant, he stopped to mail the letters, dropping them into the box quickly. He drove on through the twilight, past the hundreds of houses, their lights gradually being turned on, until he approached the city center. He drove down Summit Street looking for a place to park but saw none. At Michigan, he turned off and went several blocks, knowing that he was too far from the large stores. He turned down a street and returned to Summit, and, luckily, a car pulled out. He was afraid of backing into the space because already a car had pulled up behind him, and he began to perspire from his exertions, shifting the wheel, stretching to see that he missed the other two cars. At last he pulled into the opening and turned off the ignition, very satisfied, almost joyous at his success. Wiping the sweat off his forehead with the back of his hand, he got out of the automobile.

Late shoppers were window-shopping or hurrying places, their hands loaded with bags and bundles. Cole stopped for a moment at a drugstore, amazed at the display in the window: packages of prophylactics in neat little boxes lying next to diaphragms in their clamlike cases. A sign read: PERSONAL CONVENIENCES. True, he agreed, they were that. So customs, even in Toledo, could alter in only three years!

He went into a department store, and was shocked by the spread of goods before him: counters overflowing with sweaters, shirts, yard goods, cosmetics, shampoos, deodorants, creams, even foods and candies and nuts, so much wealth lying where the indifferent walkers could amble by, barely turning their heads at the magnificence. Cole felt like a visitor from another, backward planet, and he was sorry that he would grow used to it all, like the others, very rapidly, no longer seeing it with such excitement.

At one rack of pants he noticed a pair of blue trousers that he liked. There was a shirt in a nearby pile that he picked up. He took them into the fitting room and tried them on, a bit stunned by all of the mirrors surrounding him. The pants were a perfect size, and he turned around, looking over his shoulder at himself. *How strange that I'm encased in this particular body. Is that* me?

He told the saleslady he wanted to wear the new clothes, and she wrapped his old ones in a bag. He wanted to smile as he left her, delighted by the feel of the cloth against his skin, fresh, comforting, secure.

Outside he stood beside a couple looking at a display of angular mannequins being dressed by a young man, an occasional nude torso amid ones draped with swirls of chiffon. *Perhaps one of them is named Judy. Somebody's lovely Judy.* The young man on the other side of the glass turned his head for an instant and smiled at the three of them; he grabbed a piece of chiffon and held it questioningly toward the neck of one of the nude mannequins, indicating it as a scarf. The couple chuckled briefly and then moved off, leaving the boy to gesture at Cole, a vaguely obscene manipulation of the dummy's breasts with both his hands, as if unscrewing them. He pretended to toss them both through the window at Cole, who went along with the game, almost catching, juggling, and then pantomiming dropping the breasts, which shattered on the sidewalk. The young man rubbed his forefingers together for shame, and Cole walked away even though he knew it was merely in fun.

For a while he passed along, looking in shop windows, not finding an art shop, although he was certain one of the larger department stores would have some equipment. As he was about to cross the street, he noticed a young man in a yellow sweater and dark brown Levi's glance over his shoulder from a window down the block. He held the gaze a fraction longer than normal and then faced the glass again. Against his will, Cole felt the passion he had imagined he had laid aside swell inside his body, descend to his loins, as if a frenzied liquid were being poured into him. He was surprised to see his body stop at the edge of the sidewalk, find an excuse not to cross the street. His head swung back, and the young man in the brown Levi's met his expression a second time. He was about twenty-five, with a collegiate casualness about him, the light brown hair close-cut but the sideburns below the ear. Cole moved the bag with his old clothes to his other hand, simply for something to do, pretending to stare down in the opposite direction as if he cared about traffic, an approaching pedestrian—any lie would do. He looked back, to see the man move along the sidewalk, farther away, and he felt weak with anxiety, a slippery tickle wiggling beneath his skin. When the young man once more glanced over his shoulder, Cole followed him, surrendering to the desire.

Ahead, the man dawdled before a hardware store, bending forward, fraudulently, to see an object for sale. Cole came up to the window on the other side of the door, and when the man stepped away, Cole waited, uncertain. Could he be someone who just had an openness, a friendliness? Or could he be a cop in plain clothes? The suspicion froze him in place. But another backward look from the man sent him after him, discarding the risk.

At the corner the young man went up the block about a quarter of the way, then stopped near a bus stop as Cole continued toward him, eventually passing him, the eyes of both meeting, but carefully, very carefully. When Cole came to the end of the block, he too halted and looked back; the man lit a cigarette and seemed to wait. Cole wondered if he was expected to make the overture, or was the man undecided? He waited.

Before the cigarette was finished, the man in the brown Levi's stamped it out and came up the block, and Cole drew in his breath slightly as the man passed by, giving a faint grin in greeting. Up at that range, the man seemed older than twenty-five; his hairline was receding somewhat, and his eyes had a certain puffiness below them, although he was attractive. He walked on to a building with wide glass doors and smiled once more as he went inside.

Cole hurried to see where he was going, worrying that the man might have given up. But he was standing in the lobby reading the list of offices. Cole entered, going to the opposite side of the lobby. His mind was churning. What if the young man pulled out a card or a gun, identifying himself as a policeman? Would he merely go along with him passively? Or would he try to run away, perhaps kick at the man, a precise, vicious kick in his groin? A fat man emerged from the elevator, and Cole started, actually felt nauseous at the fright. But the man went immediately out of the building without any acknowledgment. *No, he isn't really part of a gang that entraps homosexuals for their money, maybe for blackmail. He is just another man, like me, who wants the comfort of sex, a warm body for the ease it can provide.*

Both stood in their places, until the other went up a staircase at the end of the room, and finally Cole followed. The lights had been dimmed on the second floor, and no one was around. The young man was examining a picture on the wall when Cole neared him. They said nothing for five minutes, and then at last Cole spoke. "You're an art lover, I see."

The man smiled. "It's nice, isn't it?"

Cole let his eyes fall on the ordinary landscape. "It serves its purpose."

"You live in Toledo?"

"As of now I do. How about you?"

"Yes, but I don't have any place to go."

Cole breathed more easily at the words. "Would you like to go to a hotel?"

"That's sort of expensive." He faced Cole, giving up the pretense of viewing the picture.

"I have a place," Cole said.

"Where's it located?"

"It's a house. Do you have a car?"

"Yes, it's over a few blocks, however."

"You could follow me in yours."

"I don't have a whole lot of time; I have to get up for work pretty early."

Cole didn't respond, thinking that the man might have changed his mind.

"How about here?" the man said, gesturing at the darkened corridor.

"It's sort of public."

"There's a john down at the middle."

"How much time do you have?"

The man thought to himself, hesitating, "Well, I could spare a couple of hours maybe."

"Why don't you then?" Cole suggested quietly. "It's not too far away."

"It's all right to go there?"

"We'll have to be quiet."

"I'm a quiet person." The man smiled.

"I'd like to buy a few things first, if you don't mind."

"Will it take very long?"

"Not very. Why don't you come along?"

"I have to get up at six thirty, and it's almost nine now."

"If you'd rather not go, it's all right . . ."

"Oh, the hell with it; I'll take a nap tomorrow afternoon!"

With that, they began to descend the steps, and Cole asked, "What do you do anyway?"

"I'm a teacher."

"Really? What do you teach?"

"Science—high school science. Mostly chemistry, some physics. What about you?"

"I'm . . . what am I? I guess I'm a nurse."

"A male nurse?"

"I'm just joking. I'm between jobs—that great state of potentiality."

"Why did you say nurse?"

"Oh, I'm taking care of somebody who's sick."

"A relative?"

"Yes."

"Is it very serious?"

"I'm hopeful."

Back on Summit Street, Cole said, "Why don't I go do my shopping and then meet you back in front of that department store. Okay?"

"About how long?"

"Twenty minutes at the most."

"It's a deal. My car's right down that block, not too far."

"Don't leave; I'll come for sure."

"I've got something to get myself, so it should work out fine."

"I'm sure it will," Cole replied, with a second meaning that the other acknowledged.

"By the way, I'm Jerry," he said, offering his hand.

"My name is Cole. Nice to meet you." They shook hands.

Art supplies were for sale in the store, and Cole purchased jars of India ink, pens, nibs, some charcoal sticks, some good paper, and a flat board that he could hold on his lap, the way he preferred to draw. The salesman catered to him, as though overjoyed to be able to sell some of the materials, and Cole realized that he was probably the sole customer in that department for the whole day. Coming down the escalator, he remembered the Kleenex that his father wanted and went to the drug department on the first floor. A special on chocolate eclairs was advertised a few aisles away, and he bought four of them, thinking he would take them up to his father if he was still awake.

His packages held in both arms, he waited in front of the store, while last-minute buyers scurried in and out. After five minutes, he began to worry that Jerry had decided not to return, but then from across the street he saw him advancing toward him.

"What did you buy?" Cole asked, nodding at a box.

"A birthday present for my mom. A silver goblet."

"The Holy Grail?"

"Not quite."

"I hope she enjoys it."

"I think she will. Are you all ready?"

"What if I drive by here, or over there rather? Or do you want me to drive you to your car?"

"That might be better—so we don't get separated."

"Wouldn't want that to happen."

Grinning an answer, Jerry accompanied Cole as he headed to his parking spot. "Not much action in Toledo, is there?" Cole inquired.

"You'd be surprised. There's a good bath."

"Oh?"

"It's called the Vesuvius. Nice place."

"Is it far away?"

"Just a few blocks actually."

"Is it safe? Don't the police raid it?"

"They haven't so far, not lately anyway. Either they're getting more tolerant or else the management pays off."

"Maybe I'll try that one day."

"I've had lots of good times there. Highly recommended."

"It's nice not having to pretend that our two bodies are the only ones that you or I will ever need."

"Come again?"

"I mean—we don't have to lie that our passion is not physical. I'm so weary of jumping off cliffs in the name of love."

"I'm afraid I'm not following too well."

"Most of the time people expect to be swept up in some sort of thunderous emotion, an eternal commitment. They can only get hit by hailstones."

Jerry considered the remark. "I had a lover once. All we did was fight. For three years. He kept insisting that I tell him how much I loved him—all the time."

"And so you finally stopped?"

"No, he finally said that he wanted to live with somebody else." Jerry snorted, as if realizing the comedy in the situation anew. "Maybe I should have asked him if he loved *me*, eh?"

"If you don't ask, you won't get embarrassing answers."

"It was something that just had to end, I suppose."

"Are you a fatalist?"

"No, an optimist. I've been much happier since we broke up."

"And what happened to him—the loved one?"

"I see him around. We go on, that's life."

They had reached the automobile, and Cole pointed to it. "You're very wise. No shouting, no screaming, no phials full of poison—instead we go on. I think that must be right."

"You have to be strong."

"And supple too—in order to bend down to pick up all those pieces—of yourself—from the floor."

"Correct! If you're lucky, you lose a few pieces in the shuffle, and then they don't fall out the next time."

Across the top of the car Cole asked seriously, "Do you think we mean what we're saying?"

"I mean it," he threw back, almost in defiance.

"I don't know what I mean," Cole confessed.

They then drove to Jerry's car, which followed Cole's father's Chrysler, with Cole checking frequently, making certain that the other car made the green lights. When they parked on his street, Cole made a point of putting the car far up the block so that his father would not hear them get out. The light was still on in the bedroom in the house. But as the two of them went up onto the porch, it was extinguished. "Is it all right?" Jerry whispered.

"I think he's about to go to sleep," Cole whispered back.

When they were inside, he closed the door carefully, and motioned Jerry after him. For a moment, he asked himself if he should dare to use his own bedroom, but he knew he had never truly considered doing that. He led the other man through the living room to the small room that the family had used for a bedroom for one of the boys whenever they had had guests, who usurped one of those upstairs. Now it was an unused den, with a daybed in it. Cole pushed open the door, the kind that swings both ways, and indicated the daybed. "Is this satisfactory?"

"Just what I had in mind," Jerry answered, tongue in cheek.

"Make yourself comfortable. Do you want something to drink?"

He entered the little room. "Was this a pantry once upon a time?"

"It may have been, for all I know."

"I don't need anything to drink, thanks."

"Why don't you sit down. I'll just run up and check on my dad." He put the package of art supplies and his old clothes down on a chair and carried the eclairs with him. He listened outside his father's room for a movement, and then opened the door a crack. "Pa?"

"Huh?"

"Are you asleep?"

"Just about."

"Do you want some dessert?"

"Naw, save it for morning."

"Do you want anything?"

"No, thanks."

Cole held the door a few seconds longer. "Well, good night then. See you in the morning."

"Good night." The voice trailed off.

Downstairs, Jerry was sitting on the daybed, with his hands clasped. "I'm sorry," Cole said. "But I had to see how he was."

"Is he all right?"

"Yes, about asleep."

They stared at each other, and then Jerry stood up and came closer, putting his arms around Cole's neck. And then they pressed together. The sensation was exhilarating to Cole, making him expend his breath in a half-sigh. He pulled back and dropped his hands to the other man's belt, undoing it, then running his fingers over the front. "This is the Battle of the Bulge," he joked. Jerry pushed his own fingers into Cole's pants, from behind, pulling him close to him again. "Shall I be active or passive?" Cole asked close to Jerry's ear.

He drew back. "What?"

"Just a jest. In things I've read, homosexuals are always categorized as either the active or the passive type."

"Let's say we try a little of each," Jerry said, slipping off his trousers.

"Sounds like a good suggestion." Cole undid his own shirt, throwing it at the chair where Jerry's package rested.

Jerry made an ugly face, saying in another's voice, "You know, I've heard that them queers pat each other's buns. Can you imagine anything like that? They pat each other's buns!"

"They're nothing but a bunch of perverts."

Jerry laughed aloud, and then grimaced at the noise he had made. "I'm sorry."

Cole held up an arm and listened. Nothing.

Jerry approached and said, "Those queers do lots of funny things." He put his mouth to the space below Cole's Adam's apple and licked it, running his clutching fingers slowly down over Cole's waist and hips. "I don't know what they see in it myself."

"They're merely compensating." Cole dropped to one knee and pressed into Jerry's briefs. Then he pulled on the elastic, drawing them part way off. "They don't know what they're missing." Jerry's erection swelled against the shirttails, and Cole ran his hand over the hardened flesh.

"They're fixated orally—and sometimes even anally." Jerry clucked his tongue, rubbing his palms sensually all over Cole's neck and shoulders.

Cole reached up and pulled Jerry down, raking his body across his own until they were kneeling facing each other. "They weren't brought up right," he said, sticking his tongue into Jerry's mouth and squeezing him.

"They don't have a mature sex life, remain arrested at one level," Jerry said in a moment, breathing hard, before leaning over to take Cole's nipple in his teeth, delicately.

Cole sucked air in through gritted teeth. "It'll do. Oh, yes, it'll do." And he seized the other man around the torso and held him to himself for a long time.

They both stood, on some silent cue, and finished undressing. As he dropped his trousers over the back of the chair, Jerry knocked the package containing the silver goblet onto the floor, making a mild thud. At once Cole raced to the door, opened it, and listened to see if his father had stirred. He waited for more than two minutes before he returned. "I guess he didn't hear."

Jerry looked apologetic. "I'm so clumsy all the time."

Cole looked at him, smiling. "Don't become a thief, that's all."

"Wouldn't dream of it. You've got a bad bruise on your leg. What happened?"

"Fighting crime."

"Oh?"

Cole came near the daybed. "Would you mind helping me open this. The back slips up and then down and makes another section."

Jerry came up next to him and touched his shoulder. "What do you want to make it wider for, Mister?"

Cole twisted his head to the side. "All the better to seduce you with."

"Then, by all means, let me help." Jerry went to the opposite end, and together they lifted the metal backrest, pulling out the sections that served as legs. Cole fitted the cushions into place and then arranged an afghan over the entire bed.

"How does that suit you?" Cole asked, looking at the blond hair on Jerry's chest.

"It's like something out of the *Arabian Nights*."

"A chocolate eclair, a slug of Coke, and thou."

"I'll settle for thou," Jerry said, lying on the daybed.

Cole pressed himself on top of the other man, burning inside. Their flesh strained together as if each would melt into the other. They thrust again and again, sending waves of light through them, and Cole felt he would explode even as he sensed himself grow tired, drowsy, the keen, hot pleasure mingled with languidness.

Jerry gently pushed Cole from him, and Cole asked, "What's wrong? Am I hurting you?"

"No." He straddled Cole's waist and began to blow puffs of breath across the chest, then drew in the chest hair with his lips, moving down the body until he licked the navel, causing a shudder in Cole. "Do you like that?"

"Very much."

"Well, I have to be going now," Jerry said. When Cole's eyes widened in disbelief, Jerry laughed. "I told a lie."

Cole sat up. "You fink, you! I thought you were serious."

"You wouldn't mind if I left, would you?"

"Oh, I might—a little."

"Well, then, if it's only a little . . ."

Jerry pulled back, but Cole grabbed him and made him stretch out full length. "Let me show you how little." He knelt over Jerry's legs and kissed the pubic hair, stretching both hands upwards and dragging them crookedly down the skin. He put the testes into his mouth, one after the other, and manipulated them until Jerry began to writhe, emitting a subdued moan. Then the lips surrounded the penis, and he moved slightly up and down, twisting his head to give the maximum of sensation to the other man. His saliva slickened the organ, and Jerry began to thrust, arching his back, moaning more fully. Cole rubbed the thighs, touching the testicles again, and sucked faster, feeling the crisis mounting in the other's flesh. Down he went, swallowing the penis entirely, even though it made his throat hurt, and as he slid upwards Jerry groaned, "Oh, I'm coming, I'm coming!" Cole speeded his motion, and let his eyes briefly skim across

Jerry's body, up to the door, which had been swung open; his father stood staring at him as if he were seeing a heinous murder. Cole heard Jerry saying, "Oh, don't stop now! Not now!" And then he felt the warm semen spatter across his jaw, hit his chin, and then another spasm strike his neck and chest. "Why did you stop?" Jerry asked, but Cole could not take his eyes from his father's sickened face. He was unable to move, aware of the dampness of his own skin, a rivulet of sweat working its way down the center of his chest.

"Get out!" his father shrieked, although stifling the sound to a whisper.

"Pa!"

"Get out of my house!"

It was Jerry's movement that made Cole stand up, his nakedness shaming him; he reached for something to hold in front of him, picking up a pair of shorts. "Pa! I . . ."

Jerry began to put his clothes on, watching the angry, violently flushed face of the man at the door. "I've got to leave," he said to nobody.

"Is this what you do in my house? Haven't you learned anything at all?"

"It's not . . ." Cole could not form the words, his tongue sour.

"You thought I couldn't walk, didn't you? You thought that I wouldn't see your nastiness, your sluttishness. I came down here to show you I was getting stronger. But I'm the one who gets the surprise, though why should I really be surprised? Isn't this the rotten filth that you went to prison for?"

"It's not filth."

"What do you call it then? In your own father's house! My house!" The man came closer, the exertion of walking from upstairs outlining the creases between the eyebrows, a faint perspiration at the hairline. "Look at you there—naked. And that scum sticking all over you!"

Cole ran his hand over his flesh, the semen sticking in a web to his fingers, his words strangling him. "I haven't done anything to be—that I should be ashamed of. . . ."

Already Jerry had dressed and slipped on his shoes without tying them; he seized his package and walked cautiously toward Cole's father as if afraid that he might be slapped, and then hurried out of the room, not bothering to glance back. The front door slammed in a second.

"How could you, Cole? How could you?" his father demanded.

"Pa, you don't understand—" He thought his legs might collapse.

"Understand what? That my son is a sinner. A lecher, a freak!"

"I'm not . . . I'm not those things."

"I raised a girl, or somebody who thinks he's a girl. With a man, like that! How could you *do* that?" Suddenly the voice rose to viciousness. "You're a goddamn woman! Did you wear an apron or a dress when you was flitting around the kitchen, cooking and cleaning? Weren't you cute though!"

"God, Pa, don't!"

"Doing the cooking, keeping house—you queer. My son is nothing but a queer! What's wrong with you—?"

"Pa, don't say these things!" Cole cried out desperately.

"Your mother would die again if she had seen this. You killed her anyway, you took her away from me, you goddamn queer!"

"Stop saying that! Stop it!"

"I'm ashamed I ever had you. I want you to get out of my house and never come back. Never! You'd be better off dead!"

"Pa, please. God!"

"Get your clothes on, and clear out of here. I'd rather die alone in my bed than let you touch me again."

The man hobbled as he went out of the room; the door swung almost open from the violence he used to close it.

Cole began to shiver, clutching the shorts in front of himself, staring unseeing at the packages around him, wanting to grow deaf, wanting to scream and to vomit and to die.

16

He walked along the sidewalks, his mind numb, through the tangle of houses. He kept rubbing at the places on his skin where the semen had splashed, imagining that the sharp, tart odor remained, even though he had wiped his flesh with a towel before packing his suitcase and leaving. His father had stayed in his own room with the television turned up high while Cole had crammed his clothes, mostly soiled, into the bag. He had left behind the drawing materials he had purchased, not conscious that he had done so. The faces of Angie, Bud, and Keel pounded on the insides of his skull, confused with the horrified face of his father, and seemed to pulsate from within, but never spilling free to relieve him. Now and then he stopped, trying to draw in more air, stifled, for someone had driven a rusted spike into his chest; he fumbled with the front of his jacket to pull it out, to release the dead ache.

The weight of the suitcase finally wakened Cole, its heaviness tugging at his arm. He could not tell how long he had been walking, but he saw no other people, realizing it must be after midnight. In front of him was a sunken highway, and he wondered if it was the expressway to Detroit. He stared at it, wanting to lie on the grass and sleep forever, or to hear nothing but the soft sounds of cars hurtling by. He moved alongside the fence that guarded the highway, looking for an opening. When he found none, he threw his suitcase onto the other side of the fence and climbed over it, sinking face down in the brittle grass, and lay there, unmoving, for an hour, hearing the pulse in his temple rising to a throb, diminishing, then rising again, carrying his life through the web of veins regardless of his will. He ran his fingernail roughly across the place where the blood beat, thinking how simple it would be to let the life out, to let it soak into the grass. A quarter of an inch perhaps, a slice through the sideburn into the thin layer of flesh, which would resist, but faintly, and then the agony would drain free, a trickle of regrets, fears, hatreds, passions, pains . . . dribbling away . . . flowing away like sewage.

More battering minutes passed. Only gradually Cole lifted himself up, removing some junk that had clung to his jacket. Taking his suitcase, he walked to the edge of the highway, crossed diagonally, for a better footing, down to the strip reserved for emergency stops. *I'll go wherever the car that picks me up is going. What's the difference anyway!* He waved the suitcase with one hand at the automobiles, which caught him in the gleam of their headlights, before zooming by. Suddenly he wanted to be away from there with an intensity that made him step off the safe space onto the highway's pavement, his arm shaking wildly to attract attention. But the cars would not rescue him, swooshed past as if frightened of his touch.

A car with its bright lights on dazzled him, and he moved back to safety. Dizzy, Cole shot his hand out toward a truck that was approaching, and almost groaned with relief when it started to slow down. Because of its heaviness, it required several hundred yards to come to a halt, and Cole ran frantically to it.

The driver leaned toward the window, examining him to see if he looked dangerous. Out of breath, Cole waited, his mouth agape, trying to compose himself so that the man would not leave him. "Can I have a ride?" he said.

"How far you going?" The man was Negro, with thick arms and chest.

"As far as you want."

"Okay, get in if you want. I'll take you."

Cole scrambled up the high step, still worried that the man

might start to leave. He slammed the door closed, and the truck pulled back into the traffic lane. "Thanks," Cole said, pressing his palm to his temple.

"What are you doing out at this time of night, son?"

Cole glanced at the swarthy face beside him, lit by flickering beams from cars coming the opposite way. "Where are we going?"

"Don't you know which direction you're going? This goes to Detroit."

"What's the difference? It's somewhere."

They said nothing for several vacant minutes, and then the driver offered, "I drive back and forth here all the time. Occasionally I like to pick up a fellow, help him out."

"I appreciate it, really I do." Cole knew that the man wanted to talk. "What do you carry in your truck?"

"Meat. Got a whole load back there, of nothing but meat." He grinned.

"Including us?" Cole turned his head part way, thinking of the slaughtered animals, the carcasses lying behind him in sections—ribs and shoulders and kidneys and hearts—ripped, blood-streaked, and blood-let corpses, huge, silent hulks of deadness to be devoured when they arrived at their destination. He thought of grabbing the steering wheel, aiming the truck at the base of one of the overpasses, crashing his festering mind into oblivion.

"Lots of money in meat these days," the driver added.

"In all days."

"Give a fellow a big thick steak and you take his mind off his problems, that's why."

"He's a savage!"

The man said nothing to that. "I see you got a suitcase. Where you going?"

"I don't know. Where's a good place to go? You decide."

He chuckled, but uncertainly. "I only go to Saginaw."

Cole looked at the black head again, struck by a fanciful notion. "You go by Hell?"

"Hell? What d' you mean?"

"Hell, Michigan; it's a town I've heard of."

"I'm afraid I don't go there."

"No? I thought maybe you were sent to take me to Hell."

"No, just Saginaw's far as I go."

"If you drop me off in Detroit, I'd appreciate it."

"Be glad to."

"I live there, actually."

"Yeah? I live in Ravenna myself."

"I have a place to go back to," Cole went on, feeling the tears curling down his cheeks, but he made no effort to remove them. "There's some place where I can go, how about that. Some people don't even have that, do they? Not even that. I have an apartment, and I know people there." The tears rushed down his face easily.

"I just been through Detroit, never seen much of it really."

"It's just a city. We make cars there."

"Yeah, I know," the driver answered, hesitant, noticing the streaked face.

"Have a real good police force in Detroit; they keep those criminals in hand."

"They ought to! It's getting so bad I hate to pick anybody up nowadays."

"You're absolutely right; they should burn some kind of brand into their foreheads so that the decent folks can keep away from them. A deep brand above the eye. A scarlet H—how would that be?" Cole laughed ferociously.

The Negro moved restlessly. "Pretty fair weather tonight."

Cole restrained himself, rubbing the wetness off his cheek, feeling a slippery area where the water mixed with the remnant of semen. "Yes, it's fine tonight."

"What you doing in Toledo? Visiting your girl?"

"No, afraid not."

"Your folks?"

He snapped his head toward the driver. "True. Only my folks don't live there anymore."

"What's that?"

"I went to a funeral there."

The man shook his head in commiseration. "That's a bad shame. Somebody close?"

"Yes, me."

He did not appear to comprehend. "Funerals can be real bad times; they're heartbreaking, but, then, we all have to go sometime."

"But I'm not going yet; I won't give them the satisfaction. I'm going to go on, how about that?" Cole looked over defiantly.

The driver nodded. "Been several bad accidents on this road lately. I passed one. A real mess."

"Some of us are sturdy and survive the accidents, maybe with just one leg or one arm left, but breathing. That's a virtue, isn't it?"

"I swear most of these people don't know how to drive proper."

"I won't give them my life; they'll have to take it." Cole wiped the tears on his pants, then raised the front of each shoulder to dry the rest of his face. "Do you know how close we'll come to Grand Circus Park in downtown Detroit?"

"I'm not too sure."

"Can you let me off somewhere near downtown?"

"Okay, but it won't be up on the street. Truck's too large to get back on here."

"Anywhere's all right. I want to go someplace."

"Getting pretty late. Most places'll be closed."

"This one will be open. It's better than a church."

The truck driver kept his word, and let Cole off on the John Lodge Freeway, where he walked up a ramp to the street. He stopped at a telephone booth to look in the Yellow Pages for the address. It was listed: The Elanhus Bath on Park Street. He had never been there, but several men had mentioned it as a place to go. Except for two persons, the streets were deserted, even the benches in Grand Circus Park. The water in the fountain had been turned off; a vague eerieness, a sense of threat lingered in the silence.

He found the address with difficulty, because the steambath was afraid to advertise its existence. There was no sign outside or even in the lobby of the building. But a flight of stairs led down to the mirrored, one-way-glass window. The opening slid halfway and the cashier said, "Yes?"

"I'd like to come in," Cole said.

"Have you been here before?"

"No—but I know what's here."

The face stared at him cautiously. "This is a private membership."

"I'm a member."

"You know anybody who's been here?"

"Yes, I want to come in, please." He paused. "I'm a homosexual."

"That's close enough to the password," the other man grinned. "You want a room or a locker?"

"A room."

The man took a key from a board and presented a receipt to sign. "Five dollars, please."

Cole started to sign a pseudonym, as usual, but then crossed it out and wrote his own name, shoving the slip through the window along with a five dollar bill.

"You're number four. Here's your towels."

Uncertain, Cole looked up, and the man pointed to the door. "Thank you."

A buzzer rang as he approached it, startling him at first. "Have a good time," the cashier teased.

The hall was pitch black. He fumbled for the knob into the next room, and a wave of heat hit him when he entered. A very lean man with only a towel around his waist came out of the locker room to the side of the long corridor that faced Cole. He blew a wisp of smoke over his head. "Can I help you?" he asked.

"The room." Cole held out the key.

"Number four's at the far end. The numbers come up this way."

"And the steambath?"

"Through there." He indicated another narrower aisle. "First time here?"

"Yes."

"Enjoy yourself," he said, heading down the narrower aisle he had gestured at.

"I'll try."

As Cole walked along the corridor, he could see that some rooms had their doors ajar, some open all the way. Men lay on their stomachs or backs, smoking usually, and their eyes met his, although no one acknowledged him with an expression. He passed a room without a door and peered into it. Although he could see nothing, he sensed that there were men sitting and standing within. He could hear the sound of movement in a corner.

His room was small, but clean, with two hangers for his clothes. A large air-conditioner whirred from somewhere overhead, with a monotonous humming. He undressed and placed one of the towels around himself, trying to obliterate the image of himself naked in front of his father. He stepped into the corridor, where more men were circulating by that time, peering into the open rooms, never touching each other as they passed. A gray-haired man said hello to him and he nodded in reply. The men would reach the end of the corridor and then repeat the pacing. Now and again one would stop and either enter or continue on.

There was a ledge to sit on around the sides of the darkened room, and Cole almost sat on someone, then moved farther away. As the darkness grew lighter, he made out silhouettes, two stretched out on the ledge. There was no sound, no movement, as though the forms were watching the newcomer. Cole waited, resting against the wall, fatigued. When the image of his father threatened to fill his brain, he crushed it, refusing to let it penetrate. He wanted someone to touch him, to stroke his body, soothe it. He waited.

A few seconds later he felt a pressure against his thigh; it was the hand of the prone man on the same ledge. The pressure relaxed and then was applied again. Cole felt himself swell beneath his towel, and the hand crept into his lap, then hesitated. When it received no rejection, it proceeded farther and began to massage the genitals that it discovered. The man flipped over onto his stomach and seized the penis tightly, his hand rising and falling in a rhythm. Cole reached out and ran his fingers across the man's hair, stroking the back of the neck, wanting to please him, to ease the body. Someone else rose and sat down next to Cole and put his hand on the leg, fingertipping a path through the hairs. The second man leaned over and began to fellate Cole, whose desire flamed, and he massaged the second head with his other hand. When he felt the crisis approach, he pushed gently. "No, not yet. I don't want to yet," he said, freeing himself. The man understood and began to kiss Cole's stomach. Cole could not bring himself to use his mouth on the other. He was afraid that the scene of a few hours earlier would rise, make him gag. He sat back, too exhausted to do more, surrendering his body to them.

Cole went into the showers a few minutes later, to wash the other's ejaculate from his skin, soaping himself well, standing under the stream of warm water. Another man came into the shower room and began to clean himself too. He was an innocent-eyed, handsome blond man, not over twenty-five, a golden mustache above the lips. There were no flaws in his skin, no excess pounds, as proportioned as a statue of an athlete. The bar of soap slipped out of his grasp and slid up to Cole, who retrieved it. "Your soap." He handed it back.

"Thanks a lot. You new here?"

"First time."

"Like it?"

"So far."

"Yeah. I prefer this to all the bars and parks. There's a lot less useless chatter, useless cruising."

"I don't suppose you have much trouble wherever you go."

"If that's a compliment, thanks."

Cole had only meant it as a statement of fact, but he said nothing.

The blond boy let the water beat on top of his head, talking through the stream. "We spend so much time running around and waiting, we never have enough time for sex."

"But things are different in here?"

"They are! You can have private sex if you want it—in your own room, or you can have a gang bang."

"But it's not love," Cole said, mocking himself, watching the semen draining into the hole in the floor.

"Hell, who cares! Love's no substitute for sex."

"That's a heresy. Isn't sex meaningless this way?"

"So who wants meaningfulness all the time? I want the meaning of all sorts of experiences, with a lot of different individuals. If that's meaningless, that's also tough. I enjoy it."

"What happens when you get older—and less desirable?"

"That's a long time. I see old guys in here having a good time. I even go with them sometimes. Besides, I have nothing against love. If I fall in love, that would be all right too; still I don't have to give up this other sex."

"How romantic you are."

"I know too many guys who are crying in their beers because they haven't got anybody. All it is is dissatisfaction with themselves. So they go out seeking completeness in some other human being. Naturally, relying on another person for your happiness doubles the chances that you won't get any."

"And you won't have any children either."

"That's one of the penalties—for some people. I don't see much to kids myself. I'm glad somebody likes them, though, so the world can continue. But not having kids seems to be a small price to pay."

Cole looked at the young man to see if he was being ironic. "You can't spend your whole life in a steambath."

"Who said you had to? I come here once or twice a week; I take care of my physical requirements, and then I can concentrate on my job, on my friends, read some books. Live."

"What sort of job?"

"I'm an engineer, electrical." They continued washing, their bodies turned aside.

"And what if you happen not to be attractive to many others?"

"Then you make the most of what you've got. You diet if you're fat; you exercise if you're skinny. And if you just happen to be put together unattractively, you compensate by learning . . . other things?"

"Like how to give good blow jobs?"

The blond shook water out of his ear. "Why not? Is that supposed to be nasty or something? How puritanical! If you're homely, then, by God, I say become the best cocksucker in your city. Do what you have to. People make their own hells."

"You make it sound so easy."

"It may not be easy, but it can be done."

"Is this the well-conceived philosophy of the man who stands astride the world—and lets the rest of the people suck him off?"

The man stared into Cole's eyes, perceiving the meaning at once. "I know what you're implying. There are guys, good-looking ones, I mean, who let others do all the sex work, while they just stand or lie there expecting to be done."

"It's a pecking order. Homely has to suck Unattractive and Unattractive has to suck Ordinary and Ordinary has to suck Handsome, and even Handsome does to Handsomer."

"Some guys feel that way, it's true. They have to learn to be less selfish."

"Do philosophers live their systems?"

"You seemed to enjoy my philosophy in that room well enough."

Cole looked at him, surprised. "Where were you?"

"You told me that you didn't want to come so soon, remember?"

"Was that you?"

"In the flesh." He swept his hand at his body.

"I couldn't see very well in there."

"Darkness is the great equalizer. Everybody's sexy at midnight."

Cole absorbed the idea. "So that was you?" Then he objected again: "But don't you ever feel you're unable to form a lasting union with one other person, and that's why you're promiscuous?"

"Man, who have you been reading? Next you'll be telling me that I have to have *simultaneous* orgasm, because Erik Erikson says simultaneous orgasm—heterosexual of course—is the only way to fly. Piffle! That's fine for Erik Erikson, because he likes his sex that way, but he's not in charge of my sperm."

Cole wondered if the man was as certain as he seemed, or was it bravura? "How did you get to this conclusion, or have you always felt this way?"

"When I first came out, when I was seventeen, I decided that I was not going to be one of these semi-closet queens who keep smelling of mothballs even after they've joined the gay world."

Cole smiled. "Perhaps I've bumped into a few too many hangers in the closet myself."

"There's too much hypocrisy and fear. I resolved that I wasn't going to be one of these apologetic, no-balls liars."

"So you tell everybody you meet that you're a queer, is that it?"

"Not quite. I use discretion. I admit the stupidity of the real world, I live with it, but if anybody wants to know, I tell them." The blond man shut off the shower and took his towel from the nozzle. "I can't live anybody's life for anybody else, but nobody's going to live mine for me either. Most guys are moping around feeling sorry for themselves, when they ought to be overjoyed at their freedom, at the possibilities of exploration they have."

Cole shut off his shower and began to dry himself. "Thanks for talking to me."

"Glad to be of service."

"Is this known as the Gospel according to Plato?"

"No, it's the Gospel according to Brian—me."

"I'll try to keep it in mind." They smiled at each other.

"And what's your name?"

"It was, I guess, Old Queen Cole, but I'm going to try to change it. It's Cole."

"Good luck, Cole. Maybe I'll see you around here sometime. Get to know you better," he added with a mild leer.

"It's a deal."

"Weekends are good for me," he said, putting the towel around his waist.

"Next weekend then . . . perhaps?"

"Perhaps."

"Good night."

"Good night." The young man nodded, and stepped out of the shower room. Cole felt alone, and sharply, for an instant, he hated Brian. Or was it that he hated himself?

Coming out of the shower room, Cole encountered a tall man, sharp-chinned, about forty-four, who stopped and deliberately examined him. For a moment Cole believed that the man recognized him from somewhere and he glanced back. Taking that as a signal, the man came up immediately. "Won't you come to my room, please? I'll show you a good time." A stubble of black hairs was sprouting out of his facial skin, and there was something sinister about the black eyes.

"I was going to relax for a while."

"Say you'll come. I have a room, Number eleven."

"I don't think I can right now."

"Don't go, please. I need someone." The man held out his hand for Cole's, but did not quite touch it.

Cole stared into the stark eyes, wondering if that is how he looked in the park with Bud. "I don't know," he said feebly.

"It's right through here." He understood that Cole was considering the offer and moved a couple of steps, then returned. "Please."

Cole followed him, although the man was too thin, too tall to be attractive. When they arrived at Number eleven, the man tapped on the door. "What is it?" Cole asked.

"We'll all have a good time, okay? My friend's in here."

The door opened, and a pudgy man of fifty with tousled hair motioned them inside. "Oh, good!" he exclaimed, drawing Cole inside.

In the dark, the tall man guided Cole to the bed. "Nice, isn't he?" he said to the other man.

"Oh, he's good, Charles. He's excellent." The pudgy man came close to Cole and turned him slightly, to see him sideways. "Oh, you're beautiful, a beautiful boy!"

Cole, uncomfortable, not aroused, could not comprehend the relationship at first.

"You want to lie on the bed or just stand up?" the tall man inquired.

"What do you want?" He considered leaving.

"We only want to give you a good time. Let me do you," the pudgy one said, sitting on the bed before Cole. He undid the towel gently and drew in his breath at the sight. "Look, Charles, isn't he splendid! Oh, you're splendid!" He seized Cole's hips with both arms and pulled him closer. "What do you like, eh?"

"Yes, what do you like?" the tall man added. "We'll give you whatever you like."

They both looked expectantly at him, and he could not reply, discomfited by the oddness of the situation.

"Anything you like!" the man on the bed repeated, rubbing his cheek on the thigh.

"For my birthday?" Cole joked, and the two nodded at each other.

"He's good, Charles. Oh, yes! Is it your birthday? You be our birthday boy. Do you want me to work on this?" he said, beginning to fellate Cole. The taller man pressed against him from the rear, massaging the whole front of the body, then the pudgy man's neck. Cole looked down at the man on the bed, who was masturbating his own crooked penis, and he closed his eyes, distressed, although he could not form the reason clearly in his mind. "For you, Charles," the man said suddenly, pulling the friend down so that he could continue the fellation on Cole. He fell to his knees and began to perform the same on the tall man.

So I'm a gift, Cole said to himself. *So I'm an object for them.* He restated the idea in his mind, and then realized that it was a label that he had picked up somewhere. What difference did it make? Better an object than nothing. Yes, better an object than a love. Here there was no pain, for any of them. There was uncomplicated lust. They were using one another's bodies, but thoughtfully; it was simplistic to call it selfishness. Cole twirled his fingers in the man's ears, knowing that would excite him. The heavy man stood and kissed Cole's shoulder, running his hands down either side of the body, lifting his head, yearning, for the mouth, and Cole consented, tasting the huskiness of the man's lips. Their mouths pressed slightly, and Cole remembered the man with acne, at Palmer Park, whom he had forced to pay. The memory made him draw the pudgy man to himself, and their mouths ground together. Then Cole bent slightly in order to touch the shorter man's sex and blazed his hand wildly over the penis. The tall man took him again in his mouth, and the tiny darts started from someplace deep within Cole, and raced toward the center. Shattering him, they exploded, and he felt the heavy man press, writhe against him in an ecstasy. Both their bodies quivered as they climaxed, the other man groaning several times with the shock. "Are you all right?" Cole asked.

"Wonderful," he sighed.

The tall man sitting on the bed still held Cole in his mouth, for the maximum pleasure. Finally he let go and patted Cole's sides. "Ah, that was magnificent. Thank you."

"Did you . . . ?" Cole was worried that the man was unsatisfied.

"It's okay, okay! I don't have to come now. Um, thank you, though."

"He was wonderful, Charles. Are you all right?"

"I'm fine. And you?"

"Just wonderful."

Cole took a step backwards, holding out his hand above his sticky hip, frightened that his father's face might make disgust rise in him.

"We seem to have made a mess," the pudgy man said. "Here." He grabbed a towel from the bedpost, carefully cleaning away the liquid.

Cole relaxed as the cloth rubbed the skin. "I thought this was supposed to be a steambath." Cole smiled. "Not a spermbath."

The two men exchanged looks, happy. "You'll be as good as new. There!" The shorter man patted the dried section. "Can you come again?"

Cole put up his hand, amused. "Not just now, thanks. I'd better rest awhile."

"Well, return when you get ready, if you want to. We'd love that. Right, Charles?"

"No question about it."

"We're pleased that you came to our room."

Cole felt that he should snicker at the politeness of the men under the circumstances, but he couldn't. "I enjoyed your company," he said instead.

When he left their room, he followed a sign that indicated the lounge, where a television set was showing a late movie. The young man who had been the cashier sat watching it, while another man, with his legs folded beneath him, sat reading a magazine from the reading rack. Around the room were plastic settees and chairs, with a blue rug filling the space between them. Cole took a seat on one of the settees and watched the movie, wondering if his father was watching one also, sleepless from anger or disgust. In the movie, a monster, decidedly dragonlike, had been roused from a cave and was terrifying the populace, who were all Japanese, because of its attempts to find its way to freedom. The film was near its end, for the monster had been cornered in a park near some trees and was bellowing flames, holding its own for a time against the firetrucks and asbestos-covered men who were besieging it. The man a few seats away gave a contemptuous snort, and Cole looked over, but the reaction was to something in the magazine, not the movie. The man sensed Cole's attention and raised his head. Cole turned again to the television, knowing that the man was still looking at him. When he checked a second time, the man was pretending to be absorbed in a thought. Cole rose and went nearer, wishing to talk to somebody. Because the hour was late, after one, according to the clock above the television, most of the customers had gone, and the man might leave too. "How are you?" the man, who was about forty, said, quite friendly.

"Fine. What're you reading?"

"Oh, some dumb piece about open admissions in universities."

"What's that about?"

"Some feverish types want to let anybody, prepared or ill-prepared, into the colleges."

"What for?"

"To give everybody a chance, they say. Hell, it will ruin the schools, make them as crummy as most of the high schools."

"Are you a professor?"

"No—do I give that impression?"

"You look like you might be." He noted the dark brown hair which was beginning to be speckled with gray.

"You're not too far off, actually."

"Do you mind telling me?"

"Guess."

Cole considered him deliberately, the firm square jaw, the intelligence that showed in his expression. "You're a spy from the CIA."

The man chuckled. "Gave that up years ago. Guess again."

"You're a towel salesman out drumming up business."

The smile grew broader. "Not that either. One more try."

"You're a Bible manufacturer doing illustrations for the story of Sodom and Gomorrah."

They were laughing quite heartily, and then Cole abruptly ceased. *What if he's a policeman, laughing at his own secret? What if he arrests me?*

The man stopped as well, perplexed at the quickness. "No, I'm a psychiatrist."

Cole did not believe him. "A what?"

"A psychiatrist, a head-shrinker. Don't you believe me?"

"What would one of those be doing here?"

"Shall I draw a diagram for you?"

"But I . . . Psychiatrists have to be examined before they can practice."

"Oh, I've been through all that. I have a wife and children. I'm quite happy with them. I just require a bit of extracurricular activity now and then."

Cole was astonished. "What do you say to men who come to you because of their homosexuality?"

"It depends on how much they want to leave it behind."

"Can you help them leave it behind?"

"Occasionally. Mostly I tell them to live with it."

"What if your own wife found out?"

"She won't. And if she does, that would be her decision. I'm a good husband."

The attendant glanced back with a mild frown because their conversation was interfering with the conclusion of the movie. Cole gestured to the TV set, and they said nothing while the monster snarled and scorched and crashed from some building that he had climbed to the top of. Its smoking, charred body lay in a quivering heap surrounded by the triumphant Japanese, and then very rapidly the movie was over. The attendant stood up, stretched, and asked, "You want it on anymore?"

"Not me," the psychiatrist answered, and Cole shook his head; the man switched it off. "No, I tell people to live the best way they can. Sometimes they come in pretty screwed up. What I try to do is unscrew them." He was amused by a play on the words. "Of course there are some I'd like to screw—up that is."

"And do you?"

"Never lay a hand on them, just like most doctors."

Cole twisted uncomfortably. "Do you think you can really help people when you have this problem yourself?"

"What problem?"

"Well, this . . ."

"The main problem is in thinking of it as a *problem*, something to be eradicated at all costs."

"But by being semi- . . ."

"I'm not semi-anything. I'm bisexual. The real problem is in the old-fashioned hang-up on a sharp male-female dichotomy. It's too narrow, too prissy, too ignorant of the true facts of human beings as they *exist*, instead of as they have been ordered to be."

"I thought it was wrong to isolate sex from love. Homosexuals so often do, and use just one aspect of another person, don't they?"

"So? The mailman brings the mail; the Good-Humor Man brings ice cream; movie stars dance or sing for us. Why should homosexuals have to devote their whole lives or souls to every man who provides a service?"

"Isn't sex a special kind of service?"

"Not all that special, no."

"And you're happy?"

The man sat up and slapped Cole's knee. "Why should I—or anybody else—expect to be happy? Nobody but an imbecile is 'happy.' At ease, perhaps, but not 'happy.' People demand too much out of life; they're bound to be disappointed."

Cole meditated on that remark for a long moment, while the man put down his magazine. "I don't mean to imply that I'm miserable," he continued. "But I get so tired of hearing people, not only patients, whine because they're not happier; they've been brainwashed into expecting every day to be Disneyland."

"Does sex here make you happier?"

"Definitely."

"What about those who don't have a wife to fall back on, when they get older?"

"Heterosexuals are not invariably satisfied with having the same person to 'fall back on,' as you so succinctly phrase it. You can overworry about the fading of desirability with age. That happens to all people, of all sexual persuasions."

"But with a regular partner one doesn't have to constantly seek new contacts."

"I know a lot of men who have gotten bored *unstiff* long before the promiscuous homosexuals have gotten total rejection."

"I wish I could believe you. Fully."

"I long ago stopped telling people to cling to somebody out of a desperate hope of not being alone. Loneliness, if it ever comes anyway, is not so terrible, except to those reared believing it's purgatory. They should learn that settling down with somebody merely for security can be stifling, its own purgatory."

"I've thought things sort of like these before, but I thought I was deceiving myself."

"You've probably accepted the standards which condemn your life as functionless. As long as you live by heterosexual standards, you'll perish by the needless guilt."

"Would I be better off if I stopped wanting to be like them? I might be happy—*happier*—if I didn't feel so rotten, so despicable because of what I am."

"The difficulty is in getting there." The other man grinned.

"I think I'm halfway there." If he could just cling to the man's words!

"Of course if you happen to fall in love somewhere along the lonesome trail, that's all right too. But I would say don't count on it—not the technicolored, stereophonic variety at least. Everybody thinks he's going to go over Niagara Falls in a barrel, when he falls in love. It's so unlikely."

"I know how people can convince themselves that they're in love," Cole said wistfully.

"Have you been here long tonight?"

"Not very long."

"Most have gone home."

"I guess they work tomorrow. Don't you?"

"Tomorrow I go in late."

Cole sensed that the conversation was leading to a contact between them. "It's about time for me to get home too. It's been a . . . hard day."

"Must you go so soon?" the man hinted.

"I think I ought to look for a job starting tomorrow."

"Why don't you come to my room? I'll show you my Rorschach Tests."

Cole laughed at the witticism. He hesitated principally because he felt strange going to bed with a psychiatrist; it seemed like having sex with a priest.

"I'd be very pleased if you would."

"Are you certain we can lock the door?" Cole said, to mock himself.

"Certainly. Why?"

"Oh, it's a . . . short story. It doesn't matter."

"How enigmatic!" He stood, a moderately attractive man; he wore his towel slung low across his hips and stomach.

Cole rose too and followed him to his room, where they lay entwined in each other's arms for more than an hour, and in the dark of the room, in the mutual satisfaction they enjoyed, Cole's aches and cuts seemed never to have existed. When they parted, he went to his own room and sank onto the bed, falling into a hopeful sleep.

17

⌇⌇⌇⌇⌇⌇⌇⌇⌇⌇

Rising the next day was like swimming up out of a tunnel. Groggy from thirteen hours of sleep, Cole dressed and left his small room. He had slept himself into tiredness again, but knew that his body had been refreshed. He told the attendant, a new one, that he wanted to renew his room for that day, and the boy simply grinned at him and accepted the five dollars. Already some men were present, a few room doors standing ajar, while in the lounge two men in their sixties were conversing.

"Is there a good restaurant nearby?" he asked the new attendant, a kid in a sweat shirt with a wide gap between his teeth.

"There's one across the way, not far."

"Thanks."

Outside, the weather had become chilly, windy, but the brightness invigorated him, and most of the grogginess evaporated. Quite hungry, he crossed the street that circled the city park and went into the restaurant. He ordered a salad and scrambled eggs. A couple at a distant table was having a subdued quarrel. Briefly Angie's face, as she had looked opposite him in the other restaurant, appeared. He did not try to eradicate it, and gradually it faded of its own accord. When his meal was served, he ate it with delight, feeling silly because his eyes wanted to water from his contentment. It was wonderful to be in a restaurant at four thirty in the afternoon, with only a few others around. Just being alive. While the waiter was bringing some blackberry pie for dessert, Cole bought a newspaper from a mechanical rack at the front of the building. Even the news was not so terrible that day: a new police commissioner, a story about a tenant strike in Ann Arbor, and a few odds and ends, somehow comforting in their triviality. He took a long time, finishing with coffee and a cigarette, and read, now and then glancing at the waiters, who stood in the background.

His jacket was not warm enough; yet he decided to walk around a bit, carrying his newspaper with him. He wished that there was a parade on Woodward, something gaudy and brassy, but he realized that he was between holidays. A black man was selling or giving away a Muslim newspaper on a corner, but he drew back when Cole passed. He recalled the man at the tennis courts that day with Bud. *My brother!* He expected a pang of some kind to hurt him at the remembrance, but there was nothing. He stepped briskly. "I'm stronger than I thought. By God, I'm stronger than most people." *Here I am downtown, and this time I won't worry myself about seeing Bud or Angie. I think I'm free.* Playfully he patted the hood of a car that had stopped to let him cross, repeating, *I think I'm really free.*

He joked with himself about where he was going—to the YMCA for a swim? To run around the gym? Yes, it might be good to run. Or in a field someplace—just run and run and run until his breath dried up and he sprawled in flowers and tall, sweet grass. That would be marvelous. But if he ran here, people would stare, would think he was crazy or a thief trying to escape, or he might bump into somebody. He continued the running in his mind, threading his way among the afternoon crowd. After all, he told himself, no use running into trouble.

Trouble. The police station and the court were only a few blocks farther. Mr. Schultz would be sitting there with a bow-tie on, giving well-meant advice to his charges, bland, useless advice. *I'll go for my second visit and tell Mr. Schultz just what he wants to hear, and get him out of my life.*

And Officer Keel is there in the same vicinity, complaining in some hallway about having to come to court so frequently.

But Cole cancelled the image. *I won't waste my energies, my nerves on the man. He's nothing to me now.*

Nor are you, Pa! he almost heard himself say out loud. He sat down on a bench in the park opposite Grand Circus Park, near some construction work. He made himself hold the picture of his father's harsh face, made himself still his pulse when it began to pound heatedly. *I'm strong, Pa! You wanted me to be a strong person—well, I am! You can't do anything else to me, and I can't injure you any longer. We're both free. It's much better this way. Much better.*

He stood, surprised that sweat lay under his arms. He turned around and threw his hands out, startled, because a few yards away a policeman was coming directly toward him. He waited, blinking, watching the club swing from the man's hand; it jerked up and down on its thong, caught and thrown by the policeman. "Good day," he said to Cole, who could not answer, fighting to restrain his arms from shooting out a second time. The policeman continued walking, nonchalant, and then Cole could tell that it was merely his beat; he had not been interested in Cole at all. He sank back onto the park bench, thinking that he ought to laugh with relief, but he could not manufacture the emotion. He stared at the man's back for a long time.

He spread the paper on his lap, after several more minutes, and eventually turned to the want ads, the wind whipping the pages. Under EMPLOYMENT: MALE, he saw lots of jobs for barbers, for computer operators, salesmen. *Maybe they should have "Employment: Homosexual,"* he thought; *it might be interesting applying for the jobs.* At the joke he looked up in the direction of the policeman, shaking his head at the silliness of his suspicion. The man crossed the park and was giving directions to a middle-aged woman. Cole looked at another column of ads. A store wanted someone to dress up in a costume, unnamed, for a two-week-long special. Details would be given in person. He had not really anticipated finding a job in the paper, but several employment services were advertised, and he ripped out the squares, for they might have something for him. And if not, he could leave Detroit. He could go almost anywhere in the world. He didn't have to stay there. He leaned against the bench. Almost anywhere in the world!

The construction work caught his eye—torn-up earth, probably for repairs to the roof of the parking lot underneath the street and the two parks. But there were no men working. Their tools were abandoned, pieces of pipe, like sewer pipe, were lying in a pile near where the ground had been disturbed. He got up, to get away from the ugliness of the scene. *I would pick, out of all the places in the world, to sit where I have to stare at junk.*

He made two telephone calls from a booth in the lobby of the YMCA, to find out whether the employment offices required an appointment. They did, because an interview was recommended; he arranged one for the following day since the women he spoke with said they were about to close, though both thought they might have something for him.

Then, outside again, feeling chilled after ten more minutes of wandering, Cole returned to the steambath, ducking down the stairs as if into a secret retreat. The cashier remembered him and give him his key. "You need a towel?"

"I guess I'd better," Cole smiled back at the amused irony around the boy's mouth. "Thanks."

"Wouldn't want you to be wet or catch a cold."

In his room he undressed and got under the covers and dozed, thinking that somebody was sewing parts of his body together —only the needle did not hurt; it was in fact a soothing needle in a disembodied hand that slipped back and forth and stitched the pulled segments neatly back into place. When he awakened, he grinned into the ceiling, then fixed one of his towels around him. It was already six thirty, he was amazed to discover.

The evening customers were beginning to arrive. Sitting in the lounge, leafing through an article in *Esquire*, he surveyed the men entering the room, their eyes searching. There was eroticism in the furtiveness, the silence, the continual movement, the ebb of bodies, all sorts of bodies, average and unaverage. He felt *happy*, and even his growing desire did not disgust him. He accepted the needs of his body.

Three young men entered the lounge, flicking their hands through the air wildly, and Cole believed they were effeminate until he realized that they were making no noises, but were talking in sign language. One of them was dumpy and not properly formed, but the other two looked normal. They seemed to be joking with one another and shook their heads, taking steps away from each other, coming back and bending over in silent laughter. The odd part was that they appeared to make more noise than talking people. Two of them suddenly ran off, leaving the malformed one, who stamped his foot, but did not follow them. When he turned toward Cole looking for a seat, the babylike features became evident, a misaligned cherubic countenance that could not annoy anyone because of the vivaciousness in the eyes. He came toward the chair next to Cole, and, as he sat down, he waved his fingers directly at him, then bit his thumbnail as if shy. All of his movements were extremely feminine, but not strident, not an imitation of a female; he was simply expressing himself as he was.

He sat with his hands clasped over his kneecaps, once sneaking a look at Cole, who pretended to read the magazine. The little man picked at his fingernails and dug into his ear, though he seemed content to be sitting where he was. He made Cole uncomfortable, but finally he put the magazine in his lap and spoke. "Can you understand me?"

The little man beamed and faced Cole, nodding vigorously.

"But you can't hear me?"

The man motioned to Cole's mouth.

"You can read lips?"

He held up his tiny hands to show that he used sign language, then pointed questioningly.

"No, I'm afraid I can't do it."

The hands jumped out and patted against the air, to mean that the man would teach him the alphabet. He held out his hand, and Cole gave his, repeating each symbol he was taught, sometimes paining his hand muscles to form the letters.

"Can you say something simple to me?"

Again the head nodded energetically, and the fingers moved.

"*I . . . L . . . I*—what's that?"

The other drew a *K* in the air.

"All right, *I . . L . . . I . . K . . . E*. I like! Why did you stop? *What* do you like?"

The little man pointed several times at Cole, and then covered his mouth with his palm.

Cole smiled in response, and the man raised Cole's hand to his lips and kissed the fingers. He did not know what to say. The little man motioned that he would return in a moment and rushed away in the direction of the rooms. When he came back, he carried a pencil and a sheet of paper. Taking a magazine, he spread the paper out and wrote a note: "My name is Cupey."

Cole nodded and said his own name. "Cupey?"

"Like Cupey doll at carnival."

Cole acknowledged the information by tapping the paper.

The sheet was attacked again and handed to him: "I went Erope."

"You did? When? Just recently?"

He began to say something in sign language, then remembered and wrote hurriedly: "Three weeks ago."

"How was it? Did you have fun?"

The little man made an *O* with his mouth and shook his hand fast, up close to his face, to express the enjoyment.

"What did you see there?"

The note read: "Paris, London, Amstdam."

Cole felt sad at the misspellings, the effort it took just to communicate the bare facts. "So you got around, huh? To the steambaths?"

His companion noiselessly giggled, but broke off to write again: "I meet French boy and die my hair."

Cole wondered what that meant and frowned. The man

pointed at his own brown hair and tugged on a few strands.
"You dyed your hair in Paris? What for?"

His answer was to squeeze his cheeks with both palms and
turn the head from side to side. He scribbled the word "blonde"
on the sheet of paper, and pointed back to his own hair.

"You were blond in Paris?"

"Very sexy," the note read, and Cole made himself smile an
answer.

"What became of it?" he asked.

His hands were pantomimed through his hair.

"You washed it out. Why?"

"Go back to work." A pouting expression accompanied the
note.

"Where do you work?"

He wiggled his fingers as if typing, and then tapped his own
chest.

"And you can't have blond hair?"

"Boss." The little man grimaced at the word he had written.

"So you're blond just during your vacation, huh?"

"Next year I going to Japan," he wrote.

"And will you dye your hair for that too?" When the head
bobbed up and down excitedly, Cole was saddened. A deaf-
mute whose only real fun was being able to dye his hair in a
foreign country for two or three weeks out of the year. But
the man himself was smiling, waiting expectantly for Cole to
speak further. But he really did not know what else to say to
him.

The note was given more slowly this time: "Have you got
lover?"

"No, no lover."

"Me neither."

"Better that way," he said quietly.

The other shook his head and almost pouted, and Cole could
tell the man wanted to go to bed with him; yet he felt no desire
at all.

"No, it's true. I have it on the best authority about love—my own and that of a doctor." Cole was struck by the sound—"A *cynical* psychologist told me."

The man had not been able to follow the lips and wrote: "You —doctor?"

"Me—patient. No doctor. Me, Tarzan. You, Jane."

Cupey did not catch the joke, but did not expect it to be repeated. "My birthday," he wrote on the back of the page.

"Today?"

He held up all his fingers twice.

"You're twenty." Cole tried to peer through the grin, to determine if the young man was telling a lie. "When was your last birthday—last week?"

The other frowned very severely and shook his head.

"Well, then, happy birthday!"

The man giggled. "How old—you?"

Cole looked up from the page. "One hundred and eight."

The arms were waved in dismissal, gleefully.

"No, it's true. I'm a hundred and eight tomorrow."

Suddenly his upper arm was being stroked, twice. "Am I going to become a welcome mat?" Cole asked the air. He glanced again at the little man, disconcerted by the cloudiness in the pupils, the seriousness. How was it possible that everyone had that demon inside! "You want to make the demon disappear too?"

The little man stared, recognizing something in Cole's manner that told him Cole was considering the suggestion.

"How many times have you been rejected or had to pay in just twenty years?" he muttered. "It's probably just as well you can't talk anyway; you might only learn to scream." He rose. "Come on, Cupey. Let's go to my room." Out of the corner of his eye, he saw a few heads turn, surprised. The man, who did not reach his shoulder, was quite dignified leaving the lounge. When they reached the door of the room, Cole inserted the key, then waited. "If I kiss you, will you change into a handsome prince?" he said, but so that the other could not see his lips. The small hand ran down his side, fondly. "You're right, I've given up believing in fairy tales." He turned to him. "Happy birthday, Cupey!" And he shut the door behind them.

After his shower, he returned to the lounge, where Roy Dalby was standing in the middle of the room, his bald head as sleek as ever; he was heavier than he had been in the bar. Because Cole doubted that Roy would remember him, he merely chose a seat and continued with the magazine he had been reading earlier. The bald man was holding forth as he had been in the gay bar the first time Cole had seen him, but the voice did not carry as far. In general the gestures were more restrained. But everyone was watching him.

"If you ask me, the main trouble with the economy is all this here in-fellation that's going around. Just too much in-fellation, that's the *fly* in the ointment. Things keep going up, up, up all the time; they are absolutely getting out of hand, let me lay it on you straight." He turned and seemed to recognize Cole, but he continued with his monologue to the older man he was addressing. "I know what I'm talking about; somebody's got to put a stop to it. What we need is a demonstration someplace. How about if we all go down to the City-County Building." He included those closest to him. "We'll sashay on down there and have a regular *suck-in* right in front of the fat old mayor. That'll get rid of the in-fellation, you better believe it!" Cole was very pleased to see Roy again, to hear him carrying on, making the others laugh. "Of course, we got to be careful, you know, on account of the mayor might send out his troops and run us over. They wouldn't want us to get cum all over the city's grass —though it's okay for them to spread their own shit all over the goddamn city. They don't mind that! They can fill up all the administration buildings with their own fucking muck, but they might give us trouble." Cole detected a different note in the tone; Roy seemed less funny tonight.

"Are you giving the city hell again?" someone entering asked Roy.

He turned completely. "I most certainly am! I'm about ready to give instructions on how it can tie its ass in a knot, with a pretty pink bow on it."

"What's been happening, Roy?" someone encouraged, to keep him going.

"I come and I go, I come and I go—that's what's been happening." He stood with his arms akimbo, but he struck no poses as he had in the bar.

"Been getting much?"

"A little, on the one hand. But on the *other!*" His eyebrows went up and down in a parody of lust. "Oo, what am I talking to you all for? My psychologist tells me I should not be out among you perverts! My *psychologist* that is! My very own, provided by the city of *De*troit, at a slight charge. He says I ought to spend my time in more fruitful—that is, less *fruitful*— endeavors. He says I only load my mind with lewd, antisocial ideas by hanging around you inverts! You hear me?" Roy stalked across the lounge in an exaggerated imitation of an exit. The others smiled, enjoying the humor.

"Have you made the psychologist yet, Roy?" someone called out.

"I'll have you know," he answered, coming back, "that my psychologist thinks I'm making great progress, under his very special tutelage."

"How big is his tutelage?"

Roy grinned too. "We out-verts wouldn't know, never being interested in such things. Never for a moment. I'll have you realize that I'm going to have my breasts lesson at the next time."

"Your what lesson?"

"My breasts lesson."

"What's that?"

"Titty-winks. My psychologist and I are going to penetrate into the female anatomy—to discover why I am averse—notice my improved vocabulary, please—to portions of the female body. As everybody knows, it's simply a matter of relearning the proper, normal responses. So we is going to examine the *breasts*

—plural—to see if I can't develop a semierotic reaction. Of course we're not hoping for much at the outset, but maybe by the end of the session I'll be . . . I'll be licking the pictures. Maybe that'll show some improvement."

"Perhaps you'll turn out to be a real stud, Roy."

"Gentlemen, I'm likely to develop breasts myself before I become a stud!" He smirked too broadly. "Though maybe you're right, and then I'll get thrown in jail for rape. But I'll say, 'Your Honorship, I was only practicing my homework; I sees these hugerifous *bosoms* bouncing down the lane and I got to have 'em, just got to! Your Honor, my *psychologist* told me I had to learn to redirect my interests, and I always follow his advice, because I know in my heart that he wouldn't tell me wrong! And the judge he says to me: 'Son, we got to *help* people like you. Sixty days on the rack! And if that don't work, then another sixty days, spread-eagled on a douche bowl.' "

The others guffawed, although Roy did not. "And what'll you say to the judge?" the man nearest him called.

"I'll say, 'Screw you, Your Honor.' That's what I'll say."

"Your psychologist will stick up for you, Roy, won't he?" someone called.

"He won't even stick *out* for me, let alone up. He might get all nervous and tell the judge that my trouble is that we haven't gotten to the *right* lesson yet. He'll be so disappointed, on account of we didn't get to Female Genitalia—or better known as Pussy I—though he'd be sure to point out to the judge that I was advancing at a stupendous rate, because I was about to learn to prefer female to male hair in my mouth!"

Cole winced at the remark.

"Could be my psychologist could get me off with a lighter sentence if I showed the court my good intentions. Maybe, I don't know, he could set up something to prove my progress. I don't know exactly—oh yes, I do! We could get a little platform and set it up right in front of His Honor's dim old eyes, whereupon I and a young lady of the court's choosing will proceed to hump, to the approval and applause of the assembled spectators.

And if I manage to keep it in for five minutes, they'll let me free. And if I manage to shoot off inside her, well, glory be, we both get a free trip to Bermuda, a lifetime supply of contraceptives, and a trophy inscribed with the date, our names, and Latin for *Fuckum Bonum*."

Amid the delight he had caused, Roy smiled sourly, and then moved from the center of the room. He riffled the newspapers on a table and looked over at Cole. "Don't I know you?" Roy asked, straightening his back.

"We've met."

Roy came closer. "It was in the court, right?"

"That was it."

"Mind if I sit here?" He indicated the settee next to Cole's chair.

"Please do. What's happened to you since that day?"

"You wouldn't believe it." He sat down heavily.

"I got a taste from your scene a few moments ago. You didn't go to jail, I take it."

"I might as well have—son-of-a-bitching lawyer, he's draining my blood, visits to the damn psychologist. I even got a warning at my job that my activities are being watched, and I had better not get into any more trouble if I know what's good for me."

"You should have run for it, as I suggested to you."

"You're right, but it's too late now."

"Have you been back to the bar?"

"Just once. I'm too afraid. But I get so horny and lonely I have to take the chance from time to time. I don't know how many times I've almost fixed a toilet paper roll on top of my washing machine and turned the agitator on. I even climbed up on it once, but my big ol' back hurt so much I had to give it up."

"Sounds desperate." Cole smiled.

"I'm a carnal person, I've decided."

"Aren't we all?"

"What have you been doing since then?"

"Trying to live."

"Any luck?"

"A little."

"I didn't realize how much living I was doing before all this court mess."

"Maybe you can get back to it, later on."

"I doubt it. I've been really burned. That lawyer gave me a bill for seven hundred dollars. How about that! And I have to call him every day—and usually he's not home—because he thinks—with no promises—that he *might* be able to get my record cleared. Of course that'll be another thousand dollars—it's somebody in the back, wherever that is. I've had it up to here." He drew a line above his head.

"I know this is glib advice, but you shouldn't think about it too much. You don't seem as . . . happy as you were before."

"I'm too mad to be happy."

"You can't let them beat you; you can't let them tell you how to live."

"Tell *them* that!"

"There's a danger that you'll get more bitter."

"Who me? Why, how could I say a mean thing about those people? They only want to *help* me; I heard them say it themselves!"

"Did you have a probation officer?"

"Sure did."

"Who was he?"

"Somebody name of Schultz, I think."

Cole sat up straighter. "So you had Schultz too. What did you think of him?"

"He's hard to remember."

"Did he show you a photograph of his family?"

"Yeah, did he show you that? What was I supposed to do—cry?"

"Didn't you?"

"Not likely. I didn't see anything in them."

"You mean you didn't recognize bliss when you had it presented before your very eyes?"

Roy waved his hand. "Bliss-piss! A bunch of jerky-looking relatives."

"Didn't it make you want to settle down in a bungalow?"

"Hell, no! Though the older kid in the picture looks like he may be a real comer." Roy snorted.

"No, no, you missed the point, young man. You're expected to view the magic photograph and then lie in your chaste marriage bed and perform a limited number of chaste marriage deeds."

Roy widened his eyes. "You mean I can't ride the man next door underneath the back porch no more?"

"Not even *on* the back porch."

"How about in the garage?"

"No."

"Not even if we stay under the car out there?"

"Unheard of!"

"How about if we dig a hole in the backyard and put boards over it? Would that be all right?"

"Well . . . No, that's too public. Maybe . . . if you used boards with nails and splinters in them. Or if you promise that the hole will collapse on top of you."

Both he and Roy were warm with their amusement, and they looked at each other, delighted. "You're funny," Roy complimented.

"Smile when you say that!" They laughed again. "You're probably bad for me," Cole said.

"Why's that?"

"You bring out my bitterness."

"We use it up that way," Roy replied, thoughtful.

"Maybe you're right."

"I'm real glad I got to meet you, this way. My name's Roy." He offered his hand.

"I know. I'm Cole—Cole Ruffner. Believe it or not, I have a last name." They shook hands, pleased.

"Do you come here often? I'd like to talk with you again."

"I plan to. I'd like to talk with you too."

They smiled at each other, and then Roy said, "I was going to get some steam, since that's what I paid for. Do you want to come—talk some more?"

"I haven't even seen the steamroom here yet."

"Been too busy, huh? Shame on you."

"But the steam ought to be nice." Cole got up from the chair.

"It really is. I feel all wrung out, though sort of refreshed from it." He too was standing, and together they went out of the lounge. "The steamroom's downstairs."

At the left, beyond the shower room was a staircase that descended to the basement. A green-tiled rinse pool and more showers were below. Three older men were sitting around the edge of the pool, chatting. Across from them there was a room without doors, filled with cots, each covered with a sheet and blanket. "Who uses the dormitory?" Cole asked.

"Everybody. You can sleep there if you like. Or whatever."

"Nobody seems to be whatevering at the moment."

"It's pretty far back in there. And it's still early."

"Do I hang my towel here?" They both put their towels on hooks, and Roy yanked open the door to the steamroom, which was smokey and extremely hot. "After you." Cole crossed in front of him and entered the large room. Tiers of dark wooden seats jutted out from three walls, but they were obscured by the masses of steam that emerged from two pipes high above the seats. Little eddies swirled against the cloudy bulk and fought for space. A few figures could be discerned, some stretched on their backs, several circling the perimeter of the whole room, one or two seated at different levels. The faces squinted through the denseness to see the newcomers. Already Cole felt his body drenched, even before he sat on the lowest tier. *So I have come to Hell after all.*

From a few inches away on the bench, Roy said, "Is the steam good?"

"I might melt."

"Don't do that."

Cole looked at Roy's gleaming bald head, the chin that was

beginning to sag slightly. He wanted to take him in his arms and hold him safe, from age, from death, from everything ugly—to stop time. His heart burned with the longing, and he put his hand over his brow, leaning forward.

"Something the matter?"

"Nothing . . . nothing."

One of the circling men passed very near to them, his slick body pausing for a fraction of a second. "I want that," Roy said into Cole's ear.

Cole lowered his hand. "Sell your soul to the Devil then."

"I tried to one time—but he said he didn't want mine." Roy laughed at himself.

"Try again; he's probably waiting in here somewhere."

At that moment, the three older men who had been sitting outside came in, seating themselves on the tiers opposite Cole and Roy. "Should I try one of them?" Roy asked.

"For what?" Cole asked, with heavy insinuation.

"Selling my soul, what are we talking about anyway?"

"I just wanted to be sure what you meant."

In answer Roy slapped him lightly on the back of the arm. "You're the one with the Devil's mind!"

"There's nothing wrong with having sex with one of them."

"They're so old."

"You'll be old one day, Roy. Don't be cruel now. There's so much cruelty."

Roy agreed with a faint nod, as though he were thinking. "So serious, you are."

"Let's lighten the mood then."

"What are you going to do?"

"Watch!"

When the circling man approached again, Cole stood up and stared deliberately into his face. Briefly the man was surprised, but stopped about two yards farther on. Cole noticed the other men grow attentive. The man who had stopped waited, but when Cole did not move, he went over to a metal pail near the faucet, bending down to fill it with cold water. He raised the pail over his head and doused himself entirely. The water flattened his hair onto his skull and formed a beard at the chin. When the bucket was empty, he flicked the excess water from himself and turned back to Cole, his hand at his genitals. After a moment, Cole came up to him and held out his arm toward the chest. At once the man glanced around him cautiously, but eventually forced his body next to Cole's hand. Then they encircled each other with their arms, and the bodies joined. Cole ran his slippery fingers over the man's back, and they leaned together, the man against the wall. Cole put his mouth on the man's breast, making him sigh softly. One of the older men came close to them, his hand groping his own testicles. Uncertainly he reached out to touch the man against the wall, at the waist. But the slim man pushed at the fingers to remove them. Cole shook his head and took the older man's hand and placed it on his own waist. "It's all right," he whispered. Immediately the older man began stroking Cole's back, the buttocks; he even knelt and put his head between their two bodies, taking Cole's sex into his mouth. Through the vapor, Cole saw three others get up from the wooden seats and approach. Hands flicked back and forth, and someone's mouth found Cole's throat, and he let the sensations roll through his flesh, grasping the aroused phalluses of the men on either side of him, wanting them to feel as much pleasure as he did. The other men twisted their perspiring bodies, encouraging the others to join, and Cole saw Roy hesitantly walk nearer; he held out his hand to him, taking his arm, then gently pulling him by the back of the neck until their mouths were pressed together. He ran his tongue into the silken opening, thrusting, withdrawing, nibbling at the lips until Roy moaned, impassioned, and pressed his mouth hard against Cole's. Glowing, welling, vernal, Cole sighed, as if he had only that moment been created, realizing that he was giving more relief, more satisfaction this way than through anything he had done in the daylight world.

The steambath door was unexpectedly thrown open, and two fully clothed men rushed in. "Well, for God's sake!" Keel's voice shouted. "Look at that, boys, a regular daisy chain!" The men around Cole scattered, but the other policeman blocked the exit, his hand in his pocket, as though he might have a gun ready. "You're all under arrest, in case you didn't know," Keel said, the steam reddening his naturally florid complexion. "You guys make it easy for us, all lumped so nice and neat together like that. I'm sorry to spoil your evening's fun, girls, but you're about to visit police headquarters." He stepped back a few paces toward the door, saying to his assistant, "Give me those towels." As the man handed in a few at a time, Keel threw them at the men. "Here! Cover up your cocks. They make me sick." The men bent down to retrieve the towels, tying them around themselves frantically, but saying nothing. Cole noticed that Roy had retreated to a corner, where he stood with his hands covering his face. "Come, girls, get ready for your evening out. Haven't got all night." Keel stood beside the door as they filed out. "And don't try to run outside, because we've got two more of us upstairs and one outside. You just go and get your pretty clothes on and march real delicate-like to the van that's expecting you outside." As Cole passed the man, he wanted to strangle him, to bash in the grinning teeth. "That's right, dearie, keep moving right along," Keel said directly to Cole. One of the older men started to protest, but Keel silenced him, "Tell it to the judge. Keep moving, keep moving. Come on, baldie, you aren't nothing special. Get your bare ass over here."

The other policeman was leading them up the staircase to the first floor, with Keel to the rear. "Wait! Wait!" Keel shouted to his colleague. "Let me check around down here. Stay at the head of the line, Roddy, don't let 'em get by you." Cole looked down the stairs as the man hurried toward the dormitory. From within came a few curses, mostly indistinct, and in a minute another man, in a sheet, came up to the bottom step. Again there was a sound from the dormitory, and then Keel came back, holding Cupey by his arm. "Look what I found, Roddy! A little queer hiding under the bed. He thought he was all safe, didn't you? He had the sheet all arranged to hang down, but it didn't work, you little pigmy pervert!" Cupey tried to pull his arm out of Keel's grasp, but was not successful. "Don't give me a hard time, you little creep, or I'll knock your brains out!" Keel flipped him easily into the line. "Up, up we go into the wild blue yonder," he said jovially, signaling to the other policeman to proceed.

On the first floor, scared-looking men were dressing in the locker room, with the others in their rooms, all the doors of which were open all the way down the corridor. The attendant stood uncertainly, a ring of keys hanging in his fingers, and Cole knew that the man had been forced to unlock all the rooms. "Just keep it quiet and you won't get hurt," a man wearing a towel said to two grumblers in the locker room. He was a well-built, massive man, one of the plants the police had sent in. The other one, likewise in a towel only, was watching the men buttoning their shirts and pulling on their trousers. Keel glanced down the corridor and said angrily, "Didn't you guys check that exit back there? Get the hell down there and make sure none of these fairies escape out the back door." The massive policeman ran down the hallway until he reached the exit sign, where he waited. He said something to some of the men who looked out of their rooms, but Cole could not hear it clearly. His head had begun to throb mercilessly; he thought he might faint. "Get your ass dressed," Keel said to him, but meaning all of the recent arrivals upstairs. "We've got a room," somebody said, weakly. "Well, then, go to it and no funny business. See the keys here; we can unlock all the locks! Just put on your clothes and come back in here when you're done."

In his room, Cole blinked at his clothes on the hangers. This couldn't be happening! It was a nightmare and he would wake up at any moment. Any moment now! He touched the bed, and it was real; the rough texture of the blanket shocked him as if it had been electricity. His head swelled and pulsed, something turbulent exploding inside, in some way combined with the humming of the air-conditioner. He sat on the edge of the bed, shaking his head from side to side, to be rid of the pain as well as in disbelief. The water from the steambath ran in rivulets all over his flesh, clammy, coarse beads dripping off onto the floor. He felt stunned, unable to form his thoughts, the way a beast feels when its head has been crushed with the slaughterer's hammer, the bits of brain splintering amid the screaming blood. He sensed that he ought to do something, but he could not complete the idea, could not think through the agony in his skull. "Come on, buddy," the cop who had been at the exit sign rebuked him, sticking his torso into the tiny room. "Come on, get your clothes on; we haven't got all night." Cole looked up at him, unperceiving, although he knew precisely what the man had told him. When he made no effort to rise, the man backed out of the room and Cole heard his voice moving up the hallway encouraging the others to hurry. *Why don't I wake up?* He drew the back of his hand over his thigh. Why didn't he struggle up out of the maelstrom of sleep? He fell to one side, onto the bed, and he thought parts of him were about to spill out of his mouth, pieces of his heart were going to spatter into a pool of blood.

He wondered if he had gone to sleep, because suddenly Keel was shaking him by the shoulder. "Get into your clothes or we'll take you without them." He seized the items from the hangers and flung them on top of Cole. "You can't stay in here any longer, queero; the honeymoon's over." Keel stepped back. But when Cole did not respond, he shouted, "I'll give you exactly two minutes to get into your clothes and out of this room, do you understand that?" Clumsily, Cole rose and fumbled at his things, unable to find his shorts and instead stepping into his pants. "You didn't dry yourself off, what's the matter with you? You'll catch a cold outside. You creeps don't know whether you're coming or going, do you?" Cole fastened his shirt, and became aware of Keel's thick body standing near his own; it seemed to be forcing his against the side of the bed, although he knew it was not touching him. "Don't forget your shoes," Keel said, oddly patient. Cole leaned forward to tie the laces and almost blacked out. For an instant he believed he was sliding into a chasm, but he drew himself back. "Get out there with the others, Mary," Keel ordered, lifting him by the arm.

The assembled criminals, about thirty in all, were waiting when Cole and the policeman emerged from the room. Turning back to the exit guard, now dressed, who was following them, Keel said, "You'd better go once more and look in each room, especially under the beds, so that none of these guys get away." The guard returned to the task, but Cole was too sick to watch him. "Okay, tell Masters that we're bringing them out now," Keel said to the other cop who had been a plant, also dressed by this time. The man disappeared out the front door, and Keel addressed the arrested men: "Listen, you fellows, you give us any trouble or any guff and you get smacked, where it'll do the most good, you better believe it. I'm supposed to tell you of your constitutional rights not to confess to anything without knowing that it can be used as evidence later. Not that we need any more evidence than you've given us already. Caught some of you red-cocked, and the rest of you have been frequenting a place of lewdness and indecency. Some of you guys just never learn." The policeman who had checked the rooms returned. "All set, sir."

"You mean to tell me you examined twenty-five or more rooms in that short period of time?"

"I think we got them all, sir."

"Christ!" Keel turned away disgusted. "You guys!"

"Do you want me to go and look some more?"

"Forget it! Stay here and help load these queers into the van."

The man came in from outdoors. "Okay, sir, Masters is all set. Back's open."

"All right then. Make a line on either side," Keel directed the three other policemen. "You guys," he said to the rest, "take it nice and slow, one at a time, out the door, and into the back of the van. For a nice little ride for a few blocks." Cole saw Cupey and his companions led out first; soon after he closed his eyes, not wanting to see anymore.

When it was his turn, the last, he walked out into the lobby, past one policeman, then to the sidewalk, where the van and a police car waited. A few gaping passersby had been attracted by the commotion and stared at Cole as he stepped up into the truck, which was too crowded, and so he and several more had to stand. Straps were provided.

Soon he heard someone get in next to the driver, though he did not look through the thick, barred window to see who it was. He thought he heard Keel's voice give an order, but he concentrated his attention on Roy's bowed head; he was sitting with his knuckles twisted into his eyes. The others' faces were blanched, sitting in utter silence, except for Cupey, who was whimpering.

"Are you degenerates all comfy? Won't be long, so don't let a little jostling fray your nerves. I know how delicate they are." Keel grinned into the back of the truck, his arms spread, holding onto the handle of the door. "Try not to blow each other too much during the ride over, okay? Hey, fellows, I wish to thank you all for your cooperation. You made it possible for us to have time for another raid this evening. Yep, I think we'll be just in time, once we get you processed, to visit the girls at Palmer Park. The late shift ought to be getting started about now." He looked at his watch. "Yep, we ought to be able to round up another thirty or so. You guys aren't even a challenge anymore, you know that? If they're as easy at Palmer Park as you were here, I'll be able to get home to fuck my wife before midnight. Oh, excuse me, you don't know what a real *fuck* means, do you? A nice loving woman under the covers—you queers don't know what you're missing." He leaned in a bit. "What's wrong with all of you is that you never learned to fuck right, that's it! Just never learned how to fuck right."

Cole felt his head ease, anger flooding his mind. "Shut your mouth, Keel; shut your vicious asshole of a mouth."

"Well, a little spirit from in there! Who said it?"

"I said it," Cole said, watching the eyes focus on his face.

"I'll remember you in court tomorrow, faggot. I'll remember

you." He gave Cole a look of contempt and slammed the door shut, rattling it locked.

The ride to the police station took less than five minutes. Cole swayed from the strap, saying nothing further. No one spoke, in fact. Even Cupey had stopped crying.

One of the other policemen opened the van door, and Cole saw Keel get out of the police car behind them. They were taken in by a rear entrance, into a room where they were given papers to fill out. Keel walked among the men sitting at the tables, passing out pencils, while another policeman, in uniform, inked the pad, preparing to fingerprint them one by one. "What kind of scribble is that?" Keel said when Cole handed his form back. "Fill it out legibly. And get out your identifications, all of you. Leave 'em next to you on the table, so I can see 'em." Cole took another form and printed his name and the other information required.

"Got quite a pack tonight, eh, Keel?" the Negro fingerprinter said.

"Biggest bunch of queens I've picked up all at one time."

"It's gonna take me a while to get all those prints."

"They aren't in no hurry, Monty. They've got all night long. They aren't going back to that steambath; that's done for, that's for certain." Keel caught Cole's look of hatred and came closer. "This here's got spirit, Monty. I'm going to put in a few special words to the judge about him." He looked around. "What you guys have got to learn is that we're going to wipe you faggots out, if it's the last thing we do!" He made a fist in the air and brought it down on the table loudly.

"We're entitled to a bondsman," Cole said.

"A bondsman? A bondsman? You call your goddamn bondsman yourself."

"Where's the phone?"

"You fill out that form right first, son!" he said menacingly.

"When I do, then I want to use the phone."

"Fill it out!"

"Keel, don't give 'em such a hard time."

"You stick to your business, Monty, and I'll stick to mine."
The other policeman shrugged and laid some paper toweling next to the ink pad.
"If I had my way, these freaks wouldn't get out on bond. But these bleeding-hearts are doing all the damage. I don't know why all you Marys don't pack up and move away. We don't *want* your kind here in Detroit. Why don't you move someplace else!"
Cole handed him the form the second time, his hand almost trembling.
"That still isn't right, you dumbbell. Can't you read? It says Reason for Arrest. Fill that in too. I should make you put down 'Sodomy' but I won't. Hey, all you *Homo sapiens*, fill in Reason for Arrest with 'Lewd Behavior.' Got that? 'Lewd Behavior.' That's a lesser charge than you deserve."
Cole stared up at Keel. "Thanks for your generosity."
Keel smiled as if he were going to swallow him. "Funny man, he thinks he is. You—you put down 'Sodomy.' Besides, it fits; you were one I caught in the steambath with your prick all covered with spit." He tapped the form and leaned over Cole, putting his face right next to his. Cole thought his hatred was going to overwhelm him, that he might burst something in his brain from the intensity, and suddenly he realized what he was going to do, and, with the decision, he felt agitated further, yet held the pencil quiet, calming himself, letting the plan of the killing rest only on the periphery of his mind. "Anything else to say, queero?" Keel threatened, breathing into Cole's face. "No? Why not? Lose your nerve?" He stood upright and blew wind through his lips to make a sound of contempt. "We've got us a nervous nelly, that's all he is."
One of the policemen who had been plants in the steambath came into the room. "Need any help?"
"Yeah, go around and see if these guys are filling out the goddamn form correctly."
Cole wrote the word Keel had demanded and waited for the

other officer to come by and held the paper for him to inspect. "Is this all right?" he heard his controlled voice ask.

The man checked the form. "Yeah, that's all right. Let me see your identification." Cole took out his wallet and showed his expired driver's license. "Okay, all set. You can get printed now."

Already two others were waiting in line behind the man who was first to be fingerprinted; Cole joined them, trying not to look at Keel, who had moved to a far table. Impatient now, Cole felt that his head might shred into fragments if the policeman continued to place the men's fingers so deliberately on the ink pad before him. Every digit had to be perfect, pressed one after the other.

But at last his own hands were manipulated into position. "Relax," the man advised. "Just relax." He held himself steady, watching the black substance stick to his hand. *It's holy oil* flashed through his mind. "Now the other one," Monty directed. "All right. Wipe with this." He pointed to the toweling, and Cole rubbed his fingers, but much of it remained.

"I'd like to call a bondsman, please," he said.

"Telephone's behind that counter."

"Do you know how I can get a bondsman?"

"There are all kinds of them, right across the street. There's a phone book over there."

"How much bond do I need?"

"You'd better ask Keel." Seeing Cole's reluctance, he called out, "Say, Keel, what's the bond on these boys?"

"Three hundred apiece." He turned, with his head to one side, examining Cole.

"Thank you," Cole said to Monty and walked to the telephone, feeling Keel's eyes.

"You sure you can dial by yourself, lady?" he shouted to his back.

It took him a while to find the right section, but the bondsman he called was in his office, right across the street from the police station. The man promised to come over at once, and then Cole remembered to tell him that there were three deaf-mutes who would need bond as well. "In fact, there are about thirty of us at three hundred dollars a head. I'm not sure how many want it, though." Several men overheard and called out that they wanted bond. Cole told the man, who said he would bring enough for all of them. "Thank you," Cole said, then put down the receiver.

He sat at a table again, anxious, afraid that the man would not come soon enough, that all of them would be fingerprinted, and Keel would escape. He looked around for Roy, who sat staring into the tabletop; Cupey, pinch-faced, was still filling out the card.

There were still fourteen to complete when the bondsman, a brisk, short man in a striped suit, arrived. Cole introduced himself as the one who had called, and the man nodded, professionally. "You'll have to pay me twenty-five percent of your bond, you understand, tomorrow, in court. Can you do that?"

"Yes, I can do that." He would agree to anything the man demanded. Anything. As long as he could get free now. He had to get out before Keel left.

"You'll have to sign some papers agreeing to all this."

"I will, I accept the terms."

"Don't forget you have to be in court tomorrow morning at eight o'clock. Sharp! Have you got a lawyer?"

"I'll get one."

"Well, a friend of mine—a fine lawyer—is in the office next to mine, and I can arrange for him to handle your case if you like."

Cole showed his teeth in what the other believed was a smile. "Yes, of course, let everybody get his share of the action. Yes, I'd like that. You arrange for your friend the lawyer."

"Don't forget tomorrow at eight. There's a coffee shop a few blocks up; it's called the P's & Q's. You meet me and my lawyer friend there before eight."

"Fine," Cole said, frenzied to be away.

"I'll have to go up front now and get this approved. Maybe I should wait, though, and see how many others all together want bond."

"Please, I have to leave. Can't you do mine first? It's an emergency."

"Well . . ."

"I must leave right away. I'll give you something extra tomorrow. Please!"

"What's the big rush?"

"I must leave." He stared at the man, hoping to force him with his eyes. "I promise to give you another two hundred tomorrow."

"Well, all right. Sign here. I'll see what I can do." After he got the signature, the bondsman started to walk to another part of the police station, but several others from the steambath approached him, asking for his help. He stopped and went through the same speech. Hurrying over to them, Cole insisted: "They'll pay you; they will. Don't worry about it. Just get me out of here. We all want out, but I must leave now!"

"I'm only getting these fellows settled; you're not the only one here, don't forget."

"Please!" he almost yelled.

"It's more efficient if I take these few all at one time. Saves time in the long run." He wrote down the names of the four other men surrounding him, getting their signatures, and then at last he left the room, although several more of the arrested were talking to him, saying he would return quickly.

To quiet himself, Cole sat back down at one of the tables, a flicker of a thought jarring his mind. *Someone should nail my hands to this table so that I can't get out.* He snatched his hands from the tabletop.

"So you want to get out real bad, huh?"

Cole lifted his gaze to Keel standing above him, his tie pressed tight against the Adam's apple. He did not answer.

"Cat got your tongue, queer boy?"

Cole looked down at the brown wood.

"You still got a big evening planned, is that it?"

Cole did not move his head.

"Just what do you think you're going to do, fairy?"

Cole's neck snapped back. "I'll see you at Palmer Park!"

The man did not comprehend at once, but then a slow grin swarmed out of his mouth. "You get picked up there tonight and you'll regret it, my friend. You'll regret it a long, long time."

"You'll have to find me there first."

"Oh, I'll find you, don't worry. I'll just have to look under some bush, where you'll be sucking somebody's dick."

Cole met the other's eyes. "I hate you, Keel. You don't know how much I hate you."

"The feeling is mutual, queero."

They held the look, neither flinching. Then Cole said, "Don't delay getting out to the park, Keel."

"Wouldn't dream of it. That's what freeways are for, right? To speed justice on its way."

"We'll be waiting."

"No, you won't," he contradicted, almost with pity. "You'll go out and warn the other freaks, and they'll high-tail it out of there so fast their pants'll still be tangled around their ankles."

He started to laugh, but Cole interrupted: "I'll be there; you can count on me."

"Can I count on you?" Keel answered lightly. "Good! Taking you in will be twice as much fun as getting all of these weak sisters of yours. They don't put up a fight that's worth shit."

"I'll be waiting."

"I'm going to stick you, d'you hear? I'm going to stick you." He pointed his thick finger at Cole like a gun.

From the door the bondsman's voice was saying, "It's okay then: Fauser, Ruffner, Malenenfant, Eppley, and Olivieri, you can go. But remember you have to be at Recorder's Court at eight o'clock sharp tomorrow morning."

Already Cole was signing the paper the man laid on one of

the tables. Then he straightened up, turned toward Keel, and bowed with his head. In answer, Keel made his finger explode out of his fist as if shooting Cole.

Outside in the dark Cole walked quickly toward the park that he had been to that afternoon, where the construction work was. He was afraid that the workmen might have removed the pipes. But when he arrived at the excavation, everything was as it had been, except that tarpaulin had been thrown over the materials. A number of pedestrians were walking on the streets, but no one was in the park. Cole threw off the tarpaulin and stared at the pipes on the ground, then selected two of them about fourteen inches long, three inches in diameter. He felt their weight, amazed at how clear-minded he was. *I'm going to do it,* he realized, shaking. *I'm really going to do it.* He stuffed the two pipes under his jacket, one on either side, and zipped it closed. He walked, cold, toward Woodward Avenue. For a minute he stood watching the traffic. He pressed the pipes to his stomach and held out one hand to signal for a taxi. One on the other side of the avenue saw him and halted abruptly, the driver gesturing that he would turn around.

In the rear seat of the cab, Cole felt as if he might begin to tremble; something slimey seemed to be crawling up and down his spine, and the pipes pushed out his jacket, sinking onto his lap. *It's like being pregnant,* he thought. "My children," he said softly, stroking the pipes through the cloth.

"Where to?" the driver asked when he gave no directions.

"I want to go to Palmer Park via the freeway. But I don't want to go that far."

"What?"

"Go on the Lodge Freeway, but let me off two exits up."

"Two exits from where?"

"Two exits after we get on."

"What address is that?"

"No address. Just let me off at the top of the ramp."

The driver shrugged faintly, and drove off.

But what if Keel doesn't come this way, Cole suddenly

thought. *What if he goes up Woodward! I'll miss him. And then tomorrow, unless I run away, he'll get me, send me back to jail. I was too hasty; I should have planned it more.* He was overcome with disgust for himself, and sank back into the seat, trying to clarify what he should do.

"Is that the exit you want?" The driver pointed ahead.

"That'll do. Yes!"

When he paid the man, he knew that he would remember him—the oddness of the dropoff place, the bulge in the jacket. How stupid of himself!

He walked across the ramp to the sidewalk that led to the overpass. There were not many cars below. At the center he stopped. Stretching to the downtown area was the concrete whip—the freeway. The gusts of cold air from the few cars blew up from the pit, rippling his hair. He felt his eyes sting, but he could not blink. A man crossed the street on the side opposite him, and he held his back to him, wondering if he could go through with the killing if someone happened to come by at that precise moment. When the man disappeared, Cole unzipped his jacket and took out the two pipes, putting them on the railing of the overpass, and rezipped the jacket.

So I'm almost a murderer. Well, why not. Let's give them something real to despise me for. But they won't catch me. And there won't be any trial tomorrow without the cops to bring charges. Keel will be dead. And I'll turn up at court, and they will have to let us all go, because there won't be any cop to charge us. And even if they do, Keel will be dead, mangled inside the police car, his teeth fractured by these pipes. Cole's heart swelled, and he seized the weapons with both hands, tapping them against the railing.

He wondered how much time had elapsed. A minute? An hour? He could not tell at all.

What would you say now, Pa, if you could see me here? Would you be proud of me because I'm killing something, proving my manhood? Would this please you, you son of a bitching bastard! Would this appall you as much as what you saw? No, it wouldn't, would it? You'd rather have me a murderer than a pervert. I know you would. I know it!

"I know it!" He heard himself say the words and looked down the freeway for the van and the police car, raging. He swung one of the pipes out viciously.

Cole started. He thought he recognized the van in the distance, with the police car in front of it. It would be there in a few seconds. He placed one leg over the railing, and lifted the pipes above his head, for the maximum impact. The police car came speeding toward him, his eyes riveted on it. It was the same one, he was certain. He shouted, "Come on, come and die, come on, come and die, you normal fucker, you healthy sick animal. Come on!" The police car was a few hundred yards away, and Cole squinted to see if Keel was driving, recognizing the man behind the wheel. "We're going to die," he heard himself say, a dark, unbearable coldness filling his body. "Die," he screamed, putting his other leg over the railing. He was crying, the salt running into his mouth, burning the cut on his tongue. The car below shot at him. "We both lose Round Three," he whispered, letting his body fall from the overpass, the pipes thrust out before him so that they would hit the windshield.

He landed on the hood, at the last second his arms trying to block his head, which bounced off the arms, one pipe breaking the window glass. The automobile swerved just as another car was coming up on the right. The second one was grazed by the police car and zigzagged as the driver struggled for control, but he could not hold the wheel and the car crashed into the side of the freeway, skidding along the emergency stop area, until it struck the embankment and turned over. The driver, his wife, and their son were killed at once. The police car also skidded, scraping its side along the dividing rail between the lanes. Cole jiggled up and down a few times, conscious, smearing the blood from his shattered, softened face, and then fell off onto the expressway. He crawled on his elbows over to the guardrail, sitting against it, knowing that both arms were broken. *Why don't I die?* he thought as the pain began to slash through the shock.

Why don't I die? Although liquid was dribbling from one eye, which was blotted out, he saw the limp bodies sprawled around, hanging out of the overturned second car. The police car came to a halt. There was no movement from it, but then the door opened and Keel staggered out, a trickle of blood at his nose. He looked around dazed at the men who were running from the van stopped up ahead and then at the cars that were parking to help the accident victims. Cole looked at his dark blood dripping into his lap, across the ripped, crushed hands, and screamed out loud, "My God, why don't I die!"